A DETERMINED WOMAN

Just as Edward was about to sit down, Julia rushed toward him, gave him a push backward onto the squabs, and leaped into the hackney as the horses moved forward.

"Julia!" he cried as she closed the door behind her. "What the devil—?"

He was half off the seat, half on, when she threw herself upon him and began kissing him. She smelled his skin and caught the fragrance of his soap. Her legs were tangled with his and she giggled, slipping her hand beneath his coat and feeling the heat of his skin through his linen shirt. She kissed his neck, catching the soft lobe of his ear between her teeth. Pleasure at being so close to him rolled over her in delicious waves.

She was kissing his ear softly, letting her tongue rim the edges. His breathing grew ragged and he no longer struggled to push her off him. "Be sensible," he said weakly.

"I am being sensible," she returned gently. "Given the circumstances, the most sensible thing I could do was come to Brussels to be with you." Julia tasted of his lips and thought that for this brief moment, she could be completely happy. The touch of his skin against her lips, the feel of his lips upon hers, the warmth of his body through the thin fabric of her gown, all gave her a sense of completeness she could not explain.

She was simply at home in his arms. . . .

Zebra Books by Valerie King

Valerie King

Vanquished

ZEBRA BOOKS
KENSINGTON PUBLISHING CORP.

ZEBRA BOOKS are published by

Kensington Publishing Corp.
850 Third Avenue
New York, NY 10022

First Printing: August, 1995

Printed in the United States of America

To John, Andy, and Sarah with love,
And to Bob and Nancy Collins with gratitude.

What thou lovest well remains, the rest is dross
What thou lov'st well shall not be reft from thee
What thou lov'st well is thy true heritage.
                                        —*Ezra Pound*

Prologue

Bath, England
July 1812

"How can the postilion see where he is going?" Julia Verdell cried, peering through the front window of her family's town coach. An unseasonable storm had come off the Atlantic and was pounding the western counties. The rain beat in a deafening roar on the roof of the carriage, sounding to Julia like a thousand drums leading an army into battle. Though the image of the postboy was blurred through the glass, she could see that his hat was limp about his ears and that water was pouring in a sheet down his back. "I can hardly make him out!" Julia shouted. "I wish he wasn't driving the horses so fast."

"I believe he's a new man in our stables," Lady Delabole said. "Perhaps he hasn't yet been informed of the sharp turns along this lane." She glanced at Julia and smiled. "Aren't you glad I am able to comfort you with such hopeful words?" she queried facetiously.

Julia looked at her mother and gave her an answering smile. "Nothing you could say would help me in the least at the moment," she responded. "I confess I am completely frightened out of my wits."

She was traveling with her mother to pay a call upon their neighbor, Sir Perran Blackthorn. His home was situated five miles to the south of Bath and another five miles from Lord Delabole's family seat in Somerset. The lane by the quarry was the shorter route between the houses, though less traveled and less well maintained than the king's highway. Because of the severity of the storm, Julia regretted, as did her mother, that they had chosen to take the quicker route.

Though she was eighteen, fully grown, and had enjoyed her come-out ball only a month earlier, Julia felt as if she were little more than a frightened schoolgirl in the midst of the downpour. Resisting an impulse to snuggle next to her mother's always-comforting shoulder, she clasped her gloved hands tightly together on her lap.

"We are near the quarry," her mother announced. "I knew we should not have come down this lane. The turns are too frequent, the lane too narrow. We have more than a mile of this to endure. My goodness, I have never before heard the rain so hard upon a roof." Lady Delabole glanced up at the ceiling of the coach as though she expected it to burst open, then turned to look out the window-glass to her right. "I wonder if I ought to open the door and beg the postilion to slow the horses."

"Do not do that!" Julia cried impulsively. She glanced at the beautiful bonnet sitting atop her mother's peppered black curls and added, with a smile, "Or the onslaught of rain will ruin Gabrielle's latest confection." The bonnet was a pretty sapphire-blue silk trimmed with white silk ribbons, a white ostrich feather, and an enchanting string of seed pearls looped across the poke brim. Lady Delabole's personal maid, a French refugee, was quick with her fingers and had a remarkable eye for beauty. Julia had many times wished that Gabrielle was her own maid.

Lady Delabole's eyes crinkled at the corners. "It is lovely, isn't it?" she mused, lifting an elegant hand to let the feather drift through her yellow-kid-gloved fingers.

"I wish you might lend Gabrielle to me for a time," Julia said, trying hard to ignore another bright flash of lightning and loud clap of thunder overhead. "Anna can do nothing with my bonnets and has only a tolerable knowledge of the use of curling tongs. My hair is frizzed three days out of four."

"Your hair is frizzed because it is red and curly, and the

weather is damp. I will not permit you to blame Anna, and no, you may not have Gabrielle!" A twinkle in her eye belied the firmness in her voice.

It was always so, Julia thought, her heart full of affection for her mother. She knew an easy camaraderie with her parent, which was unusual among her friends. If she could explain the phenomenon, she supposed it was because she admired her mother so much. Of all the ladies she knew, none could compare with Lady Delabole's elegant countenance, the tranquillity with which she conducted her life, the order of her home, or the kindness that was proverbially on her tongue.

She was beautiful, too, even though she was not in the first blush of youth—eight and thirty—with clear blue eyes, a slightly retroussé nose, a dimpled chin. Julia had always wished she resembled her mother. Two of her sisters did—Elizabeth and Caroline—while Julia and her youngest sister, Annabelle, sported the red hair, green eyes, and straight nose of their father. Both boys, Frederick and Robert, also resembled Lady Delabole. A fine family. A good home. Excellent connections. Surely a happy future stretched before the Delabole siblings.

The rain lessened a trifle, the road smoothed out.

"That's a little better," her mother commented, her gaze fixed on the window in front of her, her eyes narrowed slightly. "There, the rain has let up a bit." She breathed a sigh of relief, then turned to Julia. "I had a reason for wanting you to accompany me to Sir Perran's today," she began, her blue eyes appearing concerned. "You see, there is so much I wish to tell you about . . . well, about everything. But the truth is, I haven't known how to prepare you, or your sisters, for what might lie before you. England is sufficiently prosperous to sustain you, your children, even your grandchildren, but only if I can succeed in putting to rights our own affairs. Sometime during the coming sennight, I intend to speak to our solicitor about securing your dowries. You will, of course, have the heirloom jewelry which my mother gave to me. However . . ." Lady Delabole's expression grew perplexed, as though she didn't know how to continue.

Julia was surprised at what her mother was telling her. It was as though she meant to say all was not well. Yet how could that be? The family enjoyed great wealth, a fine, large mansion in the country, and a townhouse in Bath. Hatherleigh Park was well staffed, and the grounds, which had recently been landscaped in the picturesque by Humphrey Repton, were groomed to perfection. What did she mean, "putting to rights our own affairs"?

"I don't understand," Julia said, mystified. She felt uneasy and secretly didn't want the conversation to continue. The rain and thunder was enough to set her teeth on edge, but the distant, worried expression on her mother's face was a hundred times worse.

"My life has been unruffled for the most part," Lady Delabole continued cryptically, "All my children survived, and for that I will always feel grateful and blessed. It is only lately that I have begun to suspect—" She paused and checked her words. "Well, enough time, I suppose, to place a hedge against the future. Only, once we are returned home—beginning this very afternoon—I mean to instruct you as best I can on how properly to arrange your life and to answer any particular questions you might have about—about anything you may wish to know. I am persuaded it will not be very long before you tumble violently in love with one of these besotted fellows who have been reclining at your feet in the drawing room and reading poetry to you for hours on end this past year and more." Lady Delabole pinched her daughter's cheek affectionately.

Julia knew she was blushing. "When you speak of my beaux that way, how silly they seem. But I enjoy their attentions ever so much."

"Just as you should, for I promise you, once a man takes up his full responsibilities as a husband and father, all the verses he once crammed into his head to recite to his favored lady somehow fly right out his ears. I remember once asking your papa to read a little Milton to me after we had been wed for a year—Frederick had just been born—but the only answer that greeted me was a sudden and very profound snore. I never asked again. I believe he was grateful for that."

"Do you—do you love him?" Julia queried, sorry that she had let the question pass her lips, though she had often wondered.

She watched a frown slip across her mother's pretty face, then disappear. "Of course I do," she stated.

The flatness of her mother's words saddened Julia.

Lady Delabole turned to look out the window. "You can see the quarry from here, even through the rain. What a deep pit it is, and it goes on for quite some distance. Most of the stone was used to build the city of Bath. Did you know that the recent Delabole wealth is due to the foresight of your great grandfather to acquire the quarry from Sir Perran's father? Quite a stroke of genius, since until that time the family's fortunes had been diminishing steadily."

"I didn't know," Julia responded, astonished. She had always presumed the Delabole wealth had been so vast that nothing could ever touch it. She was also dumbfounded to learn that a quarry had been provisioning her family in recent years. The thought of it disturbed her. Within her circle of acquaintances, money connected to trade was considered almost contemptible. Julia suddenly felt strange as a faint dizziness passed through her mind. She sensed that her world was changing, and she didn't want it to change. "Papa receives money from the quarry?" she asked uneasily.

The carriage hit a bump and sent both ladies bouncing in their seats, each shrieking, then laughing as the chariot bounded onward.

Lady Delabole again peered out the rain-spattered window. "Yes, he does. The quarry and the rent-rolls constitute his income. He used to have a tidy sum invested in the funds as well, but all that is . . . well, never mind. Suffice it to say that without the quarry, we would be in the basket. Goodness, the rain is increasing again. I wish we were beyond these hills." She sighed and continued. "The fourth viscount Delabole had had a business arrangement with a Mr. Wood who designed much of Bath as it is today—a quite profitable arrangement. The viscount had also hoped to sell his stone to London architects; unfortunately, stone hereabouts was considered too soft for the Metropolis. Recently, I heard rumors that your great grandfather had not come by the quarry honestly, but that is such ancient history that I'm sure it no longer signifies. The entrance is not far from here—a steep earthen rampart. I know you used to play in the hills above Hatherleigh—no, pray, don't pretend you didn't!— but did you ever go to the quarry with Edward Blackthorn and his brothers?"

Julia shook her head. Thunder rattled the carriage and she winced. The air was cold and clammy from so much rain. "No, only the hills. I was always afraid of the quarry. Just as you said, it is a very deep pit."

"Such a tragedy for Edward, poor boy. Most of his family gone for so many years—and now George. I am very sorry for him. Have you written to express your condolences?"

"Of course, Mama," Julia returned earnestly, surprised that her mother would think for a moment she would forget. How could she not have done so when she had cried her eyes out for days upon receiving Blackthorn's last letter? She knew parts of it by heart, and the most touching came to mind: "I was so fortunate to be able to be with him when he passed on. He was so frail from disease—George, who was so strong, so vigorous—little more than skin and bones. He was smiling even in death. How I will miss him—his wit and his deep, robust laughter most of all."

Julia swallowed more tears. She took a deep breath and let out a heavy sigh. She would miss George Blackthorn, would miss the recountings of his antics and exploits among his fellow army officers. In every letter, Major Edward Blackthorn rarely failed to regale her with something George had done or said. Now the middle brother was gone as well as the youngest. At least Edward was still alive—a last, happy connection to a child-

hood full of fun and frolic, one that she would always treasure
as having been fine, warm, and perfect.

Lady Delabole's voice dragged Julia back from her reverie.
"Imagine Sophia Kettering marrying Harry Blackthorn and fol-
lowing the drum, when she could have had Sir Perran's wealth.
Odd the choices we make. I knew Sophia from my first season.
She was a few years older than me, but so pretty and lively. Sir
Perran was forty or so at the time, and his brother, Harry . . .
now let me see, he would have been three and twenty. Quite a
few years separated the brothers, and . . ."

The rain droned on, as did Lady Delabole's voice. Julia
knew her mother had always been fascinated by the fact that
Sophia Kettering had had to choose between the brothers. She
herself had never known her mother's friend from London, nor
Sir Perran's brother, and so she could not find much of interest
in the tale. Her only thought for the present was a strong wish
to reach Sir Perran's home safely. After all, her sole connection
to Lieutenant Colonel Harry Blackthorn and Sophia Kettering
Blackthorn had been a hoydenish acquaintance with their off-
spring—Edward, George, and Stephen.

Julia's thoughts were drawn back to her childhood, to how
she used to play in the hills, just as her mother said, with Edward
and his brothers. A thick beech forest laced with bluebells and
ferns graced the several rises that separated the large estate of
Hatherleigh Park from Sir Perran's home, known as The Priory.
King Arthur and Robin Hood had been their heroes, the fallen
branches their horses. Frequently, Julia would pretend she was
Maid Marian. The brothers had rescued her a thousand times,
and when she would tire of being carried about on their backs,
she would chase them with a stick for a sword and claim England
in the name of France as Joan of Arc. She smiled, thinking how
very much Edward had enjoyed that particular game, because
then he could finish it by tying her to a tree and pretending to
burn her alive. Sometimes Elizabeth would play, but she was
too feisty and would generally end up clobbering one of Edward's younger brothers with a stick, afterward taking a pelter

when George or Stephen would box her ears in return. Julia wished George had not died and that Edward lived in England instead of rampaging about Spain alongside Wellington.

She glanced down at the gold military braid that ran the entire front of her forest-green silk pelisse. On her shoulders were gold fringed epaulettes. The long war with France had for many years infused English fashion with a number of military symbols. Julia found wearing her epaulettes and the gold braid a comfort, especially since the pace of the Peninsular War appeared to be quickening. Major Blackthorn would probably approve of her pelisse—how odd to think of Edward as a formal, dignified *Major* Blackthorn—but she wondered suddenly if she would ever see him again.

Thunder cracked overhead, drawing her back to the present.

"How much farther, Mama?" Julia queried, her legs and hands starting to tremble.

"We are very near the rampart. Would to God the postboy would slow the horses!"

Another brilliant flash of lightning illuminated the windows, followed by a hard crash of thunder. Julia gasped, as did Lady Delabole. The horses reared up. Julia heard the muffled cry of the postilion as he was thrown from his horse. The team bolted forward, and then, as another blinding sheet of lightning engulfed the windows and a horrific crack of thunder shot through the hills, it seemed as though the entire equipage was picked up and turned sideways, then thrown flat.

Julia fell on top of her mother.

"Mama!" she screamed.

Everything happened so fast.

A long slide downward. Horses screaming, tangled in the traces, legs broken in the scramble as the chariot slid on its side down the rampart. Down. Down.

The pit was a deep, dark hole.

Julia awoke to the feel of rain on her face. The front window-glass had shattered in the accident and the rain was pelting her.

At first she couldn't remember where she was. Her head ached abominably. She was lying on top of something soft.

Her mother. She tried to move but her leg was badly cut, and because of the pain that sliced through her as she attempted to shift her leg, she suspected it was broken. She heard her mother moaning.

"I'm hurt," Julia said, ineffectively trying to explain why she couldn't move very quickly off her. They were jumbled together, lying on the inside of the door, her mother in a heap on the floor of the coach, Julia partially atop of her.

With great effort, Julia was able to extend herself onto the side window and part of the seat. She strained to place her head near her mother and saw that the white ostrich feather was smashed against her cheek. A trickle of water dripped from each rain-soaked tendril. The heavy gray sky overhead, the sheets of rain still pummeling the countryside, and the depth of the quarry all kept the coach cloaked in darkness. Every now and then one of the horses would cry and shake, making the carriage, still attached by the pole, quiver.

"Mama," Julia whispered.

She could hear her mother struggling to breathe. She leaned closer and saw that a rivulet of blood seeped from between open lips. Her face was ashen, her blue eyes clouded with pain. "So much to tell you," Lady Delabole whispered, then coughed. "My darling girl. I am too late. God help you."

"No, don't speak," Julia directed. Fear took hold of her. Was she looking at death? Oh, God, no. Please don't let her die.

"Your father," Lady Delabole whispered, her chest rising in shallow gasps. "You mustn't . . ." She moaned and tears slipped down her face. "Pain . . . dear Julia." Wildly, she searched for Julia's face. "I can't see you. I'm so . . . cold."

"Mama, no," Julia whimpered, finding her mother's hand and pressing it to her cheek.

"You must listen," Lady Delabole said, her breathing ragged. "You must . . . take my ring. Keep it close to you always. You . . . you will need it."

"No," Julia protested. "I don't want your ring. I want you. Please, Mama."

"Hush, child," Lady Delabole responded gently, coughing. "Do as I say. Take my ring now and . . . and let no one else have it. No one. Do you understand?"

"Yes, Mama," Julia murmured. She tugged at the emerald ring on her mother's right hand.

Lady Delabole smiled. "I love you . . . tell them all . . . make something beautiful for me."

Then she was gone.

The Priory, Somerset

Sir Perran Blackthorn learned of the accident later that evening over a glass of sherry. The news of Olivia's death was as unwelcome as it was untimely. When he dismissed his butler, he seated himself in a russet velvet Queen Anne winged chair, and stared heavily into a crackling wood fire for a long, thoughtful moment.

"Cursed Providence," he muttered at last, leaning forward on his ivory-handled cane. He was in perfect health and excellent condition for a man in his sixties. Really, he had no need of the cane, but he had always found a professed lameness to be of inestimable value in eliciting sympathy. Olivia had been very sympathetic and now she was dead.

Ah, well. He could easily shift his attention from the mother to the eldest daughter.

Salamanca, Spain

Near midnight, Major Edward Blackthorn held Julia's letter of condolence in his hand. He read it through again by candlelight as he sat on his camp bed. Some of the words were smudged—tearstains, undoubtedly. His own throat grew tight with grief as he called to mind the day of his brother's death. He had only hinted to Julia at how horrible George's passing had actually been.

Edward had held his brother's gaunt white fingers in one hand and wiped a film of sweat from his own brow with his other. He had made use of a perfumed kerchief, given to him by one of the officer's wives when she learned his brother was ill, which he intended to keep with him at the hospital until his fate was known.

The Spanish summer sun had proved hot through the army tent and in the close confines of the makeshift hospital. Beds were crammed end to end, the stench of dysentery and the rotting flesh of gangrene overpowering. He was perpetually nauseated and frequently held the kerchief, redolent of roses, to his nose to gain a small measure of relief.

His brother slipped in and out of consciousness, his bowels loose and bloody, his body raging with fever. Edward stared into George's beloved face, ravaged and distorted by the quick, virulent disease. Never would he have guessed, when they were children, that this would be his end, his brother thin and wasted from disease. George had always been the stoutest of them all.

And now George was dying—the last of his family. All lost to France, to Bonaparte—his mother, his father, Stephen, and now George. Stephen had perished three years earlier in the battle of Talavera. His parents had been gone since just before the turn of the century.

Edward felt George's hand move beneath his. He hid the kerchief in the palm of his hand and quickly returned his gaze to George's face. How peaceful his brother seemed. Far too peaceful.

"Is it true," George whispered, his breathing a thin wheeze, "that Wellington gave the order to attack while eating a chicken leg?"

Edward smiled. He would miss George's sense of humor most of all. "That is the word," he responded, tears filling his gray eyes. "He was chewing along as nicely as you please, suddenly let the half-eaten leg drop, grabbed a telescope, saw a widening gap in the leading French division, and supposedly said, 'That will do.' He sent his aides galloping off with his orders, and here we are."

George squeezed his hand. "Give Boney hell," he whispered. Then he released one final breath into the fetid air of the hospital tent.

As Blackthorn reread Julia's letter, sipping a glass of Madeira, he again bid goodbye to his brother, letting the tears fall where they would. When he had blown his nose and composed himself, he made a solemn vow that he would see Bonaparte destroyed or his own corpse rotting on a battlefield before he would ever give up the fight against the Corsican monster.

One

I slept, and dreamed that life was Beauty;
I woke, and found that life was Duty.
                                        —Ellen Sturgis Hooper

Bath, England
June 1814

Julia stood at the entrance to the ballroom of the Upper Assembly Rooms on Alfred Street, a blush warming her cheeks. She knew that her dampened muslin shift was still clinging to her legs and she felt sick with shame. How had it come to pass that desperation had begun to rule even her sense of decency?

But what else could she do? she reminded herself. Lord Peter Longton was proving difficult, slow upon his feet and about as amorous as a lazy cat basking in the hot sun. So she had dampened the muslin of her shift so that the gossamer gathers and folds of her white muslin ball gown, adorned with an exquisite Brussels lace, would cling provocatively to her hips. She even wore a faint rouge upon her cheeks and lips, hoping beyond hope that these subtle artifices might warm His Lordship's recalcitrant heart.

As she watched the Master of Ceremonies escorting the Countess Howarth to open the assembly by dancing the minuet, Julia found herself regretting the dampened muslin and the rouge, but not less so the terrible need that was driving her to behave beneath her sense of dignity and propriety.

Lord Peter, second son of the Marquis of Trevaunance, was the man of her choosing. His birth and breeding matched her own, he was suitably handsome, and he was in possession of an easy competence that made him an eligible match by all standards. Of course what she needed most from him were his connections—which he had in abundance—for her sisters Elizabeth, Caroline, and Annabelle.

He had been in Bath for two months now and had made her his particular object. Yet she hadn't been able to bring him up to scratch. Two months was far too long. She knew as much. If a gentleman did not offer within that allotment of time, his attentions usually wandered to the next pretty face, dimpling smile, and splay of painted fan.

Tonight she meant to flirt outrageously with him, to entice him, to command him if she could. She had to. Time had become her enemy. Julia felt a sudden prickling of tears behind her eyes, tears of extreme frustration and chagrin. She didn't want to attend the assembly rooms in this way, to be pursuing a man with such unhappy motives.

"I don't see him, Julia," Elizabeth whispered behind her fan of pale blue lace. She was standing next to her and had only recently come to learn of Julia's intentions toward Lord Peter. "I thought he had promised you he would attend the assemblies this evening."

"He did promise," Julia whispered in return. She met her sister's accusing blue eyes. "Stop glaring at me. He will be here. He will."

"He was not at the Pump Room yesterday morning at eight o'clock and, if memory serves me, he said he would be there."

Julia repressed a sigh of frustration. "I'm sure he has a perfectly reasonable explanation."

"He could have at least sent round a missive to Hatherleigh informing you of that reason," Elizabeth suggested.

Julia knew her sister was right, which only added to her general sense of misery. "He . . . he is not the most reliable man," she admitted, "But you would do me a great service if you wouldn't always be reminding me of it."

At that, Elizabeth smiled, appearing so much like her mother that Julia could do nothing more than smile in return. "I'm sorry," Elizabeth said, then continued earnestly. "Dearest Julia, are you certain you must marry Lord Peter?"

Julia felt her cheeks grow warmer still. "Hush," she commanded her younger sister, lifting her white lace fan to hide her lips. "You know I must, if he is willing. But pray say no more, if you please. A dozen ears are listening."

Elizabeth could not remain silent. "I just can't believe things have come to such a pass that you must sell yourself, like a lowborn female at a wife auction, to the highest bidder."

"What stuff and nonsense," Julia retorted. "I will not have been the first lady of quality to marry for convenience."

"But are you certain even our dowries are gone?"

Julia nodded. She had only this morning, when her sister had persisted in harassing her about her scheme to marry Lord Peter, informed Elizabeth of the dark nature of their circumstances.

Elizabeth sighed heavily and glanced about the long rectangular chamber. "Then I must see what I can do about getting myself a husband. Perhaps then I can prevent your making such a wretched mistake."

"I am not making a mistake," Julia returned firmly. "He is an excellent man, a gentleman. Besides, I should like to see you try to win a worthy man. You have but to open your mouth to express just one of your forthright opinions, and your beaus run from you like hares before the hounds!"

Elizabeth smiled fully, evidencing her even, white teeth and a twinkle in her eye, an engaging picture beneath the sparkling light of the assembly room's several tiered and quite magnificent chandeliers. "Only the fainthearted run away," she retorted, unoffended by Julia's remark. "So I don't repine in the least. A man who lacks pluck might as well stick his spoon in the wall and be done with it! I have no opinion of cowardly men."

With that, as the orchestra in the alcove above the ballroom floor played on, Elizabeth moved away, her gown of pale blue silk swaying slightly, her carriage perfect, her bright, forceful disposition causing several gentlemen to immediately descend upon her. She was always a favorite at an assembly, regardless of the boldness of her speech.

Julia turned her attention to the lovely Countess Howarth, a lady with whom she was only barely acquainted, and watched her move through the elegant steps of the minuet. Of all the ladies present, she held the highest rank and thus earned the honor of sharing the first dance exclusively with the Master of Ceremonies. Her gown of violet silk, along with the solemn and very formal blacks and whites of the Master of Ceremonies, was a perfect complement to the stately dignity of the Upper Assembly Rooms.

The curved ballroom ceiling rose high above the polished wood floor and was adorned with beautiful white stucco decorations of garlands, festoons, and laurel branches. The upper half of the walls, rising over twoscore feet to the ceiling, was punctuated with Corinthian columns. Julia had counted them once. There were forty in all, each at least twelve feet in height. An infantry line of chairs surrounded the ballroom floor, upon which sat Bath's aristocracy and gentry, visitors and citizens alike, the ladies dressed in regal Empire gowns in a rainbow of colors and the gentlemen sporting formal black or white coats and silk breeches. Several officers, recently returned from the Continent, wore dress uniforms in blues and reds, decorated with silver or gold braiding, much to the appreciation of a people grateful Napoleon had finally been forced out of France and onto a tiny island in the Mediterranean.

Fans moved slowly over warm faces, and the gentle music of the minuet seemed to keep the general tone of the conversations subdued as the solitary couple moved elegantly through the motions of the dance. Julia loved the decorous air and calmness of Bath society. As the past two years had unfolded and the true nature of her father's affliction had come to light, Julia had grown more and more to appreciate the order of the society in which she moved. Her circumstances might be chaotic, but she could rely on the constant rhythm of Bath life to keep her head clear and her thinking steady.

If only her father hadn't taken to gaming so fiercely when her mother died. Her throat grew tight with anxiety and frustration, and she immediately gave herself a mental shake. This would not do! She could not succumb to a sense of despair at the Upper Assembly Rooms.

She took a deep breath and released it slowly. She would not repine, she would not wish her life otherwise. She knew her lot was a difficult one; she had accepted that.

Still, where was Lord Peter?

Julia finally moved away from the entrance and took up a seat beside her friend Mary Brown, who teased her instantly behind her fan, which sported a painted scene of a ferry crossing the River Avon. "How pretty you look in your dampened muslin!" she whispered. "Are you wearing rouge? I vow Lord Peter will be struck dumb by the sight of you."

Mary was a spirited young lady, shorter than Julia, and her brown eyes perpetually bore a mischievous gleam. She wore her dark brown hair in Caroline Lamb's style, clipped short and wisped about the face, which suited her vibrant temperament well. Julia enjoyed her company very much.

"What an excellent friend you are, Miss Brown," Julia retorted facetiously. "I can always rely on you to remind me of precisely that which I wish undone."

"Don't be a widgeon! I only noticed your rouge because I was the one who suggested you wear it! I have been staring at you for the past several minutes, trying to determine if you had decided to take my advice. Only now, when you are sitting beside me, can I finally detect that you have done so!" She giggled. "So, pray, don't take a pet. You're as pretty as a picture, as always!"

Julia sighed with relief. "Then it is not so obvious as I believe? I had begun to think I appeared like an actress at Drury Lane."

"Not by half," Mary responded quietly. "In truth, I don't believe you need a whit of rouge. You are still Bath's reigning beauty, and why you must resort to such measures to bring Lord Peter to heel I can't imagine. He's clearly besotted and should've been begging for your hand in marriage long before now. He never stays far from your side no matter where he finds you, whether at the assemblies, the Pump Room, or the concerts. Really, if you ask me, Julia, the whole of it is a mystery."

Julia was disquieted by her friend's whispered speech. She looked into Mary's dark brown eyes and experienced a strong impulse to tell her the truth—that she rather suspected Lord Peter had come to learn the nature of her father's difficulties and was disinclined to offer for her—but she held back the words. How shocked Mary would be if she knew the extent of Lord Delabole's debts.

"It is something of a mystery, I suppose," Julia responded evenly. "But you assume that Lord Peter's heart has been engaged. I cannot be so certain."

"He is violently in love with you!" Mary exclaimed.

Yet, even if his affections are so engaged, Julia thought, turning her gaze away from Mary and again watching the countess and the Master of Ceremonies, *not sufficiently to offer for me.*

Fear worried the edges of her heart and she glanced down at her hands clasped tightly upon her lap. What if he didn't offer for her?

Surreptitiously, she slid her hand to the side of her muslin skirts and felt for the hidden pocket sewn into the seam of her dampened shift. She found the pocket and ran a quick finger over the small enameled snuffbox tucked within its depths. Inside the box was Lady Delabole's emerald ring.

A year after her mother's death, after she had come to understand the gravity of her family's circumstances, Julia had had the ring appraised and discovered that because it was a gem of the first water, it was worth a small fortune. Her mother had said she would have need of the ring in the future, but had Lady Delabole really known how great her need would be?

She now believed her mother had.

Two years had passed since the accident at the quarry, and time was pressing Julia to the point of madness. If she was not advantageously married very soon, her future would be lost, as would be any hope of seeing her sisters well settled. The daughters of Lady Delabole would be destined forever to take up posts as governesses to children not their own or as companions to elderly, infirm ladies. Except for the sisters, the Verdell family had all but disappeared from the face of the earth. There was not a single aunt, uncle, cousin, or grandparent to whom Julia could turn for help. The Viscounts Delabole, with the death of her two brothers in a yachting accident a year after her mother's death, were simply no more. Thoughts of her brothers and her mother brought tears again prickling the back of her eyes. Too much death, too much grief. If only her father had been more reliable. Now, she was in desperate straits.

Time. A lovely little ormolu clock of gilded bronze sat upon a pretty beribboned shelf in her mind and ticked away, slowly, steadily, inexorably. She alone was responsible, and sometimes the weight of that responsibility made her feel as if her arms and legs had been strapped with several layers of boned stays, until she could hardly move. Had she been required to see only to her own future, how simple her decisions would be. She would not have dampened her muslins tonight, nor even been in attendance at a ball at one of the assembly rooms. Where would she be? Julia wondered. Probably working in a milliner's shop and writing poetry, painting with watercolors and practicing her pianoforte late at night, unwed, childless, but at least enjoying her daily labors and living without fear.

She had long known she was ill placed as first in a line of four daughters. She was not suited to the task before her. Elizabeth had more fire and strength of will. Elizabeth would have seen everything settled long before now, long before the Delabole world was ready to crash down about her ears.

Julia drew in a deep breath. Such useless musings, ponderings, wishings. She knew her duty, despite her belief she was ill equipped to manage the whole business. She would do her duty to the very highest of her ability. She always had, she always would.

But did she have enough understanding to make the right choices? Did she err in pursuing Lord Peter? Would everything hold until all was settled? Where was Lord Peter? So much depended upon the leanings of his heart and upon his courage.

She felt Mary's elbow prodding her ribs. "He's here!" her friend whispered.

Julia's gaze shot toward the entrance to the chambers. Only with the strongest effort did she hold back a great sigh of relief. Lord Peter had indeed arrived and was surveying the ballroom in his quiet manner.

As the minuet drew to a close, and the Master of Ceremonies bowed deeply to his partner and the lady curtsied in return, Julia turned her attention to the man she hoped to make her husband. She watched him, pleased with his manly bearing, his calm, composed countenance, his lack of arrogance. He met the gaze of an acquaintance seated across from Julia. He smiled pleasantly and inclined his head. His manners were perfect and gentlemanly, as was his appearance. He wore a black coat and tails, a white embroidered waistcoat, white silk breeches, and black leather slippers. His neckcloth was of a simple design, his starched shirt points moderate in height; he wore only a seal and a gold signet ring. His blond hair was cut in curls about his head, dressed in a loose fashion called *à la Cherubim,* which gave him an angelic appearance. His eyes were a warm, dark brown, his general expression agreeable.

As Julia studied him, she came to believe she could be very content with such a man. Affection suddenly flooded her heart, surprising her, causing her to realize that though she was in desperate pursuit, she had not left her heart far behind her present need. The sensation soothed her prickly conscience so that when Lord Peter in his search of the ballroom found her, smiled at her, and crossed the chamber to greet her, Julia did not hesitate to rise to her feet and permit him to kiss the back of her hand.

When her gaze met smiling brown eyes, she said, "How glad I am you've come."

"Did you suppose I wouldn't?" he queried, then clicked his tongue. "You are still piqued that I did not keep our assignation at the Pump Room. Will you forgive me if I say that my curricle lost a wheel just past Pulteney Bridge yesterday morning and I have spent the past two days seeing that repairs were made to my satisfaction? You cannot imagine how difficult it is to find a wheelwright who will perform his craft properly. Ah, I see that the country dance is forming. Will you do me the honor?"

Elizabeth's words drove to the forefront of her mind: *He could have at least sent round a missive to Hatherleigh.* She wondered if it occurred to Lord Peter how much she would have appreciated such a gesture. The affection that she had experienced a moment earlier dimmed with these thoughts as she placed her hand lightly upon his proffered arm.

If only Lord Peter were more reliable and considerate. If only he would make pretty love to her, tell her she was beautiful, kiss her fingers, whisper lines from a sonnet deeply into her ear.

She understood quite suddenly, as he led her onto the ballroom floor, that she had been lying to herself about him, about her pursuit of him.

How silly!

Julia almost laughed aloud at the trick her mind had played upon her yet again. She wasn't encouraging him solely because she needed to marry him. She had dampened her muslin shift and enhanced the color of her cheeks and lips with rouge because love was eluding her, like a teasing fairy floating about the edges of her vision, hiding behind prettily gowned ladies, peeping at her from the orchestra's alcove, laughing at her from within one of the glittering, glowing chandeliers. Love was what she sought.

Could Lord Peter love her?

Did it matter?

"How charming you look this evening, Miss Verdell," he said, smiling down on her as they made their way through the dancers.

He always said as much. If only once he would vary his compliments.

"Thank you," she responded, as was expected.

Her heart sank. Mary Brown believed Lord Peter to be violently in love with her. But if his current demeanor toward her was the evidence of violent affection, Julia wondered what he would be like five or ten years into a marriage when his ardor had cooled. *The dullest dog on earth* was the sad description that came sharply to mind.

She sighed. So love was eluding her. Love had never been part and parcel of the bargain as the eldest of four sisters, anyway. Taking a deep breath, Julia set aside the deep longings of her heart, turning her mind and her will instead to the task at hand. Love or not, she must marry Lord Peter, and be quick about it!

She decided, therefore, that it was time to flirt with him, to see if she could encourage him to a greater level of devotion, one that might prompt him to offer for her hand. But just as she opened her mouth to comment upon how handsome he was, his attention was caught by Lady Howarth nearby, who begged to know how his mother and father fared. Lord Peter stopped briefly to answer the countess's polite inquiry.

When Lady Howarth moved away, Julia began again, intending to tell him how much she admired the style of his neckcloth. But as she uttered the words *how much,* he stepped away from her in order to take up his place opposite her. Lord Peter was then distracted by a lady behind him, who had fallen into a fit of coughing, and Julia's words died on her tongue. She felt strange and awkward and knew she must be the most hopeless female ever. For though she could hear the happy chatter of any number of young ladies scattered about the Upper Rooms, eagerly flirting with, cajoling, and teasing their young men, she was quite evidently not gifted with such abilities.

Julia would not give up, however, and began once again. "I have been wanting for some time to tell you, Lord Peter, just how—"

The orchestra struck the first, second, and third notes of Handel's simple country dance, and her remaining words of praise on the fit of his coat upon his broad shoulders were lost to the music.

He begged pardon, in a loud voice, but he couldn't hear her just yet. She smiled hopelessly and in the end, as the movements of the dance permitted, she gave up her attempts at flirtation entirely. She resorted instead to her usual ballroom discourse— inquiring quite politely and considerately after his family, after his interests, and after any particular subject that she knew he enjoyed. A happy benefit quickly accrued: She was able to relax and enjoy the country dance as well as the friendly conversation that followed.

By the end of the set, however, Julia was as close to marrying Lord Peter as she was to eloping with the Master of Ceremonies. Whatever was she going to do?

He released her shortly after the country dance drew to a close so that she might seek out her next partner, just as he was obligated by the customs of the assembly to partner another lady. She watched him go, wondering what the end would be of their lethargic courtship.

Later in the evening, when refreshments were served in the tearoom opposite the ballroom, Julia was just entering the octagonal antechamber, which separated the main wings of the Assembly Rooms, when she saw the Master of Ceremonies and an officer leave the ballroom directly across from her. The officer was tall, quite handsome, and walked with a soldier's stride and bearing. In the dim light of the antechamber, he seemed quite familiar to her and she wondered if he had been in Bath very long. He wore a dark blue dress coat, with red lapels and facings decorated with gleaming silver braid. He was quite athletic in appearance, his shoulders broad and tapering in a manly silhouette to a narrow waist, lean hips, and muscular thighs encased in white silk breeches.

Much to her surprise, she experienced a sudden and very powerful attraction to him, something she had never quite experienced before. Julia paused in her steps and lifted her fan to her face, moving the lace spindles quickly across her suddenly flushed features. Who was he? she wondered.

He was sun-bronzed, probably from having served in the Peninsula for many years, the deep color of his skin setting off to extreme advantage the grayness of his eyes. He wore his raven black hair tied back with a black riband. How unusual. The effect, so at variance with the classical styles worn *à la Brutus,* like her father, or *à la Cherubim,* like Lord Peter, was stunning and lent him a wild, untamed appearance. He could have stepped from the pages of Lord Byron's *Corsair.*

The blue of his dress coat indicated he might belong to a light cavalry regiment. She thought of Major Edward Blackthorn, her major, her Edward, whom she had not seen in eight long years, though she had corresponded with him regularly. She had hoped that once the war had ended he would find the time to return to Bath, to visit his uncle, Sir Perran Blackthorn, and to pay a call upon the inmates of Hatherleigh Park. But he had been attached to Wellington's staff after Bonaparte abdicated, and he had been unable to return to England as yet.

Watching the officer, who she realized bore a striking resemblance to Edward, Julia felt a sudden longing for the major. The last time she had seen him, she had been a schoolgirl of only thirteen and he a dashing young lieutenant of eighteen. He had bid her a sweet goodbye, promising to write—a promise that he had kept!—and informing her she was fast growing into a beauty. He had placed a gentle kiss on her lips. She touched her lips now, behind the safety of her fan, remembering how surprisingly soft his lips had been. How odd that she could recall the feel of his kiss after so long a time. Had it really been eight years since she had last seen him?

Her reverie was broken abruptly when the Master of Ceremonies called to her. "Miss Verdell! Do let me recommend a partner to you in a new acquaintance of mine." With the officer in tow, he was soon before her. "May I present Sir Perran's nephew, Major Blackthorn? I wonder if you recall him. He was just asking after you, saying he used to be acquainted with you when you were very young."

Julia turned to stare hard at the officer before her. Was it possible? Her mouth fell slightly agape as she tilted her head and looked into sweetly familiar gray eyes. "Edward?" she queried, not believing it was really him. "But I thought you were in London! I can't believe you're actually here. Oh, Edward, you've come home!"

How strange she felt. She could no longer feel her white silk slippers touching the floor. Was she floating?

For his part, he was staring back at her in complete amazement. "I wouldn't have known you!" he cried, extending one of his arms toward her, then the other. "Julia, my pet!"

She was not aware of her improper conduct as she threw herself into his arms. He embraced her fully, holding her tightly to him. "Edward, when did you return? You haven't been to Hatherleigh! My dearest friend! Do let me look at you!" She pulled away from him but held his arms tightly, as though afraid if she let him go he would disappear. Her thoughts were disjointed and her words followed suit. "How very dashing you are in your regimentals! You will be breaking hearts before the night is ended! Did I ever thank you for all your letters over the years? You've no idea how much I depended on them. Why haven't you called on me, wretched man? Oh, Edward!" Again she was in his arms, weeping on his shoulder and holding him tight. "Do you know how often I worried that you would be killed? But now you are here, safe and alive!"

Only after a long moment did she release him, and only then because she became aware that the Master of Ceremonies was scowling at her.

The horrendous nature of her conduct caused Julia to fly backward, out of Edward's arms. "Oh, I do beg your pardon!" she cried, dropping a quick curtsy to the disapproving and astonished Master of Ceremonies. She wiped at her cheeks and her eyes with her hands, but to little avail, and was grateful when Edward drew his kerchief from the pocket of his coat and gave it to her.

"Thank you," Julia breathed, slowly becoming aware that she was now the object of much interest. The antechamber, connecting the ballroom with the cardroom and the tearoom, was always crisscrossed with people, many of whom were now gaping at her.

Much she cared! Edward was home. He was safe. He was alive. She dabbed at her nose, her cheeks, her eyes, laughing and crying still.

The Master of Ceremonies' harsh expression softened in quick stages. "Well, well! We are all grateful Bonaparte has been banished at last. But I hope, Miss Verdell, you do not intend to vault yourself upon all our returning officers with such abandon, or I shall be obligated to scratch your name from my book." He had spoken with a warm smile and she knew she was forgiven.

"I promise, I shall not do so again."

"Very well," he returned with a twitch of his lips. "I daresay that Major Blackthorn would not refuse a cup of tea?" He lifted a brow to Julia, and she immediately took up his hint and led Edward to the tearoom.

Just as she passed through the doorway, she happened to glance past Edward's shoulder and saw that Lord Peter was watching her with a curious expression on his face. He seemed utterly astonished. She felt an impulse to go to him, to introduce Edward to him, to make certain he did not misinterpret her conduct toward her childhood friend, but Julia instantly decided against it. All she wanted for the present was to be alone with Edward for a few precious moments. If Lord Peter disapproved . . . well, she would not worry about that just yet. Time enough to gentle his sensibilities after she had become reacquainted with Edward.

Julia shifted her attention back to Edward as they entered the tearoom. She smiled up at him, happy to be walking beside him after so many years. She had so much she wanted to know, so many questions to ask, that she simply did not know where to begin. Finally, she asked the most obvious one—how long he intended to stay in Bath. He responded that he would be staying at The Priory until the end of August, at which time Wellington would have need of him in Paris.

"Two months, then," Julia responded with a happy sigh of satisfaction. "How wonderful! Then I shall come to know you again. Do say you will make an effort to call upon my father. He will be delighted to see you. Elizabeth, too, though I daresay neither Caroline nor Annabelle will remember you."

Edward expressed a desire to pay a visit to Hatherleigh as soon as he was able. "I have affairs of business in Cornwall, which will command my time occasionally, but nothing shall keep me from Hatherleigh Park . . . that I promise you."

Julia looked at him in wonder, still unable to believe he was really with her. "Do you dance well, Edward?" she asked. "In all our letters, I cannot recall the subject ever having arisen."

"Tolerably," he replied, smiling affectionately upon her.

"I should like to dance with you above all things," she stated. Now, how long had that been a desire of hers? she wondered.

He seemed amused and vastly pleased. "I wish I had known you had grown into such a beauty. I should have come back to England long before today."

She felt herself blush beneath his praise, in spite of the fact that he was only Edward after all. "Have you only just arrived?" she queried.

"A few hours past," he explained as he seated her at a table in the tearoom, then took up a chair beside her. "Any earlier and I would have called at Hatherleigh. Instead, I contented myself by attending the assemblies, hoping that our good Master of Ceremonies would forgive my not having called on him earlier."

Julia watched him fondly, listening to his deep voice with pleasure, and began marking off in her mind every spare hour she could give to him in the coming months. She was so happy to have him home, to be with him again, she could hardly speak. she watched his gray eyes narrow slightly. His thoughts were drifting; she could see as much in the expression on his face. What was he thinking? she wondered.

Major Edward Blackthorn sighed inwardly. Faith, but Julia had grown into a considerable beauty. Her face was an oval shape, her nose was straight, and her brows were arched gently over thickly fringed lashes. Yet, however pleasing these features might be, her eyes were by far the best of them all, a deep emerald-green from which a keen intelligence shone. Her lips were neither full nor thin, simply kissable. Her hair was a lustrous auburn, and given the thickness of her chignon, he supposed her locks to be very long. He wondered what her hair would be like pulled down about her creamy white shoulders and touching the swell of her rounded breasts, visible above the décolletage of her white muslin gown. A sudden desire for her swept over him once more, just as it had a few moments ago when he had held her in his arms.

How surprised he had been by the sensations that filled him when he had found her clinging to him. When he met Julia again, Edward had not expected that he would feel this way toward her—physically exhilarated. But her beauty of person, the delicious feel of her womanly body in his arms, the surprising strength of his emotions as he held her, had all caused him to want nothing more than to kiss her forcefully. How shocked the Master of Ceremonies would have been had he given in to that particular impulse!

As he looked at her now, he wished they were anywhere but in the constraining tearoom of the Upper Rooms. A little privacy and he would not have hesitated to take her in his arms and kiss her hard. Given the way she watched him with parted lips, Edward suspected that she would have received his kiss willingly.

His thoughts turned abruptly to rumors of an imminent betrothal. His uncle had told him that Lord Peter Longton, Trevaunance's second son, was very near to offering for her, an event eagerly anticipated by all of Bath society. Julia was greatly beloved in Bath, and an alliance with the Trevaunance family was felt to be her due. At the time, Edward had scarcely reacted to the news, save for a detached gratification that her future would be a grand one given Lord Trevaunance's exalted place in the Prince Regent's circle of acquaintance.

But right now, nothing seemed worse to him than Julia married to another man.

Yet of course she would one day marry, and the only really surprising aspect of it all was that she wasn't yet wed, especially given her beauty, her elegance, and her birth. Would Lord Peter make her a good husband, though? Knowing His Lordship, Edward highly doubted it. What the devil was a filly of Julia's stamp thinking, encouraging the advances of a man who hadn't the smallest strength of spine? Edward would have long since written to her of his opinion of her beau, whom he had met in London earlier in the year, but for some reason Julia had failed to make mention of Lord Peter in her letters. She had written of her numerous Bath acquaintances, of her father, of a hint of some unexplained financial difficulties, of her sisters Elizabeth, Caroline, and Annabelle, but of Lord Peter not a single dash, period, nor exclamation mark.

That was the rub. She hadn't confided in him. Yet she had been an unflagging correspondent, an anchor in his life of Spanish heat and tedium, of army dust and the perpetual presence of hordes of vultures, of the wondering, the waiting and finally the entrance into the chaos and nightmare that was battling the French. He believed he owed his sanity to her clear hand and sensible words.

She had written him dozens of letters over the years, many of which had gotten lost in the inevitable quick starts and abrupt stops of living as a soldier, year in and year out, on the Iberian Peninsula. Those letters that remained he kept close, afraid that if he lost them all, he would lose part of himself forever. Julia had come to represent England to him, especially now that George was gone. When in the midst of the aftermath of a terrible battle, having chased the vultures off a corpse that used to be a good friend and fellow officer, when his heart was set low in his soul's horizon, Edward had but to bring Julia to mind and his spirits would right themselves.

He realized now, that through all his years of service, this moment, this reacquaintance with Julia, had been an unacknowledged objective of his.

Julia sipped her tea and watched Edward's eyes. How intense his expression was. She felt an incomprehensible trembling within, as though her thoughts, not yet completely formed, had already communicated themselves to her quickly beating heart, to the butterflies in her stomach, to her trembling limbs.

She set her teacup on the saucer and returned her hands to her lap, where she clasped them together tightly. Her breathing was oddly shallow. Her lips were parted, as though to speak, but no words came forth for a long moment. Finally, she said, "You've come home." How inadequately these words expressed the sentiments that filled her heart. Julia heard the strains of a country dance emanating from the direction of the ballroom, noting from the periphery of her vision that the tearoom was quickly clearing of people. She ought to seek her partner, but she was incapable of doing more than looking at Edward.

He leaned forward abruptly and placed a hand over hers. In a whisper, he asked, "What is this nonsense I have been hearing about Lord Peter?"

Julia felt stunned by his question, as though he had slapped her lightly across the face. She averted her gaze and drew in a sharp breath.

"Are you betrothed?" he asked quickly.

She shook her head. "No."

"If he asks you—which I am told he will—do you intend to wed him?"

Julia looked at him. "I . . . yes," she responded awkwardly. A thousand thoughts seemed to rage through her mind at once—that she didn't want to marry Lord Peter at all, that she wanted her father to cease gaming, that she wanted only to race around in the hills with Edward, that she didn't want to be dutiful anymore.

He leaned back in his chair, removing his hand from over hers. "The devil take it," he murmured, frowning.

Julia's heart seemed to fail her in that moment. "My life is not so simple anymore," she said, hoping he might read her thoughts, hoping he might somehow come to fully comprehend the few hints she had dropped in her correspondence with him—that she desperately needed to marry a man of substance.

"Does your father approve of the match?" he asked.

"Yes, of course," she answered quietly.

Edward continued to frown and to search her eyes. "But he has not offered for you," he said.

Julia shook her head. "No, he has not."

A slow smile spread across his features. "Then I have not come home too late."

Julia looked at him, a great sadness stealing over her. Clearly, he had not understood her letters after all. If he had, he would never have intimated anything so hopeless as an interest in engaging her affections. She could not wed a mere Major Blackthorn, without fortune, without connections, whose only prospects involved rising in rank within the British Army, and whose end was likely to be death on a hated field of battle.

When from the doorway Mary's younger brother appeared, announcing to Julia that she was to dance the next set with him, she found herself relieved. She knew that before very long she would have to tell Edward the truth about her circumstances—but not tonight, not on the day of his return to Bath. She introduced Mr. Brown to him instead, then begged him to call at Hatherleigh as soon as he was able.

"I will," he responded.

As she took Mr. Brown's arm and moved away, Julia glanced back at Edward, who was smiling warmly upon her. She wanted to reach out to him, to touch him, to embrace him again so that she could be reassured he was really with her. He was like a specter, a ghost who had come to visit. She could not believe he was real.

Yet he was real, and she was so happy he had come home.

She returned his smile and, with her fingers, blew him a kiss over her shoulder.

Two

Later that night, Blackthorn stood in front of the fireplace in his bedchamber at The Priory. He held a fencing sword in hand, having long since cast off his black leather dancing slippers. He was enjoying the feel of the cool wood floor beneath his stockinged feet.

His blue dress uniform coat was slung over the back of a gold and white striped Empire chair and his neckcloth lay crumpled in a heap on the seat. His white shirt, open at the neck and loose about the shoulders and wrists, was still tucked into snug-fitting white silk breeches, though for ease of movement he had unbuttoned one side of the small falls. Flexing the tip of his sword, he saluted a portrait of a youthful Sir Perran, which hung above the mantel.

He began moving back and forth about the hearth, around the bed, then to either side of the massive carved mahogany wardrobe, thrusting his sword, sliding away from invisible opponents. He kept his knees bent, his feet light, his movements quick, an arm extended in proper form for balance.

The effort of practicing a thrust, a feint, a parry, caused his heart to beat rapidly. His brain cleared. He continued to move. He could think better when in motion than when sitting comfortably in a chair, his mind settling into a stupor of inattention the longer he remained inert. Besides, the inactivity of sitting and thinking somehow kept his mind pinned to Julia—the wonder of seeing her for the first time in eight years, the feel of her in his arms, his increasing dislike of her scheme to pursue and marry Lord Peter. The longer he sat, the more his thoughts became fixed on her, thoughts for the present he needed to set aside.

No, it was far better to be moving about the bedchamber. The more he moved about, the better he was able to attend to the pressing matter at hand.

He hadn't told Julia the precise truth. He had not come to Bath after all these years merely to visit the city, his uncle, Hatherleigh Park, and to attend to matters of business in Cornwall. On the bed were twoscore of documents that Wellington had given him before he left London, all of which he had studied for the past several days—dates, names, places.

After returning from the Upper Assembly Rooms, he had tossed the documents yet again on the bed and carefully reviewed several of the more recent ones, trying to uncover the trail he sought. It would seem someone connected to his uncle was a traitor, a Bonapartist in fact, a French patriot intent upon seeing Napoleon restored to the throne in Paris. Bonaparte would not remain long on Elba, of that he was convinced. The famous general had once ruled most of Europe. Was he now to be content with Elba as his sole domain? No. Impossible. Never.

Edward stopped suddenly in the middle of a quick thrust and stood upright, pointing the blade toward the floor. He drew in a slow deep breath and listened. What was it he had heard? A scraping, a sliding, a shuffling? He turned his head toward the doorway and scrutinized every sound. He breathed deeply and slowly, his lips parted slightly.

Nothing.

Yet he knew someone was beyond the door. He could feel the presence of another person as surely as he was breathing and listening. The sensation began to pass, as quickly as it had appeared. He stepped forward, his bare feet silent on the carpet, and listened again. He then ran quickly to the door and jerked it open. No one was there, only a brief shadow that might have been a man, disappearing at the end of the hall.

Still holding his sword in hand, Edward shifted it several

times, his heart racing. He felt the presence of an enemy, now *his* enemy, just as surely as if he sat astride his horse and faced the French across a wide field. Only this was not a soldier against whom he might lift his sword, but rather a man of cunning and nerve, who preferred to fight his war in shadows, in documents, in secrecy.

Blackthorn waited a moment, then strode back into his bed-chamber. All had changed, he realized. No longer was this merely an assignment given him by a superior officer, cold orders written on a piece of paper to be dispatched at will. This was now war, *his* war. Personal and deadly. But how to win a war so at odds with his training as an officer of horse?

His black hair had partially slipped from the riband and he gave it a brisk tug. His hair fell to his shoulders and he tossed the riband on top of the documents. Why had Wellington chosen him for this task? Damme, but he wasn't suited to this type of work. Better to be in command of a cavalry troop than to chase shadows. Yet he would do anything for the newly created Duke of Wellington, who in his opinion was a professional soldier unparalleled anywhere in the world.

Edward again began to move about the room, thrusting, swiping at the air, the blade of his sword singing, his stockinged feet padding softly across the gold and red carpet. How odd that all trails led to the city of Bath and to the environs of his uncle's house. But not so odd after all, when he considered the enormity of Sir Perran's connections. There wasn't a pulse in the nation, or in Europe, upon which Sir Perran's capable fingers were not firmly pressed. Though a mere baronet, the scope of his uncle's knowledge was more than most statesmen or even the shrewdest man of trade could gather. Though neither a statesman nor a man of trade, Sir Perran had still been able during his lifetime, through careful investments, to acquire an extraordinary wealth. According to all that Blackthorn had learned, hitherto unknown about his kinsman, Sir Perran was worth nearly six hundred thousand pounds invested in the funds alone. He had had no idea his uncle's wealth was so vast.

Blackthorn looked at the bed, thrusting just past a bedpost, scrutinizing the various documents scattered from one end of the red velvet counterpane to the other, and understood a little of how his uncle had succeeded in achieving his fortune. The baronet had developed a network of connections that made Wellington's company of spies seem like a paltry lot indeed. Sir Perran somehow managed regularly to gain access to nearly every field report generated throughout the British Empire.

Letting his sword rest for a moment at his side, Blackthorn reread the report stating that a plan was being developed to hire Algerian Corsairs to kidnap and murder Bonaparte. He was stunned as much by the outrageousness of such a scheme as by the fact that Sir Perran, according to Wellington, had a copy of the document as well.

Wellington's orders were clear. Major Blackthorn had been assigned to discover the identity of the French agent connected to Sir Perran in Bath, who was lifting information from his reports. The baronet was not suspect. But somewhere, probably living under his roof, Wellington believed there was an agent of either Bonaparte's or perhaps another highly placed French official who had found a means of attaching the documents that came to Sir Perran.

Blackthorn had one lead as to the possible identity of the traitor—a retired infantry sergeant who had lost an arm at Talavera and was now working in Cornwall. For the past year, Sergeant Whitwick had been employed as a Preventive Officer, a rather hopeless job in a county that enjoyed tremendous revenue from the age-old art of smuggling. In the process of performing his duties, he had managed to capture several smugglers near Falmouth, and one of the smugglers had turned out to be in possession of several conspicuous documents.

Blackthorn would be leaving in the morning to search out Sergeant Whitwick and to see what he could discover from the smuggler.

Letting his sword fall to his side, Edward again turned his thoughts toward Julia. The worst of it was, he did not want to leave Bath just yet, not when Julia was so near to accepting Lord Peter's hand in marriage. He knew once she was betrothed, she would be unable to disentangle herself from the engagement without creating a scandal. He knew her well enough, both from correspondence and from having observed her strict decorum at the Upper Rooms, to realize she was not a lady to delight in scandal of any kind. No, he did not want to leave Julia. Edward sensed the hour was critical. Yet he couldn't fail in his duty to his commander. Besides, his first duty would always be to see Bonaparte vanquished—he had vowed as much when George had died.

With perspiration dripping down his neck, he tossed his sword on the bed. It slid across several documents before coming to rest, having nearly punctured one of the pillows. He crossed the chamber to the window and threw back the heavy red velvet drapes. Opening the window, he inhaled the moist June air. God, that he might be granted wisdom to see his mission through quickly.

He looked up into the starry night sky. A breeze swept down the hill and was stiff enough to lift the drapes a little. His brow was wet from his recent exercise, and the rush of air cooled him. His bedchamber overlooked ancient, beech-studded hills, the same forest he had played in with his brothers and with Julia and her sister Elizabeth.

Through the open window, laughter floated up to him, the deep-timbred, ribald laughter of a gathering of men who were enjoying an evening without the restrictive presence of women. He had been invited to Sir Perran's card soirée, a weekly event that undoubtedly would continue far into the early morning hours. Edward had refused the invitation, pleading the fatigue of traveling, for he had arrived in Bath from London only that morning, but begged to be admitted to the next game, which was scheduled to take place the following Saturday evening. His uncle had graciously excused him tonight but had requested he greet his guests once he returned from the assembly at the Upper Rooms.

Lord Delabole had been among Sir Perran's guests. Blackthorn had greeted Julia's father, holding back, with no small effort, his shock at the man's appearance. He would not have recognized the viscount in any setting other than this one or Hatherleigh Park. His pale complexion was literally laced with veins from excessive drink and his eyes were deeply shaded in blue shadows. Only a jovial smile and gracious manners remained of the former man. After being introduced to the balance of his uncle's guests, Edward retired to his bedchamber to take a little exercise, to study the documents again, and to try not to think of Julia.

Now, as another explosion of laughter erupted from belowstairs, he rose from the chair and began once more to read through the documents. This time, he arranged them according to dates.

Lord Delabole arrived home at three o'clock in the morning, sick at heart. The carriage ride from The Priory to Hatherleigh Park had served to clear his head sufficiently, so that by the time he was heading for his bedchamber up the wide, elegant staircase leading to the first floor, he knew full well what he had done. He doggedly mounted each step, like a horse heading for the stables after a long day, intent on falling into bed and dropping off to sleep as quickly as he could. He wanted to forget the night's gaming, to dream of Olivia, to believe for a little while that his pockets were not crammed with vowels.

The servant who followed him up the stairs, holding a candle aloft to light the way, left him at his bedchamber door, where his sleepy-eyed valet received him, taking in hand his black silk cape, his fine black silk hat, and his exquisitely constructed gloves. These were the luxuries Lord Delabole could not bring himself to relinquish—expensive clothing suitable to his rank. Even the thumbs of his gloves had been designed separately, in order to accommodate the minutest disparity between them. The leather of the gloves was so thin that an awkward thrust could easily force a hole through the doeskin.

Even Sir Perran had remarked on the quality of his gloves.

How many gloves did the baronet own?

Good God! Was there a man in all of England better shod than Sir Perran Blackthorn? Golden Ball Hughes, perhaps. But he was an absurd creature, whereas Sir Perran—no, there was nothing absurd about Sir Perran, whose eyes glittered like the devil when he played at cards, like a kestrel preparing to seize his prey.

Though his blood had been thoroughly drenched and heated by the baronet's rich ports, clarets, Madeiras, and brandies, Lord Delabole's veins suddenly felt like ice at the thought of Sir Perran's piercing gray eyes. They were always shifting, moving, seeking, alert. No wonder he succeeded at card play.

Yet he was one of the most affable gentlemen of his acquaintance. Curious, that! Above all his friends, he enjoyed Sir Perran's company the most—his wit, his vulgarity at times when the moment suited. He was a damned fine host, always serving the best fare, the most flavorful wines, his silver polished until it dazzled the eye.

Lord Delabole belched. He did not meet the gaze of his valet, whom he had not paid in over six months. He let the faithful and conscientious retainer carefully remove each item of his clothing, down to his Cumberland corset.

Damned fine fare. Sleep would feel good. He would like to dream of his wife tonight, of holding her again in his arms. He would go to sleep pretending there had been no coaching accident that had bereft him of his darling Olivia, no stupid yachting accident that had stolen his sons from him. He hated the sea. He supposed deep in their hearts most Englishmen hated the sea, which kept them penned in like sheep behind a dry-stone wall for eternity. You couldn't get to France without casting up your accounts aboard a small packet to Calais.

God, but his mind was loose, drifting from one thought to the next without any sort of order. Too much of that delectable East

Indian Madeira. He had probably drunk the last bottle himself. How much had he lost tonight? He sat on the bed and his valet removed his stockings. He could recall writing a number of vowels, but how many? Was he ruined?

No, by God, no. Julia still had her emerald. Until her ring was gone, he was not ruined.

His head hit the pillow and he immediately began drifting off to sleep, holding another pillow to his chest. He pretended he was fondling Olivia's breasts. A need overtook him. Tomorrow he would pay his mistress a visit. Dirty little thing, but she pleased him and didn't cost very much. God knew he had precious little to give any woman now. Better to sleep. Lord Delabole sighed heavily and drifted into a world of nightmarish dreams of the sea, reaching up and engulfing him time and again. He tossed and turned and awoke several times, only to drift off to sleep again. When at last he slept soundly, he dreamed of Olivia calling to him, of his sons begging him to help them, to save them. But he couldn't. He couldn't even save himself as the sea swallowed him alive. He was drowning. He couldn't breathe. He drew the salty, vile ocean into his lungs.

He awoke with a start, gasping for air. In his nightmare, he had been drowning. But it was just a dream . . . a dream. Thank God it was just a dream.

Light poured in through the dark blue silk draperies that flanked each of a pair of windows in his bedchamber. He squeezed his eyes shut, trying to keep the sunlight from burning into his brain. He felt like the devil. His head ached abominably. His mouth felt as if he had been chewing on one of his pillows all night.

After a few minutes, he opened his eyes and looked up into the elegant yellow silk canopy of his massive carved bed. How many viscounts had slept in this bed? Damme, must have been all of them, the bedstead was so ancient.

His bedchamber was expansive, the furniture one hundred fifty years old and of a heavy, gleaming carved oak. The walls were covered with rich, colorful tapestries, one of them showing the exploits of William the Conqueror. The first Lord Delabole had claimed to share a heritage with William I, but he believed that was pure humbug.

His thoughts drifted to his own life, to the heritage he was passing along to his daughters. A familiar melancholy descended upon him. He had been trying so hard for the past year to turn his losses around, but it seemed the harder he tried, the further he fell into debt. The weekly card parties at Sir Perran's were taking a monstrous toll. If he hadn't known better, he would suspect he was being taken by a Captain Sharp. But Sir Perran was a man of honor, just as he was. The baronet would no more take advantage of his friends, or try to cheat them, than he would cut off his nose.

No, the cards had simply turned against him, though why he couldn't comprehend.

Probably the Madeira. He knew he drank too much when he played, but he wouldn't think of that now.

He threw back the bedcovers and slid his feet to the floor. Dressed in a long nightgown of soft white linen, he crossed the chamber to his wardrobe. Opening the door, Lord Delabole sought his coat from the night before and, finding it, removed all the crumpled bits of paper from the pockets. Once he began to add up the figures and realize the sum, he almost fainted.

Three thousand pounds!

How had it been possible for him to have pledged himself for so much? He didn't have the resources to gather together three thousand pounds!

There was only one thing he could now do. He had to press Julia to give him the emerald ring. He needed to sell it, not only to pay these debts—which were entirely a matter of honor and could not be ignored—but also to amass a sufficient amount with which to stake the next game. He was sure to win at next Saturday's game. Thank God they would not be meeting again for a full eight days. Surely by then he would have the ring in hand.

* * *

Julia sat in the housekeeper's office, deep within the nether regions of Hatherleigh Park. She chewed slightly on her lower lip, her brow furrowed as she stared down at the brief missive from Edward. It seemed a matter of business, to which he had alluded briefly the night before, had seen him aboard a post chaise and four and headed for Cornwall early this morning. He could not call upon her today, as he had wished, but would make every effort to pay his respects to her father when he returned, hopefully by Tuesday.

She knew a strong sense of disappointment. When she had awakened, with the morning sun lying about the floor of her bedchamber in perfect rectangles, her first thoughts had been about Edward and about having tumbled into his arms at the Upper Rooms the moment she realized who he was.

Even now, as she leaned his letter against a glass vase containing a jaunty bunch of violets, her thoughts, her senses, turned back to Edward and that first, impulsive embrace. How wonderful she had felt held tightly in arms, as though she had just found a part of her that had been missing for years. Julia had wanted to hold him forever, and she wondered what might have happened had they embraced in a less public place. One thing she knew for certain: She would not have released him so quickly. Not by half. No, she would have held him for hours. Well, perhaps not for hours, but for a stretch of time the thought of which left her sighing with happiness.

She drew in a deep breath, leaning back in her chair. The same sense of wonder she had experienced in that moment swept over her now—of joy, of bliss, of profound affection. She would never have believed that a mere embrace could have felt so alarmingly wondrous or have aroused within her heart all manner of sentiment and wishes she knew could never be fulfilled. All morning, for instance, she had been wondering what it would be like to kiss Edward.

She opened her eyes and blew out a puff of a breath. Better

not to encourage these thoughts, she decided for the hundredth time. Julia sat straighter in her chair and glanced at the open ledger before her. She picked up a receipt for candles and entered the figure carefully in the appropriate column. She set the receipt down. She had not done her accounts in several days. The task must be completed.

But must it be done today? Her mind began to drift again.

If only Lord Peter would embrace her as thoroughly as had Edward. How easily she could love him then. She turned to look out the small, hazy window beyond which was a view of the kitchen gardens. Weeds grew up everywhere and the chickens were again loose among the furrows. The gardeners did not have time to tend the vegetable plots. Their orders were to see to the visible portions of Hatherleigh Park exclusively, and Cook was far too busy to do more with the garden than to make certain it was sufficiently watered and drained.

What would Lord Peter think if he saw such an untidy garden? Would he then guess how desperate her circumstances were, or did he already know? Was that why he had not yet offered for her?

Julia shuddered with a terrible sense of panic. What if he did not offer for her after all? The gold ormolu clock, sitting tidily upon her mind's shelf, ticked loudly at her again. Tick, tick, tick.

Not enough time.

But there must be enough time, otherwise she would be lost, along with her sisters. Enough of this, she commanded herself. She must be courageous, now more than ever. There was enough time. There was. There was.

She brought her thoughts to order quite firmly, again sat forward in the chair, and again began applying herself to the figures that she had been scratching into the various household columns for the past hour. Her numbers were neat, even, fastidious. Each figure she entered into her books matched an accompanying receipt. She separated and stored each receipt alphabetically by creditor. Julia knew the costs of her father's household down to the last tuppence.

She had served her family in the capacity of housekeeper for quite some time. Mrs. Strelley, Lord Delabole's former housekeeper, had celebrated her seventieth birthday and had retired nearly a year and a half ago. Her father had told Julia to hire another, but when she informed him that they still owed Mrs. Strelley two months' wages and had no promise of income with which to pay another housekeeper's hire, he had stared at her blankly for a long moment.

"Whatever do you mean?" he had bellowed at last, the furious tone in his voice causing her to jump. "I have never heard of such a thing! The housekeeping funds gone! Did we not give Mrs. Strelley a gift when she departed, and yet she used us so ill that there is not a farthing left in the household accounts with which to pay for the hire of another housekeeper? I should send for my solicitor and see her imprisoned for such a crime if I thought it would not reflect badly upon our family."

Julia had been astonished at his rage and at the odd turn of his mind, to have blamed so faithful and honest a woman as Mrs. Strelley for his own excesses. He alone had drained the accounts that supported his staff. She remembered precisely when he had done so, quite at her own protests. She supposed she dated all loss of hope from that moment.

So it was, as these thoughts ran fitfully about her brain, that when her father came into the housekeeping office and demanded she immediately give him her mother's emerald ring, Julia flatly refused. He glared at her, the broken vessels on his face in sharp and ragged contrast to his sunken green eyes and bluish complexion.

"Mother gave the ring to me," she explained in a quiet voice, as she had done many times before, "for safekeeping against my future. You may not have the ring and I am only sorry you broached the subject again, for you must know in doing so you cause me great pain."

"Dash it all, Julia!" he thundered, crashing his fist on the desk that separated them. "How dare you refuse me!" The water in the vase containing the violets jiggled from the impact. Julia watched her father wince, then rub his hand as he continued. "I am your father! I am the one responsible for seeing to your future and Elizabeth's and the others! I need your ring, the fortune it represents, to . . . to make a worthwhile investment which will no doubt treble the original sum. You've no right to withhold anything from me, and certainly not some deuced bit of trumpery. Damme, young lady, give it to me at once, I insist. It is my right!"

You lost that right a long time ago, Julia thought. She was no longer angry or distressed, as she used to be when he would harass her about the emerald. She could only look upon him with pity. "How much did you lose last night, Papa?" she queried gently. She could even summon a smile. "I apprehend an appreciable amount, since you have not hounded me for Mother's ring in at least two months. Has fortune turned her back upon you again?"

He opened his mouth and huffed in bewildered exasperation. Clearly, he had not expected her good humor or her perceptiveness.

"I . . . I . . ." he stammered. "It was not . . . that is, a paltry sum, I assure you, which is not at all the reason I have asked you for the emerald. Merely for an investment. I wish to make an investment on your behalf."

Julia rose from her chair, the morning light a reflective pool on her large black ledger books. She rounded the desk, took his arm, and guided him from the chamber. His temper quieted with each step they took down the long servants' hall toward the stairs, which mounted to the ground floor of Hatherleigh Park.

In a few minutes, Julia was leading him into a long gallery overlooking a stone terrace and a wide expanse of well-scythed lawn. She opened a door and ushered her father onto the terrace. The full sun felt warm and pleasant on her fair skin, but she noticed that her father winced in the sunlight. She smiled in faint amusement at his familiar discomfiture and let her gaze rove the vista before her.

The configuration of the estate sloped ever upward from the

back terrace. Beyond the lawn, and separated by a naturally
clipped hedge of yew, rhododendrons, and a scattering of brambleberry vines, was a parkland in which grazed several fallow
deer, their yellow coats dotted with white spots. Her eye was
drawn to the steep rise of the hills beyond, thick with stately,
spreading beech trees, and upward to a deep, blue sky.

A lovely, charming view, Julia thought, the deer reminiscent
of an age gone by. At least the grounds were in decent order.
Though the household staff had been thinned to a minimum and
most of the rooms closed up, the gardens, the well-scythed
lawns, the maze to the west of the house and the numerous yew
hedges surrounding the house, all required a certain number of
strong arms to maintain. Throughout many of her feats juggling
those meager funds that remained at her disposal—from the
rent-rolls and the quarry—she had been unable to reduce the
size of the gardening staff without jeopardizing at least an appearance of ease and wealth.

When her father rubbed his eyes with his hand, her heart went
out to him. "Does your head hurt very much?" she asked kindly.

At that he released a deep, resigned sigh. "You are very much
like your mother, my dear," he said, straightening his shoulders
a little. "I have not honored her memory as I would have wished
to. It would seem that while she was alive she provided my feet
with a proper path. I didn't understand the scope of her influence
until she was gone. Nor have I done well by you or your sisters.
I have tried, but every time I succeeded in bringing my affairs
about, I seemed to lose at cards or hazard. Curious, isn't it?
Almost as though . . ." He gave himself a shake. "Well, never
mind that. You must keep your mother's ring. Perhaps you will
be better able to honor her than have I. Now tell me, how is this
beau of yours, the charming Lord Peter? He seems quite taken
with you. Has he asked to call upon me yet?"

He was smiling down at her, his expression so warm that
despite the telltale blood vessels scattered across his cheeks,
Julia saw in his face the man with whom her mother had tumbled

in love. "No, Papa, he has not, but I have not relinquished all hope yet that he will do so."

"Do not keep him dangling! You must encourage a man of Lord Peter's stamp. He'll not be brought to heel without a series of tight tugs on his leash." He pinched her chin. "You deserve such a man—his family, fortune, and connections. You are a good child, the best of all my daughters. If he does not offer for you soon, then he is nothing short of an addlepated nodcock!"

Julia looked up at him but could not smile at his little joke. Even though she saw in his eyes his sincerity and hope, she couldn't help but wonder if he fully realized that he alone had jeopardized Lord Peter's interest in her. She didn't know whether to beat on his chest and beg him to come to his senses before all was lost, or to cry out in despair at his inability to recognize the disaster he had created for himself and for his daughters. But she knew any such expression would be futile. He was too far down his troubled path to do more than bluster and argue and deny that anything untoward was amiss. Instead, she simply embraced him, slipping her arms fully about his back as she laid her head on his chest and shoulder.

For a long moment, he stood almost paralyzed by her affection. Then, slowly, he encircled her with his arms and held her tight. She felt him swallowing hard and knew he was biting back strong sentiments. But her neck grew damp anyway, where his tears landed in silent protest to how hard life had proved for him. She held him for a long time, sensing that she would probably never know such a moment again. She felt as though she was saying goodbye to him, perhaps to all that she had wanted him to be and all that he never could be.

"I love you, Papa," she whispered.

"My darling daughter" was his gentle reply as he held her close to his heart in the morning light.

Three

Major Blackthorn arrived in Falmouth early Saturday evening and proceeded straight to Sergeant Whitwick's rooms near the Customs House in Upton's Slip. He entered the sparsely furnished parlor, shaking hands with the burly sergeant and exchanging familiar pleasantries with the retired officer. The sergeant offered him a welcomed tankard of ale and within a few minutes they were discussing the Peninsular campaigns, especially the battle of Talavera.

The smell of tobacco was heavy in the air, both inside the house and out, and when Blackthorn commented on it, Sergeant Whitwick explained, "Customs is burning smuggled tobacco we recovered in a recent raid. 'Tis burned in the King's Pipe, a brick chimney not far from here."

Blackthorn nodded. "I see. You must be kept busy here in Falmouth."

"Aye, and then some," he responded easily. Whitwick smiled, revealing the absence of a front tooth. "But ye didn't come this far to sit an' chat with the likes o' me. I expect ye'll be wantin' t'see the papers we found."

"Yes, please," Blackthorn replied. A moment later, he was staring at a number of reports, written in a meticulous hand and identical word by word, almost to the jot and tittle, to several Blackthorn had brought with him to the West Country. In this he could not be mistaken, since he had reviewed the reports Wellington had given him at least a score of times.

"Good God," he murmured as he stared down at the documents, unable to believe what he was seeing. The Preventive Officer waited next to him, a heavy frown on his brow, the seriousness of the documents not lost to him.

Falmouth was a harbor town located near the southernmost tip of Cornwall at the end of Carrick Roads. Built by Henry VIII and protected by two castles, Pendennis and St. Mawes, the bustling seaport had been the headquarters of the Royal Mail packets since 1688 and enjoyed a prosperous trade because of it. Smuggling had always been part and parcel of the town, and some of the captains of the packets were known to engage in the ancient trade. Blackthorn was not especially surprised therefore that Sergeant Whitwick had stumbled across a French agent in his efforts to stop the illegal smuggling of tobacco, silks, firearms, and wines into the country.

Cornwall was a land unto itself, surrounded on three sides by the sea. The air was brisk and smelled of fish and salt. The native townspeople walked hunched, as though the sea and the wind would rise up at any moment and carry them away if they weren't careful. A sense of ancient struggle resided in the port and in the indomitable will of a people loving and fighting the land that had given them birth.

Blackthorn felt oddly at home in Cornwall and in Falmouth. Since he could remember, his life, as well, had been one of battle. His whole existence—the early years with his parents, later with an enigmatic and cold uncle, finally as an officer in the British Army—held a colon thread of survival and struggle. He had been born to fight his way through life, and the fighting had become his life, welcomed, feared, a friendly adversary, at times beloved.

To him, examining the documents was like picking up a sword. He whistled low and turned astonished eyes on Sergeant Whitwick. "These papers were on his person, you say?"

"Aye. The very ones. In a satchel he were carrying." Sergeant Whitwick was a large, barrel-chested man whose face was ridged with sun-baked wrinkles. His blue eyes sat far back in folds of squinted skin, his expression stern. His short hair was slicked flat with Macassar oil. Telltale faint blue patches along his cheeks and jaw gave evidence of a recent brawl. Blackthorn liked his openness and confidence. Instinctively, he trusted him.

"Where is the man? At the Customs House? I wish to speak with him."

"The good Mr. Mawls is in t'other room," the sergeant said, jerking his thumb toward the door behind him.

Blackthorn looked up and glanced at the door. "What?" he cried. "Not in your bedchamber!"

Sergeant Whitwick smiled broadly. "Aye! The lockup is full, and I weren't about to let anyone else guard him."

Blackthorn looked at the door, painted a pristine white. "Well, then, let's see what he can tell us."

The prisoner sat in a chair by the drapeless window, the pink-gray twilight casting a rosy hue on his peppered hair. He was salt-worn and seaworthy, thin and agile, his face darkened by the sun. He was bound to the chair by so many ropes that it was all Blackthorn could do to keep from laughing outright at the absurdity of the picture. At the same time, the smuggler's bonds were a proper reflection of Sergeant Whitwick's thoroughness. He would have been an asset to any regiment, and he was sorry that the loss of his left arm had bereft the British Army of a capable soldier.

"Sergeant Whitwick tells me you're not French," Blackthorn stated.

"Nay" was the direct reply. "I've lived in Falmouth all me life."

"Why have you been engaged in smuggling military documents out of the country, then? Are you aware you jeopardize the lives of English soldiers in doing so?"

The man stared up at him, his expression angry. "I only done what I was told to do. I've said as much to Sergeant Whitwick. I didn't know what was in the packages."

"Are you telling me you never once stole a glance at the contents?"

He shook his head. "M'family's starved in these hard times.

I don't ask questions. The gent always paid handsomely. I didn't poke my nose where it didn't belong."

Blackthorn turned to the sergeant. "Is this his story?"

"Aye."

"What do you think? Is he telling the truth? Or would you like to persuade him a little?" Blackthorn had no sympathy for the man before him who, since he appeared to possess some intelligence, must have more than once suspected that his cargo was of questionable content.

Sergeant Whitwick turned to the small, wind-burned man and smiled faintly. "I've a number of persuasive tricks, Major. You have but to give the word and I'll tend to this fellow right smartly."

Blackthorn leveled his gaze at his prisoner. "What say you, Mr. Mawls? Do you wish for Sergeant Whitwick to employ his 'tricks' on you?"

Mr. Mawls lifted his chin slightly. His hazel eyes, red-rimmed from lack of sleep, remained firm and steady. "Sergeant Whitwick may do what he pleases. But I tell you I didn't know what I was delivering. Plain and simple."

Blackthorn stared down at the man. He had disciplined soldiers under his command a hundred times over the years. He knew when the truth was being told and when it was not. Mr. Mawls was telling the truth.

"Tell me everything you know about the man who gave you these documents."

"He's not tall—that is all I can tell ye. I never saw him in the light, and he held a handkerchief to his mouth when he spoke and wore a hooded cape. He came up to me at the cove, whispered what he wanted, gave me several guineas, and left."

"How frequently?"

"Twice a month."

"What was your responsibility?"

"To see the parcel mailed to Italy."

"How long have you been in his employ?"

"Five years."

"Good God!" Blackthorn murmured. "Do you expect to see him again soon?"

"Sunday, next."

"Will you help your country?" he asked.

Mr. Mawls's gaze shifted away from Blackthorn. He turned to look out the window, the faint gray light barely illuminating the smuggler's features. "I will do whatever you ask of me. There is just one thing I wish to know. Am I to hang for this crime?"

"Treason is punishable by hanging," Blackthorn responded slowly.

Mr. Mawls looked back at him. "But I didn't know, I swear it! And I've six babes to feed."

Blackthorn scrutinized the man carefully, seeing into his mind, trying to weigh the balances of his life—the hardships, the laziness, of which he saw nothing; the good fortune, of which he saw even less. "If you are careful in your assistance to the Crown, I might be able to see that you receive a sentence of transportation instead."

Mr. Mawls again shifted his gaze to the window. "I'll do whatever ye ask" was his response. No apologies, no repentance. He ground his teeth lightly and then began to hum a sea chantey. Disinterest was in his narrowed eyes and his voice. Life had been very hard on Mr. Mawls.

Blackthorn returned with the sergeant to the parlor and discussed the possibilities with him. His cook served a thick fish soup, bread, and more ale for dinner, after which Blackthorn retired to the Dook Inn for the night.

During the following two days, he and the sergeant visited the cove at which the smugglers had been captured and at which Mr. Mawls and his faceless employer normally conducted their business. By the time he began his return journey to Bath, a simple plan had been set in place, in which Mr. Mawls would keep his next meeting with the traitor.

Mr. Mawls's parting words remained with Blackthorn: "Be careful, Major. He's a sly one."

* * *

On the following Tuesday morning, at the precise hour of eight o'clock, Julia and her maid strode into the Pump Room adjacent to the magnificent Bath Abbey. Her sisters had not accompanied her, since they were engaged in selecting pattern cards for new ball dresses. Julia had been torn between staying with them and helping with the sewing, or observing her weekly ritual of attending the Pump Room. She chose the latter for two reasons. First, she hoped to see Lord Peter. Second, she needed very much to retain a sense of order to her life when disaster sat so closely on her doorstep.

For many years, she had been in the habit of climbing aboard her family's town coach, with usually one or more of her sisters or her maid in tow, and traveling the five miles from Hatherleigh Park to Bath on Tuesdays to take the waters. Imbibing the vile-smelling drink was the first of several amusements that occurred in established succession, followed by a trip to the bookseller's, where novels, plays, pamphlets, and newspapers were consumed for later discussion; a tour through the millineries and toyshops, and finally a visit to Mr. Gill, the pastry cook, to enjoy a bowl of vermicelli, an apricot tartlet, or a jelly. If the weather permitted, she would add to this round of activities a promenade through the Orange Grove. Only then, when the whole of Bath's morning regimen had been enjoyed, would she return to Hatherleigh Park.

As she entered the Pump Room, however, Julia couldn't refrain from quickly scanning the assembled personages and searching for Lord Peter's friendly, handsome countenance. Twice, she let her gaze rove the gathering. Her mouth grew dry. Once more, she surveyed the gentlemen present.

Her heart plummeted. He was not here. She couldn't credit her eyes. Where was he?

She felt suddenly dizzy with fear. She had not seen him since she danced with him at the Upper Rooms four days prior. He had not called upon her at Hatherleigh during that time, and

Julia began to suspect that her conduct toward Edward at the assembly rooms had offended him. Of course the hour was still early and Lord Peter might even now be on his way to the Pump Room. If he did arrive, she decided she would speak to him about Edward and explain how it had come about that she had embraced him so scandalously at the assembly.

Her fears partially allayed, Julia bid Gabrielle seek her own amusements as she in turn began greeting her numerous acquaintances. Mary Brown soon drew Julia apart from her friends. "I could not help but notice you were scrutinizing every man present," she said in a whisper. "I can only presume you have not heard that Lord Peter has left Bath and is gone to Wiltshire to visit his parents."

Julia blinked down at her friend and felt her former dizziness steal into her mind. "No, I had not heard," she stated quietly, panic seizing her. "Thank you for telling me."

Mary looked at her and frowned. "You have become quite pale," she said. "Do you wish for my vinaigrette? Whatever is the matter?"

Julia shook her head. "No, I am perfectly well . . . just a trifle stunned. He hadn't mentioned he was leaving."

"I have given you a shock and I am sorry for it. Had I known you would be so deeply affected, I would have told you more gently. Mama informed me only this morning when her housekeeper—who has several friends in employ at the White Hart, where Lord Peter was staying—told her both of his departure and"—she paused and smiled mischievously at Julia—"his intention of returning quite soon. He left two of his portmanteaus with the landlord."

"Two of his portmanteaus?" Julia queried, hope again rising within her.

Mary smiled broadly and nodded.

Julia could barely contain the relief these last words afforded her. "I see," she murmured.

"You are very much in love with him, aren't you?" Mary

responded quietly, placing a hand on Julia's arm. "Pray don't demur . . . I can see that you are."

"I . . . I suppose I am," Julia returned, prevaricating. She could see that Mary wasn't in the least conversant with her true motivations and hoped she never would be. She turned slightly away from her friend and looked about the Pump Room, all the while attempting to compose herself. But she could not keep her thoughts from dwelling on the meaning of Lord Peter's departure.

What did he intend to accomplish by making such a sudden journey to Wiltshire? Again she felt sick with worry. There could be only one purpose: Lord Peter meant to discuss with his parents his interest in a certain *Miss Verdell* of Bath. With this thought, Julia realized she had been living in a dream. Did she suppose he would have asked for her hand in marriage without consulting Lord and Lady Trevaunance? But how absurd! Of course he would, and what would the marquis tell his second son? She thought it would depend entirely on what His Lordship knew of her father's gaming habits.

"He will return," Mary assured her, somehow sensing her friend's dispiritedness. "You mustn't despair. Besides, how can you be unhappy when you are wearing such an exquisite confection?" Mary's gaze shifted to Julia's bonnet. "Would that my maid had such an eye and such skill!"

Julia looked at Mary and smiled, grateful that her friend had changed the subject of their whispered confidences. She concentrated on setting aside her fears and turned her attention instead to Mary's expression of awe, as she scrutinized Gabrielle's handiwork. Few if any of the excellent milliners in Bath could compare with her abigail's ability to figure a bonnet. Gabrielle's present creation bore a large poke brim of apricot silk, gathered, puckered, and ruched into a charming swirl over the crown and decorated with small, artificial white gardenias. Julia wore a matching apricot silk pelisse trimmed with a narrow band of ruffles about the high neck and the hem. A white beaded reticule dangled from her wrist. From beneath the hem of her pelisse a delicate rim of white muslin gave a hint of the gossamer morning gown hidden underneath the smooth silk.

"You may give your compliments to Gabrielle," Julia said, "but for the present, as you can see, she is besieged." With her gaze, Julia gestured toward the statue of Beau Nash, which was situated on the east wall high above the assemblage for all to view. Below the statue of the man who was credited with bringing order, decorum, and wealth to the city of Bath was Gabrielle and at least a dozen friends and beaus. Since the Pump Room was attended by all classes, Gabrielle, with her dark brown curls, dancing dark brown eyes, and lilting accent, never failed to attract a bevy of admirers, many of whom were artisans, clerks, and young men of trade. Julia suspected the day would arrive when she would be bereft of her superior abigail, losing her to Cupid's arrow.

Mary commented on Gabrielle's various conquests, and as her gaze scanned the several ladies gathered to the left of the alcove housing the famous statue of Nash, she gave a shriek. "Kitty has arrived from Lincolnshire! I wasn't expecting her until Tuesday next. Did you hear she has become betrothed?"

"Yes, it is wonderful news. I wish her joy."

Mary glanced at Julia and smiled wickedly. "You detest Kitty Stoneleigh," she whispered. "I suspect *joy* is not what you wish her at all."

"On the contrary, I wish her every happiness," Julia insisted. "If her tongue wags too much to please my sense of propriety, I am still able to be happy for her good fortune."

"Oh, very well! Be dignified and proper if you must. I suppose you will not come with me then to greet her?"

Julia gave her head a shake. "I haven't yet taken the waters. Now do go to Kitty before you swoon from anticipation!"

Pulling a face, Mary bid her drink a glass of water in her stead, then quickly crossed the long chamber. Julia turned her attention to the famous waters of Bath. She approached the counter and requested from the serving girl the three prescribed glasses. An older man standing next to her, dressed in the brown box coat and breeches of a man of trade, swallowed his first glass and came up sputtering. He turned to her and, with blue eyes wide with astonishment, stated, "Why, it tastes of warm flatirons! And I was told it would cure my gout! Humbug! Pure humbug!" He then refused further glasses, politely tipped the pumper, bowed to Julia, and limped from the building.

Julia could only smile. He was right about the taste of the water, which sprang from deep within the earth. He was neither the first nor the last who would complain about the flavor of the supposedly medicinal waters.

Regardless of the smell or the taste, Julia took the waters because it was the fashion in Bath and because she had always been part of Bath society. She would have far preferred to reside in Bath, as her family had while her mother was alive, especially during June and July, when the town was full of Londoners and the warm weather tempted everyone to walk along the Orange Grove and the Parade. In the summer the city was alive with conversation, fashion, and the latest news from abroad.

But not long after her mother's death, Lord Delabole had given up his townhouse in Queen's Square. Initially, Julia had thought it was because he couldn't abide living in a house where his wife's hand was so thoroughly seen in every piece of furniture, every selected drapery fabric, every painting hung upon the numerous walls. Hatherleigh Park was the result of many generations of contribution. But the townhouse in Queen's Square had been a reflection exclusively of Lady Delabole.

However, not long after the townhouse had been given up, Julia came to understand the truth. Shortly after his wife's death, Lord Delabole had taken to gaming excessively and very soon had no longer been able to afford the maintenance of two residences.

Julia accepted the three glasses of water from the cheerful serving maid and began her own trial of endurance. She would have liked to have pinched her nose, but instead she took a deep breath and quickly imbibed the first glass.

Then the second.

She let the third glass sit upon the counter for a long moment. If she drank too quickly, she often felt nauseated afterward.

She turned and surveyed the jovial group now gathered about Mary. Mary herself was betrothed to a man of birth and breeding, whose annual income was in excess of five thousand pounds. She would want for nothing during her lifetime. Kitty's recent betrothal was to a cousin who was heir to a great property in Lincolnshire. Kitty's future as well was likewise neatly secured.

Julia felt envious suddenly, something she rarely experienced. Both ladies were talking rapidly to one another, to the exclusion of the three gentlemen in attendance upon them. The young women were undoubtedly discussing wedding plans. If only her future was settled as well!

Julia thought back to her confrontation with her father about the emerald ring. Though she was grateful she had been able to withstand his demand for the ring without forcing an argument, the encounter had left her shaken, her fears of the future returning in full force. Having observed the desperate expression on his face during the ensuing days, she had again become fixed on doing all she could to arouse Lord Peter Longton's interest in matrimony. Occasionally, Edward had crept into her thoughts—her desire to see him again—but so pressing was her sense of urgency, Julia found herself consumed by her need to marry as quickly as she could.

If only Lord Peter had not gone to Wiltshire.

She sighed, turning toward the doorway, wishing him to appear yet knowing he wouldn't. As it happened, just as she turned, a man did arrive at the Pump Room, a man who fairly filled the doorway with his broad shoulders, soldierly bearing, and well-muscled legs. Her heart simply turned over in her breast, quick tears rimming her eyes at the sight of her friend from childhood.

Edward.

He had returned on Tuesday, just as he said he would.

Years of affection rose within her, flooding her heart and, in quick stages, obliterating thoughts of Lord Peter. How was that possible? she wondered vaguely, when moments before she had felt incapable of dwelling on anything besides the desperation of her circumstances.

But now Edward was here, and so different was his place in her life that his presence swept away all her immediate needs, replacing them with the warmth of a hundred childhood memories. She felt lit from within all over again, just as she had felt at the assembly rooms on Friday. Had she not been in the midst of a crush of people, she suspected the strength of her sentiments would have once more caused her to fall into his arms, to embrace him, to welcome him home yet again.

How handsome he was as he caught her gaze and smiled at her, a dazzling, warm smile, full of promise.

Edward Blackthorn, soldier and man, not the boy she had loved but a man. He was not wearing his regimentals this morning, but instead sported a dark blue riding coat, buff pantaloons of soft buckskin, which fit his muscular legs to perfection, and gleaming Hessian boots.

When he entered the Pump Room, Julia could not keep from glancing about the crowded room to see how his arrival was affecting her many friends. She was not surprised to find that he was being ogled by at least a dozen young ladies, along with several matrons. For those who had not yet been informed of his presence at the Upper Rooms, she knew from long experience that the same questions were being raised in one mind after another: Who was this man? What were his prospects, his connections? What about his birth, his breeding, his family, his character? And, most importantly, was he married? She heard the whispers begin, followed by the responses—the explanation of his late attendance at the Upper Rooms, his close connection to Sir Perran, the speculation that the baronet might one day make his nephew his heir.

Giddier young ladies wanted only to know how well he danced and whether he could easily be conquered and added to their courts. But matchmaking mamas each wanted answers to the same sensible, critical questions: Would he make her daughter a proper husband? Would he manage his wife's dowry with care? Would he see to the future of their children?

This was the crux of the society in which Julia lived. Fortune and management were everything. The lack of either was, if not complete disaster, then a life of hardship and diminished prospects. A man without a fortune was unlikely to wed a well-dowered young lady, and an impoverished miss was unlikely to marry a gentleman of fortune and property. The rules were clear, if at times brutal.

Julia wondered if Edward was fully aware of the interest his arrival had occasioned and what he thought of it. When she turned back to him she found his gaze heavily upon her, his gray eyes cloaked and scrutinizing. Though he was still smiling, she could not help but wonder what his thoughts were.

Blackthorn had no interest in the ladies who, with artful smiles, were attempting to attract his notice. From the moment he had descended Sir Perran's town coach, he was intent only on finding Julia. When he had left Sergeant Whitwick on Monday, every other thought on his return trip to Bath had been about Julia—why she was determined to wed Lord Peter, could he have a future with her himself, did he have enough time to win her affections before she became betrothed? He needed to see her again, to discuss the whole of it with her, to find out if more than mere friendship could exist between them.

When he caught sight of her standing at the counter with a full glass of water in front of her, the rest of the lofty chamber seemed to disappear from view. He saw only her. She was a vision in apricot silk, from the top of her pretty bonnet to the hem of her pelisse. A very simple, powerful emotion rolled over him like a great ocean wave, dragging him down, pulling him along, turning him head over heels until he was dizzy with wondering where the devil he was.

Yet he knew precisely where he was. He was in Bath again. He had returned from a successful trip to Cornwall and had come back to find Julia. Had he already tumbled in love with her? The sensations that swirled through him, around him,

within his heart, were strong indications that he had. What if he
was mistaken and he was merely caught up in a momentary
tendre that would pass within a fortnight or two? What if he
persuaded her to relinquish her pursuit of Lord Peter, only in
the end to leave her when he returned to the Continent? He was,
after all, a soldier, and his first duty would always be to his
country. Could a woman, any woman, truly be an integral part
of his life?

Edward didn't know what to think or even what he ought to
do. When he had returned from Falmouth on Monday, his first
question to his uncle had been to ascertain whether Julia had
succeeded in bringing Lord Peter up to scratch—was she betrothed?

His uncle had narrowed gray, calculating eyes at him and,
after a moment's pause, responded that he believed Lord Peter
had left Bath for several days to meet his father at a friend's
house in Wiltshire and to his knowledge there was as yet no
betrothal.

Blackthorn remembered that upon hearing these words an
overwhelming sense of relief had descended upon him, as
though heaven had opened a window and poured a blessing over
his head. He watched Julia now and was struck again by how
beautiful she was. Her fetching bonnet obscured her lush auburn
hair, except for a delicate fringe of curls that she wore across
her forehead. In the brighter light of day, he saw that her complexion was singular, undoubtedly the envy of all of Bath, a
pure, clear, creamy white tinged with a color very similar to the
silk of her bonnet. He wanted suddenly to be alone with her. In
his mind, he was kissing her cheeks, drifting his lips over the
softness of her skin, tasting the cream of her complexion. He
was holding her in his arms, her womanly body warm against
his. He was kissing her. He found that his deep affection for her
was transforming into a desire to hold her, to kiss her, to make
love to her. As he advanced into the room, he decided that if he
accomplished nothing else today, he would kiss Julia Verdell . . .

and see what his heart would say to him and what Julia's heart might speak in response.

Edward lifted his beaver hat from his head as he approached her. She smiled sweetly, seeming to lose the seriousness that had characterized her countenance when he had first laid eyes on her. She appeared young suddenly, and it occurred to him, upon remembering how she had looked at the Upper Rooms when he observed her dancing with various partners, that for the most part her expression was somber, as though she was weighed down with concerns not typical for one her age. Edward wondered if something was amiss.

When he reached her side he bowed to her. She responded in kind, dipping a quick, playful curtsy. Edward did not hesitate to take her hand in his. He pressed her fingers, and the answering pressure affirmed the affectionate expression on her face. What was she feeling for him? he wondered.

"I was hoping you would be here this morning," he said. "My uncle told me you came to Bath especially on Tuesdays, so I did not bother stopping at Hatherleigh to find out whether you had gone. I see my uncle was right."

Julia's heart was suddenly full of sunshine, her former cares all but forgotten. "Yes, I always come to Bath on Tuesday," she responded.

How glad she was Edward had come. Her womanly heart reached out to him, teasing her mind with thoughts of what life might be like with him. Her heart picked up its cadence, her knees began to tremble, her mind raced forward. She was in the hills with Edward once more, only instead of playing games from childhood, this time his arms were wrapped tightly about her as he laid her on a bed of bluebells. He was kissing her madly, passionately, telling her how much he loved her, touching her.

"Julia," she heard him whisper as he took a step toward her. "What are you thinking about?"

The daydream began to vanish as Edward's face came crisply

into view. She looked up at him and sighed deeply. "Of what can never be, I think," she replied.

She knew that his prospects were hopeless where she was concerned. If only Sir Perran intended to make Edward his heir, then she could give full rein to the wishes of her heart. But to her knowledge, Sir Perran had other plans. Rumors had abounded for months that the baronet was about to take a wife in order to provide an heir for The Priory.

Bringing her thoughts and her heart to order, Julia turned back to her third glass of water. Taking it in hand, she smiled at him. "I have only one glass left to drink, and then I will want to know how your business fared in Cornwall." She lifted the glass to her lips and quickly began drinking the contents.

"How do you bear it?" Blackthorn queried. "I would swear I was smelling the brimstone matches of a tinderbox!"

Julia nearly choked on the last droplets of her final glass and came up sputtering. "How unkind of you to be joking when my mouth is full. As for the water, I don't know how I bear it, either. I suppose I am used to it. But I have it on excellent authority that these waters will cure any manner of ailment."

"Are you ill, then?" he queried, his gray eyes warm and teasing.

"You know I am not," she responded, laughing.

"Then I can't imagine why you persist in drinking these horrid-smelling draughts even if they have beneficial qualities, a claim I am inclined to doubt."

"Because my mother always did," she answered simply. Julia tipped the serving girl, then slipped her arm through Edward's and drew him away from the crowd about the counter. "I'm so glad you've come home. Seeing you here has brought my childhood back to me. Every time I look at you, I see the past. For how many hours did you and George and Stephen cart me about on your backs? You made the best horses, and for several years after you were too grown-up to play with me, I quite refused to ride any of the ponies in our stables."

"We had great fun as children, sharing the hills between our homes."

"We did, indeed we did." Julia fell silent, thinking of his brothers, missing them. "I only wish George and Stephen were still alive. I am ever so sorry for your losses."

"And I, yours," he responded quietly, pausing her in her steps and turning her to look at him. He held her gaze solemnly for a long moment, an unspoken but shared sadness passing between them. After a time she offered him a faint smile. He took up the hint and, glancing at her silk pelisse and at the white beads embroidered upon her reticule in meticulous fashion, gently broached a new subject. "You seem to be prospering," he said. "Are your sisters well, and your father? Is Hatherleigh as elegant as I recall?"

Julia remembered now that he was still laboring under a misapprehension. She knew she needed to speak to him about the difficulties before her, but she didn't know how to begin. Instead, she answered his query politely. "All are in excellent health and Hatherleigh is still the prettiest house in all of Somerset." She wanted to say more, but she couldn't find the words.

He cocked his head slightly and narrowed his eyes. "I see your beau has not yet returned from Wiltshire."

Julia lowered her gaze. "No, he has not," she said.

He lifted her chin with the palm of his hand, forcing her to look at him. His gray eyes held her gaze steadily. "You could do better, you know, far better."

Julia was distressed. "You have no great opinion of him, then?"

"No," he responded. "I fear that I don't."

"Well, that is quite lowering," she said.

"What do you mean?"

"I was hoping for your approval and your blessing," she told him. Julia could see she had surprised him. "Will you come home with me today?" she asked. "There is something I wish to show you . . . at Hatherleigh."

Four

After disengaging Gabrielle from her many friends and admirers, Julia ushered her maid into the Delabole family coach and gave the postboy orders to return to Hatherleigh Park. Gabrielle's first response to her sudden removal from the Pump Room was one of mild surprise, but shortly afterward her dark brown eyes twinkled. *"Très bien,"* she said in her pretty accent. "Now I shall be able to help your sisters. Annabelle has ruined more than one length of silk without my hand to guide her!" A moment later, and the coach was rattling down the street.

Julia turned her attention fully to Edward, lifting her apricot silk skirts as he helped her into Sir Perran's glossy burgundy and black traveling coach. The postilion wore the baronet's livery of gold and scarlet, the horses were black and matched to a shade, the squabs were thick and comfortable as Julia sank down into them. Edward took up his seat beside her as the carriage moved forward, and the entire equipage was soon passing by Bath Abbey.

Julia's attention was riveted to her friend from childhood. She looked at him curiously, trying to place herself within the strides of his life. What was it like to be a soldier? She had heard about the war, had read articles in the newspapers about the various battles throughout the years. She had known officers who had come home maimed, and many families had lost younger sons early in the war, serving at sea under Nelson, or later in the Peninsula under Wellington. The war had been, and clearly still was, a very close, personal matter to Edward. What was it like, she wondered, to be in the midst of battle, to have a horse shot out from under you, to watch your fellow soldiers perish before your eyes, to march for hours on end, to obey orders you would as lief not? She could only imagine what his life had been like for the past several years, at the same time she was curious as to what he planned to do now that the war against Bonaparte was over.

"Do you intend to sell out?" she asked.

He shook his head and frowned. "I am not convinced Europe will be at peace for long."

"Then you are of Sir Perran's opinion that Bonaparte will not remain on Elba . . . that perhaps the allies should have sent him to a more distant place of exile?"

"Yes, I am of the same opinion," he returned firmly.

Julia saw the tightening of his jaw and the hardness that entered his eyes as he surveyed the passing honey-colored stone buildings. For a moment, she felt as though she was looking at a stranger. What did she know of Edward after all?

"Do you believe there will be yet more years of war?" she queried, wanting to know his opinions and to understand him better.

"Possibly. No one can know for certain," he replied, looking back at her. His black brows were drawn together in a sharp frown, his gray eyes intense as he spoke. "All depends on how France responds should Boney escape from Elba and attempt a resurgence. The Bonapartists and the army are fanatical where their emperor is concerned. But the rest of the nation is fatigued from so many years of war—they will not welcome Bonaparte readily. I will say only this: Should the army rally behind him yet again, the war will resume regardless of the sentiments of the French populace."

Julia was startled by the intensity of his expression, and she realized he was every inch an officer. She felt strength emanating from him as though it were a tangible thing. Her mind wavered between admiration for the man Edward had become and a fearfulness that he was not long for this earth. How frequently could a man tempt fate by riding into battle without finally succumbing to that fate?

She touched the sleeve of his blue coat as if by touching him she could keep him anchored to the earth.

He covered her hand with his own. "Have I frightened you?" he asked.

She nodded. "A little. I have only known you through your letters. A written description of a skirmish or a battle is a far cry from what your soldiering life must be like every day. Until you arrived, none of it seemed real. But seeing your face and the look in your eyes when you speak has forced me to realize you have, in fact, been living beneath the Spanish sun, riding your horse, obeying orders, seeing to the men under your command. Edward, are you ever afraid?"

At that he smiled, his expression softening a little. "Yes, every time my regiment confronts the enemy. A man would be a fool to feel otherwise."

Julia shrugged her shoulders a little, trying to rid herself of the qualms that were prickling her nerves. "But as an officer, aren't you normally positioned farther back in the lines so as to be protected?" She looked at him hopefully, but was stunned when he gave a crack of laughter.

"Any officer who deliberately and consistently attempts to engage the enemy behind his troops will soon find the ranks deserted," he responded. His smile faded and his expression grew more serious as he continued, "In the midst of a battle, the men need to be infused with courage. Wellington himself is everywhere during the course of an engagement—he has had innumerable horses shot out from under him over the years. You cannot know what it means to see your commanding officer risk his life at such a time, and I can certainly do no less for the men who depend on me."

Was it her imagination, or did Julia hear cannons roaring, white powder-smoke billowing into the air, the steady, earsplitting staccato of rifle fire? Overcome with the images that raced through her mind, she turned her wrist and grasped the hand that was covering hers. Edward responded by squeezing her hand in return.

"It is not so very bad," he said, a faint smile on his lips as he attempted to reassure her. "For you must remember, we always go into battle with a purpose: to keep an ambitious man from ravaging more countries than he already has. All my consolation for whatever happens during a cavalry charge is fixed on my desire to see Bonaparte vanquished forever."

Julia held his hand tightly, her gaze locked with his. She felt his confidence, his sense of purpose, and her fears transformed into a strong desire that he give some of his strength to her. Would that she was able to confront her difficulties with as much force of will as Edward seemed to possess.

He drew her wrist slowly to his lips. She wanted him to kiss her, to impart his courage to her. She watched in fascination as he placed a kiss on the line of skin that appeared just above her lavender kidskin glove.

Julia found it difficult to breathe. What if those same lips, which were teasing the tender skin of her wrist, should touch her lips? A quick wave of desire brushed over her and she sighed. She wanted him to kiss her.

Her heart quickened. All thought deserted her; she could only feel. Slowly, he kissed her wrist a second time, then turned her hand over and feathered kisses over her pulse. Again a delicate rippling of desire flowed over her, through her, only this time with greater intensity.

"Edward," she purred, his gray eyes steadfastly holding her gaze.

She wanted him to kiss her. She wanted to feel his lips on hers. She wanted his courage, his strength. She leaned close to his shoulder and tilted back her head. "Edward, I wish that you could stay with me forever."

"My darling Julia," he whispered.

Gently, he settled her hand on her lap, turned slightly toward her, and slipped his arm across the back of the squabs. He looked deeply into her emerald eyes and felt himself being drawn into her. Slowly, he leaned toward her and placed his lips lightly on hers, barely touching her. Edward felt her tremble as she placed her hand on his chest. He encircled her with his arms and pulled her close. With the tips of his fingers he stroked the soft skin of her cheek. He heard her moan faintly and the sound, a dove's coo, brought desire rushing suddenly through him.

He kissed her more firmly, holding her more tightly to him. Edward reveled in the softness of her lips and of her skin. She felt warm, familiar, and so alive. Julia returned his kiss willingly, passionately. The budding love he had felt for her at the Upper Rooms—was it only four days ago?—began to blossom. He was full of wonder at the sensations growing within him, at the sweet rush and swirls of passion moving inside him, urging him to hold and keep her close. He wanted to kiss her again and again, to embrace her, to make love to her. Edward wanted her with him, now and always.

Julia was caught up in a swell of emotion so powerful, her mind seemed to disappear. She couldn't think, she could only revel in the feel of his lips, the touch of his hands. She felt as though he were breathing life into her with each feathery kiss he placed on her lips, her cheeks, her eyes. Her heart beat strongly and quickly in her breast, her fingers tingling as she lifted her hand from his chest and touched his face. Desire curled deeply within her, rising up to her heart. She wanted the moment to continue forever; she wanted to be held by him, to be kissed by him again and again. Was this what it was like to be in love? Was it possible to tumble in love so quickly, or had she always been in love with Edward Blackthorn?

She thought back to her childhood, his kisses mingling with the sweetest of memories . . . memories of Edward racing about the hills as Robin Hood. Even as a young girl Julia had wanted to be Edward's wife, but she had always believed such thoughts belonged just to her girlhood. Now she was not so certain.

The carriage lurched suddenly, forcing them apart, and the moment began to dissipate. Gently, he drew back from her and placed his cheek alongside hers. He did not release her, but held her close to him as the coach swayed along the macadamized road leading to Hatherleigh Park. Julia's eyes filled with tears.

He had come home. She was so glad he was home, that he was with her. All her cares seemed to vanish in the warmth of his embrace. For the first time in years, she felt safe and deeply content.

Releasing her at last, he looked into her eyes and smiled. "There," he whispered. "That is what I wanted to do at the Upper Rooms but couldn't because of the proprieties."

"And I would have let you," she responded quietly. "Once I was in your arms, I wanted to hold you for hours."

"Why are you crying?" he queried as he tenderly wiped away two tears that had trickled from her eyes.

"I didn't realize how much I missed you until now."

Julia let herself drift into his eyes, losing herself within him for a long moment. "Edward, if only everything were different . . ." She wanted to say more, but the words eluded her.

He frowned. "Something is wrong, isn't it?"

Julia leaned back against the squabs. He released her, slipping his arm about hers and holding her hand tightly. She fell silent, averting her gaze away from him. He didn't prompt her further.

Blackthorn turned to look out the window as the carriage bowled swiftly along the lane. The surrounding hills were a brilliant June green, and at the edges of the woods topping the hills, bluebells peeked from the forest floor. A stream that fed the River Avon ran alongside the road nearly the whole distance to Hatherleigh. The mid-morning sun cast shadows at a stark angle across the opposite hills; the leaves of the beech trees sparkled in the summer sunshine.

His thoughts traveled forward as he wondered what it was Julia intended to show him at Hatherleigh. He tried to imagine what had brought such a troubled expression to her lovely green eyes, but only certain doubts came to mind. She had made mention in her letters that her father had not been himself since his wife's death, that he drank and gambled more than he ought.

But Edward could name a dozen such men whose similar habits had resulted in nothing untoward, and he hoped Lord Delabole's drinking and gaming had not gotten entirely out of hand. He remembered his own astonishment at the sight of the viscount the night of Sir Perran's card soirée. Was it possible Lord Delabole was all to flinders? But how could that be? His uncle had always said the Delabole wealth was enormous. Could a man, lost in his grief for a beloved spouse, lose an entire fortune in card play?

Because his own circumstances were so straitened that his officer's pay barely sustained the appearances of gentlemanliness, Blackthorn couldn't credit anyone being so foolish as to gamble away a fortune—and so large a one at that. No, something else must be wrong, but for the life of him he couldn't image what.

As the majestic lines of Hatherleigh Park came into view, the castellated rooftop a golden bridge against the verdant hills beyond, Edward's thoughts turned away from Lord Delabole. The ancient mansion, with no less than twenty bedchambers, was set in a parkland that appeared completely natural. Several years ago, Julia had written to him of the landscaping efforts of Humphrey Repton, but until now, he hadn't understood how beautiful the effect could be, as though nature had done the labor by herself in the gentlest and most pleasing of arrangements.

Passing through the gates that led to a long avenue, Edward was struck by the beauty of the pink rhododendrons lining the drive. Dozens of fine plants had been placed in a loose, scattered array ever closer to the mansion, which had the effect of drawing the eye toward the house. Row upon row of windows glittered in the sunlight. He was impressed, as he always was, by the stately beauty of the ancient stone dwelling. What was before his eyes, he wondered, but a reminder of Lord Delabole's vast wealth?

Appearances.

He was reminded of the dilemma facing him at The Priory.

Someone in Sir Perran's employ was not just a servant, but also a French agent.

Appearances.

He thought back to his interview with the smuggler and his return trip to The Priory. During the journey, he had reviewed all that he had learned in Falmouth, comparing the documents found in Mr. Mawls's possession with the documents he had taken with him to the seaport. He could only conclude that someone working at The Priory had meticulously copied the documents. But who? His secretary, perhaps? When he had arrived home on Monday, his first effort was to visit Mr. Ladock, who had an office next to Sir Perran's study. In just a few minutes of conversation, he was able to catch a glimpse of the secretary's handwriting—a script that did not match the documents recovered from Mr. Mawls. Mr. Ladock was not a French agent.

Who then? Who in Sir Perran's employ—and to all *appearances* a faithful servant—was engaged in spying for Bonaparte? On Saturday, when he would again return to Falmouth, Edward hoped he would uncover the identity of the spy.

For the present, he would listen and observe the comings and goings at The Priory.

As the coach drew to a stop before the front door of the mansion, he turned to look at Julia's profile and noticed that a somber expression had returned to her face. Edward was so affected by the sight of her sad appearance that he slipped his arm about her and gave her shoulders an encouraging squeeze.

She smiled halfheartedly up at him. "Come," she said in a whisper. "Now you will know everything."

A few minutes later, he was standing beside Julia in Cook's weed-strewn vegetable plot. "I don't understand?" he queried, a deep frown on his brow. "Why haven't your servants attended to this?" He waved his hand over the rangy rows of cucumbers, cabbages, and peas all laced with a fine web of grassy weeds.

"We haven't sufficient staff."

Edward looked at her sharply. "The devil take it!" he cried. "Have things come to such a pass?"

Julia nodded and bid him follow her. She led him to the kitchens, where only Cook and one scullery maid kept the family and the remaining servants fed, then told him of Hatherleigh's diminished staff. Within the house there remained the butler, Grigson, who had been with the family for over three decades; a footman; an upstairs maid; an undermaid; Julia's abigail, Gabrielle, who had served Lady Delabole; and another personal maid, Anna, who besides dressing Julia's sisters also mended the linens. Outside the house, a gardener and three laborers tended the formal, landscaped portions of the grounds, and a head groom maintained a small stable of only five horses, with one young man serving as groom and postilion.

"Only these? For a house this large?" he asked, dumbfounded.

"Most of the rooms are in Holland covers, by my orders. Papa did not wish it so but I was firm. Which of the few remaining servants would have time to keep the draperies clean? Who would dust and polish the furniture with beeswax? As it is, I have acted as housekeeper for over a year. We have been unable to afford one since Mrs. Strelley retired." When he stared at her in utter astonishment, she continued. "I don't mind the labor—in truth, I enjoy it very much—but I do not hesitate to tell you that meeting with tradesmen who wish to see their accounts settled at once has been a sore trial."

"Whatever has happened, Julia? Have the rent-rolls failed? I know that throughout England, the Corn Laws have created disaster in many counties."

"No, it is nothing of the sort. The farms are prospering well enough, though I wouldn't say they are thriving."

"What then? Have you suffered losses at the quarry? I was given to understand that the quarry made a handsome profit annually for your father."

"The quarry has suffered in recent years, primarily because of poor management. I believe with a little effort, better contracts could be arranged, but that is not the source of our troubles."

"Then what? Do not tell me . . . has your father attended my uncle's card soirées more frequently than he ought? I now recall that in your letters you hinted at something of the sort."

Julia felt her throat constrict. She rarely spoke of her circumstances, but when she did give voice to the truth, somehow she felt the troubles surrounding her more keenly. "My father has regularly attended Sir Perran's card soirees and really any invitation extended to him, from a friend or otherwise."

From the kitchens, Julia led him up the stairs to the ground floor. Edward walked along beside her in silence for a time. When he spoke, his voice was solemn. "I had no idea. I only wonder that my uncle permits your father to continue in his excesses—at least under his roof. Surely, he can't be ignorant of what is going forward, yet he has said nothing to me. Julia, I am so sorry. Is there anything I can do?"

She looked up at him, deeply grateful for his concern and for his offer of assistance. "I only wish there was," she responded quietly. Passing through the Long Gallery, which overlooked the terrace, she said, "My sisters are longing to become acquainted with you again."

"I can hear their laughter coming from beyond those doors," he remarked, turning to peer down the gallery toward a pair of carved oak doors.

"The morning room. That's where we do our sewing and share the latest tittle-tattle." When she heard Annabelle cry out, Julia added, "Though we are not generally given to squealing while we ply our needles."

When one shriek then another could be heard from beyond the morning room doors, Edward cried, "What the deuce—"

When Julia reached the doors, she threw them wide and bid him enter.

The lofty square chamber, decorated in a deep blue silk-damask, was in a state of feminine chaos. Yards of white muslin, sheer tulle, rose silk, fine print calico, and ribbons in a dozen shades were draped over the scattered chairs, sofas, and tables. In the very center of the room was Gabrielle, her vision hindered by a pad of soft white cambric held in place over her eyes by a length of lace tied into a jaunty bow over her brown locks. She groped in quick steps toward unseen players.

"Elizabette?" she cried, unable to say the soft *th*. "Annabelle! Caroline! You mustn't hide! You must play fair, *n'est-ce pas?*"

"Gabrielle!" Julia called out, laughing. "Did you not tell my sisters that Major Blackthorn was coming to call?"

Gabrielle instantly whisked the kerchief and lace from her head, her brown eyes alive with laughter as she greeted her mistress. "No, mademoiselle . . . I quite forgot! The moment I entered the room, Miss Annabelle put a kerchief over *mes yeux*. I was playing before I could think! I am so sorry! I shall go now." She glanced at the major, her eyes twinkling with mischief. A faint blush suffused her cheeks as she giggled, bobbed a quick curtsy, and hurried from the chamber.

Elizabeth crawled out from beneath one of the shrouds of rose silk, her black hair mussed from her adventure. From a kneeling position, she smiled up at Edward. "Hello, Major Blackthorn," she called to him. Two more heads peeped from beneath the fabric, one red like Julia's, the other black like Elizabeth's.

Blue eyes and green eyes looked from Julia to Edward in utter confusion. "So you are Julia's major!" the youngest one cried. She was on all fours as she turned to Elizabeth. "He is very handsome, Lizzie, just as you said."

Caroline, who was kneeling beside Annabelle, clicked her tongue. "You will embarrass the major if you say such things." She was a sweet-tempered young lady who was always aware of the feelings of others.

Elizabeth crawled from beneath the silk and gained her feet. Standing squarely before Edward, she lifted her chin and held his gaze steadily, a twinkle in her eye. "Do you remember me?" she asked.

"Yes," he responded with a half-smile. "You used to hit Stephen until he cried. Then George would box your ears and you would run home as mad as fire."

"You do remember!" she returned ecstatically. "Those were the best days of my life. I swear they were!"

Edward looked at her in surprise. "The best days?" he queried. "Sounds like you're pitching a bit of gammon, if you ask me."

"Somerset and Bath are dull beyond bearing," she announced firmly. "More than life itself, I wish I were a man. I would go to sea and never return. I would."

"I believe you, Miss Elizabeth," he said, smiling warmly down at her. She was a little shorter than Julia and just as pretty, though in an entirely different way.

Elizabeth smiled broadly upon Edward, then embraced him. "I am so glad you've come to Hatherleigh," she declared, kissing his cheek in a sisterly fashion. "I hope you mean to visit us frequently. We do not have as many guests as we used to. Something about practicing economies." Upon this last statement, Elizabeth's gaze shifted uneasily to Julia.

"It's all right," Julia assured her in a whisper. "I have explained all to . . . er . . . Major Blackthorn." Privately, she was perfectly comfortable addressing him by his Christian name, but she knew in public he would always be a formal Major Blackthorn or, simplified, Blackthorn.

Having crawled from beneath the rose silk, muslin, and tulle, the younger sisters now made themselves known to Edward. The third sister, Caroline, peered up at Edward and carefully searched his face. She then extended her hand to him. In her soft voice, she said, "I have been trying to recall you, Major, but I cannot. I daresay I was too young to remember you when Julia was acquainted with you."

"And I could not have been out of leading strings!" Annabelle announced. "But later on Julia told us all about your adventures, when Caroline and I were older. What famous fun! I wish I had been old enough to steal away from the nursery! Old Nurse used to become the crab over poor Julia until she would cry. Did you know that Julia was convinced she would marry you when she was fully grown? Even after you'd been gone several years, she still spoke of hoping to wed you." Annabelle had just turned seventeen and was the youngest, and she had not entirely learned to be circumspect in her speech.

Edward turned to Julia. "Indeed?" he queried, a soft smile lighting his gray eyes. "Is this so?"

"A silly schoolgirl's *tendre*," she returned evenly. "Nothing more, I assure you, so you may now remove any peculiar notions from your head which may have just entered it."

Edward regarded her warmly, the smile remaining in his eyes. After a moment, he looked from one sister to the next, then to the chamber full of feminine industry. "Has Lord Peter visited you when you are thus employed?" he questioned.

Julia was clearly taken aback by his question and gave a shake of her head. "No, he has not."

"Were I he," he said pointedly, "nothing would charm me more than happening upon such a happy familial scene as this."

Julia lifted her brows in surprise. So he was charmed by the disorder of the morning room. She considered Lord Peter for a moment and knew that he would very much dislike so much confusion in a home—the chaos, the nonsense, the young ladies actually having involved a servant in their play, the fact that they were playing at blindman's buff when they shouldn't have been playing at all.

She was about to thank him for expressing such a warm-hearted sentiment, but Annabelle spoke first. "Major, perhaps you would like to play our game with us?"

Before he could protest, Annabelle had drawn up a chair behind him, climbed up on the chair, and was quickly tying the kerchief and lace about his eyes.

He did not protest in the least, and for that Julia was immensely grateful.

Five

Blackthorn remained the rest of the day at Hatherleigh Park, beginning his stay by playing blindman's buff until all the sisters were exhausted from laughing. Later, in the crimson and gold drawing room on the first floor, he sang duets with Annabelle while Julia accompanied them on the pianoforte.

Caroline and Elizabeth listened appreciatively to their performances but were by no means idle. Each sat in a chair near the brightest window and, with bent heads, plied their needles in careful rows of tiny stitches. They were making their own ball dresses, a habit the sisters had acquired a year before when it became impossible for Julia to pay the dressmakers in Bath. He was astonished by their industry and equally so by the fact that though they labored steadily, not one word of complaint crossed their lips.

"Do you design all your gowns?" he queried of Caroline, when she held up for his inspection a gown of white silk overlaid with an embroidered sheer tulle. Edward had moved to stand over her shoulder, the afternoon light sparkling on her black curls.

She looked up at him and smiled from clear blue eyes. "Yes, but only after we've carefully considered the latest creations in Ackermann's and *La Belle Assemblée*. Of course, Gabrielle usually has the best ideas. Then we make our own pattern cards, cut the fabric, and hope for the best. I don't think we've ever had a complete disaster, though once I cut one gown several inches too short in the skirt and we had to construct no fewer than five rows of ruffles to make it sufficiently long. And do you know that after having worn that particular gown, I have begun to see more ruffles about the hem."

"Then you have created a new fashion," he announced, teasing her.

Caroline blushed and wrinkled her nose. "Do you think so? Oh, you are just funning. Julia said you enjoyed teasing." She grew serious for a long moment, then leaned toward him slightly and gestured for him to draw near. When he had lowered his ear to her lips, she spoke in a low voice. "I wish you would persuade my sister not to pursue Lord Peter. He is a pleasant enough fellow but she doesn't love him, though I daresay she has convinced herself otherwise. The truth is, I know he will never be able to make her happy. Julia may seem rather dull, but you don't know her as I do. She would perish living as wife to such a proper, self-absorbed creature."

Blackthorn could not have agreed more, but having come to understand the desperate nature of the sisters' situation, he now comprehended fully Julia's interest in marrying Lord Peter. Knowing neither Caroline nor Annabelle were completely informed of the seriousness of their predicament, he did not feel he could discuss the subject with her.

"She knows my sentiments," he responded at last, drawing back from her slightly. "Which do not differ significantly from your own. I promise, should the occasion arise, I shall attempt to divert her from such a marriage."

Caroline turned to look directly at him. "Don't be deceived, Major Blackthorn," she said, holding his gaze steadily. "Once Julia has got an idea fixed in her head, she will only release it through much persuasion."

At that, Blackthorn smiled. "Then I must begin persuading her."

Later, when the three younger sisters retired to dress for dinner, Blackthorn had an opportunity to speak privately with Julia and decided to address the very concern Caroline had so earnestly presented to him.

He moved to join Julia, who was standing beside one of the tall windows overlooking the terrace, the lawn, and the beech-covered hills beyond. He looked out at the deer feeding just past the neatly scythed grass and flowing hedges. "Such tranquillity," he murmured.

"It is lovely," Julia returned. "The Delaboles have lived here for over two centuries. But not much longer, I fear. Papa has actually spoken of letting the house, though I don't know where he intends to remove us."

Blackthorn turned to look down upon the auburn curls and fair features of his childhood friend. In her emerald eyes were shards of anxiety, reflected in the creases along her brow. He knew a strong desire to smooth away the tiny wrinkles, but instead took hold of her hand and held it firmly in a brotherly manner.

After a long moment, he said simply, "Don't marry him, Julia, even should he have enough bottom to make you an offer. He is not worthy of you."

Julia looked down at the windowsill and mentally made a note to have the undermaid take a cloth to the dusty ledge. A small cobweb veiled the corner. She sighed. "I suppose the point is moot until he does offer for me. But, Edward, I don't believe you value him sufficiently. He is a good man."

"All right," he conceded. "Lord Peter Longton is a good man. But he cannot make you happy."

"I have long since given over my happiness as the primary object. In fact, my only intention is to do all I am able to do to make him happy. I hold him in great affection, indeed, I . . . I love him in my way. But how do I explain to him that my family is utterly destitute?"

"If you cannot tell the man who would become your husband that through no fault of your own you are penniless, then I can offer you no stronger case for refusing his offer in the first place. And if you'll recall, you did not hesitate for a moment to tell me of your difficulties."

"But that is quite another matter! I have no designs upon you."

"Why should it matter, though?" he asked tenderly. "If he loves you—and how could he not!—he oughtn't be concerned about your family's misfortunes. If he can't separate you from your father's mistakes, then he doesn't deserve to possess even one hair of your head, let alone your hand in marriage."

Her green eyes glimmered as she looked up at him, a soft smile touching her lips. "How very kind of you to say so," she purred. "You are an excellent friend, Edward. A most excellent man."

He lifted her hand to his lips. "And that is quite the nicest thing you have ever said to me." As he met her gaze, a warm sensation flowed over him in gentle waves. She was so beautiful with the northern light setting her features aglow. Edward didn't understand all that he was feeling as he pressed his lips against her fingers. He heard a faint sigh pass her lips, and her eyes began to shimmer with unexpected tears. An unspoken understanding passed between them. No matter what happened, they would always be friends. Always.

He drew her fingers up to his lips and, holding them curled within the palm of his hand, kissed them. She lifted her other hand to his face and caressed his cheek. Her tears remained brimming on her lashes. He wanted to kiss them away. He wanted to take her in his arms, to hold her tightly against his chest, to protect her.

"Julia," he whispered.

It was in part a question, but no words followed to complete his thought, his query. He didn't know what he was asking. He could ask her nothing. He couldn't even ask for her hand in marriage. He could give her nothing.

"It doesn't matter," she whispered.

She understood even when he didn't.

Julia laughed lightly. "Silly man. You used to look at me in just that way when I would fall and skin my knees. I appreciate your concern. I cherish your concern. I brought you here because

I wanted you to understand how difficult my circumstances are and why I do what I do. But I don't look to you to whisk me safely away to your castle."

"I haven't even got a cottage," he responded, and for a moment they laughed together. "Do your sisters know how badly circumstanced you are?"

"The younger know a little, but a few days ago I told Elizabeth everything. Perhaps I should have informed Caroline and Annabelle as well, but I felt that even if I had been unable to enjoy what remained to me of my girlhood and innocence, they should at least have the opportunity to do so."

"Who has supported you all this time, then?"

She thought for a moment, her fingers a gentle feather on his cheek. "Memories of my mother, I suppose. Yet I don't repine. Edward, I promise you, I don't. My lot is not so very bad when you consider the sufferings of so many in these hard times. I have but to think of the children who are in the coal mines to know that if the worst that has come to me is that I must marry a man not of my particular choosing, then I would be foolish to complain." She paused for a long moment, her voice suspended by tears, strong emotions passing across her lovely face. Her voice broke as she continued. "Gabrielle lost her whole family to the guillotine. I cannot imagine the terror, the horror of what she has endured. So you see, once placed in perspective, for me to rail against fate would be an absurdity."

"You are too good." His throat felt tight.

"No," she whispered, giving her auburn curls a quick shake. "Nonsense. Do you suppose there are not times when I am more angry than grateful? I have been known to throw a fit of the hysterics on occasion, particularly after the tradesmen have come to call. They have a great deal of patience, but you cannot imagine the frustration I feel when I cannot discharge our debts to them. To me it is a matter of honor as great as the honor you gentlemen feel when you are playing at cards and cannot redeem your vowels." She drew in a deep breath before continuing. "Annabelle was right about one thing: I always loved you. Just tell me that you understand why I am making the decisions I am, then I can be content."

"I do understand. I do. I promise you I do. I just wish there was another way for you."

"If I were alone, of course I would not go down this road. But I am not alone. I have Elizabeth and Caroline and Annabelle to care for, and I will do my duty by them. That is what is required of me. In the same way that you will sacrifice for your regiment, I must fulfill my duty to my sisters in a similar manner."

"I wish I could help you."

"I know you do. And your wish of helping me will sustain me."

Only then did he lean down and place his lips on hers. He meant to comfort her. In no way did he intend to repeat their passionate encounter in the carriage earlier that day. But what began as a tender touch of his lips against hers quickly burst into a bright flame of desire. She was soon wrapped tightly in his arms, giving kiss for kiss, straining against him, holding him fast, whispering his name upon his lips and deeply into his ear. He plundered her mouth, taking possession of her in the only way he could. Edward wanted her as he had never wanted a woman before. Had he even the most meager competence, he would have begged her to become his wife.

Julia did not understand what was happening to her. A moment earlier she had been explaining why she would marry Lord Peter, and now she was permitting Blackthorn to taste of her mouth, to hold her so tightly against him that she could feel evidence of his desire. Knowing that he wanted her seemed to arouse her own passion, so that she began speaking his name in whispers after each kiss.

But she could not have Edward Blackthorn, even as a lover. Such were not the convictions of her heart. How wrong it was to permit him such liberties even now, to respond to his touch with such abandon when she could never be his wife. Julia felt his hand suddenly on her breast, and the sensation, so steeped in desire, nearly caused her to swoon. At the same time, she realized she must end what could never be fulfilled. She caught his hand and prevented him from touching her further.

"You mustn't, Edward," she breathed, then kissed him again.

He again tasted of her lips and her mouth. He was breathing raggedly as he kissed her over and over. "I know," he whispered between kisses.

She didn't want to let him go. She didn't want to stop his advances, but nothing could come of torturing him or herself. So, at last she pulled away from him and, with a smile, told him softly that she was certain he had pulled some of her curls apart and that she would need Gabrielle to repair the damage.

He let her go without protest.

Later, Blackthorn dined with Julia, her sisters, and Lord Delabole. The viscount conducted himself jovially, except when he thought he wasn't being observed. At these times, Blackthorn noticed his features would fall into a state of acute misery.

Lord Delabole drank heavily through dinner, and when the ladies retired to the drawing room, he finished a bottle of port after having seen a single glass served to his guest. His tongue became loose and he rambled on about former glorious days when his stables were full. He spoke of his wife, half the time as though she were not dead, the other half with tears in his eyes. He held the conversation exclusively to himself, Blackthorn never saying a word, merely smiling, nodding, and shaking his head at appropriate times as Delabole's discourse meandered from one subject to the next.

Later that night, when Julia bid him goodbye privately, he said, "Had I had the least doubt about the extent of your troubles, your father's appearance and speech would have removed them all. God keep you, Julia." He placed a last, lingering kiss on her lips, looked deeply into her eyes, and wondered what, if anything, he could do to help her.

* * *

At dusk the following evening, Sir Perran Blackthorn lifted a glass of sherry to his lips and took the barest sip. He let the wine rest on his lips for a moment, then drew the smooth, nut-flavored liquid into his mouth to pass along his tongue. He never hurried anything. That was not his way, any more than it was the sun's way to descend in a quick, brilliant flash. To move relentlessly and purposefully was a design reflected in nature in many ways. There was and had been an inexorable quality to his life, just as the sun would set regardless of anyone's wishes otherwise. So he sat in a chair on his terrace and lifted his glass to the setting sun.

The terrace that opened off Sir Perran's bedchamber on the first floor of his mansion had been constructed for only one purpose: to catch the hills opposite his house glowing with the light of the descending sun. The manor faced west, sitting at the base of a hill in a narrow valley that the baronet owned. A stream flowed through his property, which eventually found its way to the River Avon.

In late afternoon, at any time of the year when the sun was able as now to break up the perpetual drift of clouds coming off the Atlantic, the beechwoods glittered like stars.

At these times, when he could survey the magnificence of creation, he knew a most profound sensation of peace and well-being.

How many years remain? he wondered.

Longevity was his heritage. His grandfather had died at ninety-two and his father at eighty-eight. At sixty-seven, he supposed he would live for many more years to come, years in which he would finally be able to enjoy the fruits that he had been cultivating year upon year since he was sixteen.

He smiled, letting his gaze drift up into the deepening blue sky above the hills. Pure, virginal satisfaction coursed through him. He leaned his head back into the winged chair, closed his eyes, and just as he had savored his sherry, he drank in the precious taste of triumph that he now knew.

He had seen Lord Delabole drive up the avenue ten minutes

ago. He could only want one thing, and Sir Perran could think of few things he was more likely to enjoy bargaining for than the viscount's request.

He heard a faint coughing behind him and a dart of irritation pierced the sublimity of his thoughts. "You are disturbing me," he stated quietly. He was not a man to lift his voice in anger.

"I most humbly request your pardon, Sir Perran, but Lord Delabole has arrived, quite unexpectedly, and begs an audience with you."

He let his displeasure rest heavily in the air. Though he was not able to see his manservant, he was certain that the nerve just below Beeston's eye was twitching. His hazel eyes were undoubtedly round with distress and unblinking. How odd that of late, he did not even have to see the results of his actions to believe in their effect and to enjoy them.

When he heard the slight shifting of worried feet on the stone terrace, he finally spoke. "You must inform His Lordship that if he will be patient, I shall join him presently. Take him to my study. Do not offer him refreshment. Has a fire been built up in that chamber?"

"No, Sir Perran."

"Good. Let it remain unlit. That is all."

That is all.

He smiled to himself, satisfied at how well his plans were progressing.

Sir Perran watched the last rays of the sun dart off the beech leaves. Stars began appearing like clusters of diamonds. He had always been able to appreciate the beauty around him. How curious that he had been given such an exacting eye. And how incredible that Delabole had produced precisely the woman to fulfill his objectives . . . in every possible way! Really, it was miraculous.

Julia Verdell would never displease his eye. She was an auburn beauty who displayed to advantage in any drawing room, in any assembly room. She carried herself as though supporting a crown, head erect, shoulders and back perfectly aligned, gait

slow and measured. How the devil she had sprung from Delabole's loins, he would never know. If Julia was graceful, her
father's agitation and inclination to drink had given him a reck-
less step and a posture that made him appear as though he was
walking into a strong wind. She had acquired his fine bones,
however, for Lord Delabole had once been a devilishly handsome young man. But too much wine had deepened his eyes in
his sockets and broken vessels on his cheeks. His dashing appearance had long since been attributed to the years of his youth.

He again sipped his sherry, a burning drift upon his lips and
tongue. He wondered what Julia would think of him as her husband. Twenty years ago, he would have presented a striking,
formidable countenance. A little careful seduction and she
would have tumbled in love with him. Now, even though he kept
himself fit—he only feigned the need for a cane—his hair was
pure white, the skin wrinkled at the corner of his gray eyes, his
complexion marked in places with unattractive dark splotches.

Julia would undoubtedly think him an old man, especially
since he moved about with a cane and a limp.

How much better to have her now, though. She would have
demanded a great deal from a younger husband, but a man of
his years could easily command her. A lift of his brow and she
would still her tongue. Command was what his years had
brought him.

Sir Perran's thoughts turned to Delabole waiting in his study.
He again smiled, permitting himself a chuckle or two. The pleasure he would soon experience was everything to him. He eased
back in his chair, watching the final light from the sun disappear
entirely. He sipped his sherry and waited.

An hour later, he entered his study on his slow tread, supporting himself in part with his burnished, thick-handled cherrywood cane.

"Sit, pray sit!" he declared, smiling at his guest, when Lord
Delabole rose to greet him. He glanced about the chamber, decorated in a muted amber velvet, approving the chill of the room
and the single candle lit at Lord Delabole's elbow.

Assuming his most astonished expression, Sir Perran exclaimed, "Good God! What a pass my home has come to! No fire, the lighting as dark as a dungeon, and not even a comfortable glass of Madeira to warm your bones!"

He turned to the tapestried bellpull by the door and gave a hard tug. "Do you have as much trouble with your servants as I, m'lord? I vow, there are days I would turn them all off without a reference if I thought I could do better. But alas, they seem to be generally a lazy lot. If I get rid of an old one, the new one is worse."

Lord Delabole smiled nervously. "A lazy lot, indeed," he responded.

Sir Perran repressed a sigh of satisfaction. He could see that the viscount was caught between strong emotions—a need to placate his host, and a fury that he had been kept kicking his heels for an hour and that without the least attendance to his comforts. Delabole sat by the fireplace in one of two amber velvet-covered winged chairs. He thrummed his fingers on the arms of the chair. One knee was shifting about as though it did not belong to him at all. He clearly needed a drink.

What a worthless man, Sir Perran thought. Julia is worth twoscore of the likes of him. She certainly didn't deserve to have a rain of coals brought down on her head, but then neither had he at the tender age of sixteen.

Vague memories of watching Delabole's grandfather, a man of shifting morals, march through his own father's quarry and simply turn him out came back to him in a hot wave. The quarry was on ancient Delabole land, he had proclaimed, and had never belonged to the Blackthorns in the first place.

Just like that, a fortune stolen, all legal, all right and tight.

A kind of heat worked in his chest, melting his sympathies to a pool of unusable elements. He drew in a deep breath and coughed. Sir Perran moved slowly toward the vacant winged chair and sat down with great care, favoring his right leg. "How do you go on, m'lord?" he queried. "Have you not been resting well of late? You seem a bit fagged. I always rest these days, whenever I can. Many take the waters in the Pump Room, but I find rest will cure what brackish waters can't." He laughed, and to his satisfaction, Lord Delabole laughed nervously with him.

Sir Perran chatted cordially with the viscount for several minutes, until his man arrived. The butler wore the red and gold Blackthorn livery. His hair was powdered and tied up in a black riband. His expression was stoic, save for a twitching beneath his eye. When he bowed to the baronet, Sir Perran glared at him. "How is it that a man of Lord Delabole's consequence has been left unattended in my study this hour and more? I gave you strict orders to provide him a little Madeira and to build up the fire. Do you not receive your pay at my hand? Well, do you not?"

"Yes, Sir Perran," the servant responded, bowing low. "I do beg your pardon if an oversight—"

"An oversight," he returned, raising his voice slightly. "What an impertinent fellow you are! I wish the fire laid immediately, a bottle of Madeira and two glasses brought forthwith, and at least a dozen candles. The chamber is a tomb." His choice of words pleased him and the heat returned to his chest, spreading through his stomach in warm tendrils of pleasure.

"Yes, Sir Perran," the servant responded, unwilling to meet his master's gaze as he backed from the chamber. His complexion was suitably pallid.

When the door was closed, he smiled. "Won't do a bit of good. Do you happen to know a butler of some sense? I am desperate, you can see that I am. I don't suppose you will be relinquishing your man in the foreseeable future? Now, there is a servant who has learned his trade and plies it to perfection. What is his name?"

"Grigson. Damn fine man! Been at Hatherleigh for ages. In fact, didn't he once belong to your grandfather? Quite some time ago, that, eh?"

"Yes, indeed, now that you mention it." He held Delabole's gaze steadily, watching the viscount's eyes shift uneasily. Sir Perran immediately changed the subject. "How are your daughters?" he queried. "I suppose they will be at the assemblies on Friday, though I daresay Miss Verdell will outshine them all."

"Ah, yes, my dear daughters, my lovely Julia! They are all perfectly well and I do thank you for asking, though I must say there is not a one of them who is not a trifle silly now and again, as all young girls are wont to be, with the exception of Julia, of course." A look of warm affection entered his eye. "She is so much like her dear mother and becomes more and more so each day. You remember Lady Delabole?"

"Who does not? A great lady, indeed, God rest her soul. To think of her perishing in the quarry like that, as though some sort of retribution was at work." Not wanting Lord Delabole to think on this remark too much, he hurried on. "Does Julia have any suitors of merit these days?" He knew the answer. Only one man seemed to have turned her head of late, and he was such a halfling that Sir Perran did not give him even a moment's distress. The first hint of trouble, and Lord Peter would turn tail and run.

Lord Delabole smiled broadly for the first time since the beginning of their discourse. "It is all but settled," he said. Sir Perran knew it was a bald lie, but if he had been in Delabole's place, he would have said precisely the same thing.

Sir Perran nodded. "Lord Peter will bring great consequence to your daughter and will undoubtedly provide the younger ones all they will require to connect themselves well in marriage. You ought to be pleased and proud. Of course, no one is more deserving than your fair Julia." He laughed lightly. "Were I twenty years younger, faith, I would be tempted to offer for her myself. As her husband, I could certainly have provided my father-in-law any manner of assistance he might have needed. Which brings me round to the point, and I trust you will not be offended if I say that your visit comes as no surprise to me. I imagine you have come to ask for help and I promise I will do whatever I possibly can, so, please, be candid. Do not withhold even the smallest concern from me. What is it you need?"

He could see that he had startled the viscount and was glad for it.

The servant scratched on the door before Lord Delabole could speak. He brought with him two footmen to tend the fire while he poured the Madeira for Sir Perran and his guest. After the gentlemen were sipping the rich wine, the butler began moving smoothly about the chamber, lighting several candelabra and seeing that the fire was properly tended. When the thick logs, collected from the Home Wood, were blazing high in the hearth, when he refilled the glasses and the chamber was properly diffused with candlelight, only then did he withdraw with his footmen, bowing again to Sir Perran and closing the door silently behind him.

Sir Perran approved of his butler more than he would ever let him know. Beeston had been with him for five years now, and during those years not once had he grown arrogant or overconfident in his abilities. It took so little to keep him properly in his place that the baronet thought it probable Mr. Beeston would be with him the remainder of his days.

Turning his attention back to Lord Delabole, the baronet began again. "Now," he said kindly, watching the viscount carefully, "tell me everything."

Lord Delabole set his jaw and launched heavily into an accounting of his estate. He had overreached himself, he said, and the funds that he had acquired from the latest selling off of his lands were simply and quite mysteriously gone. He referred to some vague possibility of thievery within his household but did not pursue it. He knew he had written vowels last Friday night, but the devil of it was he hadn't the funds to cover them. He was sure that the forthcoming game on Saturday night would see him fixed up all right and tight. But for the present . . .

Sir Perran's whole being now glowed with a heat so pleasurable that he only wondered Lord Delabole did not take notice of it. Surely there must be some visible sign of precisely what he was experiencing. If only he had someone with whom he could share the triumph that played within his body like a fine violoncello in the hands of a virtuoso, then his delight would be complete. He thought of his father and of his grandfather, of the stone quarry, of the life wrenched from him at sixteen, of his years on the high seas, of making a small fortune in prize money, of retiring in his forties to Bath with a baronetcy bestowed upon him by a grateful king, of creating a network of spies, of learning the skill of cunning investments, of making a massive fortune.

His whole life was about to come full circle in a most glorious fashion.

"So you are in need of a few hundred pounds, then?" he asked, knowing full well the viscount's gaming debts were closer to three thousand. He watched Lord Delabole's countenance pale.

With an attempt at a light tone, the viscount chuckled. "Were it only that simple. But it would seem that I require three thousand to discharge last night's debts and then, of course, a proper stake for Saturday."

Sir Perran sipped the Madeira, just as he had the sherry earlier, letting the dark wine rest on his lips, then slip along his tongue before sliding down his throat. He narrowed his gaze at the viscount. "I wish that I could simply give you all that you require but—and pray forgive me for being so blunt—years of harsh experience with men of every stamp have taught me that the best of transactions can be hindered by a lack of foresight. For instance, should you lose in your play on Saturday—though I am personally convinced you will not—how do you mean to repay me?"

He kept his gaze fixed upon the viscount, his hand rolling over the ivory handle of his cherrywood cane in a single fondling movement.

Lord Delabole cast a despairing glance toward Sir Perran, then quickly looked away. He did not answer for a long moment as he stared at a globe of the world across the study, near the doorway.

Sir Perran leaned back into his comfortable chair and smiled.

"I thought it likely you had not considered the possibility of failure. But I must. I owe it to my children, who will one day inherit my fortune. Ah, I see I have shocked you, and possibly now you are wondering about all the rumors. Yes, as it happens, I do hope to take a wife—a young wife—very soon. But as I was saying, I owe it to my children to keep all for which I have steadily labored intact. Let me make you an offer, therefore, which I trust you will not find displeasing. I would have your eldest daughter for the handsome sum of five thousand pounds, which, from what you have said, will be an excellent beginning for you."

Lord Delabole's attention was caught. He jerked his gaze from the globe back to his host, his mouth falling agape. "My daughter?" he asked, dumbfounded. "For the use of five thousand pounds I must give Julia to you?"

"Well, yes. Do consider that should your daughter produce a son, he would inherit Hatherleigh. The women in your family have not been left out of the entail, have they?" He watched the baronet give his head a shake as though caught in a nightmare. "Well then, we would both benefit—a son of mine, a grandson of yours to walk the halls of Hatherleigh. Are you not enchanted by such a vision?"

Lord Delabole's face had turned a vivid red, the veins along his cheeks and nose a burgundy lacework against the bluish hue of his skin. "Damn you," he whispered. "I'll not sell a child of mine to anyone, nor my estate—"

"Not even what is left of it, eh?" Sir Perran broke in firmly. He wanted Delabole to consider how badly he had managed his inheritance. He let him wallow in his anger for several minutes, before giving his head a shake and taking Delabole down an entirely different path. "Good God! I believe you have completely misunderstood me. Did you suppose I meant to take one of your daughters for the loan? My good man, it is no such thing. I've bungled it! So I have! Permit me to explain. I would suggest to you that should you lose on Saturday night—by some incredible mischance of fortune—then I would be willing to

offer for Julia in order to bring all your daughters beneath my
protective wing. You would never need to worry about their futures again. Should you win—which I am convinced you will—
well, then, you have only to repay the five thousand from your
winnings. What do you say? I have the money here now, if you
wish to strike a bargain."

At that, Delabole seemed startled. "What?" he cried. "Under
your roof?"

"I always look to the eventualities."

"Then you expected my call?"

"Let us simply say that by the rather forlorn expression on
your face when you quit my house the other night, I hoped you
would turn to me for assistance." He rested his cane against his
leg and stretched his hand out to the viscount. "Have we struck
a bargain?"

"Julia is in love with Lord Peter," the viscount returned uneasily. Clearly, he was mollified by Sir Perran's *explanation* of
his offer. "What of Elizabeth? Or Caroline?"

Sir Perran shook his head. "After having known Julia, it is
your eldest or none."

"I shall win," Lord Delabole returned, extending his hand to
the baronet.

Sir Perran gave him a friendly smile and a firm handshake.
"Of course you will. Now, let us not speak another word on the
subject. Will you dine with me? I believe my chef has prepared
his unusual recipe for lobster patties. He would be gratified to
know that a man of your consequence was partaking of his efforts."

When Lord Delabole graciously accepted, Sir Perran again
slipped his palm over the thick handle of his cane and stroked
it gently. All was as good as settled.

Six

On Thursday morning, Julia sat beside Edward, directing him along a crisscross of lanes that led to her favorite meadow. Edward drove an old-fashioned cart with large, cumbersome wheels but a bed sufficiently wide to support Elizabeth, Caroline, and Annabelle, as well as an enormous wicker basket replete with a bounteous quantity of victuals, champagne—which he provided with his uncle's compliments—china plates edged in a deep royal blue, crystal goblets, silver forks and knives, linens, and a blanket for their alfresco nuncheon. The current plight of the family did not permit the attendance of a servant, but Julia didn't care, nor did her sisters complain in the least. If anything, the absence of a footman to wait on them lent a relaxed air to the outing.

Sitting in the back, their skirts of muslin, cambric, and calico, consecutively in pink, white, and yellow, the younger sisters surrounded the basket like flower petals. They sang bright ballads of love in pretty harmony, laughing when one of the wheels would hit a rut, giving them a severe jolt that caused their melodies to turn to squeals.

The sounds of summer, Julia thought happily, familiar sounds that reminded her of earlier family picnics when her mother was alive and her father's feet were planted firmly on the ground. Even though her thoughts were suddenly full of her mother, she would not permit herself to be unhappy, not today, not when her heart was so light and free of cares.

She glanced up at Edward. His fine beaver hat shaded his

face from the bright sunlight. He looked down at her and smiled, softly, tenderly. Because her sisters were facing backward, they could not see that he held the reins in one hand and had entwined his fingers within hers with his other. His touch, how closely they were seated together, the warmth of the sun on her skirts of pale green muslin, all served to bring a rush of desire pouring over her. She wished she was alone with him. She wanted to be kissing him again and again—as she had yesterday, when he had taken her on a surprise trip to Cheddar Gorge, a holiday that had occupied the entire day.

When he turned his gaze back to the road and she directed him through the next gate, her thoughts wended their way back to the previous day. Julia felt a blush rise on her cheeks.

Yesterday.

Yesterday, Edward had arrived unexpectedly and had stolen her from the breakfast table, her sisters encouraging her to go with him. After hastily donning a light blue silk pelisse, a white silk bonnet, and sturdy half boots of soft kid, she clambered aboard his curricle and begged to be told precisely what his intentions were.

He held the horses in check. "I wish to take you to Cheddar to see the gorge. It is quite one of the most beautiful places in all of England. I know it is scandalous of me to be asking you to accompany me unattended, but I thought we might pretend to be husband and wife." A smile lit his eye.

How scandalous to travel anywhere without a maid to lend her countenance!

But how wonderful to be alone with Edward. She had never done anything quite so daring in her entire life.

"I have never been to Cheddar," she said, wondering whether she should go.

"My brothers and I used to walk the entire distance—I believe it was nearly thirteen miles—from Barton, past Winscombe, skirting several farms until we reached the gorge. We would sleep the night in Cheddar, then reverse the entire pilgrimage the next day."

"Edward," Julia said, placing a concerned hand on his arm. "I cannot possibly march thirteen miles, however lovely the vista might prove to be once we arrived there. I can manage three or four, but beyond that I fear I will become greatly fatigued. And indeed, though I believe you would conduct yourself as a gentleman, I don't think we ought to spend the night in Cheddar!"

He laughed outright. "I never meant to suggest anything so bold as staying the night, nor had I the least intention of forcing you on such a walk. I thought we might drive directly to Cheddar. The cliffs and the gorge are nearby. So, what do you say? Will you go with me?"

How could she refuse his invitation? Especially when he lifted her hand to his lips and kissed, not her fingers, but the very center of her palm. Even though her hands were covered in white kid gloves, he might as well have placed his lips against her skin. A warmth curled through her chest; desire to be in his arms again took possession of her. He was making her a promise by kissing her in such a passionate manner, making it now impossible for her to refuse even if she had truly wanted to.

The entire day had been idyllic, the weather all sunshine, puffy clouds, and deep blue sky. The breeze, as they traveled, was neither hot nor cold, but wrapped them up in a cocoon of bliss. They enjoyed a plain nuncheon at the village, partaking of the local cheese that had been a product of the area since the twelfth century. Boiled potatoes, slices of roast beef, a sturdy bread, and a glass of Madeira completed the meal, followed by a bowl of delectable strawberries.

They had left the curricle at the inn and walked the distance to the gorge. Julia was awestruck by the pale gray limestone walls of the gorge, which seemed to reach up forever into the sky. Her neck grew weary with straining as they walked and walked, enjoying the beauty of the whitebeam and ash trees, which seemed to thrive on the limestone that characterized the whole of the Mendips. They were alone. He held her hand the entire distance, or sometimes she would release his hand to take his arm. The quiet of the day, their companionable enjoyment of each other, the sublimity that always accompanied a good walk, were all soothing balms to her soul. She felt as though strings within her chest, like those belonging to the violin, were suddenly unloosened from a too-tightly wound scroll. She felt at ease and wished, as she seemed always to wish when she was with him, that the day might go on forever.

"Are you very tired?" he queried gently as they began their return through the gorge.

She shook her head. "Not a bit. Truly. Thank you for bringing me here. You've given me a wonderful respite from my daily tasks. I'm so very grateful."

He smiled down at her and she met his gaze; it seemed as if the whole day became centered on this very moment between them. How easily she fell into his arms, almost as though she had done so her entire life. In the shadow of the limestone cliff, he kissed her deeply and thoroughly, possessing her mouth as he had before. Edward untied her bonnet and before she knew what had happened, he slipped it from her curls and let it drop on the grassy path next to him. He caressed the side of her neck with his hand. She touched his hand and did not protest when his fingers drifted lower to caress her breast. She wanted him to; she wanted Edward Blackthorn to touch her as a man touches his wife. She knew she could never have him, and perhaps for that reason she permitted the liberties she knew to be wrong.

The day disappeared, as did the world, her cares. Julia knew only the touch of his lips, his tongue, his hand. She was drifting downstream on a current that steadily took her onward. Holding him close as his fingers touched her, she drew apart the ribbon that secured his long hair. Julia let the ribbon fall and slipped her fingers deeply into his hair.

His kiss became more urgent as he pressed his body against hers. She felt his desire for her. She kept her mind closed to every thought except the one she wanted to hear: *For this brief moment, Edward is mine.* Julia let her hands drift, slipping them underneath his blue coat. His white shirt was slightly damp with perspiration and she found the sensation pleased her. She let her hands drift even more, and he answered with a moan of pleasure as he kissed her hard in response.

"Julia, my darling," he whispered against her lips.

She was lost; she could not respond with words. She pressed herself against him.

Then he stopped kissing her, almost abruptly. He was breathing almost laboriously and Julia discovered she was too. He did not release her, but held her in a tight embrace.

"What are we going to do?" he queried in a throaty whisper.

Only then did a dozen thoughts fly into her mind, those she had prevented from disturbing her before—thoughts of her father, of Lord Peter, of the weed-strewn kitchen garden. She clung to him. How hopeless, how useless.

"There must be a way," he said. "I will find a way for us to be together." He drew back from her, holding her gaze fiercely as he gripped her by the shoulders. "Julia, you must listen to me. You must trust me. I will find a way, but I need time."

"I want to trust you, Edward, I do. But I have run out of time."

"Surely your father is not completely ruined. Surely there is something to be salvaged yet."

"I . . . I don't know. But I have a strong instinct that our situation is precarious, as though my whole family is perched on the edge of a great cliff and that the merest breeze will push us off, one and all."

"Regardless," he stated firmly, still holding her by the shoulders, "you cannot marry Lord Peter or anyone. You are mine, from this moment on, though I daresay you were mine from the time I carried you about on my back—"

"Or tied me to the tree and pretended to burn me alive?" she said, smiling through sudden tears.

"Yes," he answered, taking her into a warm embrace and holding her fast. "I love you, Julia. I love you."

"I love you, my darling Edward."

After a long moment, he finally released her. Picking up the white silk bonnet and black riband, they had continued their walk, gazing more into each other's eyes than taking pleasure in the beauty of the gray limestone cliffs about them. On the drive home, she had begun daydreaming about a future with Edward—a fine family, a cottage by the sea, a small farm. He would sell out, of course. She would give him a dozen children.

Julia had fallen into a stupor of love during that walk, which had remained with her. After arriving home, she saw nothing except her wishful dreams of a life with Edward.

Now, as the cart hit another rut and her sisters' singing voices spiraled upward yet again into girlish squeals, Julia was brought happily back to the present.

The horse plodded along, still guided by one of Edward's hands, his other hand giving hers a squeeze.

"What were you thinking?" he queried gently. "You were silent for quite a pace."

"About yesterday," she responded.

He looked down at her and smiled affectionately. "You are so lovely, Julia. I wish I could take you to London, if for no other reason than to make all my friends mad as fire that I was actually able to win such a devilishly pretty lady." He sighed, obviously quite content.

At last the cart arrived at the meadow, which stretched out in a long sweep of knee-high grass to the base of the hills where Julia and Elizabeth along with Edward and his brothers used to play. The hills were gently sloped and forested with oak and beeches, through which were scattered a thick, fragrant carpet of bluebells. A stream cut through the middle of the meadow and it was here that Edward drew the cart to a halt. He unharnessed the horse and would have led him to drink, but Caroline insisted on performing this task, as well as rubbing him down with handfuls of the grass. "I was always fond of horses. You cannot imagine how sorry I was when Papa sold off most of the stables. I lived there everyday and became the worst trial to Chilton."

The brown gelding tossed his head as though in agreement with Caroline. When she had led him partly into the shallow, clear stream, Edward responded to Elizabeth's request to help them with the cumbersome wicker basket. It was proving too heavy for the ladies, even with Julia at one end and Elizabeth and Annabelle at the other.

He relieved Julia of her end and, with relative ease, lifted the basket to the ground. Annabelle pounced on it with glee. "I'm famished!" she announced, flipping open the lid. "Besides, the whole way I have been smelling the apple tartlets Cook prepared for us. What torture!"

The meal consisted of cold chicken, hot pigeon pies kept warm with heated bricks wrapped in linen, pears in a lemon sauce, fresh-baked bread and creamy butter, brambleberry jelly, and apple tartlets. Julia savored each bite, sipping her champagne in between. The bubbly wine, the fresh air, and the easy camaraderie created a lazy, comfortable atmosphere. Caroline read poetry aloud between a spoonful of pear and a bite of bread—Wordsworth or Byron.

When Annabelle began putting the food away and Elizabeth fell asleep on Caroline's lap, Edward begged all the sisters to join him for a walk in the beech and oak woods. "Oh, indeed, yes, do come," Julia cried enthusiastically, pulling hard on the ribbons of her straw bonnet and tossing the hat gently into the back of the cart.

Elizabeth lifted her head. "What is it?" she queried with sleepy eyes. "A walk in the woods? Perhaps later. I would much prefer to sleep." She immediately settled back down onto Caroline's lap.

Annabelle slapped down the lid on the wicker basket and jumped to her feet. "Of course I'll come!" she cried.

But Caroline caught her brown and pale yellow calico skirts and prevented her from doing more than taking a tumble on the blanket. "Silly goose!" Caroline told her with a meaningful expression. "Don't you remember you promised to read to me when I was finished? And, I am finished." She presented Annabelle with her thin volume of poetry.

"But—" Annabelle began, staring at the book in confusion.

"You promised," Caroline wheedled. She turned to Julia and said, "Do go on! Annabelle will remain with us."

Only then did Annabelle turn her green eyes toward Julia. Comprehension flooded her face in a pink blush. "Yes . . . yes, do go on! I did promise Caroline. How . . . how thoughtless of me."

Julia understood her sisters perfectly and did not know whether to feel vexed or grateful. Their ploy was more than obvious. Whatever must Edward think of her? Would he believe she had arranged the whole of it? At the same time, she wanted nothing more than to be alone with him.

For that reason, she shot Caroline a grateful glance and turned brightly on her heel. Catching Edward up by the hand, she hurried him away.

They crossed the meadow in less than a minute, and by the time they reached the base of the hill, a race was in progress. Julia lifted up her light green muslin skirts and began gliding up the gentle slope as quickly as she could. She might be in the habit of walking two and three miles a day, but running up a grade—even if it was not horribly steep—soon saw her taking deep, gasping breaths, her steps feeling as though she were slogging through mud. If she had any consolation at all, it was that Edward was not far ahead of her, though he did not seem to be struggling for air as ferociously as she.

She caught bluebells in her flying pale green skirts and white muslin shift beneath. From the corner of her eye she could see their blue heads bobbing in her wake. The leaves of lower branches plucked at her hair, which had been pinned into a chignon. With each pass of a branch the pins began to loosen, and soon her auburn tresses were dangling about her shoulders and flipping against her back with each awkward running step she took. Up and up she ran, until the forest began to thin and the grade was not so steep. The bluebells were thickest at the top, and before Julia knew what had happened, Edward turned in his stride toward her, dashed at her from her left, caught her neatly about the waist, and pulled her down onto a bed of bluebells.

She was laughing and gasping for breath at the same time. "I could have beat you!" she cried, then gasped again.

He laughed at her, lying just to her side. "Listen to you!" he cried. "You can hardly breathe." His chest was also rising and falling rapidly, but not like Julia's.

"I know. I know," she cried, laughing again and gasping. "This is so absurd but so wonderful." She looked up and, through the branches of beech leaves, could see a sky of the deepest blue. "Have you ever noticed how on a hill the sky seems closer and more vividly blue than on low, level ground. Why is that, I wonder?" Her gasps began to subside.

When she looked at Edward, she saw that his gaze was fixed on the rise and fall of her breasts. Her gown was cut very low and there was little of her he could not see. Desire overtook him, and Julia forgot about the color of the sky.

He shifted his gaze and she met warm gray eyes, full of passion and love.

"Kiss me," she whispered.

He touched her face with one hand while supporting himself on his elbow. His thumb touched her lips, which she parted, and he kissed her, fully, deeply. At the same time he moved on top of her, and the press of his body against hers filled Julia with desire, prompting her to wonder for the first time what it would be like to be joined to him, to be one with him. She slipped an arm about his neck and another about his back.

As he kissed her, his hands again began to trace the lines of her body, the swell of her breast, the curve of her waist, the line of her hip. She could feel him lifting her skirt. He slipped his fingers beneath her garter and stroked her leg inside her silk stocking. Pleasure swirled over her.

He left the confines of her stocking and stroked the length of her thigh. His kisses became more fervent as his hand felt the nakedness of her flesh beneath her muslin shift. There was nothing to prevent him from knowing her, she realized.

He groaned as he touched her, his lips sliding from hers to

ease down her neck, her throat, to drift over the swell of her breasts.

"Julia," he whispered. "I love you. I wish you weren't so soft, so beautiful." He kissed her breasts. "You smell sweetly of roses."

After a moment, he replaced her skirts and slipped off her to lie beside her.

"Why do you stop?" she asked quietly, running her hands through his long black hair, which had escaped the riband.

"If I don't, I shall force myself on you whether you protest or not. And I don't want to. I want you in my bed as my wife." He covered her breast with his hand and stroked her gently, lovingly. "We will know great pleasure one day, I promise you."

Julia felt her heart, as well as her body, straining toward him. She loved him so much. She always would. If thoughts of her current predicament rose to challenge her happiness and her wish for a life with Edward, she set them aside. For the present, he was loving her, and she would be content with that.

Seven

Later that evening, when the house was quiet, Blackthorn sat in Mr. Ladock's office, the door to Sir Perran's study ajar. He was having difficulty concentrating, thinking, planning. His thoughts were jumbled, his need to contrive a future for himself and Julia punctuated by the awareness that within his uncle's house resided a French agent who had been actively stealing information from Sir Perran's documents for at least five years.

Earlier that afternoon, when he had promised Julia he would devise a solution to her difficulties, Edward hadn't allowed himself to consider the serious nature of her dilemmas. His promise had been based solely on his desire to be with her always. Now that he had had an opportunity to study the problem, however, he was in a quandary. She felt her need to be immediate, yet the only practical solutions that came to mind would require months to bring about.

The best of his ideas, he believed, resided in the quarry; of that he was convinced. His uncle had expressed his opinion that a fortune remained yet to be made in Delabole stone, indicating at the same time that the business had suffered due to poor management resulting in a lack of contracts for the limestone.

Blackthorn had numerous contacts of his own from which he was certain, with a little effort, he would be able to procure a sizable contract or two. He wanted to begin right away, but affairs at The Priory had taken a turn during his absence.

Upon returning from Hatherleigh Park, he had found that someone had been in his bedchamber and had examined the documents Wellington had given him. Was he now jeopardizing his mission, perhaps even his life, by being distracted by Julia's difficulties?

He had discovered the intrusion as a result of having lived a soldier's ordered existence for years in the Peninsula, an order designed for quick retreat or advance—whatever his superior officers required. His batman kept his clothing and other personal articles in meticulous arrangement . . . an arrangement he had enhanced with a subtle trap.

On the floor of his mahogany wardrobe, he had placed a leather envelope that contained the critical documents. On top of the envelope, he had settled three pairs of rolled stockings, one end of each pair inverted over its mate. Next to the stockings and envelope, he had arranged his boots in a row—Wellingtons, Hessians, white top boots. Over the stockings he had lain his fencing sword, the arc of the handle toward the back of the wardrobe.

When he examined the arrangement at the bottom of his wardrobe—by habit, since his arrival at The Priory—each item appeared to be exactly where he had left them. Even the sword sat at its original, precise angle. But what couldn't be seen by the eye was the embroidery of his initials on the center pair of stockings, because they were rolled up. He had removed the center pair and found they were not the embroidered ones after all. The stockings to the left were embroidered. Someone had meticulously removed each article to get to the leather envelope but had failed to replace the stockings properly.

When he had examined the documents again, all was in order, by date, just as he had left them. Mr. Mawls had been right: Whoever the agent was, he was a sly one. Yet not sly enough, it would seem.

Now, as he sat in Mr. Ladock's austere chamber, he heard a lady giggling softly, followed by Mr. Ladock's voice, a gentle murmur in the stillness of the late hour. They were coming toward the office. Blackthorn considered leaving, but decided it might be to his advantage to surprise and disconcert the secretary with his unexpected arrival.

A moment later, the secretary and his lady appeared in the doorway. Mr. Ladock held the woman tightly about the waist, smiling into her eyes. She had a hand on his cheek, returning his smile. They were oblivious to him as they entered the chamber.

"Good evening," he called to them both as he rose from a chair by Mr. Ladock's large, document-laden desk.

The lady, whom Blackthorn recognized as an upstairs maid, gasped.

"What the deuce—" Mr. Ladock cried out, startled. "Oh, Major Blackthorn. Do forgive me, but you gave me such a start." He then flushed to the roots of his brown hair at having been caught with the maid. Immediately, he whispered a word into her ear. She retreated in quick order, her footsteps silent across the thick amber and black carpet of Sir Perran's study.

"Did you wish to see me?" Mr. Ladock queried, his color remaining high.

Blackthorn shook his head. "No. I came only for a bit of solitude."

"To my office?" he questioned, a frown deepening across his brow. He was a tall, thin man with a pointed nose, black eyes, and dark brown hair. His complexion, except for the moment, was pale. He was probably five and thirty years of age. He stared at Blackthorn, the expression in his eyes offended.

Blackthorn smiled. "I am in love," he returned, intending to confuse the secretary. "How else can I explain how the devil I ended up here?" He then took in his surroundings—the beautiful wainscoting that decorated the office, the desk, the cupboard of tiger maple across from the desk—and shrugged.

Afterward, he further confounded the secretary by quitting the chamber. Before he had crossed the study, however, Blackthorn quickly retraced his steps and peered through the opening of the half-closed door. What he saw there surprised him. Mr. Ladock was leaning against the desk, his hands flat on the smooth wood, his complexion as white as a cambric kerchief. He looked as though he was about to be ill.

Blackthorn entered the office and closed the door behind him. He stepped into the chamber and, in a curt voice, asked, "What's wrong?"

Mr. Ladock, lost in thought, jerked his head up to look at him. A sheen of perspiration had broken out on his forehead. "Nothing," he whispered.

"Is your heart pounding, your stomach boiling? I've seen soldiers who have looked just like you while facing the enemy across a battlefield. So don't tell me *nothing* is wrong, for I won't believe you. What is going on in my uncle's house?"

The question seemed to stun Mr. Ladock, a look of horror in his dark eyes. "Nothing, I tell you! Why won't you believe me? It is you who should be answering that question. You gave me a fright when I found you in my office. That's all that is amiss. I'm . . . I'm not made of stern stuff, if you must know."

Blackthorn crossed the room and shoved the secretary hard on the shoulder, causing him to fall awkwardly into the chair behind the desk. "Humbug," he stated, staring hard at Mr. Ladock. He perched himself on the side of the desk and crossed his arms over his chest. "Now, tell me what's going on."

"Nothing," Mr. Ladock insisted in a small voice. When Blackthorn continued to stare down at him, the secretary began to swallow hard, his nostrils flaring and deflating like the gills of a frightened trout. Finally, he blurted out in a whisper, "I . . . I think someone has been taking things from my papers . . . that is, Sir Perran's papers. At first I thought it was a trick of my mind, but later I began to suspect that something was afoot. A paper would be missing in the morning, then reappear where it should be in the evening. Not often, mind you, but often enough to set me wondering."

"How long have you been in Sir Perran's employ?" he asked.

"Six months."

"Is that all?" Blackthorn questioned, surprised. "What happened to your predecessor?"

Mr. Ladock blanched. "He was killed. He fell from his horse while out riding, not far from here. Struck his head."

Blackthorn looked into haunted eyes. "You've begun to fear for your life," he said.

Mr. Ladock leaned forward and put his head in his hands, nodding slowly. "I was so ecstatic about getting this position—secretary to Sir Perran Blackthorn! You've no idea how many years I've hoped for the opportunity, prayed for it! And now . . ."

Blackthorn watched the frantic movement of his long, slender fingers through his brown hair. "What sorts of papers do you find missing?"

He paused for a long moment before answering. Then he looked up at Blackthorn, his expression somber. "Only those having to do with the allied forces in Europe. Whoever is doing this has no interest in the Americas, South Africa, India, or the Far East."

"Mr. Ladock," Blackthorn said, "will you please tell me if you find anything missing in the coming days?"

"You're here because of this," he stated, some of the color returning to his face. He took in a deep breath and tears rimmed his eyes. "Yes, of course I will."

"Not a word to anyone, if you please."

"No, of course not," he responded, sniffing. Taking a kerchief from his pocket, he blew his nose hard.

Blackthorn reached out and placed a hand on his shoulder. "A little courage, my good fellow, and we'll see this through—trust me. But again, not a word."

Mr. Ladock smiled faintly and nodded. "I'll be all right," he murmured.

"Of course you will," Blackthorn returned.

Julia.

She heard her name spoken as if from a great distance. She ignored the voice as she ignored everything. Even the usual cacophony of sounds from the Upper Assembly Rooms beat at

only the fringes of her hearing. It was Friday night and the multitude had arrived. The orchestra, stationed high above the assemblage in its usual alcove, was between pieces.

Julia's gaze was transfixed. A wind roared through her mind.
Every thought now had only one object. Edward had just walked
through the doorway of the ballroom. Now her life could begin.

Stop dreaming, she commanded herself. From the time Edward had returned Julia, her sisters, and the lumbering cart to
Hatherleigh late the previous afternoon, she had been trying to
reason with herself, to take charge of her errant sensibilities.
Julia kept reminding herself of the disaster looming just beyond
the horizon, but her mind refused to acknowledge anything other
than Edward's telling her she was to trust him to help solve her
difficulties so that they might be married. But he had not given
her even one hint of a solution upon which she might pin her
hopes.

All she had to do was trust him, he had said, and she did. At
least, she did in part. But when he had gone, two tradesmen
were waiting in her office to speak with her. Not an especially
unusual occurrence, except that they had come because they had
heard rumors that Lord Delabole was in debt to the moneylend-
ers for some five thousand pounds. Julia had nearly swooned
and only kept from falling by placing her hands firmly upon the
desk in front of her.

"Rumors," she had stated. "Nothing more."

She had listened to their concerns for some time. But she
repeatedly assured them that regardless of the rumors and
whether there was any truth to them, she would not let her father's debts go unsettled forever. She had ended with: "I have
myself certain prospects which will undoubtedly resolve these
matters before the summer has ended." Julia watched each man
breathe a sigh of relief. She knew what they were thinking—rumors were also rife that she would very soon be betrothed to
Lord Peter.

The experience had shattered the fragile yet wondrous air of
peace and contentment that had surrounded her since her trip

with Edward to Cheddar Gorge on Wednesday. When the men had quit her office she had leaned back in her chair, feeling like one who has suffered a severe blow.

She had been lying to herself again.

How could Edward begin to comprehend the scope of her difficulties? Would he ever understand that these were matters of honor to her? Yet how, if she married him, would she ever be able to discharge so many debts?

She shook off the unhappy memory and let her gaze drift hungrily over Edward. He appeared as handsome as ever, in a coat of black superfine cloth, a white vest, black pantaloons, and black dancing slippers.

She fanned herself slowly, her eyes peering at him from just above the tips of lace spindles. He was busily occupied greeting a number of ladies and gentlemen. The ladies smiled, pulled at their earlobes, dipped coquettish curtsies, and unobtrusively permitted their eyes to rove his broad shoulders, narrow waist, and strong, athletic thighs.

The gentlemen shook his hand firmly. Some whispered in his ear—how he laughed in response, a full, warm laugh that rolled across the ballroom floor and struck her over and over in waves of painful bliss. If the ladies flocked about him, the men did no less, a circumstance that held her attention rivcted to him. This was very rare.

How grateful she was that she could observe him, at least for a few seconds, without hindrance. She didn't know what to do or what to think of his pleas that she entrust her future to him. Her thoughts were a jumble, her emotions no less so.

Julia. The voice, more insistent this time, begged for her attention. Still, she ignored it.

Did she love him, truly? Of course she did. Perhaps to the point of madness. He had kissed her, he had touched her in places she shuddered to admit. He was the essence of her dreams and the nightmare of her waking hours. He was everything she wanted but he lacked what she needed most. She feared him . . . feared the way he made her feel, as though duty were nothing and desire everything. She had never, ever before felt this way. Never.

At times, she hated him for disturbing her ordered world.

Yet, she longed for him to smash the order of her world to bits forever.

She felt as though her mind were being pulled very taut, then plucked and strummed and sliced by a ruthless musician and his bow. She would be in Bedlam soon.

Would to God that Edward had never come to Bath!

Yet all she could think of was how much she wanted to dance with him, to feel the soft vibrations the touch of his hand played on her skin. She wanted to kiss him again.

Julia! The voice called firmly to her. She ignored it still.

He was laughing again. The sounds hit her chest.

"Look at me," she whispered, her breath, redolent of tea, returning to her from the nearness of her fan. Edward obeyed, searching the room with quick, alert eyes as though he had heard her. He found her. His gaze took hold of her. He physically turned more completely toward her, straightening, staring, tensing. Desire implored her from sharp gray eyes.

She lowered her fan without thinking, until it touched her lips. He returned a faint smile to her. The wind in her mind roared stronger still. She could hear him speaking, she could hear his voice from yesterday: *Julia, I love you.* The words of a lover. The pleasing hands of a lover. Her abdomen grew taut, her heart weak, her senses dizzy. She closed her fan and let it dangle at her side. She wanted him to see her fully, her gown of rose silk caught high to the waist in the Empire style and overlaid with sheer gossamer tulle, the décolletage of the bodice, the rise and fall of her breasts in response to him. His gaze swept over her, his eyes darkening.

Julia! The voice snapped at her. "Julia, here is Lord Peter, prepared to dance with you! Are you weaving air dreams again? Faith, child, but you will give His Lordship a very odd notion of you. Do attend to me!" Lord Delabole then laughed nervously. "Your prettiest curtsy, if you please."

She could no longer ignore her father's voice. Julia turned toward him, toward Lord Peter, her mind still too full of Edward to do more than regard the marquis's second son blankly and extend her hand to him. "Good evening, Lord Peter," she offered from long, careful practice, the wind still holding her mind captive. When had he arrived? How was it she had been oblivious to his return from Wiltshire. "I beg you will forgive my hapless manners."

Lord Peter took her hand, and as she curtsied to him, he brought her fingers to his lips, then kissed them fervently.

She could not credit it! The whole assembly room would soon be whispering about such a passionate kiss. He had never before kissed her like that. Always, he had been so polite. Chagrin and excitement twisted through her. What did he mean by kissing her fingers so boldly? Would he come up to scratch at last? Now? When she didn't want him to, yet when she needed him to, oh, so desperately, regardless of Edward's hasty promises?

She was so surprised she could have laughed, especially when, as he straightened from his bow, he drew very near her, took strong hold of her arm, and wrapped it possessively about his own.

A sennight earlier, her heart would have soared at such an attention. But now, as she looked into his face, his brown eyes became blue; his blond hair, wisped angelically about his face, turned coal-black; and the sweetness, the gentleness of his expression, transformed into something liquid and fiery. Edward.

Edward.

Julia blinked. She blinked again, clearing *his* image from her mind. If only the wind would cease, she thought distractedly as Lord Peter, still holding her arm tightly, led her out for a country dance. If only Edward hadn't come to Bath. Everything was in such order. Everything so perfect, so necessary. Surely Lord Peter had received his parents' blessing.

* * *

Sir Perran Blackthorn took Elizabeth Verdell's hand in his and squeezed it, then winked at her and called her a vixen. "You should not say such wicked things of your sister, my little one," he said. He had spoken lightly, but there was nothing airy about the fury seizing and constricting his chest. He took a deep breath and commanded his features to obey him. He smiled upon Julia's nearest sister.

"You do not believe me!" Elizabeth cried, a pretty smile on her lips, her expression bold and teasing. "But I saw Julia with him Tuesday afternoon, in the red salon. He had been with us nearly the entire day. We—my younger sisters and I—had left the chamber to dress for dinner. I had forgotten my reticule and returned to the crimson and gold drawing room, only to find them . . . er . . . together. Really, it was quite splendid, if you don't mind my being so bold. They were locked together in an embrace so . . . well, suffice it to say, Julia is in love with your nephew. She always was, you know."

When she had first whispered her secret to him, Sir Perran had believed Elizabeth was telling one of her teasing whiskers again. But by now he knew she was speaking the truth. He had witnessed for himself Julia's besotted, lustful state—her green eyes aglow above the horizon of her lace fan as she met Blackthorn's gaze, the fan dropping to touch her lips provocatively, the fan falling to her side.

He directed his gaze toward his nephew, rage seeping into his veins. How very much the boy looked like his mother, that worthless woman. Time to take him down a peg or two!

"You do not believe me?" Elizabeth queried, still in a secretive whisper. She was of such a forthright disposition that frequently Sir Perran had wondered whether he had made the right sister his object. "Then why do you think she made up for herself such a . . . a *womanly* gown—one that clings to her as she dances, without even dampening her muslin shift beneath as ladies sometimes do? I have never known her to be so . . . so bold. Not Julia!"

Sir Perran dropped his gaze from the sight of his nephew and slipped a cambric kerchief from the pocket of his burgundy velvet coat. He began to cough, very carefully, purposefully. He knew Elizabeth was clever enough to discern his sentiments once he gave the smallest hint what they might be. A numbness had stolen into his face because of the truth—that Julia's heart threatened to betray his careful schemes. But with his features so frozen, he would not be able to tell the lies he needed to tell Elizabeth. So he coughed instead of trying to feign a smile and an easiness he could not at present summon.

Damn Julia! Offering herself to Blackthorn across a ballroom floor for everyone to see, conducting herself like a courtesan, a heedless London Cyprian. He had never thought of her as one who might have desires and passions. How complicated her conduct now made everything. He coughed again.

"Sir Perran, shall I fetch you a cup of tea? Are you all right? Your complexion is very high!"

He looked into solicitous, round blue eyes and again wondered if he had chosen the right sister. He took a deep breath and leaned back in the velvet-covered chair at the edge of the ballroom floor, rubbing his hand slowly over the ivory head of his polished cherrywood cane. "If I were a few years younger, I would insist upon dancing with you, Miss Eliza, if for no other reason than to prove to you I am perfectly well. Do not make overly much of a cough or two! And do not open your eyes wide—for I am reading in your thoughts that you believe me to be falling into a decline, but it is no such thing, I assure you!"

She smiled. A luminous smile, her creamy white skin set off to perfection by coal-black hair. How different the sisters were—Elizabeth and Julia. Julia's hair was a brilliant red, cast with shades of pink in summer's light, like her father's. Her eyes were a rich green and almond shaped, her auburn brows delicate arches, her nose straight, her face oval. Elizabeth and her raven's hair was as much a contrast to Julia as she could be—and just like her mother's. Her black brows were dramatically arched, her nose slightly retroussé but quite appealing, her chin firm—a pronounced and accurate reflection of her character. Elizabeth was strong. Yes, very strong.

But it was Julia who knew her duty. She would do her duty. He could never rely on Elizabeth to do as much.

"So tell me, Miss Eliza, is there not a gentleman here tonight who has tempted your heart?"

Elizabeth's eyes crinkled as she smiled at his question. No artifice. He liked her very much. "Not one," she replied almost bitterly. "Not ever. I have begun to wonder if I even possess a heart. The closest I have come to experiencing a lasting attachment was to my friend, Charles Everard. Do you recall him?"

"The baker's son?" he queried, surprised. "Oh, you are full of mischief."

Elizabeth lowered her voice. "You mustn't tell anyone my secret. But we used to wander the hills for hours at a time, ever since I was old enough to climb trees and guttle fish from the streams hereabouts. He went to sea when he was fourteen. I receive a letter from him nearly every two months. He is now two and twenty. He is in the Mediterranean. I have not seen him in ages."

"Yet, you do not love him?" Sir Perran asked, curious.

Elizabeth chuckled. "I wish that I could say I did, for I believe it would be quite romantic to tell my friends such a secret—that I loved a young man my father would never permit me to marry. But alas, I am merely fond of him as I would be of a brother. But what of you, Sir Perran? In all these years, you never married. Do you know how much an object you have been for all the matchmaking mamas hereabouts? From my earliest years, when I could comprehend what was being said between sips of tea, you were always the subject of grave ponderings and desperate hopes."

"You mean my fortune was," he responded, waiting to see her reaction.

Elizabeth placed a mocking hand aside her cheek. "Whatever do you mean?" she queried in facetious innocence. "I recall only hearing of your charm, your elegance of bearing, and your abilities on the ballroom floor."

He smiled. She was a delightful combination of innocence and wisdom. He thought one day she would make the right man an excellent wife, one who could appreciate her forthrightness, her wit, and her sensuality. She might condemn her sister for wearing so intriguing a gown, but even clothed in virginal white as Elizabeth was, with only a hint of her pretty bosom exposed above a row of ruffles, the energy with which the young lady spoke and moved, her full, womanly lines, were as seductive in her modest white as Julia was in her revealing gown. There was a wildness about Elizabeth that, in his younger days, might have captivated him.

A young man approached Elizabeth, his polite stammers amusing to Sir Perran. But, with her usual buoyant grace, she accepted his invitation to join him in partaking of a cup of tea. As she rose, she turned and smiled down upon Sir Perran once, quite brilliantly, then permitted the young man to spirit her away. Would that Elizabeth had been born a few years earlier!

He felt his loins stir. Odd. He couldn't remember the last time he had felt the smallest inclination in that respect. He shrugged the thought away. Sir Perran had always believed passion to be a man's Achilles' heel, and early on he had hardened his heart against such desires. Better to attend instead to the matter of most pressing concern—Edward Blackthorn.

When had the rascal found sufficient time to seduce Julia? His aggravation was profound as he observed his nephew watching Julia go down the country dance. His thoughts adjusted themselves in quick stages when it occurred to him that not only was Blackthorn *not* a real threat to his schemes, but his obvious *tendre* for Julia could only serve to enhance the pleasure he would take in the moment Lord Delabole gave Julia to him.

He sighed inwardly and deeply, though he trained his expression to indifference. The fact was, he would see his nephew dead before he permitted him to wed Delabole's eldest daughter. Nothing was going to deprive him of his revenge. Nothing.

* * *

Lord Delabole watched his daughter go down the country dance with Lord Peter. He wavered between pleasure at the sight of Julia receiving such pointed attentions from one of the most eligible gentlemen in Bath, and fear that something would arise to destroy Lord Peter's interest in her.

He felt nervous, uneasy. His gaze drifted to a large white ostrich feather tucked into Annabelle's red curls, then shifted abruptly to Sir Perran's cane and the hand that was always methodically rubbing the handle, as though he were perpetually polishing it. Then he glanced distractedly at the alcove housing the orchestra, finally returning his gaze to Julia's glistening red curls. He wished something a little stronger than tea was served at the assemblies. His mouth felt dry, his nerves raw. He tried not to think of the bargain he had struck with Sir Perran.

Julia caught him watching her. She smiled, thinly, the hint of a frown creasing her brow.

She knows, he thought. But she can't possibly. She might suspect, but she can't know all of it or even most of it. Where does she keep that emerald ring of hers? The only jewelry left of her mother's. If he could find the ring, he could use it to hedge his play tomorrow night in addition to the money Sir Perran had loaned him. He might even be able to exchange the ring for that part of the bargain he had struck with the baronet for Julia's hand in marriage should he lose.

But where was the ring? She must keep it someplace very secret, since he had searched her bedchamber and the housekeeper's office over and over again. Yesterday afternoon, while she and the rest of his daughters had been enjoying an alfresco nuncheon, he had again searched her bedchamber but had found nothing.

He watched his eldest daughter, trying to understand her mind. She danced with great beauty, just as her mother had. His thoughts floated as Julia floated along the floor. She would keep the ring close to her.

Her reticule. The thought simply popped into his mind.

One of her reticules. Of course.

His mind whirled and spun about several times.

Of course. He had never bothered to examine anything as obvious as her reticules. His search had included only what he believed would be the most clever and cunning of hiding places, but never anything as simple as a reticule.

A sensation of great relief poured through him, followed swiftly by a piercing blade of guilt. Julia's emerald ring was the only heirloom left to any of his daughters. Olivia had given it to Julia the day she died in that wretched carriage accident. All the rest he had had duplicated in paste, the originals sold off, one after the other, in an attempt to restore his fortunes. Olivia would never have approved of course, but dash it all, she wasn't here any longer, so her opinion no longer mattered.

Thoughts of his beloved wife caused his head to suddenly pound. How unbearably hot the ballroom became. His heart filled with a quick, overwhelming sickness that turned his feet toward the entrance to the ballroom. His stomach began churning. Lord Delabole picked up his steps, ignoring those who called a greeting to him. He reached the octagonal entrance hall. He heard a burst of laughter erupt nearby—a ribald joke.

He passed through the entrance to Alfred Street, drank in a gulp of air, but it was too late. He vomited onto the pavement, his mouth full of water and bile, and as he looked down he could see specks of blood reflected in the light from the nearby oil lamps. He leaned against the hard, rough stone of the building. Lightning flashed. A crack of thunder erupted overhead and a hard rain suddenly pelted him, disguising the tears that began coursing down his cheeks.

Olivia. If only you hadn't perished in that stupid accident. You held me together in every way. Without you, I've come apart, bit by bit. My darling, my darling.

He remained outside, letting the rain wash over him, hoping that it would cleanse him of his many sins.

"May I call upon you tomorrow, Miss Verdell?" The country dance had ended and Lord Peter had escorted Julia to the side of the ballroom, where she would await her next partner.

"I would enjoy that very much," Julia responded, looking up into warm, tender brown eyes. *He is in love with me,* she thought, her sensibilities oddly flat and disinterested. How curious that she felt so little, when a few days ago she would have been *aux anges* to have seen such a light in his eye. She smiled faintly and continued. "I have been hoping you would come to visit my family at Hatherleigh for some time. Papa will be grateful for the attention."

He possessed himself of her hand, just as he had done earlier upon greeting her. Again, he placed a fervent kiss upon her fingers. Julia drew in her breath. She knew with utmost certainty that Lord Peter had just committed himself to her.

"Perhaps it is your father whom I should call upon tomorrow," Lord Peter said softly, searching her eyes.

Julia nodded, trancelike. "I shall tell him you wish to speak privately with him," she returned, wanting him to know she understood his meaning.

"Excellent," was his response.

He released her hand and bowed to her. He would have turned away to go in search of his next partner, but at that moment, Annabelle, her white ostrich feather bouncing with her hurried movements, rushed up to Julia and slipped an arm about her waist. "You must come at once!" she whispered, her face creased into a dozen lines of fright. "It is Papa! Major Blackthorn is with him. He found him on the pavement outside—and it has been raining!"

Eight

"Oh, no," Julia cried. She did not so much as glance at Lord Peter, but quickly hurried away, following Annabelle's lead. It was only when she reached the octagonal entrance hall and turned to beg Lord Peter's assistance that she discovered he had not followed after her. Julia knew an instant of profound disappointment. Didn't he realize she needed him?

But these thoughts were quickly set aside when she found Edward sitting in a chair beside her father. He was nearly as wet as the viscount and supported him with a firm arm about his shoulders. Her father was trembling. Edward was helping him drink a hot cup of tea.

Elizabeth and Caroline were already with Lord Delabole, as well as the Master of Ceremonies and two servants ready to perform whatever services were required. All eyes turned toward Julia as she and Annabelle joined the group. "Papa, what happened?" she asked. "Are you all right?"

Lord Delabole shook his head. "I don't know," he responded with a disoriented frown. "That is, I am certain I am perfectly well. How very odd. I went outside to take a breath of air, and the next moment Major Blackthorn was lifting me to my feet. It was raining! Can't conceive what happened."

Julia shifted her gaze to Edward's. "Has our coach been summoned?" she queried softly.

He nodded, his expression grim, his gray eyes holding her gaze steadily. She understood him. He was gravely concerned, just as she was.

"Never fear, Papa," she said, turning her attention back to her father. She patted his shoulder gently. "We shall have you home and tucked between the sheets before the cat can lick her ear."

"Thank you, yes, that would be best," he murmured.

Two hours later, Blackthorn waited for Julia in the study on the ground floor of Hatherleigh Park. He stood beside a highly polished desk of tiger maple and traced the exotically grained wood with the tip of his finger. His thoughts were dark and scattered, leaping from one impossible truth to another—Lord Delabole's erratic health and his penchant for gaming, Lord Peter's obvious love for Julia, Mr. Ladock's nervously imparted news that another document was missing.

What a wretched coil, his mind cried. What was he to do? Julia needed him here, but he must be in Cornwall on Sunday to see if he could entrap Mr. Mawls' employer.

Only, what was he to do now with Julia? Would she understand his pressing need to leave?

Blackthorn left the maple desk and crossed the chamber to stare out the windows facing a lawn, which sloped steeply downward. He could not see far beyond the small rim of light cast by the two branches of candles in the chamber, partly because it was still raining and partly because the light was simply not strong enough to make a significant impression on the dark landscape about the manor. The sound of the rain was an unrelenting drone on the windowpanes. The cold air emanating from the glass cooled his face, but did nothing to divert his frustration or his bewilderment at how he was to manage both his affairs in Falmouth and Julia's immediate needs.

He heard steps on the stairs and quickly moved to the doorway, which opened onto the entrance hall. He saw Julia and the surgeon slowly descend the stairs, the doctor speaking in a low, fatherly manner to her, holding her arm tightly in his own. She appeared deeply distressed, and as she got to the bottom of the stairs, he saw that tears sparkled in her eyes.

"Thank you so much, doctor," she said, as together they arrived on the black-and-white tiled floor. "I am so grateful you could come. I . . . I needed to hear your assurances. You've no idea."

He smiled down upon her and patted her arm. "I know your father well, Miss Verdell. Dare I prophesy that tomorrow you will not be able to keep him in bed?"

At that, Julia brushed away her tears and chuckled. "Undoubtedly."

"And if for some reason he is worse—though I sincerely doubt he will be—you have but to send for me and I shall attend him at once."

"You are very kind. Thank you."

Grigson held an umbrella for the doctor as he opened the door and assisted the surgeon to his carriage. When the butler returned to the entrance hall, Julia asked him to bring a decanter of brandy to the study for Major Blackthorn.

Once Grigson had disappeared down the hall, Blackthorn guided her into the study. "Tell me everything," he commanded, his hand just touching her waist as he drew her near the fireplace. The study was a long, rectangular chamber, which housed several suits of armor situated like sentinels between four sets of windows. The windows were draped with gold velvet over underdrapes of sheer muslin. Valances of green velvet trimmed with gold fringe had been casually looped across brass rods decorated with cast eagles. The effect was stunning and very much in the current fashion mode of ancient Greece. Scattered throughout the chamber were green velvet sofas and chairs, either winged or in the Empire style, of gold and white striped silk. On the floor was a patterned Aubusson carpet in green, gold, and black.

Julia seated herself in one of the Empire chairs and recounted to him everything the doctor had done and said. Perhaps a fever of the brain, perhaps a touch of the ague, yet no real symptoms of either. Hopefully, he will not develop an inflammation of the lungs. A melancholia, perhaps. Who can say? A little laudanum to help him sleep.

Blackthorn watched her. She sat forward on the edge of the chair, her hands clasped tightly on her lap as she spoke, her gaze fixed on the geometric patterns beneath her feet. The colors were at odds with her rose-colored tulle gown, just as her distress, evident on her features, had distorted her pretty face.

In the glow of the dim candlelight, Edward stood before her and looked down at her soft auburn curls, seeing a woman battling all by herself. He knew a compassion for her, one he felt for the simple reason that he had many times before been in similar painful situations—though in the guise of various military campaigns and battles. The circumstances were different, but the struggle was the same: to overcome. He had promised to help her, but how? He wouldn't even be with her in the coming days.

Edward knelt before her and placed his hands over hers. He bid her look at him. "I want to help you," he said. "You are not alone." She looked at him as though seeing a stranger. He did not understand the distance in her green eyes.

"I should not have permitted Papa to escort us to the Assembly Rooms this evening. He should have remained at home, resting. He sleeps so little, you see."

He rose from before her and drew a matching chair forward, so that he might sit next to her.

Grigson arrived bearing a silver tray, two snifters, and a crystal decanter of brandy. He set the tray on a table at Blackthorn's elbow, then quit the chamber.

Blackthorn poured two glasses, handed her one, and bid her drink.

She took the rounded glass in long, elegant fingers, so skilled upon the pianoforte, so able to interpret Handel, Haydn, Mozart, and Bach dramatically, so useless in preventing the disaster about to fall down on her head. Julia took a sip, then another, then another, her gaze still fixed on the carpet. She was silent, but he could see by the tense shifting of her eyes over the green, golds, and blacks that her mind was racing on and on. The brandy would slow down her thoughts, her fears, he thought.

Blackthorn waited, sipping the brandy himself, letting its warmth radiate through his veins. His clothing was still damp from the rain that had drenched him during the few seconds required to lift Lord Delabole to his feet and support him inside the Assembly Rooms. Edward had seen the viscount leave the ballroom hastily, his complexion ashen. He had found him barely two minutes later, facedown on the pavement, soaked to the skin. He didn't know what was wrong with the man, but he suspected that his mounting debts might be conquering his mind. He wished there were some way he could help Julia's father, but there was so little he could do for anyone these days—no time, no money. Yet, there must be something he could achieve, even if only temporarily, to relieve a little of the pressure so rife in the house. But would anything he might do be enough? He had plans, good plans where the quarry was concerned, but he could see Hatherleigh Park needed help now, tonight, this week.

He swigged down a generous mouthful of the brandy. His life had been measured by this—too little, too late. Always. Here it was again. What could he do to aid Lord Delabole that would be neither less than what was needed nor given at too late an hour in the game to be of any value?

A feeling very much like impotence raged through him and he emptied the snifter, settling it with a harsh clink on the silver tray. "It is not your fault," he stated, perhaps as much to himself as to Julia.

She looked up at him, her brandy only half consumed. "I know," she responded. "But it still feels as though I might have done something to prevent his collapse."

"He will be better tomorrow. I'm sure of it. He will sleep all night."

She gave him a smile, appearing to summon her courage. "Of course he will. He has a remarkable constitution, you know. If he has not been the same since Mama died, who can blame him? I only wish—" At that she covered her face with her free hand.

Edward took hold of her hand. "My darling," he whispered, "don't distress yourself. Look at me. You must have courage. Now, listen. I am going away, but—"

"What?" she cried, clearly stunned. "When? For how long?"

"I shouldn't be gone more than a couple of days—my affairs in Cornwall again." He didn't understand the look of horror on her face. "I promise you, I shall return as soon as I can, and then we shall begin to search for a way out of this coil. The truth is, that until I have settled these urgent matters in . . . er . . . Falmouth, I am not entirely free to act as I deem best. But Julia, if you will be patient, if you will trust me, I am persuaded we shall soon contrive to put an end to all your troubles. Somehow, together, the deed can be accomplished."

Because of the strange look in her eye, Edward knew she was not convinced. He patted her hand and placed a gentle kiss on her cheek. "And now I think it is time I left you so that you can slip into bed and give yourself over to a deep sleep. You, too, will feel better in the morning."

Upon this speech, Julia rose, her shoulders slightly slumped with fatigue, her expression resigned. "You are right, of course. Of a sudden I find myself fagged to death. Do you wish to remain the night? I am certain Grigson will be happy to have a bedchamber made up for you."

"No, thank you," he responded. "I must return to my uncle's home. He is expecting me to bring word of Lord Delabole. If I do not come home, I know he will fear the worst, and I would not willingly put anyone through such unnecessary anxiety and grief."

She did not try to persuade him, but rang for Grigson. When the Delabole traveling chariot drew up at the door, the butler employed his umbrella again to help Blackthorn ascend the coach without being entirely deluged by the hard rainfall.

On the following morning, Lord Delabole sat upright in bed and watched his door, his heart pounding in his head. He was still feeling queasy, probably from his collapse of the night before or perhaps because of the laudanum. He swallowed and felt worse yet. He heard footsteps and now his heart thundered in his chest. His valet entered the bedchamber, gave him one brief, pointed nod of his head, then went about his business.

Lord Delabole threw back his bedcovers and slipped from the bed. He stood up, then immediately sat back down on the edge of the bed. Faith, but he was still dizzy. After ignoring his valet's inquiries as to his condition, he finally rose to his feet. He drew on the burgundy brocade dressing gown, which his man was holding out for him, shrugged himself into it, then tied the belt securely about his waist.

He moved quickly, or at least as quickly as his tender stomach and dizziness would permit him. He turned left down the hall, passed the first door that used to be his wife's bedchamber, then stopped before the second door. Without hesitating, he walked in and closed the door briskly behind him.

Julia was not here; her bed had already been made up. He scanned the bedchamber quickly with one sweeping glance. How powerful he felt. He had an objective, and once he had set his mind to achieving it, nothing could stop him.

He found what he was looking for sitting in plain view. He could have laughed aloud at his own stupidity for not suspecting the obvious, for there, resting in a little heap, was one of Julia's reticules, probably the one she had used last night, made of white satin and embroidered in a butterfly pattern with seed pearls.

He crossed the room and gingerly opened the reticule. Poking through the contents with his fingers, he felt a shock of dismay go through him. The ring wasn't there, only a vinaigrette, a snuffbox, a small mother-of-pearl comb, a pair of peacock embroidery scissors in a small velvet casing, and a small ceramic pot of rouge.

The viscount heaved a sigh. No ring. A vinaigrette, a snuffbox, a comb, scissors, rouge. He frowned, staring at the reticule. He felt the fabric, wondering if perhaps she had a secret compartment. His heart leapt within his chest. She did, by God, she did!

His excitement rose, for there was something oval within. He found the hidden seam, slipped his fingers through, and withdrew the object.

Damn. It was merely a brooch, which, when snapped open, contained a carefully tied lock of what was probably his wife's hair. He ignored the worthless broach and set it aside on the table.

A vinaigrette, a snuffbox, a comb . . .

Wait a minute. Julia never took snuff! He pulled the snuffbox from the depths and flipped it open. His eyes filled with tears at the sight of its contents. The emerald ring simply glittered in the morning light. He kissed it. He kissed the snuffbox. Then hurriedly stuffing the ring into the pocket of his dressing gown, he replaced the snuffbox and drew the strings of the reticule together, patting the sides a little in an effort to emulate the bag as he had first seen it. He turned and crossed the chamber.

When he got to the door, he listened carefully. Failing to hear footsteps, he opened the door abruptly, entered the hall, then closed the door behind him. He forced himself to walk confidently just in case one of his daughters had seen him enter Julia's bedchamber. But when he realized no one was about, Lord Delabole breathed another sigh of relief and returned quickly to his bedchamber.

Once there, he ordered his valet to see him dressed quickly. "I must leave the house unseen. You understand?"

The valet nodded.

At eleven o'clock on the following morning, Julia stood in the recess of a window, one hand holding back the gossamer muslin drapes just enough for her to see Lord Peter arriving in his glossy Stanhope gig. He drove an exquisite piebald team tandem and in every respect looked like a man of fashion. Settled on the seat beside him was what appeared to be a posy.

She was waiting in the green salon, a smaller, more intimate chamber located on the first floor of the mansion and overlooking the yew maze to the east of the property.

Her heart should have been fluttering in her breast. After all, the man she had hoped to attach to her side was coming to call in order to ask for her hand in marriage. Instead, she felt completely dead inside, incapable of any kind of emotion.

Following her father's collapse and Edward's informing her he would be away from Bath for several days, something within her heart had shattered. Julia held little hope now of her circumstances working out with any manner of ease. Her father had insisted he would see to the future of his daughters, but he was so ravaged by his excesses that he could scarcely care for himself, not to mention those dependent upon him. As for Edward, he was a dream and nothing more. He spoke of helping her find a solution to her troubles, yet his own concerns—whatever they might be—took preeminence. She knew his intentions were generous, just as were her father's. But what really mattered, ultimately, was action.

And so it was, as these thoughts rattled through her head and she could hear the wheels of Lord Peter's carriage rumbling along the drive, that she set her mind yet again to the future she had decided upon so many weeks ago.

She turned back, into the chamber, and scrutinized the masculine room that had always been a particular favorite of her mother's. The chamber had been decorated *en suite* in a forest-green damask silk, accented with gold. Even the walls were covered with the expensive fabric, a molding of darkly stained mahogany breaking up the expanse of walls into smaller sections, each of which housed a painting of a famous racing horse, or a Pollard coaching scene, or a hunting scene. The effect was dramatic, rich, and very masculine. She knew enough about Lord Peter to comprehend that he would be affected by the paintings. Horses, racing, the auctions at Tattersall's, the latest innovations in carriages, C-springs, harnesses, and saddles—these were the life and breath of this man. All the sofas and chairs were nearly two centuries old. As a general shape, each was square and lacked the softer lines introduced during Queen Anne's reign. However, the arms and legs were adorned with intricate carvings. Enhanced with the dark green damask silk fabric, the overall presence of the furniture was both comfortable in appearance and again decidedly masculine.

Light from four windows illuminated the room in a cool glow, while sunshine streaming in from two last windows brought the green of the fabric and the gleam of the wood to life.

Julia had chosen her gown with care. She matched the chamber, wearing a gown of a striped dark green and white silk, which sported puffed sleeves, a high Empire waist, and was cut low across the bosom. She should not have worn the gown for receiving a visitor. It was scandalously décolleté. But Julia would take no chances today, not when her future and that of her sisters depended upon Lord Peter's motivation and courage.

Lord Peter stood in the entrance hall and permitted the aging butler to take his hat and his gloves. Everything he had seen thus far impressed him, not the least of which was Lord Delabole's manservant. His father, the Marquis of Trevaunance, had once told him that a family's butler could tell you all you needed to know about a family.

"Your name, my good man?" he queried, addressing the butler.

"Grigson, m'lord," he said firmly, but in the quiet, dignified manner of a well-trained servant.

Lord Peter was pleased and some of his anxiety dissipated. Last night, after he had hinted to Julia that he wished to offer for her hand in marriage, he had begun to regret his hasty speech. He truly didn't know why he had said it, except that when he had seen her staring at Major Blackthorn as though he were a god, all his former conviction that he ought to carefully proceed with his courtship of Julia—perhaps offering for her in six months time—had simply and completely deserted him.

He had felt like a fool. He knew she was distressed that for

all his attentions he had still not asked to pay a call upon her
father, but that had not been his concern. If his budding love for
her continued to blossom, if her interest remained strong and
pointed, if she showed an increase in affection for him, then he
would of course make her his wife. Who wouldn't want to?

He had come to Bath simply to see her. During the Season,
Frederick Brown had so dazzled him and many others with his
descriptions of the charming Verdell sisters and the extraordinary beauty, in particular, of the eldest, Julia, that Lord Peter
had decided to see for himself if Mr. Brown was pitching gammon or not.

But when he arrived in Bath and laid eyes on Julia, he knew
a sensation of excitement so pure that from the first day he had
made her the object of his attention. He would never forget seeing her partaking of the waters at the Pump Room, oblivious to
the crowd who frequently turned her direction merely to look at
her, drinking the vile waters without even a wrinkling of her
nose, greeting her friends with an elegance of manner unequaled
even in London, and appearing like a veritable goddess in a pale
blue silk bonnet, a matching pelisse, and a charming reticule
dangling from her wrist.

His vision of his future had shifted in that moment. He would
marry her; he would take her to London where she would charm
all the great men and all the famous hostesses. He would know
an increase in stature simply by holding her on his arm. His
father would respect him for his choice, his mother would praise
him, and above all Harry, his older brother who would one day
inherit Father's rank, titles, wealth, and properties, would be engulfed in jealousy. Harry had been obliged to wed a lady of
inferior beauty because the estate entailed upon her marched
alongside the Trevaunance county seat. Not that Lord Trevaunance had insisted upon the match—not by half, for he was a
considerate father; Lord Peter would give him that. But Harry
couldn't abide the thought of not acquiring for his family that
particular parcel of land. Harry was greedy.

But if Harry was greedy, what was *he?* Lord Peter wondered.

He wanted to bring something to the family's consequence as well, and here was something he could bring—a beauty of the first stare—but at what price? A month earlier he had begun to hear the rumors of Lord Delabole's gambling habits. He had heard that even his daughters' dowries were gone and that very soon it was likely Lord Delabole would find it necessary to let Hatherleigh Park. Because of the serious nature of these rumors, he had gone to Wiltshire to see his parents and to discover what they knew, if anything, of Lord Delabole's circumstances. His father had had it on the best authority that the viscount hadn't a feather to fly with. He had also counseled his younger son against the match, quite strenuously.

Lord Peter looked about him and saw the elegance and polish of the black-and-white tiles, the well-maintained wainscoting surrounding the entire entrance hall, the glossy wood of the stairwell. A round inlaid table, gleaming of beeswax and adorned with a beautiful arrangement of bluebells and ferns, sat in the middle of the large square entrance. He saw nothing either in Grigson's demeanor or in the housekeeping that would indicate the rumors were indeed true.

"I trust His Lordship is expecting me?" he queried of Grigson.

But at that the butler tilted his head slightly and said, "Miss Verdell has requested that she speak with you privately first— that is, if you have no objection?"

"No, of course not," Lord Peter returned, surprised. He had expected to address Lord Delabole, to explain the precise nature of his personal resources so that he could prove his ability to care for his daughter. At the same time, he knew a prickling of anxiety. What was amiss? Had Julia changed her mind? Did she not want to marry him after all? He swallowed hard. Whatever his misgivings about her father might be, he felt sick with dread at the thought she might in the end reject his suit. He followed after Grigson, mounting the stairs in a quiet rhythm that matched the even gait of the butler.

Nine

Julia was still standing by the window when she heard Grigson's scratching on the door. Biting back bitter tears of fierce anticipation, she bid him enter. How long had she waited for this moment? Two months? Not long by any standard, yet so much hung in the balance that she might as well have been waiting for years.

The door opened, and she found herself clutching the skirts of her green striped morning gown. Grigson announced Lord Peter, who stepped across the threshold, then the butler silently closed the door.

The chamber was neither lofty nor expansive, yet miles seemed to separate her from Lord Peter. He was dressed immaculately in a blue coat, pale yellow waistcoat, buff pantaloons, and gleaming Hessians. He carried the posy in his hand at an awkward angle. Clearly, he was not used to offering bouquets to ladies.

"Hallo," he called to her, a faint smile on his face.

Julia stepped forward, crossing the room to greet him, her steps leaden. He seemed reluctant to move, as though afraid to do so. "Very punctual," she responded with a smile. "The clock had just struck eleven when you were drawing your gig to the front door. A husband ought to be punctual." She had tossed this sally from her lips, waiting for his reaction, to see if he grew even more frightened or if he warmed to the idea.

She watched his shoulders relax immediately and a gleam

enter his brown eyes. Julia released a very long but silent breath of air.

"Yes, a husband most certainly ought to be punctual," he returned. He lifted the posy for her inspection. It was a cluster of violets. "I hope these please you."

Julia took the flowers, then touched the tip of her nose to one of the soft petals. "Very much so." She then slipped her arm about his and guided him toward the sofa near the fireplace. "Do sit down. I believe we've much to discuss."

He sat down on the sofa and she took up a seat in an ancient chair next to him, so that she might see his face. A frown creased his brow as he looked at her. "Tell me," he said, "is your father well? I understand he was taken ill outside the Assembly Rooms last night. I would have attended you, but I knew you would wish for your privacy above all things."

Julia looked at him for a long moment, wanting to tell him he was very much mistaken and that what she had desired most from him was his strength and support. However, she knew now was not the time to discuss the matter with him. Instead, as she set the posy on a table at her elbow, she answered his question. "The doctor believes Papa is merely fatigued and that a little rest will restore him to health."

"Excellent," Lord Peter responded sincerely, leaning forward. "I am greatly relieved. Which brings me back to my purpose in calling at Hatherleigh today. I had intended upon speaking with your father and requesting your hand in marriage formally, but I am grateful that you wished to see me first. There is a matter of some delicacy that I would as lief put to you as attempt in any manner to discuss with Lord Delabole."

Julia folded her hands on her lap and forced herself to breathe easily. "I would have it so," she responded. "You seem hesitant, as though something is troubling you sorely. However, I believe I can guess the sum of your thoughts."

He leaned back against the soft cushions of the sofa and sighed. "Do you remember about five weeks ago, when we spent the day in the city visiting the Pump Room, the coffeehouses . . .

reading the newspapers . . . touring the Abbey? That was one of the finest days in my whole existence. When I had first laid eyes on you, I thought you the prettiest creature that had ever been born in all of creation. But that day, three weeks later, I believe would mark the budding of deeper, purer sentiments toward you."

Julia remembered the day clearly and how utterly pleasing it had been to be in his company. They had exchanged views on a dozen different subjects that morning. She had discovered in Lord Peter a similar love of art and music, a shared belief that the Corn Laws were bad for the country as a whole, a compassion for the suffering of the poor, a desire to contribute to society something, as yet undefined, of value and worth. It was only afterward that she had firmly decided Lord Peter would be the man for her. Here was a man she could love—or so she had thought. Here was a man who would answer her family's particular needs.

"I became convinced, my lord," she said, looking deeply into his eyes, "that we would be able to know a real, well-founded happiness in one another. I had never enjoyed myself so much as during the whole of that day."

His features grew more animated and he again leaned forward in his seat, so that he might reach over and trace her folded hands with his fingertips. "Know, then, that the painful subject I am bringing forward has nothing to do with you, my opinion of your worth, my love for you. And I do love you, Julia. Very, very much. But a week after our lovely day together, I began to hear unsettling rumors about your father. I have continued to hear them since, and each worse than the last . . . that he is a gamester." The gentle touch of his fingers became a firm grasp as he covered her joined hands completely with his. "Tell me I am not wounding you beyond repair by speaking thusly?"

In spite of her determination otherwise, her throat was so tightly constricted with tears that she could not for a moment speak.

"I have caused you pain and I did not wish to do so," he whispered. "Do you know nothing of which I am speaking?

Have I been so crass as to have brought to your notice something hitherto unknown to you? Pray that I have not!"

Julia shook her head and swallowed hard. She took a deep breath, then began. "The rumors are accurate and probably do not reflect the worst. My father has lost his entire fortune. My dowry disappeared months ago, along with my sisters', and all the heirloom jewelry is nothing but paste."

His hand was still protectively covering hers. "I had heard that Lord Delabole was considering letting the Park."

Julia nodded. "It is inevitable."

"Then you are in desperate straits." He held her gaze firmly.

"I will not hold you to a betrothal only hinted at," she said. "Were I in your stead and had just learned what you have learned, I would not want to enter such a marriage hastily or without counsel."

He smiled a little. "I have already sought counsel from my father. He recommended I leave Bath at once, that such a connection would be foolhardy since your father's creditors would very likely permit him to continue his excesses in anticipation of attaching my father's bank accounts." This was spoken bluntly but truthfully. "In short, he advised against such a connection, but then since he does not know you, he cannot comprehend the advantages of this match for me."

"Will you wed against his wishes?"

"He has left the decision entirely up to me, though he assures me that beyond a settlement in your favor—ostensibly to settle any debts outstanding at the day of our nuptials—he will not offer a tuppence more."

Julia blinked. For the first time she realized that though she had doubted Lord Peter for the past month, it would seem that during that same period of time, he had been carefully and judiciously examining every aspect of a potential marriage to her. She allowed herself to smile and most of the constriction in her throat disappeared. "You have taken the trouble to pursue the possibility of a match with me, and even after having come to understand the potential difficulties of such a connection, you

are still here. I don't think you could have proven the strength
of your affection for me more profoundly. I am deeply gratified.
Then you do not blame me?"

"You?" he asked, astonished. "How can any blame attach to
you? Besides, everywhere I turned, your character spoke for
itself. None of your friends and acquaintances, even Sir Perran
Blackthorn, fail to extol your abilities, your devotion to your
sisters, your careful management of Hatherleigh Park since your
mother's death."

Tears burnt her eyes. Somehow in his accolade, he had consoled her for all her suffering of the past two years in a way she
had never before been consoled. She slipped from her seat and
dropped to his knees. "You have been so kind," she wept, looking
up at him through her tears.

"Dear, Julia," he said, stroking her cheek with his fingers. He
then rose, lifted her to her feet as well, and kissed her. His lips
were firm, his embrace solid and soothing. If she found herself
comparing the feel of his kiss to Edward's, she quickly set aside
such a traitorous thought, concentrating instead on all the ways
she meant to make Lord Peter an admirable wife.

Drawing back from her slightly, but still holding her within
the circle of his arms, he asked, "Miss Verdell, will you do me
the honor of becoming my wife?"

She smiled up at him. "Indeed, yes, I will."

A few minutes later, Julia agreed with her betrothed that he
would speak with her father immediately. She rang for Grigson
and when he arrived, she bid him request Lord Delabole to join
her in the Green Salon as soon as possible. She could not keep
from smiling brightly upon the butler and saw a disturbing light
enter his eye. "I'm not certain," he began uneasily. "That is, I
am sorry, miss, but it would seem that His Lordship is not at
home. The head groom informed me he left some time before
your guest arrived, and no one knows where he went or when
he is expected to return."

"I see," she said, vexed with herself. Her father was in the
habit of coming and going as he pleased and rarely informed

her when he meant to leave the house. She ought to have at least confirmed his plans for the day.

When Grigson quit the chamber, she turned to Lord Peter. "Will you stay for nuncheon? Perhaps my father will return soon. I do so wish for you to speak to him. But now I recall that in all the shock of last night—with his collapse—I forgot to tell him you were coming to call, and I didn't see him this morning. I am sorry."

"It doesn't matter," he responded. "Today, tomorrow, or the next. It is only a matter of time. And yes, I will stay for nuncheon."

But as soon as her sisters had been informed of the purpose of Lord Peter's call—and Julia's acceptance of his proposals—she regretted having asked him to stay. They were all civil to her guest, of course—not one of them would set aside their manners, no matter what the nature of their sentiments toward a guest—but Julia could see by the penetrating looks cast her direction that each disapproved of her betrothal.

When her father did not return by three o'clock, Lord Peter bid farewell to his future bride and his soon-to-be sisters-in-law. But the moment his carriage was heard on the drive, they pounced on her.

"How could you," Elizabeth cried, "when you have flirted so boldly with Edward Blackthorn? And do not say it is a lie, for I saw you last night, looking at him across the ballroom floor as though you wished for him to take you in his arms and . . . and kiss you! Yet today you accept Lord Peter's offer! And don't tell me it is because of our *circumstances,* for then I truly will be vexed!"

"What circumstances?" Annabelle asked. "You mean because Papa has not prospered on the Exchange? But that happens to everyone now and again." Julia had explained their diminished circumstances to the younger sisters by saying that their father had lost some of his investments on the Exchange.

Julia glared at Elizabeth, then turned to Annabelle and said, "Pay no heed to your sister. As for Major Blackthorn, I knew from the start that we could not have a future together, and . . . and he told me last night that he is leaving Bath."

"No!" her sisters cried jointly.

"Yes. That is, he said he had business affairs to resolve in Cornwall. He . . . he said he would be gone for several days."

"But he intends to return, doesn't he?" Caroline asked softly, her expression painfully sympathetic.

Julia looked at Caroline and nodded. "But it will make no difference. He has no prospects, none at all. You all know as much. He is a soldier, and an impoverished one at that."

Annabelle had fallen deeply silent, and when Julia looked at her she realized something was wrong. "What is it?"

Annabelle blinked rapidly. "Nothing . . . That is, I heard something last night. Sir Perran told me. I thought it was a joke, but now I begin to wonder."

Julia felt strange. "What? Please speak. Tell me what he said."

Annabelle blinked again. "Only that he thought his nephew had gotten involved with smugglers. And they do operate out of Cornwall, don't they? And Major Blackthorn was always . . . well, always adventurous, wasn't he?"

"Well, yes, I suppose so, but I can't imagine that he would involve himself with smugglers. Not Edw—that is, not Major Blackthorn. Besides, what Major Blackthorn does or does not do cannot signify. A match between us is quite impossible. As for Lord Peter"—here she lifted her head, straightened her shoulders, and continued—"he and I share many similar pleasures and views, and I mean to make him a good wife. He . . . he knows of Papa's unfortunate losses *on the Exchange,* but he doesn't care." She met Elizabeth's gaze squarely. "So it is all but settled. Lord Peter has but to request my hand of Papa, and we shall be married."

How simple it all sounded, even to her own ears.

But where was her father? At dinner, Julia learned he had returned briefly, dressed for Sir Perran's card soirée and, having ignored her request for a few words with him, quit Hatherleigh without having spoken to her. She supposed her good news would simply have to wait until the morning.

The sisters enjoyed a quiet evening together, and as Julia began to openly discuss plans for her wedding and for her future, she was happy to see that one by one, Elizabeth, Caroline, and Annabelle began to enter into the joy and excitement such a fine connection would mean for all the Verdell sisters.

Later that evening, when Julia retired to her bedchamber for the night, she bathed in a steaming bath fragrant with rose oil, breathing deeply and easily for what seemed like the first time in years. She was so happy that she dismissed Gabrielle early, saying she was certainly capable of drying off and slipping a nightgown over her head. Gabrielle expressed her gratitude and quit the room.

Julia sank deeper into the bathtub. All was settled. Her future was settled. Her sisters would have as many London seasons as they could wish for. She would reside in London, which was where Lord Peter preferred to live; she would become a great hostess; she would see each of her sisters established in happy marriages; her life would be good, her life would be beautiful, and her mama would be proud of her. Now she could begin, as her mother had requested just before she died, to make something beautiful for her.

She was so certain she had made the only wise choice that Julia suddenly rose from her bath and, though dripping wet, quickly opened her reticule and withdrew the snuffbox. She wanted the emerald ring on her finger as a way of bringing her mother close to her; as a way of saying to her departed parent that she had been a good and dutiful daughter; as a way of believing she had succeeded in the most important object of her life: achieving a good, even an excellent, match.

She snapped open the lid and blinked.

The ring was gone.

Suddenly, she couldn't breathe. It was as though she had been hit in the chest, the wind knocked from her. She gasped for air, her throat and eyes burning with pain. *My ring,* her mind cried. "Oh, dear God, where is my ring?" She searched her reticule, unable to credit that the worst had happened.

How had *he* found it? She knew he had searched her room

before, but she had been clever and had left the ring in a place where no one would guess she kept it—in her reticule, in her snuffbox. Julia was desperate with panic.

She noticed that her brooch was sitting on the dressing table. Only then did she stop in her erratic movements. If her brooch, which had been concealed in a hidden pocket with the handmade reticule, was actually sitting on her dressing table as though it always sat there, then he had searched her reticule, opened the snuffbox, found the ring, and taken it from her.

Julia tried to tell herself that it didn't matter. That she was betrothed to Lord Peter, her future was settled, and even if Lord Delabole had taken her ring, it could no longer make a whit of difference to her future. But somehow, she knew the loss of the ring did matter, though she couldn't explain to herself why she felt this way.

She turned back to the tub, but she no longer wanted to soak in the hot water. She didn't know what she wanted to do, except cry perhaps. Her mother had given her the ring. The emerald had come to mean so much to her—the way in which her mother had provided for her even in the face of an improvident man, the symbol of her relationship with her mother, the security of her future apart from any man.

Now it was gone. She felt naked and unprotected, just as naked as she was standing in the middle of her bedchamber, with water still dripping from her and forming slippery pools on the wooden floor. Julia began to shiver. She had to get dressed before she succumbed to a chill and fell violently ill. She drew a warm nightgown from her wardrobe and absently used it to begin drying off. When she realized what she was doing, she laughed, though bitterly, and tossed the nightdress onto the pool of water on the floor. Finding another gown, she slipped it over her head.

Her ring was gone.

Gone forever. She would never see it again. Never.

She blew out the candle beside her bed, climbed under the velvet counterpane, and because of the fatigue of the day's jostling emotions, she fell sound asleep.

Ten

Lord Delabole leaned his head out the window of his traveling chariot and bellowed for his postilion to slow down. God, he'd had far too much wine and brandy. The persistent sway of the carriage was causing him to feel ready to cast up his accounts.

When Major Blackthorn had requested Lamb's Wool—good God, but the man had a hard head—he had appreciated the gesture. The hot ale drink was far preferable to Sir Perran's cherry brandy, especially when he was doing all he could to keep his gaming wits about him. Still, it seemed he had gotten foxed long before all play had ended.

He wasn't even certain how he'd gotten into his traveling chariot, though he had some recollection of Blackthorn leaning over him. Oh, yes, now he remembered. Blackthorn had all but thrown him over his shoulder, carried him through the house, and tossed him in his coach. He would have to thank the major in the morning. Blackthorn had said something, too, but the viscount couldn't remember what it was. Oh, yes, *All was well.* What a curst joke that was.

Lord Delabole held his head in his hands. He shouldn't drink so much. He tried to recall the last hours of play but couldn't. He remembered laughing a great deal, as did the other men present—except Blackthorn. For some reason, the major barely laughed or smiled all evening. Instead, his sharp gray eyes seemed fixed on him more often than not. How odd that he won Julia's ring. He had tried to sell the ring in Bath, but when he was unable to get a figure anywhere near the gem's true worth, he decided to use it as a stake in the game. Now even the ring was gone, and he was ruined.

If only his head would clear. The sound of the wheels grinding into the dirt lane that separated the two estates droned on and on. He felt droplets of water on his face.

Good God, was it raining? Lord Delabole narrowed his eyes and looked out the window, but he couldn't see anything; he just felt the wet drops against his skin. He tried to lift the window, but the effort sent the blood rushing from his head. He slid backward onto the seat.

When he awoke, he didn't know where he was. He was being jiggled in a strange way and his satin breeches were soaked. He could feel water dripping in rivulets down his legs. He looked up and tried to focus.

Where was he? It was so dark. What was pelting his legs? Why was he wet? Was it rain or the ocean? The darkness loomed over him. He tried to swallow but couldn't. He couldn't breathe. A terrible panic began growing in him. He was suffocating. He groaned, but no one heard him.

"Help!" he cried, but his voice came only in a raspy whisper. "Help!" he cried again, a little louder, but the rain must have prevented anyone from hearing him. He sat up and gave a hard push at the wall next him. He slid through the sudden opening that appeared—the door to the carriage! Too late! He tumbled over and over, felt a blinding pain slice through his head, then nothing.

The next thing he saw was an expanse of black-and-white tiles. He smelled something foul, like vomit. He couldn't keep his stomach still. He heard snatches of words.

"Foxed. Fell out of the carriage while 'twere moving at a spanking pace. He's bleeding."

"Get a sticking plaster and awaken two of the gardeners to help get His Lordship to his chamber."

Grigson's voice. Somehow knowing Grigson was nearby distressed him. His earlier panic rose again within his chest, but he didn't know why. His mind began to drift. He thought of

Olivia, and a warm, safe sensation enveloped him. Olivia had always anchored him into society, into life. He had depended upon her so much. No one really knew that, except Julia perhaps.

In the summer when his home in Somerset was heavy with the smell of roses from Olivia's garden, he missed her the most. Even in winter, her potpourri recipe filled bowl after bowl throughout his house. She was a rose, so delicate beneath his kisses, so entwined in his arms when he made love to her, so prickly when he drank too much or gambled too much. She had kept him in tow and he had gladly given himself into her safe-keeping. He had always known his weakness. Olivia, Olivia . . .

How much later it was, he couldn't know. Two hours, perhaps three. He was in his bed, in his nightshirt. How many men did it take to undress a drunkard? he wondered absently. His mouth tasted vile. He smelled of vomit. What time was it? Couldn't be four yet. The servants weren't stirring.

Lord Delabole sat up, feeling the effects of too much wine already beginning to burst like fireworks in his head. He slipped bare knees over the edge of the bed. His legs ached. Why? Oh, yes, he'd fallen out of the coach. He touched his left cheek and felt a heavy scrape along his cheekbone. He'd have to call for the surgeon.

What was he doing now? There was something he must do at once. Oh, yes, of course. A gentleman's most solemn obligation in the face of disaster.

But first he had to get dressed. He couldn't perform his duty in his nightshirt. That would be most indiscreet. Should he send a letter to his mistress? Would she even care? No, of course she wouldn't.

Making use of a tinderbox and brimstone match, he lit the tinder and then the candle on his nightstand. Slowly, he rose to his feet and unsteadily moved to his wardrobe. Opening the polished oak doors, he found the coat he wished to wear. A fine coat, fashioned by Stultz, of course. Many preferred Weston, but he thought Stultz had a better hand. A white shirt, nicely starched points, white waistcoat, black pantaloons, black knit stockings, black slippers. How his hands shook as he dressed himself, the buttons of his coat requiring ten minutes to fasten. How the devil was he to achieve a decent arrangement of his cravat if his hands continued to shake so badly?

From the depths of his wardrobe, he withdrew a bottle of brandy. He uncorked it and drank deeply, his tongue thickening with the flow of the liquid. He sat down on the bed, holding the bottle pressed between his legs. His whole body was shaking. He drank again, his vision clearing a little. When at last the shaking stopped, he recorked the bottle and slipped it back into place among his many slippers.

He moved to stand before the long gilt-edged mirror, next to the wardrobe, and with the practice of many, many years, he carefully wrapped the neckcloth about his neck, arranging the folds with great care and tying the ends into a crisp knot. Touching the scrape on his cheek, he wondered if there would be much blood.

He stepped back from the mirror and examined his appearance from head to foot. He brushed his hair briskly, then dashed rosewater over his face and hands. He still smelled the vomit. He wished he had had a chance to bathe, but he couldn't be concerned with that now. He wanted to be done with his dutiful task before the servants were about. He gave a gentle tug on each sleeve in turn, then pulled lightly on the bottom of his waistcoat. Nodding to himself in approval, he looked into his eyes. For the first time in months, he really looked at himself and was horrified by what he saw. His eyes had nearly disappeared into his head. He looked like a ghost. Would Olivia even know him?

He smiled to himself. Of course she would.

Lord Delabole turned away from the strange reflection in the looking glass and headed toward the door. Exiting his bedchamber, he descended the stairs to his study. He wrote a brief note to his solicitor and one to Julia, then drew his prime set of dueling pistols from the bottom drawer of his desk. He smiled fondly upon them, remembering the silly duels he had engaged in when he was younger, still in his salad days, much before Olivia's time, when he thought himself at home to peg in a scarlet brocade box coat, lace at his wrists and throat, yellow satin knee breeches. Clocks on his stockings. His hair thickly powdered and tied with a red silk riband. Lord, a macaroni born and bred.

He had been wounded once in a duel, a flesh wound, and had thought himself dying. How his friends had laughed at him, at his hysterics. He'd made such a cake of himself! How was it Olivia had ever seen an ounce of manliness in him?

He knew he had to be a man now, however. He had struck a bargain with Sir Perran, which he never intended to keep. He would not permit the baronet to have his beloved Julia. He would not be known as a man who had sold his daughter. His death would buy back all his debts and his daughter's hand in marriage.

He primed his pistol, leaned over the desk, and placed the gun to his head. He thought of Olivia.

Julia awoke out of a deep sleep, the kind of sleep that clung to her so ferociously she could barely open her eyes or move her limbs. She didn't know what had awakened her, though she heard movement in the attics above her bedchamber. Perhaps one of the servants, upon arising, had dropped a basin or something. Oh, yes, a loud noise had awakened her. Nothing to signify.

She turned on her side and could not keep her eyes open. What an odd dream she had been having. She had been dancing with Blackthorn and he had said, *I see your unhappiness.* Then he had kissed her. His lips had been so soothing, so sensual. She still felt as though she could feel them on her own. But she wasn't unhappy. Her whole life was settled tidily. She could rest now.

She heard more footsteps, running this time. One of the gardeners or maids had probably gotten up late. Neither Grigson nor Cook would tolerate tardiness. She heard a door slam, then a woman cry out, a sort of wailing sound.

Julia sat suddenly bolt upright, sleep deserting her completely.

Something untoward had happened. She slid from her bed, her heart beginning to hammer. What was wrong? She heard Grigson shouting orders. Another door slammed shut. What was happening! Doors were never slammed in Lord Delabole's home.

Someone was hurt or had taken ill in the night. She thought of her sisters—Elizabeth, Caroline, Annabelle. Julia ran from her bedchamber and sought each of their rooms in turn. Both Elizabeth and Caroline were sound asleep. Annabelle was sitting up rubbing her eyes, her mobcap angled comically off her head. "What is it, Julia? I heard a sort of crying sound."

"Go back to sleep, pet. I think one of the servants is ill. I am going to see what I can do to help."

She returned to her bedchamber and put on a warm woolen dressing gown. Slipping her feet into embroidered slippers, Julia moved immediately to the stairs and began to descend them. She could hear a woman sobbing, and when she reached the landing halfway down, she saw that Cook, dressed for the day in a gown of black stuff and a long, starched white apron covering the entire front of her gown, held a kerchief pressed to her face. She was crying uncontrollably. A gray-faced Grigson held a candle aloft with one hand and patted her shoulder with the other. He was whispering in her ear.

"What has happened?" Julia heard herself ask. How strange that her voice seemed to echo down the stairwell. She had never noticed an echo before.

Both servants turned to stare up at her. Cook immediately stopped crying and wiped her face with her apron. Grigson turned bodily toward her. "You should return to bed, child," he said. He was old enough to be her grandfather, but she was no longer a child.

Julia continued to descend the stairs. She felt peculiar. All sleep had long since disappeared from her brain. She could see that Grigson was approaching the stairs and that he was speaking, but she couldn't hear him. Instead, she was hearing the noise that had awakened her.

A thumping. No.

A pounding. Someone had been pounding on the door. No.

Gunfire. There was never gunfire about Hatherleigh Park. Never.

Her mind wouldn't work properly. "Is my father returned yet from Sir Perran's?" she queried, avoiding the butler's somber gaze. She reached the bottom step.

"Please, miss, return to your bedchamber. Let me tend to your father."

"Is he ill?" Somehow, Julia knew she was asking a stupid question, but the right one evaded her.

"Yes, I'm 'fraid so. Please, go back to bed. Enough time in the morning to deal with this."

She looked Grigson directly in the eye. He was perhaps an inch taller than she, so Julia did not even have to lift her head to hold his gaze steadily. "Is he dead?" she asked in a tone barely above a whisper. Finally, the question had come. But why had she asked it?

"He's still breathing," Cook said, taking a step toward her. "But we don't know why."

Only then did Julia look at the doorway to the study. Candlelight spilled from the chamber into the entrance hall. She walked toward the yellow light and crossed the threshold. She saw her father slumped over his desk of tiger maple.

Grigson spoke from behind her. "I've sent Chilton to fetch the surgeon."

"Oh, Papa," she whimpered, not moving at first. "Why didn't you let me help you?" She crossed the chamber slowly and came round next to him. She leaned over him and placed her cheek against his. He was still breathing, but erratically, his face lying in a thick pool of blood. His flesh was warm to the touch. She began rocking slowly against him, cradling his shoulder with her arms. "I love you so. I never stopped loving you."

* * *

Blackthorn stared out the window of his bedchamber at the Dook Inn. The Cornish sky was light gray, high clouds obscuring the sun beyond. He had arrived just an hour earlier and had bespoken nuncheon, which would be brought to his rooms. In a few hours, he would send word of his arrival to Sergeant Whitwick, but not before he had eaten, shaved, and slept a little. The appointed hour was ten o'clock in the evening, past dark. The sun would travel only so fast across the sky.

The journey from The Priory had been uneventful. The posting houses along the southerly road through Somerset, Devonshire, and Cornwall were at a peak of efficiency, his coach having been drawn by one fine team after another the entire distance. Thank God the government was paying his posting fees, however, or he'd be in the basket by now.

As he watched a gull circle overhead, then sweep toward the large, natural harbor, he slipped his hand in the pocket of his coat and fingered the emerald ring he had won from Lord Delabole the night before. His heart grew sick at the memories the emerald returned to him—of Sir Perran's card game, of watching the viscount disintegrate in sure, quick stages after his third bottle of port, and later, of watching him collapse in a drunken stupor. He had done all he could to win the ring and had succeeded, believing it likely the emerald had once belonged to Julia. He had decided then and there, when her father had staked the ring in a critical game, that he would see it returned to her. Blackthorn smiled, for on the journey south he had decided he would surprise her with the emerald on their wedding day.

But what to do about the viscount? Lord Delabole had played recklessly, even mindlessly. Blackthorn had wanted to take his uncle aside and beg him to stop the plundering of the poor fool, but such were not the rules of his society. All he could do was take the viscount in hand, carry him away from the table after he had signed a score of vowels, promise the old man that *all would be well*, toss him into his carriage, and send him home.

He had wanted to follow after him, to see that he arrived safely, but he couldn't. Once he had seen Delabole into the carriage, Blackthorn had excused himself from the remainder of the night's play, reiterating to his uncle his need to attend yet again to his business affairs in Cornwall.

Now he was in Falmouth, preparing to capture a French agent, yet his thoughts were still fixed upon Julia. He took the ring from his pocket and examined it. The green gem glittered in the gray light. He was reminded of Julia's lovely eyes, and suddenly he missed her beyond measure. He was amazed by the strength of the sentiments that flowed through him at the mere thought of her. He wanted her in his arms again; he hated that he had had to leave her. But soon he could devote day upon day to her, seeing to her happiness, setting about the resolution of her difficulties, holding her, kissing her, loving her. He would then begin to prepare her for her life with him.

Once Europe had settled down for good, Blackthorn meant to request duty in India. Wellington had begun his career in India, and for himself, he wanted to experience firsthand the exotic land, as well as to serve his country's interests. Julia would love India. He was sure of it. He knew her well: There was a spirit of adventure in her even if her current difficulties masked her true nature. Yes, she would love India very much.

But for now he would wait. He would complete his mission and he would see the chaos at Hatherleigh Park ended.

Near dawn on the following morning, the French spy, who had been secreted among the rocks of the cove since dusk of the previous evening, watched as Major Blackthorn and a large, burly man whom he did not recognize finally gave up their vigil. They emerged from the underside of an overturned boat, stretching and cursing, their voices against the quiet lap of waves and silence of the gray-pink light an amusement to his French soul.

He shifted his attention to Mr. Mawls. The poor fellow appeared quite miserable, he thought with a smile, as he watched the major and the large man thump their boots in a lively manner against Mr. Mawls's sleepy buttocks. He had had to sit in the cold night air, by himself, eventually curling himself into a ball, falling asleep, and snoring for several hours. Really, the entire scene had been fodder for a farce. He had enjoyed himself hugely, especially since he had had the usual foresight and good sense to bring along a blanket, a bottle of wine, a thick wedge of cheese, and a loaf of bread.

He now had the information he had been seeking, namely whether his good Mr. Mawls had been discovered—and indeed he had!—and whether Sir Perran's *dutiful* nephew had actually returned to The Priory after so many years of disinterest to pay a loving visit upon his uncle, or whether he had come back to fulfill a different office altogether, one ordered by the British Army. How interesting that the latter had proved true.

Well, well, he thought, neither surprised nor dismayed.

It had only been a matter of time after all. But so much time! Never would he have believed he could have served in Sir Perran's employ for so many years and not have had his identity uncovered long before now.

When the major had arrived some ten days earlier, he had been impressed by the officer for many reasons. For one thing, he presented a fine figure of a man, a strong, healthy specimen designed for war. For another, he appeared utterly unmoved by the enormity of his uncle's wealth. If he thought the major the wrong man to have been given the task of ferreting out a spy, he had set aside this opinion, intending not to underestimate the man's abilities. After all, Major Blackthorn had survived one engagement with the enemy after another, and it did not follow that a man who had kept from getting killed on the Peninsula lacked intelligence. Far from it. It was an easy thing for a witless man to get himself shot.

But beyond his intelligence, Blackthorn was passionate about what he was doing. He wanted to rid Europe of Bonaparte for-ever—he had made no secret of his wishes on that score—and was convinced war would return to France as long as Napoleon resided so close to the Continent. Passion, in the agent's opinion, was what bent the currents of the world.

But did Blackthorn comprehend the passion of a French spy? He thought it unlikely. How could a British soldier understand a Bonapartist? He couldn't, which he believed would work to his advantage. Major Blackthorn couldn't know, therefore, that he would die, if he had to, in his attempts to restore his *empereur* to the throne.

As Blackthorn and his compatriot took Mr. Mawls away, he kept himself hidden for some time. Near noon, when the cove had been empty for hours, he slipped from his hiding place and began his return on foot to his cottage some three miles from Falmouth. He was dressed as a fisherman, and no one would have supposed from his appearance that he was actually an upper servant in Sir Perran Blackthorn's household. The cottage was near the cove. Once there, he changed into suitable clothes for traveling. An hour later, the cart he had hired in the town of Penryn arrived to take him to a posting house. When he was finally aboard a post chaise, he let out a deep breath. Relief swelled over him. Now he could be more secure.

Just as the post-chaise quit the edges of the town, however, he felt a strong instinct that he was committing a grave error by returning to The Priory. He ought to beg the postilion to return him immediately to the inn, and afterward, he should make every effort to seek passage on the next ship leaving Falmouth. He sensed the moment was ripe and that his fate might just be decided in an unhappy manner if he remained in England. Though he leaned forward in his seat, ready to bid the postboy to turn the carriage about, he stayed the order.

He couldn't go, not when Saturday evening, before he had left for Falmouth, he had found three more documents in Mr. Ladock's office that he knew would be of inestimable value to Bonaparte—one of them indicating a growing sympathy between the Prussians and Russians over territorial claims. Such an alliance could ultimately afford Napoleon the opportunity he was seeking to reclaim France.

No, he couldn't leave England. Not just yet. He would secure these three documents and at the same time arrange for a boat to meet him at Polperro Harbor. Yes, that would do to a nicety. For precautions, he would hint to Susan that he intended to take a holiday in Falmouth, just in case Blackthorn somehow discovered his identity and followed after him.

Besides, he wanted to make love to Susan one last time before he left The Priory forever. Dear, delightful Susan, whose fear of him since the last secretary's unfortunate demise had made her a willing pawn in his capable hands.

Eleven

At noon of that same day, Monday, Sir Perran stood beside a table in his library, covered with cloths and laden with a multitude of dishes from which he would sample a delectable nuncheon. He savored the aroma of Yorkshire ham, filet of sole in oyster sauce, roast beef, duck, peas, broccoli, potatoes, and cabbage, all rounded off nicely with a steaming tureen of turtle soup. Jellies, sweetmeats, biscuits, and a platter of carefully arranged fruits promised a satisfactory end to the meal. On a separate table, alongside which stood a footman, a bottle of his finest champagne waited patiently.

Anticipating the delights of the meal was a large part of the enjoyment for Sir Perran. He was very content.

A half hour earlier, Beeston had given him a letter from Hatherleigh Park, from Julia—had Delabole already informed her of her duty?—and word that belowstairs the viscount's groom was awaiting a response before returning to the Park. Naturally, he had not opened the letter immediately. He was savoring reading its contents as much as he was delighting in the bouquet of the splendid fare on his table. He leaned over and smelled the soup. Perfect. He would send his compliments to his chef. Really, a perfect meal to be enjoying on a Monday after such a perfect card soirée two evenings prior.

All had gone as planned, except for one small irritation: Blackthorn had won the emerald. Sir Perran doubted his nephew knew how much the gem was worth. Still, the ring hardly signified. All that truly mattered was that Delabole was no longer in possession of a gem that could have staked him for two or three more games and so prolong his own game, which he was ready to bring to a tidy close. After enjoying this meal, he meant to drive over to the Park and begin the delicate process of taking Julia to wife.

Sir Perran chuckled. He was very happy. He ordered his footman to uncork the champagne, listening to the loud pop with a sensation rather like glee. He felt young, alive, as though he was just beginning the best adventure of his life. He would enjoy removing Delabole from Hatherleigh and moving in. He would take over management of the quarry, which had become stupidly unprofitable in the past five years—but not surprisingly. Delabole had a slack hand, along with his many other faults. But Sir Perran would soon set all to rights. He would gather in, with enormous satisfaction, the inheritance stripped from him so many years ago—good God, over half a century ago. The best, however, would be owning Hatherleigh, a condition he would require in exchange for settling Delabole's debts. Hatherleigh Park was an ancient house of extraordinary beauty. He deserved to own Hatherleigh, he and his descendants.

He sighed deeply, again chuckling. A man could die of so much pleasure, he thought with another smile.

Sir Perran seated himself and settled the letter beside his plate, then began the process of smelling, savoring, selecting. He directed a glass of champagne be brought to him. Sipping the bubbly wine, he tasted the sole, a sliver of broccoli, a slice of potato. Another sip of champagne. He knew how to live. He would teach Julia how to live. She would give birth to his sons, *his own sons,* a dozen of them. She was young and strong and came from good birthing stock. He would live to see ninety and then some. He might even survive to see his grandchildren.

A little roast beef, a little duck, a spoonful of turtle soup, a cabbage leaf. More champagne. He was a powerful, wealthy man who could command anything he wished.

He glanced at the letter. From Julia. Why not from Delabole himself? Was it possible that oaf, Delabole, had already told

Julia of the agreement? The man lacked finesse. It was not the least necessary for the viscount to be so hasty after all. To browbeat any female with the knowledge that she would now be required to marry a man clearly thrice her age would hardly promote a propitious beginning.

He thought of Hatherleigh's groom waiting belowstairs. Why had Julia required an answer?

His curiosity mounted.

One more bite of soup and he decided not to wait any longer.

He picked up the letter, broke the red wax seal, and unfolded the single sheet of paper. In a sweep of his eyes, he read the contents.

As my father's dearest friend, you will want to know that the losses he has sustained steadily for so many years have finally taken a toll—his own life, in fact. He shot himself with a dueling pistol just before dawn on Sunday, yet did not die immediately. He finally expired around eight o'clock this morning. Please believe that I hold no one to blame except my father. You have always been a most generous neighbor and friend, and I knew you would want to know as soon as possible. Services will be conducted tomorrow at eleven. Yours, etc., Miss Verdell.

The turtle soup still lingering on his tongue turned as bitter as bile and he spat it out.

Delabole shot himself.

He reread her bold words a dozen times: *He shot himself with a dueling pistol.*

Sir Perran felt as though a thief had broken into his house and robbed him of every groat he owned. He placed a hand to his chest; he made himself breathe. He tried to think but couldn't. Anger began to rise up within him like the curling tendrils of smoke at the onset of what would be a roaring log fire. Up and up, his rage curled, wisped, and grew, until the smoke choked his head.

He had been cheated of his revenge. Cheated, like a Flat by a Captain Sharp. Robbed. He hadn't wanted Delabole dead, he had wanted him alive—to see for himself the superiority of the

Blackthorns. Alive, for God's sake! Alive to know what it was to be stripped of all that was of meaning and value to you.

His anger burst into a roar of rage and Sir Perran rose from the table. In one mighty movement, he overturned the table and all its food, cutlery, china, and crystal. The plates and dishes shattered; the food splayed across the carpet in a gross sea of turtle soup dotted with lumps of meat and vegetables, fruit and biscuits.

"God curse Delabole and all who came from his loins. God curse them all!" Picking up the letter, he crumpled it fiercely in his hand. He turned to find the footman staring at him, his face white, his dark brown eyes bulging in terror. Sir Perran pointed at him. "Not a word of this to anyone. If I hear even a whisper from another quarter of what has happened in this chamber, I shall have you turned off without a reference and see that you never find a place in service again! I expect you to take the blame—you tripped and knocked the table over—do you understand?"

The terrified footman nodded briskly.

"Now clean this up! And not a word!" Sir Perran commanded, his limp entirely forgotten as he strode toward the door in long, angry strides.

An hour later, he found himself sitting on the terrace outside his bedchamber. His temper had settled and his rage had cooled. He exposed the letter, which he had kept imprisoned in his hand, and pressed it out flat on his lap. He read it through several times. Julia had no reason to wed him now. He had no leverage with which to force her hand. None.

He strummed his fingers on the letter, propping his elbow on the arm of the chair and dropping his chin in his hand. He must think. There must be some way to complete his objectives in spite of Delabole's useless suicide. Julia would have need of help now.

Suddenly, he smiled. He could help her, he thought wickedly. He could help her a great deal. He could help her to see that the only way out from under the burden of her father's enormous debts was to marry him.

Sir Perran breathed a sigh of relief. Sometimes the most obvious solutions were best. A little of his former glee returned to him. In fact, when he began to consider it, how much better to have Delabole dead after all.

The next few days for Julia passed by as though she were in the midst of a bizarre dream. Each hour brought something different to her—as in a dream, when the image of a lake could suddenly be replaced by the vision of a knight fending off a dragon. One moment she was standing with her sisters, all shrouded in black crepe and weeping, listening to but not hearing the good reverend usher Lord Delabole into the next world; the next moment she was receiving the condolences of her many friends who had driven to Hatherleigh to console her. Then she was alone in her bedchamber, lying flat on her bed, crying and crying; then she was dressing for a dinner she did not wish to eat; then she was speaking with Sir Perran about letting the Park; then she was sleeping; then, on the following morning, she was receiving the tradesmen and their condolences, but knowing full well they were also silently requesting that their bills be settled; then she was speaking to the servants about the future—she wasn't certain, but, yes, she was considering letting the Park, in which case they would remain in service. Julia remembered wishing that Blackthorn was with her, comforting her.

All the while, as she moved through each dreamlike hour and day, she wondered why Lord Peter did not come to her. Where was he?

At the same time she had sent Sir Perran word of her father's death, she had also dispatched an urgent request to the White Hart Inn for Lord Peter to come to her, informing him of the tragedy that had befallen her and that the funeral would take place on Tuesday.

But three days had come and gone. Julia didn't understand

what had happened. Lord Peter had not attended the funeral. He had not so much as sent a concerned word to her. Didn't he understand how badly she needed him to support her during her grief, to honor his promise to her? Where was he?

Early Thursday afternoon, after Sir Perran had told her that months were frequently required to find a suitable lessee for any property as large as Hatherleigh Park, Julia felt she could wait no longer and ordered the carriage to be brought round. She would go to the hotel. She was certain that if she could see Lord Peter and speak with him, then she could determine why he had failed to support her. She was ready to forgive him for his inconsiderate conduct. He must be feeling terribly guilty by now.

But why hadn't he come to her?

When she arrived at the White Hart, she found that she was trembling as she addressed the short, balding man in attendance at the desk. She wished to speak with Lord Peter.

"I'm afraid you have come too late, Miss Verdell." He knew her. But then, who in Bath did not know of the striking Verdell sisters?

"I don't understand?" she queried. Her mind felt strange, as though it had become very soft and dense.

"He left yesterday morning. And since I know you to be a particular friend of his, I shall tell you what he told me—that his esteemed parent, the Marquis of Trevaunance, had been invited to the Pavilion in Brighton for several weeks and wished for his son to join him. How could such a dutiful son as Lord Peter refuse?" He spoke kindly but firmly, his blue eyes sympathetic. "His Lordship was such a gracious, good-hearted guest, he will be sorely missed, I promise you."

Julia could only stare at him in disbelief. "He is gone to Brighton?" she asked stupidly.

"Yes, Miss Verdell. He is gone and pointedly stated that he feared he would not be back for some time." He then cleared his throat. "We were all very saddened to hear of your recent loss. Lord Delabole often visited friends here at the White Hart.

A very jovial, generous man. Always tipped the servants rather extravagantly. He will be remembered kindly, I assure you."

Julia nodded dumbly, her mind still as loose as an undercooked pudding. She bid him good day, then left the hotel. All the way home, she couldn't think. She stared blankly out at the surrounding countryside, all hopes of an acceptable solution to her difficulties now gone, her heart wrenched from its delicate moorings as she renounced her happy opinions of Lord Peter's character.

Was she any better, though? She had made him an object, not because she loved him, but because he could give her what she needed most. In return, she had promised herself she would love him and make him a most admirable wife. But would that ever have been enough to sustain his happiness through the trials and tribulations of a long marriage?

The point was moot. She would never know. Lord Peter was gone.

When she arrived home, Julia permitted herself a glass of sherry in the Green Salon. She would give herself over to the despair of her situation for one hour, then she would turn her mind fully to solving the horrible dilemma that now faced her.

She had just finished her glass when she heard a carriage on the drive. She wondered who would be paying a morning visit so soon after the funeral. Julia rose from her green silk damask chair and moved to the window. When she pushed back the muslin drapes, she looked down onto the drive and saw a man in a black hat and blue coat jumping lightly from his curricle.

Edward.

Her heart nearly jumped into her throat at the sight of him. Hope soared suddenly in her breast. He held his horses until he could turn the equipage over to a footman, then literally ran into the house.

She felt so strange, both delirious to see him again and guilt-ridden that since the time he had last spoken to her on Friday night, she had won and then lost Lord Peter. How could she receive him with the strong affection that was at the present overwhelming her, when she had so recently been betrothed to another man?

Julia set her glass on the mantel and waited. She wore a gown of black silk, a color she would wear for at least six months. She tugged at her curls but knew that even if her hair was arranged properly, the whole process of grieving had affected her appearance. There were bluish circles beneath her red-rimmed eyes and a tight unhappiness to her mouth.

In the distance, she heard him mounting the stairs two at a time. A moment later, the door burst open. Edward flung his hat and gloves on a nearby sofa, crossed the chamber, and took her heartily in his arms. "I just arrived home," he said, a little out of breath as he rocked her. "The moment my uncle told me of your disaster, I came over."

"You did?" she asked, stunned. How different he was from Lord Peter. Julia held him tightly, tears already flowing down her cheeks.

"Don't cry, my darling. I'm here."

"Where were you? Where did you go?" Thoughts of Cornwall and smuggling tugged at her mind. Was it possible Sir Perran's suspicions were true? If they were, did it matter?

He drew back from her slightly, but still held her in a firm embrace. "Cornwall, and no, my efforts were not entirely successful. I'm not certain what I will need to do next to settle a most prickly business! But that shan't affect you and me. I promise. My . . . my affairs are almost tidied up, and then I can devote the whole of my attention to you and your sisters. But tell me how everything stands."

As he drew her to the sofa where only five days earlier Lord Peter had offered for her hand in marriage, she told him all that he wished to know. He had many questions—about the death of her father, about the tradesmen in particular, about her efforts to let the Park.

"Papa's debtors have been polite, but I know it will not be long before I am besieged with demands of payment. Edward, I don't know what else I can do. For . . . for years I had had one last little nest egg that I had been able to keep from my father, but somehow he discovered it and used it to play at Sir Perran's. Your uncle has been very kind and is guiding me in my efforts to find a lessee for the Park, but he let it slip that Papa owed him five thousand pounds. I must repay him, but how?"

At that, she noticed Edward had grown tight-jawed, his gray eyes dark with anger. "I hold Sir Perran to book for this mischief. I was there. My uncle should have stopped the play long before the night ended."

"I don't blame him," Julia responded. "My father alone was responsible for his conduct."

"A man can be encouraged down any path," he returned, holding her gaze steadily.

"But at some point, a man must refuse, if the path is hurting him. I will not fault Sir Perran, especially in light of his kindnesses to me and to my sisters since Papa's death. Do you know he even offered to settle one of the tradesmen's debts? I refused, of course."

Edward seemed mollified. He took Julia's hand in his and brought it to his lips, placing a kiss on her fingers. He then turned toward her and, catching her lightly at the neck, leaned over and kissed her fully on the mouth. The sensation, so full of passion, again brought tears to her eyes. After a moment, he drew back from her. "I have missed you sorely these past few days. You don't know how much I hated parting from you on Friday, knowing I would be gone following the card game, that I had to go, but knowing you needed me here."

He tried to kiss her again, but she wouldn't let him, placing a hand on his chest. "There is something I must tell you, Edward."

He frowned slightly. "Of a serious nature, I perceive."

"I believe it is. You see, after my father's collapse on Friday night, and after you told me you would be gone for several days—to Cornwall—I made up my mind about something. At the Assemblies that night, before Papa became ill, before you found him on the pavement outside the Upper Rooms, Lord Peter asked to pay a formal visit upon my father."

"What?" Blackthorn cried. "Good God, do not tell me he actually came up to scratch! You refused him, of course."

Julia looked at him and thought it very strange that he simply assumed she would have done so. Didn't he understand even a little of the pressures she had been enduring and still was? He might say that he was ever so sorry to have left her and to have gone off to Cornwall even when he knew she needed him, yet he had gone. He had gone. He had left her to fend for herself, and so she had.

"I know you will not credit it or comprehend even a part of it, but I did not refuse him."

He seemed taken aback, even shocked. "You are very right . . . I don't understand."

She rose from the sofa and moved to stand by the fireplace, her thoughts rushing madly about in her brain. Edward was angry and part of her was angry as well. If only he could understand her a little.

He rose to join her by the hearth, an expression of deep disapproval on his face. His gray eyes pierced her in their intensity. "Did we not agree that if we combined our abilities, we would be able to discover a way out of this fix?"

"You wished it so," she responded simply. "You have tried to assure me a dozen times that you could find a way, and a dozen times I believed you, until I was at home and Papa confronted me with yet again another of his excesses. I . . . I felt compelled to accept Lord Peter's offer."

Julia averted her gaze and looked down at the green and gold patterned carpet on which they were standing. Edward was wearing black top boots, polished to a gleam. If only he had not left her on Friday.

She clasped her hands together and gathered her thoughts. "On Saturday, I found myself almost numb with panic," she began, finally lifting her gaze to meet his. "Lord Peter and I came to an agreement that he would speak with Papa, gaining his consent for our marriage. Later, when all was settled formally, we would announce our betrothal. But early the next morning, after Sir Perran's card soirée, Papa shot himself. . . ." How strange that she could speak these words so unemotionally. "The funeral was held on Tuesday, and Lord Peter neither responded to the three letters I sent him nor attended the funeral, though many were in attendance whom I had not personally contacted. He must have known of father's death. A few hours ago, I drove to the White Hart in hopes of speaking with him, to discover what had prevented him from coming to me, but I was told he had gone to Brighton for the remainder of the summer."

At the end of her speech, she turned away from him and moved back to the window where she had been standing when he had first tooled his curricle up the drive. Julia looked out at the gray day, a thick layer of clouds overhead threatening rain very soon.

She heard his muted footsteps on the carpet as he crossed the chamber to join her by the window. His breath was on her ear as he stood behind her. "You know my opinion of Lord Peter, and he has confirmed that opinion. Yet he does not concern me, nor does his absurd offer to you which he did not honor. What troubles me is that you trusted me so little."

"You weren't here and you've only now just arrived." Julia was tired, battle-weary. "Perhaps I was acting hastily. I don't know. But when I weighed all the various aspects of the situation, I could come to only one conclusion that seemed to bring me any peace at all: I must wed Lord Peter, if he would have me, so that my sisters' futures would be safe."

"Why won't you trust me? I am not without connections and influence, as I have told you. I am convinced I can restore prosperity to your quarry, which would go far in seeing your sisters established."

"What of my father's debts?"

"Julia, I don't know at this moment what can be done, but I am persuaded the situation is not hopeless, not if we join forces and see the task accomplished together. Only tell me this, do you love me?"

He took her chin in hand and turned her face so that she had to look up at him. She found herself staring into clear, imploring gray eyes. He was taking her down a path, one she wanted to travel more than any she had ever before encountered.

"Do I love you?" she whispered. "Of course I do, now and always. It is just that I feel so hopeless. Try to understand— Elizabeth, Caroline, Annabelle."

"Enough," he commanded her gently. "For the present, see only me and the future you want with me. You are worn down by grief and fear, so much so that you are not seeing the best part of what lies before you."

Julia looked at Edward, permitting herself to see only him. She forced the cares that had been dogging her incessantly for the past two years to slip away. Losing herself in his eyes, she wanted only him. She didn't care what manner of life they would have together, rich or poor; she wanted to be with him—him alone. "When you are here, Edward, everything seems so simple."

He smiled contentedly. "Much better," he murmured. He drew her gently into his arms and kissed her.

For the first time in several days, her heart felt light again and she was floating as she gave herself fully to his embrace, to the persuasion of his promises, to the feel of his lips upon hers. How safe she felt, how protected, how free of cares.

Edward released her after a long moment and drew her back to the sofa. He bid her sit beside him, and before she knew what he intended he was kissing her again, passionately. Part of her wanted to protest, yet she couldn't, not when the sensation of being kissed and held tightly by Edward was so sweet, so soothing. Julia forgot about her beloved father, about his debts, about the future.

Edward began tugging at her curls and her chignon fell apart, her auburn hair cascading about her shoulders. He lifted her hair to his lips and kissed the long curls. Slipping his fingers through the hair at the back of her neck, he kissed her yet again.

His fingers found their way down her back to her waist. He pulled her toward him, but the awkwardness of their positions prevented him from holding her close. Always he was kissing her, teasing her lips, her mouth. Desire began to rise up in her sharply as it never had before.

She wanted him, she realized with a start. She wanted him to be her husband now, in this very room where Lord Peter had spoken his words of love and devotion, only to leave her when it suited him. She wanted Edward now. She began unbuttoning his coat; he was quick to take up her hint. Releasing her, he removed his blue coat and his waistcoat.

Instead of simply kissing her again, however, he leaned over her and slid her beneath him. How much more comfortable and pleasing it was to be able to slip her arms about his neck, his back, his waist, to hold him close to her. He kissed her fully, deeply, lovingly and with such passion.

He was a tender, exciting lover, his hands touching her with a feathery lightness that forced her breathing into shallow gasps. He kissed the fullness of her breasts above the black silk bodice and, with both hands, held her tightly about the waist. Desire curled deeply within her. He lifted her skirts, and a moment later was joined to her.

She was surprised at how she felt as he drew back slightly, looked lovingly into her eyes, and asked if he was hurting her. "No," she whispered. "There is only pleasure." She had heard that the first time could be painful, but there was no pain for her.

He moved into her, firmly, deeply, his hips striking a rhythm that spoke of the whole pulse of the earth, as it had always been, as it always would be. She lifted her head, searching for his lips. She found them and he crashed down on her, pleasure and desire igniting. She slipped into his rhythm, allowing waves of pleasure to break over her with each roll of his body against hers.

Edward was loving her, taking her, possessing her. Julia

closed her eyes, her mind becoming loose and free. Every thought was of him, of what she knew of him, of being children together, of having wanted to be his wife in every way since they were young.

The waves came faster now, her thoughts drawn down and down, waiting, hoping, wondering. She heard him moan, followed by her own labored breathing, pleasure flowing over her again and again, rising to a sharp pinnacle that took her breath away. Julia wanted to cry out, but his lips were on hers and her moans joined with his. Every part of her felt alive and full of wonder as he began to slow his movements and finally stopped. She felt his kisses against her neck. Desire, less urgent but still so pleasing, clung to her. When he tried to move away from her, she begged him to stay, holding his waist tightly.

"My darling Julia," he whispered into her hair. "We will be married very soon, regardless of an appropriate mourning period, and you will not refuse me."

"I will not refuse you," she said, believing she could now do whatever he wanted of her. Permitting him to take her had been a way of promising herself to him forever. She could trust him now completely.

Sir Perran closed the door. He had followed his nephew to Hatherleigh, but apparently Major Blackthorn had been unaware. How stupid not to have at least locked the door. Anyone could have found them entangled like that, fully clothed, the springs within the sofa squeaking methodically. He would have found the whole of Blackthorn's adventure amusing had he been ravaging one of the maids. But when he realized his nephew had just taken the woman he meant to make his wife, a kind of blinding madness had stolen into his mind. He had watched and listened because he couldn't do anything else. He was too stunned to move. How easily she had been seduced.

When the sofa grew quiet, only then did he command his senses enough to close the door.

The whole of it was so odd. He had even waved Grigson away at the last moment, before the butler would have announced him. But then, he had seen Julia's lust for his nephew at the Assemblies on Friday and he supposed he had wanted to surprise them. It was amazing what you could learn about people when you simply surprised them, by something you might say or by simply opening a door upon two people closeted together.

Sir Perran returned to the entrance hall and called for his carriage, saying nothing to an astonished Grigson. He could have remained, but he was afraid that the anger he was holding at bay toward his nephew would rise up within him, as it had on Sunday—God curse his own foolish temper!—and he would do something he regretted.

Better to remain calm in the presence of others. Better to think through all that he had seen, all that he knew of the entire situation, before planning anything.

As he climbed aboard his traveling coach and a footman snapped the door shut, his thoughts turned to his brother. He didn't want to think about his brother or his brother's wife, but it would seem now Edward had forced him to do just that.

Circles. He thought of circles. The sun, the moon, the earth, the endless round of the seasons, birth, life and death, vengeance and revenge, the tides going out and coming back in, the way life demanded beginnings and endings, more beginnings, more endings. Around and around, eternally. Circles.

He had loved once, completely, furiously, at times with a powerful jealousy. The woman had had sharp blue eyes that had devoured him the moment he first caught her gaze. Her hair had been coal-black, her expression alive, vibrant, strong. He had pursued her, wooing her with flowers and Milton and every conceivable ploy used by man for centuries to win the reluctant lady of his choice. He had even seduced her, finding that she was as responsive to him as it appeared Julia had been to his nephew.

How great the irony of that. For in the end, the woman he loved had been Edward's mother. And now, as if fulfilling the circle in order to create in him a kind of virile madness, *her* son had taken Julia from him, the only other woman he had ever wanted.

But it was not over and he would have her. As heaven was his witness, he would have her and he would be avenged.

Twelve

Later that evening, when Edward arrived back at his uncle's house, he found himself in the devil's own temper. He crossed the polished planked flooring of the elegant entrance hall, snapping off each of his York tan gloves in quick succession. He was as mad as fire about the death of Lord Delabole. He had never been on intimate terms with the viscount, so he could not claim a profound feeling of loss, but he was Julia's father. Her pain was what drove him to bark at Beeston, requesting to know the precise location of the baronet.

Beeston lifted a brow, clearly surprised by Blackthorn's tone of voice. "I believe he is in his study," was his clipped response.

Blackthorn threw his gloves into the bowl of his hat, tossed it to Beeston, and headed to Sir Perran's study.

Once outside the door, he paused for a moment, drew himself into his most soldierly bearing, and knocked on the door. Heeding Sir Perran's summons to enter, he turned the handle, gave the door a shove, and a moment later stood before the baronet. "A word with you, sir?"

Sir Perran was seated in one of the amber winged chairs near the fireplace, several branches of candles lighting the chamber in a warm glow. He gestured for his nephew to take the chair opposite him. Blackthorn seated himself and would have launched into a cataloging of his many complaints, but he realized Sir Perran's eyes were closed and that he was waving his hand rhythmically in the air and humming.

"Sir?" Blackthorn queried, wondering what the deuce his uncle was doing.

"Vivaldi," he murmured by way of explanation. "Ever since I was a child, I could recall an entire sonata in my mind and hear every part played by the various instruments, a gift I have developed and enjoyed over the years. By the way, I should like to give you a hint: You really ought to be more careful how you conduct your . . . er . . . *flirtations,* m'boy."

Blackthorn, first lulled by his uncle's odd childhood reminiscence, was then startled by the unexpected admonition that followed. "My flirtations?" he asked.

Sir Perran opened his eyes and looked directly at him. Blackthorn experienced an odd sensation of familiarity so striking that he felt gooseflesh rising on his neck. Sometimes Sir Perran could appear so much the image of his father that he fancied himself looking at a ghost. But they were brothers, so of course the resemblance was not unnatural. Still, the peculiar sensation remained with him.

For a moment he forgot why he had come and the subject at hand, until Sir Perran continued. "The next time you decide to fondle Miss Verdell in the Green Salon, I suggest you lock the door. What if Grigson or one of the servants had found you? Fortunately, it was I who chanced upon the pair of you. I trust you mean to wed her. I have come to look upon Julia and her sisters both with great affection and a sort of fatherly concern."

Blackthorn remained silent. He was dismayed that he had been so indiscreet that the intimacy he had shared with Julia had been witnessed by his uncle, but he would make no apologies at this eleventh hour. Instead, he addressed the only significant issue at hand. "Of course I mean to wed her. We are betrothed and we intend to speak with the vicar tomorrow. What do you suppose I am, a blackguard? A rogue? Would you believe me capable of seducing an innocent? In case you are not informed of my character by now, I am not so vile a creature."

"Good" was all Sir Perran said, as he closed his eyes and again began weaving his hand through the air. " 'Four Seasons.'

Nothing quite as beautiful has been composed since. I am not half as enchanted with Bach or Mozart as I am with Vivaldi. Now do go away and leave me to my air dreams. I was keenly overset by discovering you with Miss Verdell."

But Blackthorn had spent many years as a boy in his uncle's house and knew Sir Perran well. He would always remain something of a mystery, but he knew enough not to be set from his objective by a curt dismissal, as though Blackthorn were still a schoolboy. "I am sorry for the shock I have given you," he began somewhat mockingly. "But I did not come to your study to discuss Julia with you. Instead, I wish to know why the devil you permitted Delabole to continue playing after he was so foxed he didn't know an ace from a queen. Even your friends, Lord Yarnacott and Mr. Loxhore, had grown miserably uncomfortable with the last hour of play in which one of us or you won the remainder of his stake. It was unconscionable."

"Whether last Saturday night or six months from now," Sir Perran said, opening his eyes and frowning at Blackthorn, "it would hardly have signified. He was a gamester and so deeply entrenched in his excesses that it was only a matter of time before he ruined himself. I just never thought—never dreamed—that he would take his life."

Blackthorn could tell from the distressed expression on Sir Perran's face that he was deeply disturbed by Delabole's suicide. The baronet leaned forward in his chair, his previous ease lost in the tensions of the conversation. He picked up his cherrywood cane, which had been reclining against his knee, and gently rubbed the ivory handle with the palm of his hand. He was agitated and averted his gaze as he spoke.

"I should have stopped him. I know that. I shouldn't have kept a bottle at his elbow, but I thought I was being a good host, and he always demanded more when he found the bottle empty. He was as bad as Charles Fox—four bottles a night, when he was alive and caught up in the heat of play. I know you tried to allay the inevitable with your call for Lamb's Wool. I confess I was a little shocked. But by God, it was worth it, though, to see the expression on Yarnacott's face. He can't abide the stuff. Thinks it's only for commoners. Quite caught up in his own conceit, that one. You brought him down a peg or two when you drank to his health. How can a man refuse to drink to his own health? Didn't seem to half mind the brew after that." Sir Perran chuckled faintly and finally settled back in his chair. He was silent for a moment, then added, "I meant to return what I won from him that night. I will, of course, see that Julia receives the figure."

Blackthorn did not know what to say. Julia had spoken of her father owing Sir Perran some five thousand pounds, but he now realized his uncle had no intention of demanding the sum from her. Far from it, or so it would seem. "I am glad you mean to help her, uncle," he stated quietly. "Julia is grievously distressed and your generosity will go a long way to relieving her mind."

Sir Perran's features grew quite serious for a moment as he acknowledged Blackthorn's expressed appreciation with a nod. Finally clearing his throat, he gave the subject a turn. "So tell me, Edward, what is all this business in Cornwall? A bit havey-cavey, what?"

Blackthorn found he was grateful to drop both the matter of Julia and of Lord Delabole's death. The mere mention of Cornwall brought vivid memories surging forward in his mind, of overturning the rancid fishing boat under which he and Sergeant Whitwick had remained hidden for hours on end and nudging Mr. Mawls with the toe of his boot. The smuggler had been chilled to the bone but snoring as contentedly as if he had been in his own bed.

Blackthorn had chosen to remain in Falmouth for three more days and nights. Each night, he and the sergeant had taken Mr. Mawls back to the cove and repeated the vigil in hopes that the spy would arrive. But in the end he had not.

Finally giving up hope, Blackthorn decided to return to Somerset. Once arrived and resettled in his bedchamber, he had spoken with Mr. Ladock about activities at The Priory. The revelation that since Tuesday three documents had disappeared, then reappeared, made it clear that for those days, the agent had not been in Falmouth. But what about Sunday or even Monday? Was it possible the spy had discovered the arrest of Mr. Mawls and had used a second means of transporting his information across the Channel? What to do next? he had wondered.

A few moments cogitation had given him an idea he wanted to pursue. What if the spy had gone to Falmouth but had somehow divined their trap? He would then have simply returned to The Priory and taken up where he had left off, and perhaps searched for a new connection in Cornwall. It would follow, then, that the agent must have been seen by someone when he both left and returned, but by whom?

When he had left Mr. Ladock's office and met his uncle in the drawing room where he was partaking of tea, however, Sir Perran had informed him of Lord Delabole's horrible and untimely death. He had had to set aside his desire to find out who might have been absent from The Priory on Sunday. Julia had needed him.

He glanced at his uncle now, who in turn was watching him from narrowed gray eyes. He wondered how much of his mission, if anything, he ought to reveal to the baronet. Rather than address the situation directly, he asked, "How many servants are in your employ? About thirty?"

Sir Perran lifted his brows, clearly surprised by the question. "I believe so," he responded, giving the top of his cane a slide of his thumb. "Why do you ask?"

He held his uncle's gaze steadily and decided for expediency's sake that he must now involve Sir Perran in his efforts to capture the spy. "I believe one of them has been stealing your documents, copying them, and sending them along to our Corsican friend now residing in the Mediterranean."

Sir Perran's mouth fell agape. "What?" he exclaimed. "Whatever do you mean? Are you speaking of a spy? In my home?"

"I know that you receive information from all over the world, not the least of which the military field and diplomatic reports.

Why would it surprise you then that someone could be secreted in your home for nefarious reasons?"

"I don't know," he replied slowly. The expression on his face appeared as though his thoughts were being tied up into a string of little knots. He was clearly dumbfounded by what Edward was telling him. "How do you know this? Good God! My home. A spy. Well, I suppose it would be possible, but by God . . . the thought of it! Our troops . . . good God, you've given me a fright. Are you telling me that this is what you've been doing in Cornwall? Seeking out spies?" He stared at his nephew as though he were seeing him anew. His gray eyes were wide with wonder and consternation.

Blackthorn instinctively knew he had made the right choice in telling Sir Perran of the nature of his activities in Falmouth. "I trust in your discretion."

"Yes, of course," he responded promptly. "A spy. And how long have you known of this? Then are you saying that this is the reason you have returned to The Priory after so many years?"

Blackthorn narrowed his eyes slightly. "I won't mince words. I've come home solely because Wellington ordered me to."

"I see." Again Sir Perran seemed stunned.

Blackthorn looked at him, his own thoughts taking a jump to the right. "You hurt my mother once," he stated, surprised that he had spoken the words aloud. Never before had he addressed the nature of his enmity toward his uncle.

Sir Perran's color faded as he looked at Blackthorn. A sticky silence reigned in the amber and black study. He ground his teeth together. "Your mother wounded me deeply," he said at last, his gaze unblinking. "She . . ." With great effort, he bit back the words that gathered in his mouth and set his jaw to working strongly. He could not finish his thought.

Blackthorn saw his uncle's anger, the dislike, even the hatred on his face. How dare such a cold man hate his mother, good, sweet, kind lady that she was! He rose to his feet abruptly. The conversation could not continue, that he knew. If Sir Perran was angry, Blackthorn felt years of rage suddenly rise up within his chest.

He moved away from the chair and stood by the window. It was raining. He took deep breaths, three of them, trying to calm his spirits. Odd that so few words could bring all his anger climbing to the surface of his heart again. He was a little boy once more, watching his mother cry after Sir Perran had spoken harshly to her. Her pain had become his, but he didn't know what to do with it. So he took deep breaths and with his eyes followed the raindrops as they made trails down the window.

After a quarter of an hour passed and his temper had subsided, Blackthorn returned to his chair and found his uncle had also composed himself. He was again humming a sonata and drifting his hand through the air. He sat down and cleared his throat. "I must apologize," he said quietly. "I had not intended to overset you. I don't know why I even brought Mama's memory forward."

"I've forgotten all about it," Sir Perran responded quietly.

Blackthorn looked at him, at each indifferent feature, and believed his uncle had. He then addressed the former subject. "What I wish to know, what I need to know, is whether any of your servants were absent from your home on Sunday."

"You had best speak with my housekeeper. She will know precisely who was gone and for what length of time."

"I have your permission, then?" he asked.

Sir Perran nodded, his eyes remaining closed.

"You will speak of this to no one?"

"To no one," he replied. "Now, pray leave me. I find our conversation has greatly fatigued me."

Blackthorn rose immediately and quit the chamber.

Sir Perran heard the door click shut and he opened his eyes. Almost immediately, the tears began to fall. He withdrew his cambric kerchief from the pocket of his coat and mopped his eyes, but the tears flowed on and on.

"Bah! Too much sensibility!" he cried aloud.

But for some reason, he could not stop the tears.

As Blackthorn made his way to the nether regions, seeking the housekeeper's office, he wondered how it had come about he had actually exchanged words with his uncle about his mother. The curt and quite brief exchange had left him feeling vulnerable. He wished he had kept the words unspoken. But what was done was done and now he must address a different concern entirely.

He found the housekeeper in her large, meticulous office, dozing in a rocking chair by the fireplace. She was a tall, thin woman by the name of Mrs. Petroke. Her hair was gray, and she kept it pinned tidily into a small bun at the back of her head. Her door had been ajar when Blackthorn approached it, yet she had not responded to his polite queries.

Entering the neatly furnished chamber, he touched her gently on the shoulder. Unfortunately, she awoke with a start and jumped from the chair, which caused it to rock wildly, bang into the back of her knees, and draw her into its rhythm with a stunning plop. Blackthorn couldn't help but smile at the humor of the hapless occurrence, at the same time catching both arms of the chair and steadying it to a halt.

"Oh, dear! Goodness gracious!" the woman cried, staring up in bewilderment and fright into Blackthorn's face. "Why, Major Blackthorn, whatever are you doing?"

When she clutched her shawl about her shoulders, he immediately backed away from her and flung out his hands protectively. "You are quite safe from me, I assure you," he said hastily. "I meant only to steady your chair. The door to your office was open, otherwise I would have knocked, and you did not immediately respond when I addressed you. Pray calm yourself. Do you want a little sherry or brandy perhaps?"

The lady, her small brown eyes bulging with fear, nodded several times in quick succession. Blackthorn crossed to the bellpull and within a few minutes an undermaid arrived. A few minutes more saw Mrs. Petroke sipping a small glass of cherry brandy, her color returning to her face in quick stages.

"Better?" he queried.

Mrs. Petroke nodded. "I am so sorry, Major Blackthorn. I was having the most absurd dream about flying through the clouds, and then suddenly the chair was rocking wildly and you were standing over me." She took several deep breaths and began to collect her wits. "At any rate, before I begin babbling like a fool, tell me what has brought you to my office and in what way I might serve you?" She was a gentle-tempered woman who had treated him and his brothers with great kindness when they had resided at The Priory so many years before. She summoned a faint smile, which encouraged him to continue on his quest.

"What I am going to ask you," he began, "must remain in strictest confidence between us. May I have your assurance on that?"

Her eyes opened wide again. "Indeed, yes!" she cried. "Of . . . of course! Of course!"

She listened attentively as he explained briefly his need for information regarding the whereabouts of Sir Perran's staff on Sunday. He hinted only vaguely at the possibility one of the baronet's staff might be involved in a rather harmless way with smugglers, choosing not to alarm her with information about spies and national secrets.

Mrs. Petroke was on her feet immediately, expressing her dislike of smuggling even though she was fully conversant with the fact that many approved of the activity, believing the excise taxes on most imported goods far too dear. She checked her household books, and after placing a pair of spectacles on her nose and setting a branch of candles directly over the books, she ran a quick finger down two lists of names.

She began shaking her head. "Not a one," she offered at last.

"What?" Blackthorn queried, stunned. "Are you certain? No one had the day off on Sunday?"

She lifted her brown eyes to hold his gaze steadily. "Sir Perran

prefers his staff to gather on Sundays in the chapel, where services are held for all."

"Were any absent due to ill health?" he asked.

"Two of the younger maids were in bed with . . . er . . . the
headache. But I assure you, I checked on each of them frequently
during the course of the day."

Blackthorn thought it unlikely a woman would prove to be
his spy, anyway, and was satisfied with Mrs. Petroke's information about the girls. "What about Monday?" he asked, thinking
it possible that the spy might have left late Sunday unobserved.

She turned the page in her book and read through her lists
again. "Two of the grooms were gone to Bristol in the morning—I saw them leave only because I happened to be walking
through the Home Garden. They were supposed to have returned
by eight in the evening, but you will have to speak with the head
groom if you wish to verify whether they actually did. As for
the house, neither Beeston nor myself permit the servants to be
off on Sunday or Monday. Tuesday, Wednesday, and Thursday
are the preferred days—and then, only a half day is permitted."

"I see," he responded, his gaze dropping to the wrinkles on
her thin, fine-boned hands. "Well, I have trespassed on your
evening long enough. Thank you so much for being of assistance."

"You are quite welcome—and might I add, *Master Edward,*
that it is quite pleasant to have you home again. I was sorry to
hear of your many losses, especially dear George! Always a favorite!" Tears of fondness and affection brimmed in her eyes.

On impulse, he stepped round the side of her desk and placed
a gentle kiss on her cheek. "Pray don't tell my uncle I've been
kissing you!" he admonished her teasingly, then quit the chamber.

The hour was late when Sir Perran retired to his bedchamber.
He found that once more his valet, Sutcombe, was laid up with
one of his excruciating headaches, which only a heavy dose of

laudanum seemed able to relieve. He was therefore dependent upon one of the footmen who had been trained by Sutcombe to assume his duties whenever a menacing headache afflicted him.

He had just lowered himself into a bath fragrant with oil of roses, which he had found to be one of the most pleasing rituals of his life, when he suddenly realized something was amiss.

"Sutcombe was ill on Sunday last, as well as Monday morning, wasn't he?"

"Yes, Sir Perran," the young servant named Ramsley responded.

"Good God," he murmured, staring up at the ceiling.

"Is the water not to your liking, Sir Perran?" Ramsley queried, slightly flustered.

Sir Perran didn't answer him but continued staring, his mind working in brisk twists and turns. His valet, a French agent? Was it possible? He felt sick with dread at the thought, since the first drifts of his mind took him to one battlefield after another. All these years—and it would have been years, since Sutcombe had been with him for five or six, he could not quite remember!—at any rate, all these years information would have been leaking from his house. How many British lives lost because of it! Hell and damnation!

His next thoughts were of an entirely different nature. He wanted to be of service to his country but, damme, he didn't want to inform Blackthorn of the agent's identity. He wanted nothing to do with his nephew's success on his mission. If anything, he would like to see him disgraced.

But as he shifted his hips in the steaming water, his mind turned sharply. He had followed the wars against France and Napoleon year after year and had supported financially, in every way he possibly could, every European government in its efforts to stop Bonaparte—in particular Portugal, once Wellington had seen the French armies cast out of her lands and into Spain. The thought that Bonaparte might have been benefiting from his private documents, at the very same time, made him utterly despondent. What a terrible irony, he thought, if it were true. And all this time Sutcombe must have been laughing at his efforts, at his many boasts that Bonaparte would not last forever on the French throne.

But how clever Sutcombe had been, he thought. Never once had his man betrayed his sentiments by so much as a twitch of an eye.

"Remarkable," he murmured again, lifting a silver brow.

"Sir?" Ramsley queried.

"Nothing. That is . . . fetch my nephew."

When Ramsley stared down at the soapy bath water, Sir Perran could see he was shocked. "You ought to learn from Sutcombe not to reveal your opinions by the expression on your face. Now, fetch Major Blackthorn at once! Oh, and Ladock as well. His doxy, too, if she's with him."

The tone in Sir Perran's voice sent Ramsley flying from the chamber.

A few minutes later, Sir Perran received his guests while sitting up in his tub of rose water, his arms draped over the sides, his eyes intent as he glanced from his secretary to Blackthorn to the upper maid called Susan. He ground his teeth together, then ordered Ramsley from the room before he began.

Once the door was closed upon the bewildered footman, he directed his first question to Susan. "Where is he gone?" he barked.

The maid, a pretty young woman with round hazel eyes, jumped at the sound of his voice and immediately burst into tears.

"Where has he gone?" Sir Perran shouted again, which caused both Blackthorn and Ladock to look in astonishment from the baronet to the maid.

"Who be ye referring to, Sir Perran?" she queried through her sniffles. The baronet could see she was trembling with fear.

"Is Sutcombe gone to Cornwall?"

"Aye," Susan whispered, wiping her face on the sleeve of her gown of brown stuff. "He spoke o' Falmouth. A holiday."

Mr. Ladock, who had previously been standing quite close to

the maid in support of her, now took a step away. "How do you know as much?" he queried, his dark eyes beset with the sudden pain of one who has just discovered himself betrayed.

"He forced me," she whimpered.

"Then you were the one who took the documents—and all this time . . ." His face was gray as he stared, disbelieving, at the maid.

She lowered her gaze to the floor. "He hurt me . . . he made me do everything. I didn't want to. I was afraid."

"Sutcombe, then?" Blackthorn asked, directing his question to Sir Perran. "Your valet?"

"The man has been ill for years—always with the headache— and I believed him!" Sir Perran splashed his bath water with both hands and sent a large portion flying from the tub. His lifted his knees, which rose from the water like white islands. "Damme, miss, tell us everything, or by God I'll see you hanged for treason!"

At that, the maid opened her eyes wider still, as well as her mouth, and with a shriek fell backward into a dead faint.

An hour later, Blackthorn was in a post-chaise heading south toward Falmouth.

Sir Perran retired to his bed, his thoughts torn between distress that he had harbored a traitor in his home and satisfaction that his nephew was gone at last. For several minutes, he reflected on the former, on the extraordinary fact that he had housed and fed a spy beneath his roof for so many years, along with the accompanying ramification that through his ignorance of Sutcombe's activities, he had himself been a tool in keeping Bonaparte rampaging about Europe. His agitation was great, though futile at this late hour. Yet he had never once suspected Sutcombe's true identity. The man's accent was flawless and he was the best valet he had ever had—so cool and well-ordered, so indifferent to any of his attempts over the years to disconcert the fellow. In other words, Sutcombe had been a perfect French agent.

Sir Perran could have heaped mounds of self-recrimination upon his head, but he was of a practical turn. What had happened had happened, and there was nothing to be done or undone at this late hour. After a time, therefore, he forgave himself entirely for having placed his country in jeopardy and turned to a more pleasant train of thought—the fact that Blackthorn was gone.

Sir Perran chuckled with pleasure. He would now enjoy precisely the opportunity he required to win Julia's confidence. Regardless of the intimacy she had shared with Blackthorn, Sir Perran knew that she would do her duty by her sisters first. All he had to do at this juncture was help her to see that the only way she could fulfill her duty was by marrying him. If his nephew returned before he had succeeded in leading her to the altar, then his task would be a trifle more difficult, but in no way impossible.

So strong was his confidence that he could manipulate the whole of the situation that he leaned back against his pillows with a contented sigh and, for a long moment, regarded a missive lying propped up against a tall, lit candle on the table at his bedside. His contentment deepened. The letter had been written by Blackthorn and was addressed to Julia. Beeston, knowing his duty, had most properly turned the letter over to his master instead of delivering it to Julia. Sir Perran had ordered Beeston to forget ever having seen the letter, and should Major Blackthorn inquire after it in the future, the baronet would profess an ignorance of the missive and Beeston would claim to have seen it delivered to Miss Verdell all right and tight. Who could prove their misdeed? No one. And the whereabouts of the missive would thereafter remain a mystery.

Sir Perran smiled. He enjoyed intrigue and power more than anything. Though he could admire his nephew for holding in his breast a proper affection for his country, though he valued Blackthorn's willingness to die for England, he still thought him a fool.

He adjusted his nightcap and smoothed out the gold bedcovers over his chest and stomach, then finally took the letter from the table. He broke the seal and read the contents. The text was neither long nor short, but as full of romantic nonsense as it could be. In addition, Blackthorn informed his beloved not only of his need to attend to matters of business in Cornwall again, but also that should the occasion arise, he meant to see what he could do to secure at least one contract for Delabole stone before returning to Bath—he had connections in Cornwall and Devonshire and was confident of success.

Sir Perran lifted a brow. He hadn't considered the possibility of his nephew being quite so industrious. At the same time, he thought it likely that if Blackthorn pursued this second course of action, he would be absent from Hatherleigh for an even longer period of time than Sir Perran had initially hoped.

He nearly laughed aloud with joy.

Fate was with him. He was sure of that now. He had wanted justice, and it would seem the heavens were about to grant him the justice he sought.

With infinite pleasure, he held the letter over the candle and watched as the thin paper burst into flames, the dancing line of fire eating up the paper and leaving behind a curled black refuse. Holding the missive by the seal, he ignored the singeing of the hair on the backs of his fingers. When most of the paper had been burned, he settled the charred remains on the candlestick. He then blew out the candle, thinking with delight that the smell of smoke could be a heady aroma, indeed. He fell asleep with visions of Julia speaking her vows at the altar and promising to obey him so long as she lived.

Thirteen

On the following morning, Julia awoke from a night of peaceful dreams, sat up in bed, and stretched lazily. Flopping back on her goose feather pillows, she smiled. Falling asleep the night before, she had committed every moment of her afternoon with Edward to memory. Her confession of her betrothal to Lord Peter, then the sweetness of Edward's kisses and the passionate way he had made love to her, then the long time spent exchanging vows of love and devotion afterward. They had formed a loose plan, one that she thought might just work.

On the morrow, he would drive over from his uncle's house, pick her up, and together they would go to the vicar and make arrangements to be married privately. Afterward, they would visit the most needy of Lord Delabole's creditors and see what could be contrived to stay a collection of his debts, since it would likely be demanded that Hatherleigh be sold at auction.

Julia, as the eldest surviving child, had inherited Hatherleigh Park. In all the distress surrounding her father's death, she had not realized that she was now the owner of the magnificent ancient house. Most of the lands had been sold off by now, but still, some fifty acres, the house, and all attending outbuildings belonged to her. The sale of the house would discharge most of Delabole's debts, but it seemed to Edward that by letting the house for five or ten years, a significant portion of these debts could be retired. In addition, Julia now owned the Delabole quarry, which Edward believed could be made to turn a tidy profit with the right connections.

"And I know my uncle will want to help you," Edward had said. "He holds you in considerable esteem and has said he wishes to be of assistance to you. I only wonder that he permitted your father to continue attending his card soirées when he knew of his propensity to lose at cards."

Julia remembered that Edward had grown very quiet for a time. He seemed distressed, until she again reiterated that the place of gaming meant nothing to her father. He gambled because he gambled. Yes, he had lost his fortune—and probably a portion of it to Sir Perran and his friends. Yet, how often had Sir Perran come to Hatherleigh in order to give her father a severe dressing-down about his habits? A score of times, perhaps more. And each time her father would restrain himself for a fortnight, then he would be invited to an acquaintance in Bath and would return home drunk, his pockets stuffed with vowels. No, she could not blame Sir Perran.

Edward had seemed mollified, yet she sensed he was not as convinced as she that his uncle was guiltless.

As Julia lay in bed, she felt wondrously at peace. She was sad that her father's affairs had come to such a pass that he would feel he had no alternative but to end his life. A ripple of guilt passed through her. The truth was, she felt relieved that he was gone. No longer would she have to wonder and worry and fret about her father's comings and goings. He could sink their circumstances no further than they were; he could no longer badger her for a ring he had already stolen from her. Yes, she felt guilty, yet not. Had he lived, how would he have discharged his debts or seen to his daughters' futures? No, what was done was done, and she would not repine.

Later that afternoon, when Sir Perran came to call, she received him in the crimson and gold drawing room. He seemed surprised by her manners. "You seem almost happy, my dear. And I have not seen you so lighthearted in a very long time."

She sat opposite him, serving tea in her black silk mourning gown, sitting forward on a red silk damask sofa. She was pouring a cup of tea, a silver teapot angled over the cup, but at his words she paused and looked at him. "Do I?" she queried softly, feeling a faint twinge of guilt, which she quickly set aside. "I suppose I am; though if I told you the reason, you would probably think poorly of me."

"I can guess," he said gently, accepting the cup from her. He laid his cane alongside his white and gold striped silk chair and sipped the strong, fragrant tea. "A little more milk, please," he requested, handing the cup back to her. Julia added the milk, watching him until he nodded. She returned the tea to him. He smiled, very contentedly. "Now let me attempt to comprehend you. The shock of your father's needless death has begun to subside, and though you miss him, the troubles he brought to his home, which have lain so squarely upon your shoulders, can get no worse than they are today. You are beginning to realize that your life can commence and you feel relieved—but not without experiencing occasional bouts of guilt."

She sat very straight while he spoke, her own cup of tea poised halfway to her lips. "How perceptive you are," she said, a little in awe of him. "Those were precisely my thoughts. But I have a confession to make, one about which you are probably already informed."

He smiled faintly. "You and Edward are to be married."

She nodded, smiled, and sipped her tea.

His gray eyes glittered in the afternoon light streaming in from the window at Julia's back. "You do not intend to wait the proper mourning period?"

She shook her head. "It seems pointless somehow, since Papa has so plunged us into scandal by taking his own life." She found herself surprised at how easily she could speak of his death, as though it had happened years ago instead of just a few days past. Julia realized in a moment of insight that for the past two years, for months and weeks on end, she had been shedding her tears of grief for her father. In a way, he had been dead to her for a long time.

"I suppose I should do the same if a similar, most unfortunate experience had ever afflicted me," he returned easily. "By the way, you do know he is gone."

Julia only barely withheld a gasp as she clattered her cup against her saucer. "Gone? You mean Edward?"

"Yes," he offered blandly, taking another sip. "To Cornwall again, I suppose. He always was a rather adventuresome sort of man. Even as a child, he would dart off here and there and be gone for hours at a time. But tell me, how do you mean to survive, you and my nephew? He has scarcely a farthing to call his own. I trust the two of you have discussed your future."

Julia was so thrown by learning Edward had again left her that she didn't stop to consider whether it would be appropriate to discuss their plans with Sir Perran. Instead, perhaps in hopes of setting aside the doubts that suddenly assailed her, she launched into a recounting of their every scheme.

Sir Perran encouraged her to talk, offering perceptive questions about the quarry, about letting Hatherleigh, about the remaining acreage, so that even had she felt a mild reluctance to reveal their ideas, his gentle manner of praising her sensible train of thought, then making suggestions of his own led her on and on, until he knew everything. "So you see, given time, we should be able to bring about what is left of the Delabole legacy."

"An admirable plan, except . . ." He paused, his brow furrowed.

"What is it?" Julia asked. "Please tell me. Do not fear that I will dislike anything you feel ought to be said at this juncture. We are both of us, your nephew and I, untried in these matters."

"Well," he began firmly, "yes, you are. For one thing, it may take a year or two, as I have said before, until you are able to find a suitable lessee for the Park. And as for the quarry, at one time it was functioning at peak operation because Bath was growing so quickly. But unless I much mistake the matter, fewer and fewer truly genteel Londoners have begun to frequent our beloved Aquae Sulis. You are perhaps too young to have noticed a change—Bath is as it always has been to you. But when I was young—oh, my dear! Everyone went to Bath."

He seemed to fall into a brief reverie. Julia set her cup on her saucer and placed both pieces of pure white china on the table in front of her. She admired Sir Perran so very much that if he thought the difficulties before her might still prove insuperable, then how would she manage? "I see," she said softly.

"Oh, now there! Look what I have done. I have dashed your hopes. No, no! You mustn't listen to an old man like me. I'll tell you what I'll do, especially since that nephew of mine has disappeared again and left you to your own devices. Why don't you and I go into the city tomorrow and call on a few friends of mine, a Bath official or two, and see precisely what the possibilities are where your quarry is concerned?"

"Would you do that, indeed?" she asked, her heart light again. "That would be wonderful. How very kind you are."

He rose from his chair, supporting himself with his cane. He rounded the table that separated them and stood over her. Sir Perran took her hand in his and lifted it to his lips. "My dear, I would give you the world were it in my power." He then held her gaze for a long, lingering moment. "In fact, there was a time when I . . . but this is nonsense. Only believe that I will do anything to see you happy."

How strange of him to say such things to her, she thought, almost as though he was in love with her. And the look in his eyes! But this was such an absurd notion that she dismissed it entirely. When they had agreed on the time he would stop by and take her up in his carriage, he left.

At dusk of that evening, Blackthorn's coach rolled through the grassy valley just outside of Polperro, which deepened and narrowed with each turn of the wheels. Small white and cream cottages either clung to the hillsides or fronted the River Pol—more a brook than anything greater—that coursed through the center of the valley. The river arrived at the sea, opening up to a wide harbor surrounded by steep hills. The small fishing village looked like a town all piled up on itself, and the harbor mouth was so narrow that in rough weather the sea could be shut away from the village by stout timbers fitted into slots.

The journey south had been tiresome and frustrating. Blackthorn had not trusted the maid's information that Sutcombe was returning to Falmouth. From the start of his journey, he had inquired at every posting inn whether a man of Sutcombe's description had been seen passing through. The valet's quiet, elegant demeanor and fashionable clothes set him apart, making him a traveler easier to remember than most.

He had spent two hours at Bodmin in the heart of Cornwall, determining through his efforts that the spy had taken a sharp, unexpected easterly turn. Sutcombe was no fool. The villages of Liskeard and Looe finally led him to Polperro Harbor and to the end of his journey. There was nowhere else for the spy to go.

The sun was setting quickly and before long Blackthorn would have no light with which to discover Sutcombe's whereabouts. The streets were so narrow that he was forced to leave his carriage at a tavern and continue the remainder of his trek on foot down the steep, cobbled streets. He carried a pistol with him, which would be useful for only one shot. He had no idea whether Sutcombe would be armed. Blackthorn headed for the harbor, where row upon row of small fishing boats were anchored, pilchard fishing being the primary industry of the coastal hamlet.

But smuggling was a pastime for many of the inhabitants as well, especially anyone unconcerned about the nature of his boat's cargo such as a man requiring transportation to the Continent. Unfortunately, the houses, shored up with stone, butted against the harbor. The individual dwellings had sole access to the boats and to the sea. Polperro was an exceedingly private community and perfectly situated for smuggling.

Sutcombe had chosen well. A walking tour of the small town convinced Blackthorn his task was only half complete after all.

He returned to the tavern and requested information of a reluctant landlord, who served him a pint of ale with a cold gleam in his black eyes.

The landlord stared hard at him for a long moment, then directed him to two men seated in a corner of the tavern. "Preventive officers" was all the man would say.

Blackthorn turned to observe the two men who were watching him curiously. He did not hesitate to approach them and, in low tones, explained the essentials of his difficulties. One of the men grew animated. He was of medium height and rather plump, with laughing blue eyes and a red stubble on his chin. "I saw the man you were looking for," he said. "He rode in on a cart, conspicuous in his fine clothes. But it was his air that struck me—quite above his company. Curious that, and to think him a spy. But he didn't stay in Polperro. He headed west to Lansallos. There's a church there, a mile away, and a stretch of sandy beaches below."

"How long ago?" Blackthorn queried, his heart sinking.

"An hour, mebbee two."

He didn't wait to exchange pleasantries, but hurried from the town and began a swift march along the cliffs in a westerly direction, the light failing in quick stages. The beach below the church at Lansallos was empty. He continued on, walking for another half mile or so. From a cove below, he could see a faint glow on a small, jutting stretch of sand. His heart began to beat soundly in his chest as it always did before a battle. He picked his way down a well-worn path, the salty sea air in his nostrils, and quickly reached the bottom. There he saw two men standing together, a few yards from the surf, a lantern between them.

Blackthorn recognized Sutcombe at once, even with his back to him. He was a short, sturdy man with the bearing of a prince, as befitted a gentleman's valet.

The beach was composed of part rock and part sand. Crossing it would be an awkward business. He dropped down just behind a grassy outcropping and loaded and primed his pistol. The men were little more than thirty yards from him, but the constant crash, roll, and drift of the surf kept them unaware of his presence. His heart was now pounding in his throat as he held his pistol carefully in hand.

The men stood at ease, speaking in low tones, apparently unconcerned that they might be discovered. A fair-sized fishing boat lay anchored just beyond the unnavigable waves and a small rowboat sat angled on the rock and sand, the surf tugging at it gently but ineffectively.

Blackthorn watched the men embrace as though old friends. He began to cross the beach toward them, picking his way through soft, sandy places among the rocks, his body tucked in, his head bowed, his pistol held low but in front of him.

"Mon dieu!" the stranger suddenly cried out, as Blackthorn reached the perimeter of lantern light. The stranger gave Sutcombe a shove, pushing him out of harm's way, at the same time drawing a knife from a belt at his waist. He lifted the weapon with a swift jerk, preparing to throw.

Blackthorn fell to his left and fired at the man at the same time. He felt the blade whiz by him and clink into the rocks and sand beyond. The stranger fell backward into the sand near the boat. He didn't stir.

Sutcombe now faced Blackthorn. "So you've come for me, is that it, Major Blackthorn?" the valet cried.

"Yes," Blackthorn returned coldly, dropping his now-useless pistol and walking steadily toward him. A glimmer caught his eye and with a quick glance, he ascertained that Sutcombe was armed with a knife bearing a long, thin blade.

Blackthorn set his jaw and prepared for battle. As he walked toward Sutcombe, he tossed his hat aside and removed his coat, carrying it in his right hand for protection against the knife. "You will return with me, Sutcombe—or whatever your name might be. Your work is finished here and in France as well."

Sutcombe dropped into a crouch. "I'll not go," he responded, digging in his heels and leaning forward. The yellow light from the lantern cast the relief of his face in eerie shadows, the expression of his dark eyes cloaked in the uneven darkness. He gave a brisk tug on his hat and sent it flying into the sand, afterward removing his coat.

Blackthorn stopped eight feet away from his prey. The sensations of the surf beyond, the salt-laden wind through the fine white linen of his shirt, the soft sand beneath his feet, all disappeared as he, too, folded into a taut crouch. He moved to the right, Sutcombe to the left. His eyes never left Sutcombe's face. His heart began to pound in his chest.

Sutcombe smiled faintly.

Blackthorn moved slowly, his coat clutched tightly in his hand. He moved behind the lantern, which now separated him from Sutcombe. The oil wick, protected by glass from the breeze, burned steadily. From his peripheral vision, he watched the blade shift and turn in the spy's hand, not nervously but in a practiced manner. Blackthorn saw the confident movement. His throat began to throb with fear. He could die tonight, came a thought, which he quickly banished.

He had only one chance to vanquish the skilled man before him. In a quick movement, he darted to the right of the lantern, turned his side to Sutcombe, and, with a rapid jerk, swept his coat over the blade.

The coat fell away from the knife as Sutcombe lunged toward him. Blackthorn caught his wrist. The spy fell on him, his knee gouging his right thigh. Blackthorn groaned in pain, rolled, and pushed Sutcombe on his back, struggling to keep the blade at bay, his hand still gripping the spy's wrist tightly.

The next moment was a blur, as his eyes and nose became crusted with wet sand the spy had thrown at him. Blackthorn couldn't see. He felt Sutcombe's wrist close in on him. He sat up and straddled the spy, using both hands to keep the valet's powerful arm from sliding the knife home.

He forced Sutcombe to roll with him to the right, setting the arm with the knife off balance. Blackthorn released one of his hands and felt in the sand for a rock or a jagged shell. He still couldn't see. He found a rock and as Sutcombe slipped away, he lunged and struck out instinctively toward the man's head.

He connected, with what he didn't know, and immediately fell back, wiping his eyes with his shirtsleeve.

He was on his knees when his vision cleared sufficiently to see Sutcombe, also on his knees, reeling forward, clutching his head. The spy shook his head, clearing his senses, searching for but not finding the knife in the sand about him.

Blackthorn dove toward him. Sutcombe cried out, fell backward out of his reach, and grasped the lantern. He threw it in a quick movement but it missed Blackthorn, shattering instead against the boat beyond, sending oil and fire in a smoky hiss over the damp wood.

Blackthorn fell on his enemy and drove his fist into the side of Sutcombe's face. He was breathing hard. He felt the spy's thick fist pound his own chin. Blackthorn flew to the right, into the sand.

Sutcombe scrambled on top of him and with a heavy fist slammed into his face. Blackthorn felt a gray mist descend over his mind as another blow to his cheek brought a rushing sound that filled his head.

He fought to retain consciousness, but his will began to slip away. He heard Julia's sweet voice deep within his mind. Where was she? He had to get back and help her. She was desperate for his help. He began to strike back, thwarting blows wildly. *Julia.* Anger filled him that this man meant to separate him from Julia forever.

"Vive l'Empereur!" the spy cried victoriously.

The words came to Blackthorn through a wall of pain, drawing his rage into a shaft of hatred. He saw Bonaparte, living comfortably on his little island with his sixty-five servants, and he caught Sutcombe's arms and hissed into his face. "Death to your emperor," he cried.

Blackthorn was no longer one man, he was *every* Englishman intent upon ending the reign of a madman. A spirit of heat and victory flooded his veins. He was light, resilient, a star shooting through the heavens as he lunged at the vile man before him. The madness that filled him became a devil's wind in the sand.

Against the flames now shooting up brightly from the burning boat, Blackthorn struck the spy again and again, fending off his blows as though he knew precisely beforehand where each one would land. He didn't feel his feet. As he moved about, his boots were one with the sand and the earth. He watched Sutcombe pick up a shard of glass, and with a deft movement he kicked his wrist and the glass fell harmlessly away. Sutcombe's face was bruised and bloody as Blackthorn pursued him. The spy stumbled backward, the blows he returned ever more awkward and ineffective.

He was dazed and fell into the sand, on his side.

Blackthorn moved to stand over him, his own fists bloodied and cut. Only then did he see that Sutcombe had found the knife. As the man thrust his arm awkwardly toward his legs, Blackthorn jumped lightly back.

It was over. Sutcombe remained inert, breathing raggedly. His face was half in the sand as he looked up from swollen, bleeding eyes and smiled. He gazed into the night sky. Stars shone brightly, the moon just rising in the east. The man began murmuring through thickened lips. Blackthorn thought he heard, "A pleasant night to die."

"You're not dying, at least not tonight," he returned curtly. He was about to step on Sutcombe's wrist and dispossess the spy of his knife, when Sutcombe suddenly rose up onto his elbows and drove the knife into his own throat.

Blackthorn turned him over and quickly withdrew the knife, but saw that his aim had been true. He would be dead within a minute or two, if that long.

Sutcombe watched him. His lips moved, but no air could pass from his lungs to give voice to his words. Blackthorn knew what he was saying, however. There could be no mistaking *Vive l'Empereur.* Bonaparte was beloved among his army.

He sank back into the sand and clasped his bloodied hands about his knees. He began to shake and to weep as Sutcombe's lifeblood departed his body, forming a pool in the wet sand.

Fourteen

On the following day, when Julia returned from her less than fruitful excursion to Bath with Sir Perran, she sank down on the edge of her bed, her bonnet dangling to the floor from long black ribbons, her gaze settled on a strip of golden light that shone onto the floor of her bedchamber through a narrow aperture in her drapes. She could see dust swirling around within the beam of light. She whisked her bonnet absently toward the beam and watched the dust boil and swirl a little more. Julia felt like a speck of dust at this moment, turned over and over by the mere whisk of a bonnet, by the kindly expressed regrets of the city manager that there was little building at present in Bath, by an agent who shook his head sadly a dozen times over at the impossibility of letting the Park.

"Years, Miss Verdell," the agent had said. "I'm very sorry I can't offer you even the smallest hope of something sooner."

Sir Perran had been supportive and kind, even offering his shoulder for her to lean on when he saw her eyes filling with tears. What would she do without him? He had even hinted again that were he younger . . . She supposed he meant he would offer for her, kind soul that he was. It was no wonder that her father had counted him chief among his friends.

But what was to be done now with her own trying circumstances?

If only Edward were here, Julia thought. She stretched out on the bed, letting the ugly black silk bonnet drop to the floor. Gabrielle had been kind enough to fashion several bonnets for

Julia, as well as for her sisters, but nothing could make her feel happy about wearing black. Her fair skin and auburn hair seemed to turn gray when pitted against black. She despised the color; she wished never to see it again.

Julia turned on her side and felt tears begin to collect in the corners of her eyes, some seeping over the bridge of her nose to eventually trail into her hair and dampen her pillow. Whatever was she going to do?

Sir Perran did not immediately return to his home after seeing Julia safely delivered to Hatherleigh. Instead, he had a brief mission to accomplish and made his way back to Bath, where he paid a call on the postmaster general. After a brief exchange of pleasantries and a simple explanation of what he required of him, Sir Perran gave his old friend a gift of one hundred pounds—a tidy sum that he knew was likely to appeal to the man's avaricious wife. In exchange for his *gift*, the postmaster general promised to lend his attention to a matter of the utmost delicacy—the withholding of certain letters from Hatherleigh Park. By the time he bid *adieu* to his friend, Sir Perran knew he could now expect to receive all the mail sent by Blackthorn to Julia.

How simple life could be with just a little money and a kindly word or two.

A week later, when Edward had neither returned to Bath nor sent a letter to Julia explaining the reason for his sudden departure—indeed, what now seemed to be his complete disappearance—she began to grow anxious. She could understand a week's delay on a matter of business; she could even forgive him for being so thoughtless as to not have informed her of his comings and goings. But when eight days became nine, then ten and eleven, her heart began to grow cold and hard. With the passing of each hour, with the increase in frequency of the as-

saults of the tradesmen, with the continued kindnesses of Sir
Perran in marked contrast to Edward's absence, a veneer of stone
began forming about the tender feelings she held toward the
man she had already permitted to rob her of her innocence.

Smuggling. Sir Perran had uttered the word with a despairing
frown. "What else could it be?" he had asked her, apparently
as perplexed as she.

She didn't know. To some degree, it didn't matter what the
devil he was doing. All she knew was that she needed him here
and he was not here, and she hadn't the vaguest idea of where
he might be or where she might reach him if her circumstances
became desperate.

Sir Perran, on the other hand, had scarcely left her side. If he
was not in attendance on Julia and her sisters at Hatherleigh, he
invited them to be his guests at The Priory. He complimented
all of them on their elegant morning gowns and bonnets that
they had fashioned themselves; he applauded enthusiastically
their performances on the harp and pianoforte; he provided a
string ensemble for their enjoyment. And the food he served
strictly for their pleasure was beyond description.

He teased Annabelle about wrinkling her nose when she
laughed; he gave Caroline permission to make use of his stables
whenever she wished, which was frequently, to be sure; he spent
hours playing backgammon and cribbage with Elizabeth, who
seemed to delight in teasing him. He was in every respect the
father Julia had needed but never had when her mother died.

When a fortnight had passed and Sir Perran at his most solemn
offered to relieve her of all responsibility, she was neither surprised nor entirely opposed to the match.

The arrangement was suggested from affection and from a
belief that he could provide the security she and her sisters so
desperately required, especially in the face of his nephew's unin-
terested conduct. He wished for children, of course. She would
provide them, of course. He would dower each of the sisters
handsomely and would see to every particular of their futures,
especially guaranteeing a London season next spring. He would

settle all her father's debts. Julia thanked him effusively for his generosity and kindness; she told him she would give him an answer in a few days.

A week later, in mid-July, Julia awaited her sisters in the morning room. She felt life changing all about her as she glanced about the square chamber. The room was the same as it had always been, a pretty combination of draperies, chairs, and sofas upholstered in a lovely deep blue silk damask, laid against tables and chairs of a gleaming cherrywood. But she felt the chamber was different somehow, because she was different, and the eyes through which she was looking were no longer eyes of hope. Yet she was not sad, merely accepting of what she now realized had been the inevitable all along.

Her sisters entered the chamber, each dressed in somber black silk. She bid them take up a chair about the round table, which sat below a portrait of the family as it had been some five years earlier—mother and father, two hopeful young brothers, four sisters—and for the first time she explained to them at length precisely what the true state of their affairs were. She dwelt lightly on their father's unfortunate habits, especially since the manner of his death had already forced to some degree a revelation of the conduct that had precipitated his suicide.

Elizabeth, who was already fully informed, stared at the silver epergne in the middle of the table and remained silent. The younger sisters both appeared as though Julia had taken a heavy stick and had begun beating them with it.

Caroline's blue eyes filled with tears. She couldn't speak. But Annabelle's jaw grew stiff. "We are ruined?" she cried. "Utterly? How could Papa have been so improvident? I don't understand. You always used to practice economies, and I thought you were being overly cautious simply because Mama had died. Why didn't you tell me? Julia, you can't know the bitterness I've harbored toward you these past two years, not permitting me to go to the dressmaker's in Bath any longer—and I so loved having my gowns made up by our modiste!" Her speech was disjointed, her green eyes darting from one sister's face to the next. "We are ruined?" she repeated again, apparently wanting to make certain she had indeed understood what Julia had just said to her.

Julia nodded. "Perhaps I should have told you sooner, just as you've said, but I did so want to find a way out of this bumblebroth without disturbing your lives completely. I felt it was my duty to protect you as much as I could."

Caroline dabbed at her tears. "Yes, you most certainly should have told us. When I think of the fripperies I have purchased this past year alone—"

"What fripperies?" Annabelle cried. All three sisters stared at Caroline in disbelief. Of the four young ladies, Caroline rarely bought anything of a frivolous nature.

She sniffed. "I bought a locket in January, and . . . and just before Christmas some silver lace merely because . . . because it sparkled!" She began sniffling again.

Caroline was astonished when all three sisters laughed at her.

Elizabeth reached over to her and pinched her cheek playfully. "How could you have been so thoughtless!" she cried, facetiously. "Why, I am persuaded we shouldn't be ruined at all if you had not let that silver lace catch your eye! Silly goose!"

At that, Caroline smiled and blew her nose. "I suppose it does sound rather absurd. It's just that I . . . I had no idea. Dear Julia, whatever do you mean to do, especially since—"

She could not finish the thought. Even Annabelle squirmed in her seat slightly. Julia saw that all eyes were turned in her direction, wondering, wanting to ask about Edward but afraid to.

She took a deep breath. "I suppose it is very simple after all: Major Blackthorn is simply not as reliable as I had at first supposed. I had wanted him to be someone I could depend upon—so very much!—but alas he is not such a man." Speaking the words aloud caused her throat to tighten ominously. She averted her gaze out the window, which overlooked the green lawn and parkland beyond. The deer were still feeding in the tall grasses behind the groomed hedgerow. She took a deep breath, ordering her mind to feel as tranquil as the scene outside.

"I love him," she stated. "You all know as much. But I suppose some things are simply not meant to be. I have not withheld knowledge from him, either. He knows of our circumstances. So, perhaps he became overwhelmed, as Lord Peter did, with the enormity of our problems here and has simply failed to return. Can anyone blame him? Were I a man and the woman I loved carried with her a mountain of debt and a scandal that will always attach to her name, would I have the courage to remain at her side? I don't know. All I know is that I shall miss him terribly."

At that, Elizabeth rose from her chair and placed her arm about Julia's shoulder. "It isn't fair! I know how hard you tried to keep Papa in check. But what of the emerald ring? If you still have the ring, perhaps we, together, could open a shop. We certainly have enough sewing skill among the four of us to clothe all the fashionable ladies of our acquaintance. Gabrielle would certainly come with us, and you know how everyone has always exclaimed over her bonnets. Have you thought of that?"

Julia looked up into Elizabeth's hopeful face. It was a wonderful, appealing idea. But her experience with Sir Perran warned her that however enticing a notion might be, until you thoroughly investigated all the obstacles involved, you couldn't possibly know whether such an idea would thrive.

"We could charge a fortune, too!" Annabelle cried, her green eyes sparkling. "Certainly enough to live on."

Julia patted Elizabeth's hand, that still embraced her shoulder, and reached across the table to take Annabelle's hand in hers. "And who would marry you, Annabelle, and give you the children you have talked about ever since you were old enough to know from whence they came?"

Annabelle opened her mouth to speak, then clamped her lips shut. Who would marry her? A lady of gentle birth engaged in trade, whose father—though a peer of the realm—had shot him-

self in the head because of gaming debts he could not discharge.
"No one," she answered sorrowfully, awareness striking her
hard. "At least no one of my acquaintance."

"Precisely," Julia responded gently.

"I shall become a governess," Caroline announced.

Julia chuckled. "Unlike Annabelle, you start whenever a child
enters a room, and you ought to know that governesses are not
generally permitted a run of the stables."

"It doesn't matter," Caroline returned firmly, clasping her
hands tightly together on her lap. "Earlier, you spoke of duty.
But you are not the only one to have a duty in this situation. We
are all afflicted in the same way by Papa's death. We should each
then work to find a way out of this morass. I, for one, shall
become a governess."

"Well," Elizabeth said, "I would by far prefer to shave my
head bald than do any such thing. If I could, I would style my
hair *à la Brutus,* dress up in a man's clothes, and sign aboard a
ship."

"I still think we should open a millinery or a dressmaker's
shop," Annabelle said.

Julia now presented her idea. "I have a much simpler and
much wiser solution. One that I had never even dreamed would
come my way. Not once had it occurred to me that there might
be a man—a gentleman—waiting on the fringes of my society,
with sufficient wealth to settle our troubles forever and who
would be willing to offer for me. But so there seems to be."

"Indeed!" Elizabeth cried, stunned yet hopeful.

"Who is it?" Caroline asked, bewildered.

"Is he a man of sufficient fortune to repair so much damage?"
Annabelle asked, her practical side asserting itself.

"He is wealthy beyond measure."

All three sisters stared at her, utterly confounded. Julia smiled,
realizing that just as not one of them could begin to guess to
whom she referred, she had never considered Sir Perran as a
potential suitor or husband.

"Sir Perran has asked for my hand in marriage," she announced. "I mean to accept of his kind offer, but I wanted all of you to first know why, then to believe me when I say that I am persuaded no man will be kinder or more generous than Sir Perran."

She could see by the expressions on each of their faces that she had shocked them completely.

"No," Elizabeth cried, immediately distressed. "You are in love with his nephew."

"Oh, no," Caroline said, shaking her head, tears again starting to her eyes.

"You mustn't," Annabelle added, tears springing to her eyes as well.

Julia was shocked. She hadn't expected such an immediate negative. "Don't be goosecaps at this eleventh hour," she adjured them firmly. "I can't imagine why you have responded with such unhappy expressions. You can see he is the perfect solution. Please stop weeping! Elizabeth, Caroline, Annabelle, I need your love and support in this moment. Marriage to a man older than my father was not part of my girlhood dreams, but so it must be and will be. And I will be happy, I promise you."

Elizabeth rose from the table and left the room without saying another word. Annabelle began to weep aloud.

Caroline continued to shake her head. "You don't know him," she said urgently, leaning forward in her chair.

"What do you mean?" Julia queried, astonished. "I know him very well. He alone has stood beside me during these past months since father died."

"Blackthorn will return," Caroline declared. "I am convinced of it. Something has gone awry to prevent him. That is all. You must wait. He will have a reasonable explanation. Julia, you must wait. He is the man to trust, not Sir Perran."

Julia was bemused, particularly since she rarely saw Caroline so agitated. "Where do these ill opinions come from?" she asked. Diverted for a moment by Annabelle's sobs, she withdrew a kerchief from the sleeve of her black gown and handed it to the youngest sister. Returning her attention to Caroline, she continued: "You have seen Sir Perran every day, every week, for years. Why are you hinting that he is not trustworthy when all evidence suggests otherwise?"

Caroline looked away from Julia and took a deep breath. Her blue eyes took on a faraway appearance, as though she was searching for the truth within herself. "I don't know," she murmured at last. "It is an instinct only. Perhaps it is because he was never married before and I find that very odd, no matter the reasons he has ventured for remaining so long unwed."

"Do you suppose he does not like women, then?" Julia queried softly. She had wondered as much herself upon occasion.

"No, I am not suggesting anything of the sort," Caroline returned, a faint blush creeping up her cheeks. "It is just . . . well, I have seen him look at you from time to time, and there is often something in his expression of . . . of calculation. I cannot explain it."

"Calculation?" Julia laughed, for she was dumbfounded by what she was hearing. "To what purpose, then, would he possibly be working to have designs upon me? He has known of my circumstances from the first—before Mama died. How can a man have anything but an honorable purpose and affection in his heart in asking a lady to marry him when such horrible scandal and debt attaches to that lady?"

"I don't know," Caroline responded, looking deeply into Julia's eyes and causing a spattering of gooseflesh to travel down her neck and side. "I just believe it is so."

Silence reigned in the morning room, except for the sound of Annabelle's gentle sobs. After a moment, the youngest sister blew her nose and summed up the entire conversation: "You will be marrying an old man."

Three days later, when Edward still had not returned to her, Julia married Sir Perran in the old Norman chapel near his manor house. Only the sisters were present. The occasion was solemn, everyone dressed in black because of Lord Delabole's death, and joy eluded the day.

Julia had done her duty. And she would continue to do so, as long as she lived. The vows she had spoken to Sir Perran she intended to keep forever.

Three days following the ceremony found Julia in the library at The Priory, arranging long-stemmed red roses in a white vase. She stood near the windows that overlooked the fine avenue of beech trees leading to the front door of the house. Humming a favorite ballad, "How Sweet in the Woodlands," she bid her thoughts remain within The Priory walls and attendant upon her new duties as mistress of the lovely manor house. If her thoughts strayed, nine out of ten to Edward—wondering where he was, if he would return, and what he would think of her when he discovered she had married his uncle—she simply bid such errant, unhappy reflections to cease. She was married; she had made the only decision possible under the circumstances, she would be happy, and Edward would one day find it in his heart to forgive her.

Julia paused in her task and glanced around the elegant chamber. Books climbed from floor to ceiling, tangible evidence of Sir Perran's commitment to building a fine library. Apricot silk draperies complemented a plasterwork ceiling painted in a matching color. On the gleaming planked floor, a carpet of rich hues—apricots, golds, deep blues—ran the length of the long rectangular chamber. Comfortable winged chairs in a midnight blue velvet were gathered cozily about an empty fireplace, a promise to Julia of the pleasures she would find by drawing near on a wintry evening in front of a warm, well-built fire, with words her sole companions on adventures intellectual, romantic, moral, and spiritual. She thought it likely she would spend much of her time in this welcoming chamber.

A sound caught her ear, of a horse's hooves pounding the gravel of the drive. She glanced over her shoulder out the window and saw a man on horseback, galloping at full speed down the avenue. Julia felt suddenly overwhelmed with physical sickness.

She gasped and her hands jerked, the vase shattering over the table, white china shards and red roses swimming in a pool of water.

There was no mistaking the man astride the horse. Edward had come home.

Fifteen

Blackthorn was delirious with joy. He had accomplished so much in so little time that he could hardly wait to speak with Julia and tell her all.

When he had first arrived in Somerset, he had traveled straight to Hatherleigh Park, but his reception had been curiously strained. Grigson had been entirely elusive as to Julia's whereabouts and had directed him to speak with Elizabeth. Yet Elizabeth had been even less forthcoming, her expression deeply troubled by his sudden appearance. She had refused to respond to his inquiries regarding Julia's health, her happiness, or the condition of affairs at Hatherleigh, stating as though by way of explanation that her sister had gone to his uncle's house and she was certain he could find her there.

But what was there in this to so distress Elizabeth?

Blackthorn, for one, was not surprised his betrothed was visiting Sir Perran. She had always counted his uncle among her friends. But he couldn't help but wonder what the devil was wrong with the inmates of Hatherleigh. He supposed Julia would tell him once he found her.

When he turned over the reins of his horse to one of Sir Perran's footmen, Edward bounded up the three shallow tiers of golden stone steps, that rose to the front door, bid a curt hallo to Beeston, then asked sharply where Miss Verdell might be found.

Beeston lifted a stunned brow, opened his mouth to speak

and, after apparently choosing to refrain from his initial response, said, "I believe she is in the library, arranging roses."

"Indeed," Blackthorn replied warmly. He thought it generous of her to be arranging flowers for his uncle, yet how very much like Julia always to be thinking of the pleasure and comfort of others.

Joy filled his heart at the thought of her, of her excellent character, of her passionate nature, of her desire to become his wife. He waved aside Beeston's offer to announce him. Taking the stairs two at a time, Blackthorn was soon in the library, crossing the room on a run, delighting in the astonished expression on her face as he took her swiftly in his arms.

He kissed her thoroughly, then drew back to look at her for a long, hungry moment. Falling into her beautiful green eyes, he forgave her instantly for not having responded to the numerous letters he had sent her. He had stayed in Polperro for three days and, with the assistance of the preventive officers, had tended to Sutcombe and his compatriot. Later, when his affairs took him to Plymouth, he remained there an entire fortnight, hoping to receive word from her. He had sensed something was amiss and felt he ought to return to Hatherleigh immediately. But he stayed the impulse, determined to have at least one contract for Delabole stone in hand before heading north to Somerset.

Oh, but how sweet it was to hold Julia in his arms after so much time had passed. Again he kissed her, thinking that as soon as he had held her long enough, when he had embraced her until he was satisfied, he would whisk her off to the vicar and set a day for their nuptials.

Only after he had kissed her neck, her cheek, her nose, her eyes, did he come to realize something was wrong. Julia was not the yielding creature he had left behind, who had so enveloped him in passion that he had taken from her what he should not have.

How stiff her arms felt across his back.

He drew back from her slightly so that he might look into her eyes again, this time to discern her thoughts. But she wouldn't meet his gaze. She released his back and clasped his forearms tightly with her hands, but there was no love in her touch. Only distance and fright.

"What is it?" he asked abruptly. "What is wrong? Why will you not look at me?"

"I can't," she responded in a whisper, her complexion ashen.

"Look at me, and none of this gammon, if you please! Julia, look at me!"

Julia lifted her gaze slowly, until he was regarding green eyes so lost, so hopeless, that panic seized him.

"Oh, you've been hurt," she said, taking in the fading bruises on his face. "Edward, what were you doing all this time in Cornwall? Were you . . . were you involved with smugglers?"

"Well . . . yes," he replied, frowning.

"You mean you've taken to smuggling, then, because you are impoverished?"

"Good God, no! Of course not. As it happens, I was sent by Wellington to uncover a French agent who has been smuggling documents out of England. He turned out to be my uncle's valet. But all of that is settled."

If Julia was pale before, her complexion turned white, the expression in her green eyes acutely miserable. "I didn't know why you'd gone," she murmured. "Even if I'd known this much . . . your purposes in going . . ."

The panic he felt earlier grew in quick stages. Why hadn't she written to him? "Never mind that now. Only tell me what is going forward! Why do you look at me like that?"

"I am not free," she responded, still on a whisper, her eyes widening, a sob catching in her throat. She tried to draw back from him, but he caught her around the waist and held her against him.

"What do you mean? Speak, Julia! What has happened since I left? Why did you not write to me as I asked you to? I waited a fortnight in Plymouth, but nothing. Tell me, what has happened that you look as though you are holding a specter in your arms!"

"I . . . I don't know what you mean. You waited in Plymouth?" Her pretty face was a mask of confusion.

"Oh, hallo, Edward."

Startled by the sound of his uncle's voice, Blackthorn turned toward the doorway and watched Sir Perran enter the library. "Uncle," he responded flatly by way of acknowledgment. He was irritated that his uncle had so rudely interrupted what even a simpleton would comprehend was an understandably private moment. "Would you excuse us, please?" he continued. "I must speak with Julia. It would seem something is distressing her." Much to his surprise she tried to pull away from him, but he held her fast, not wanting to release her, afraid for some reason to let her go.

His uncle's response surprised him as well, for he did not leave the library as Blackthorn had requested. Instead, Sir Perran continued advancing into the room, moving carefully among the dark blue velvet-covered chairs, taking pains that his cane did not strike the fine wood legs as he passed by.

"Perhaps Julia is distressed because you are holding her in an intimate embrace, and she knows that to be very wrong," Sir Perran finally spoke up.

"We are betrothed, as you very well know," Blackthorn responded, feeling strangely anxious. He could not fathom the unspoken tension in the chamber. "And we shall be married as soon as the vicar will oblige us. So pray—"

"I'm 'fraid not, m'boy," Sir Perran interrupted. "Julia can't marry you now. It is quite impossible."

At that, Blackthorn turned his full attention toward his uncle. "You don't mean to cast a rub in our way, do you?" he asked. "You can't forbid our marriage, if that is what I am hearing in your words and manner."

The baronet smiled as he reached the window. When he was standing beside Julia, he glanced down at the nearby table. "An accident?" he queried. "Are you all right, my dear? Have you hurt yourself?"

Blackthorn, too, looked at the table, which was scattered with roses, white jagged pieces of china, and pools of water. He realized that in his excitement at seeing Julia again he had failed to notice she had broken a vase. Water was already forming white marks in the wood. He was disturbed by the sight of it, but he wasn't sure why.

"No, not in the least," she murmured in response to Sir Perran's query. Her gaze fell to the carpet and remained there. "I am perfectly well, I assure you."

Blackthorn returned his gaze to Julia and, frowning, scrutinized the submissive expression on her face. She had not lifted her eyes to Sir Perran when she responded to his question, and he realized that something in her demeanor toward his uncle was completely altered. Gone was the friendliness that had formerly characterized her discourse with the baronet. Present was respect and servility. He couldn't comprehend what was happening.

Blackthorn wasn't certain what compelled him to release Julia, but he did. When he stepped away from her, Sir Perran moved close and, after slipping a possessive arm about her shoulders, kissed her cheek. She smiled thinly in response, her gaze flitting for an instant to his face, then returning as quickly to the carpet.

"You have come home too late, nephew," Sir Perran said, turning his attention upon Blackthorn and watching him narrowly from cloaked gray eyes. "I don't know what you expected Julia to do when you hadn't so much as written to her over the past several weeks or otherwise informed her of your whereabouts during your adventures. I, of course, told her you had gone to Cornwall again, on a matter of *business,* but even I would never have believed you would be absent from Bath for over a month. Surely your *business* did not take so many weeks to conclude. We had all given up hope that you would ever return."

Blackthorn felt as though a sword had just been slipped between his ribs, yet there was no pain, only a numbing sensation. "What do you mean, I haven't written to her? I have composed a score of letters and mailed them post, one each day since I was gone. What the devil is going on?"

At this last part of his speech, Julia lifted horrified eyes to meet his. He cocked his head, in utter bewilderment, as he stared back at her. "Did you not receive my letters, Julia?" he cried, aghast. "Have you not known where I was all this time?"

Julia shook her head. Her mouth fell agape; tears filled her eyes. "It became unbearable," she breathed.

"Well, it doesn't matter," he assured her quickly, taking a step toward her, his hand outstretched. He touched her arm gently, the black silk of her gown cool beneath his fingers, then he continued. "I have come home now, and I have the most famous news for you. I told you you must trust me." Blackthorn reached inside his coat, slipping from the inside pocket a thin sheaf of documents. "I have got no less than three contracts for your quarry stone. A bridge in Wiltshire, improvements on a manor house in Devonshire, and the construction of a canal not far from Bath. I told you I was not without influence."

He extended the papers to her, but she remained mute and unmoving, staring at the documents as though they had just caught fire and she couldn't touch them. "What have I done?" Julia cried. She then glanced like a startled hare toward Sir Perran and, with her eyes brimming with tears, whispered, "I'm sorry. I didn't mean to . . . to sound ungrateful. Would you please explain everything to your nephew. I . . . I will be in my bedchamber." Then she ran from the room, a hand to her mouth.

Blackthorn stared after her. What did she mean, *her bedchamber?* What was it Sir Perran needed to explain to him?

He looked back at his uncle, his heart suddenly pounding in his chest.

Sir Perran's eyes were still inscrutable as he slowly rubbed the handle of his cane. "I expect you to behave like a gentleman about this. The fact is, Julia and I are married. The deed was accomplished a few days past. I'm sorry, m'boy, but you have come home too late. I was able to give the sisters what they needed—it was as simple as that. Of course, I wish now that I had had a little more confidence in you"—he nodded toward the documents still outstretched in Blackthorn's hands. "But since you had failed to confide in me your plans and in what manner you hoped to achieve your purposes, I did what I felt was best, given the circumstances."

Blackthorn felt the blade of the sword, tucked neatly between his ribs, begin to twist and turn. His uncle had known why he went to Cornwall, at least in part, yet had not encouraged Julia to wait for him. "You married her when you knew I was in love with her . . . when you knew I had already taken her as my wife?"

"Be reasonable," he stated. "You have so little, after all, to give her. I have everything."

"I have this to give her!" He shook the papers in his uncle's face. "And I have a lessee for Hatherleigh as well. Good God . . . all these rumors I had heard about you taking a wife." A thought struck him. "Was it Julia all along?" he asked, somehow already knowing the answer.

Sir Perran grew very quiet, the cloudy expression in his eyes dissipated, until Blackthorn stared back at a hatred so dark, so fierce, that the gray of his eyes appeared black. "Yes," he responded flatly. "For these two years and more. Though I had never expected you to arrive at The Priory and tumble in love with her. You nearly overset my plans."

"Why did you say nothing to me?"

"It would not have served my purposes to have alerted you."

"Alerted me?" Blackthorn asked, feeling as though he were caught in the quagmire of a nightmare from which he could not escape. "You speak as though you perceive me as your enemy. Is that how it is, then?" His mind rolled back. He was a mere lad at the time, in this very chamber, standing beside his mother. He remembered how Sir Perran had looked at her—one moment with great longing, even desire, and the next with enormous hatred. Was it possible Sir Perran had carried forward that anger from mother to son?

The baronet turned away from him, choosing not to answer

his question. Blackthorn watched his uncle limp from the chamber. His first thoughts were disjointed: *The old man can't live forever—one day Julia will be mine. On the other hand, I could end his life today. Nonsense. I would hang for the crime, then where would I be? And what of Julia? Why didn't she believe in me, trust me? Yet, she hadn't received my letters. Why? What of the letter I gave to Beeston? What of all my letters?*

"Edward?"

Julia's soft voice broke into his thoughts. He turned toward the doorway and saw that she was standing there deathly pale in contrast to the black silk of her gown. "I must speak with you," she said, taking a small, hesitant step toward him.

He was still holding the contracts for the stone, along with the letter of agreement from an Admiral Mickleover who knew the Park well and wished to retire there. Blackthorn looked at the documents, thinking they had become an unbearable weight in his hand. He shifted his gaze back to Julia; her expression was frightened and anxious.

"You must understand," she pleaded. "I didn't hear from you. The tradesmen and Sir Perran gave me no hope that our scheme would succeed. What else could I do? You've been gone nearly a month."

He didn't know how it was he found the strength within him to make his feet move, but so he did. He walked toward the door, never once taking his gaze from her. The contracts were stretched out in front of him like a short-sword. When he arrived at the door, he thrust them toward her. She took them, frowning.

"You don't really need these anymore," he told her, "but call them a wedding present. As a point of honor, however, since I made these agreements for you in good faith, would you please see that they are discharged in a timely manner? Acquiring these contracts took a great deal of persuading on my part. I had to give personal assurances to each purchaser that the Delabole quarry could deliver its stone on time. It would seem, among other things, that the quarry has gained a very poor reputation for delivery in recent years. Now that I think on it, I believe the opinion to be an amusingly ironic one in this moment, don't you?"

"You're not being fair. You never truly understood the responsibilities I bore."

"And you never trusted me sufficiently to wait for me."

"Why didn't you at least have the courtesy to call upon me at Hatherleigh before leaving for Cornwall? The only reason I knew of your departure at all was because your uncle informed me of it. Even a parting letter would have given me cause to hope."

"My business was extremely urgent," he began. "And I did write you a letter—I promise you, I did. I left it with Beeston. Why you did not receive it, I can only wonder." Was it possible the letter had never been delivered? Could his uncle have come across the letter and, with the intention of wedding Julia himself, failed purposely to see that she received it? Blackthorn began to suspect his uncle of duplicity of the worst kind. Yet what did it matter now? He had married Julia out of hand and that was that.

He looked at her for a long moment, the despair of his loss beginning to settle deeply and painfully into his heart. He would have slipped past her and left The Priory then and there, but he remembered suddenly the emerald ring. Withdrawing the ring from the deep inner pocket of his coat, he handed it to her.

Julia gasped. "Where did you get this?" she cried, her face crinkling into a dozen harried lines, her eyes brimming with sudden tears.

"I won it from your father the night before he died. I had always supposed it belonged to you or perhaps was a piece of your mother's jewelry. I had intended upon returning it to you today—as a surprise—thinking if you wished for it, I would place it on your finger on our wedding day."

She took the ring from him with trembling fingers, tears now streaming down her cheeks. "The day of Sir Perran's card soirée, my father managed to find where I hid the ring. He had left Hatherleigh before I knew he had taken the emerald from me, else I would never have permitted him to keep it, not to mention to stake it in a card game. In the end, I never expected to see Mother's ring again. How ironic that it was in your possession all this time. Do you realize that had I had this ring with me before you left for Cornwall, I would never have married your uncle? You see, it is worth a tidy sum." With the sleeve of her black gown, she dabbed at her wet cheeks.

He looked at her for a long, thoughtful moment. "Perhaps it is best that I did not give the ring back to you earlier, Julia. What, then, would I have come home to, if for this entire month past you have doubted me? No, I believe it is better that I learned in this early hour that your faith in me was so frail. I must go now. God keep you."

Blackthorn moved swiftly past her and headed toward the stairs. Only when he was riding hard down the avenue, with the wind against his face, did he give vent to the anguish inside him.

Having returned to the window in the library, Julia was again standing by the water-soaked table. The roses were wilting among the white china shards. Absently, she withdrew her kerchief from the sleeve of her gown and began to pat the table dry. She heard Edward's heartfelt cry as he galloped away from The Priory. In complete despair and misery, she turned to the window and slapped her hands against the panes in front of her. Julia was watching her life, her happiness fly away from her, yet there was nothing she could do but let tears of frustration pour down her cheeks in deep and profound regret over the choice she had made.

Sixteen

"Oh, *mon dieu,* my lady!" Gabrielle cried, peeking over Julia's shoulder. "Sir Perran will be very angry!" Her dark eyes crinkled and she giggled.

Julia met Gabrielle's gaze in the reflection of the looking glass and smiled in return, her eyes misting with an excitement and a joy she could not easily contain. "He will be exceedingly angry," she returned. "But tonight, I don't give fig."

"The major will want to kiss you beneath the mistletoe!" Gabrielle cocked her head and smiled mischievously. "No, no, my lady, do not *frown me down,* as you English say. You should think like a Frenchwoman. In such an unhappy marriage, you should take a lover. You married for convenience—not at all unusual in your society. But in France by now, you would have had a lover, unless of course Sir Perran was everything you wished for." She lifted her brows almost expectantly, as though she hoped to receive Julia's confidences on such an intimate subject.

Julia clicked her tongue. "You are being very impertinent, and I ought to have you turned off without a reference for suggesting I tell you something so private about the man who pays your wages."

" 'Tis not enough simply for a man to pay the wages, to receive love and respect. He must be kind as well. And he is not kind to you. You should leave him. He is a beast."

Still holding her gaze, Julia could not let this pass. "You mustn't say such things to me. Please, Gabrielle, if we are to be friends . . ." Somehow, since her mother's and now her father's death, her abigail had become much, much more than a mere servant in her household. She was gentle and kind, consoling in the face of loss, yet spirited and bold. Gabrielle alone knew the extent of her unhappiness and her suffering. She had become both friend and mother to her.

"I know. I know," she said in what to Julia's ears would forever remain the most charming French accent. "But tonight I cannot help myself. You are too young, too pretty to be a captive in this house—in your own house! And why does your husband insist on living here at Hatherleigh? The Priory, she is a beautiful mansion. I simply don't understand *monsieur*. And how he worships Hatherleigh! I have never seen such a madman. *Do not touch this! Do not move that! Where is the painting that was here yesterday? Nothing is to be moved!* I suppose if the ceilings began to leak, he would cry out, *Do not fix them!* I begin to think he is crazy."

Julia smiled faintly. "Perhaps he is, but tonight I find I don't very much care whether he is or not."

She shifted her gaze from Gabrielle, many of whose opinions she shared, and surveyed her appearance. Her long auburn hair was caught up in an elegant swirling chignon, a delicate wisp of curls across her forehead, a spray of artificial white roses and green leaves adorning the crown of her head like a tiara. Her gown was of an exquisite royal-blue silk, with an undergown of apricot satin, that she and Gabrielle had fashioned, quite secretly, against her husband's wishes.

Six months had passed since her father's death, which meant that an appropriate season of mourning had been observed. More than anything, she wanted to leave off wearing her blacks. Sir Perran had already given permission for the younger sisters to order colorful ball dresses of their own choosing—provided he approved the fabrics and styles beforehand. But as his wife, he wished her to remain in black. The gown he had had designed for her by a very fashionable modiste in London was of a fine quality black silk, but had been made high to the neck and bore a long, heavy train that would have made it impossible for her to dance. No one wore trains any longer! Once in a while, a demi-train, but never anything as garish as the one hanging from the tip of her bedpost some seven feet in the air, all the way to the floor.

He had told her she would appear regal. She knew he simply did not want her to dance tonight—not tonight, not ever.

And tonight she must dance!

Tonight Edward was attending his uncle's lavish Christmas ball, the ball at which Sir Perran was at last introducing his young wife to his many friends and acquaintances. The only thought, the only hope, that had sustained her during the months since her wedding, was of one day seeing Edward again, of speaking with him, of dancing with him. And tonight she would dance within the circle of his arms, twirling around and around the ballroom beneath the dappled light of three massive chandeliers.

Perhaps then a little of the unhappiness of her marriage might subside.

Julia examined her reflection. Would Edward find her pretty tonight? In the looking glass she saw a tightness in her features that had not been present even during the years of trouble with her father. How odd to think that her marriage had somehow affected her more than all her prior worries.

Her initial intense grief for her father had abated surprisingly quickly. By September she had come to realize that in the two years preceding Lord Delabole's death, she had been grieving for her father almost as though his true death had taken place on the same day as her mother's. In essence, she had shed so many tears of loss by the time of her father's suicide that when he was actually placed in the vault alongside his wife, most of her grief had already been spent. The ensuing months had seen a final reconciliation within her heart of all his weaknesses and strengths. She had forgiven him his excesses and could now remember him fondly as the father who, when she was little, had placed her lovingly on his knee and read to her; had caught her up in front of him on his horse and galloped down winding, shady country lanes; had taught her quite successfully to skip rocks across a stream, in a game called Ducks and Drakes.

Julia remembered him fondly now, as she saw him in the features of her face, the light complexion of her skin, and the rich auburn of her hair.

She thought of her mother and felt less content.

Her words came back to her: *Make something beautiful for me.*

But what? Julia wondered. She was caught in a loveless marriage to a man whose only pleasure in life was saying yes or no to the requests made of him. He commanded her in every respect, from her daily round of dutiful obligations and occupations, to her sisters' attendance to music, painting, and language lessons.

What was beautiful in this? Without love, even Hatherleigh Park's stately elegance and beauty seemed a cold, disinterested pile of stones.

She sighed, ignoring Gabrielle's harrumph of impatience as the maid turned away from the looking glass. Her abigail had suggested she take a lover. Was this her purpose in wearing a gown cut low across the bosom? Was she hoping to entice Edward? Julia did not want to answer questions that prickled like needles against her conscience.

Whatever the case, at least tonight she was not wearing black. Sir Perran, of course, would be furious at her disobedience and would undoubtedly insist she wear black for another six months—and as a dutiful wife, she would oblige him. But tonight, regardless of his iron will or his temper, she would wear her royal-blue and apricot gown. She would dance, she would be happy, and she would beg Edward to forgive her.

Later, when Julia stood in the doorway of the crimson and

gold drawing room where her husband and her three sisters had
gathered before supper, the effect of her appearance was immediate and startling. All three of her sisters gasped. Not one of
them was ignorant of the strong grip Sir Perran kept on his young
wife. They turned toward him, mouths slightly agape, eyes wide,
expressions anxious.

Surprisingly, Julia found she was not afraid. What was the
worst he could do to her after all? He had never lifted his hand
to her; he was not so base, so brutal. But even were he to threaten
to harm her, tonight she didn't care what happened to her, only
that she wore the gown of her choosing in defiance of her husband and that she danced with Edward.

Sir Perran eyed her strangely, his gray eyes narrowed, his lips
pinched together. He did not speak for a long moment as she
approached the gold and white striped silk winged chair in which
he sat, his cane leaning against his knee, the chair turned partially toward a roaring fire surrounding an enormous log.

Her sisters had decorated the mantel with yew, holly branches,
and ivy, which trailed to the floor on either side of the wide
fireplace. Candles had been lit across the mantel and the appearance was one of Christmas beauty and warmth, an ambience
at odds with the emotionally cold atmosphere prevalent in the
very air of the chamber.

"You dare" were the words he uttered when at last he chose
to speak. She stood before him proudly, determinedly, refusing
to shift her gaze from his for so much as a particle of a second.

Julia despised him in this moment. She didn't want to; she
had never hated anyone in her life. But right now, in spite of
how charmingly Hatherleigh Park had been decorated, how sa-
vory the food, how well staffed and tended all the chambers of
the enormous mansion, she hated him for wanting only to exert
his will over her.

"Yes," she responded slowly, never flinching. "Tonight I dare,
because I am sick to death of wearing black. Tomorrow I shall
again don a color I detest, out of respect for you, but tonight I

had rather you turned all your friends and acquaintances away from the door than wear the gown you commanded me to."

Silence reigned all about her. She was certain each of her sisters had simply stopped breathing.

"Then I shall do so," he stated flatly, his eyes narrowing further.

Julia heard Annabelle gasp. Of all her younger sisters, Annabelle had been looking forward to the ball the most. For six months, the ladies had been denied the society of Bath to which they were accustomed, and tonight would have been the first reprieve from what Sir Perran had insisted was only a proper expression of mourning. But Annabelle had had perhaps the least attachment to a parent who had rarely been concerned with her comings and goings. Her greatest pleasures had always been found within the society of her friends, to whom she was greatly devoted.

Julia could not relent, however, not even for sweet, lively Annabelle.

She lifted her chin slightly and again addressed her husband. "You must do what you deem best, but I shan't change my mind or my gown."

At that, he seemed surprised as he lifted a gray brow. His eyes took on a familiar, calculating expression. Having come to know him intimately over the past months, Julia had concluded that within her husband's brain were two scales upon which he weighed and balanced every action he considered taking. In the narrowing of his eyes, she watched solid, leaded ounce weights being shifted from one scale to the next as he held her gaze and speculated on undoubtedly a dozen recourses he might take in opposition to her rebellious conduct. She watched him set one notion after another aside. When he averted his gaze from hers and looked down at the handle of his cane, which he fondled lovingly, she knew he had finally balanced his scales.

"You will have to forgo the London Season I promised you and your sisters. That is all I will say."

Again she heard Annabelle gasp and Elizabeth murmur, "Oh,

no." Attendance at the annual spring event, which took place loosely from March through June, was critical to the future of every young lady of birth and breeding. During the Season, the *beau monde* gathered in a seemingly endless round of balls, fetes, soirées, and assemblies, all designed to provide Cupid an opportunity to work his will. Dozens of marriages invariably ensued.

Julia held her ground. "You mean you will refuse to honor the chiefest of our marriage contracts—seeing that my sisters enjoy sufficient Seasons in London that they might be settled advantageously—because I will not wear the gown of your choosing?"

He looked up at her and smiled thinly. "Precisely. But it is, after all, your decision. Should you choose to wear the gown I want you to, then I will promise most magnanimously to forget all about this most inappropriate and unfortunate affair and will of course take you and your sisters to London."

Julia had already made up her mind what she would do, but she wished to know her sisters' opinions. She turned toward Elizabeth, who was seated in a chair opposite Sir Perran. Julia noted that Lizzie's gown of deep rose silk overlaid with sheer tulle enhanced to perfection the blueness of her eyes and the blackness of her hair. She watched a wicked smile overtake Elizabeth's entire face as she met Julia's gaze squarely and said, "You have never appeared to greater advantage than in this moment. I've always thought blue became you exceedingly well. In my opinion, you should never wear black. Never."

Julia's heart was filled with sudden warmth and gratitude. She mouthed the words *thank you* to Elizabeth, then shifted her gaze to Caroline.

Her next youngest sister was seated on a red silk damask sofa, a novel lying open upon a pillow on her lap. She wore a gown of white silk, beaded with seed pearls in a delicate scalloped line about the bodice and hem. "You ought always to wear just those particular shades of blue and apricot," Caroline stated simply, her blue eyes glowing with warmth and affection. She smiled, then returned to reading her novel, settling her elbow on the arm of the sofa and tucking her curled hand into her cheek, as though nothing untoward was happening.

Julia's heart was now overflowing with happiness. It was one thing to set her will against her husband's; it was quite another to do so with the support and encouragement of her sisters.

But when she made a semicircle and turned toward Annabelle, she saw that her youngest sister was in a temper. Gowned in a dark forest-green silk softened by an overdress of tulle, Annabelle had risen from her gold silk chair and was glaring at Sir Perran. For the first time since challenging her husband, apprehension flowed through Julia. She opened her mouth to speak, to stay the words she could see poised on Annabelle's frequently sharp tongue, but she was too late.

"I think you are cruel and mean-spirited," she cried. "I used to think you were the kindest, most generous man of my acquaintance, but not any longer. And not just because you say you will not take us to London, but because from the time you married my sister, you have behaved like a perfect scoundrel . . . and nothing less."

"Annabelle!" Julia called to her sharply, stunned by her sister's unexpected outburst.

But Annabelle ignored her eldest sister. She approached Sir Perran on a quick march, her green eyes aflame. "You know you have! Only, why? Whatever has she done to you to have warranted such cruelty?"

He lifted both brows. "In just what way have I been *cruel* to your sister?" he queried sarcastically. "By paying your father's debts? By taking all of you under my wing? By providing you with pretty ball dresses, a roof over your heads and some of the finest English cooking to be found in Albion?" He clucked his tongue at her. "Poor little Annabelle. To be so ill used, for your sister to be treated with such cruel indifference. What a monster I have become."

But Annabelle lifted her chin proudly. "You hold your fortune over our heads like . . . like a guillotine. I vow, every piece of bread I eat while under your beneficence tastes of bile. And you may go to the devil . . . and your Christmas ball along with it." With that, she dropped him a mocking curtsy, gave her green silk skirts a flip, and quit the room.

Julia watched her youngest sister go, feeling that in these few, brief sentences, Annabelle had described to a nicety the precise state of her home and her marriage, as well as the source of her unhappiness. She was drawn back to her husband by the sound of his laughter.

"What a delightful child," he said, chortling happily. "Now, see what you have done, Julia? She will remain in her bedchamber pouting throughout the whole evening, and all because you would wear a charmingly décolleté blue gown in hopes of seducing my nephew. I am vastly amused. In fact, so much so that I almost might reconsider my refusal to take the lot of you to London. But alas, my decision in that respect must be final." He then looked at her squarely. "For you must learn that if you will not obey me in everything, you will have to suffer the consequences."

Julia passed behind Sir Perran, moving to the rosewood pianoforte that sat in a corner near the fireplace. "My dear husband," she began quietly as she sat on the stool and arranged her skirts, "do you prefer Haydn or Bach?"

"Would it matter what I preferred this evening?" he queried. "It would seem you are intent upon pleasing only yourself, though since you are asking, a little of Bach would be much to my liking."

Julia drew forth her portfolio of music, which she had painstakingly copied herself from ragged, aging sheets of music that had at one time belonged to her mother. She smiled to herself, withdrew from among her favorites a Handel contredanse, and began to play.

When the baronet turned around, peering at her from the side of his winged chair in an accusing glare, she ignored him. She knew she had sacrificed the only objective of real value to her— getting her sisters to London for their first Season—but tonight she didn't care. Perhaps it was selfish, but tonight her heart would not be denied. She must see Edward, and in the manner in which she wished to be seen by him.

Besides, she had already begun formulating a scheme by which she would attempt to persuade Sir Perran to relent in his decision to refuse her a London season. Not that she had in six months been able to persuade him from any decision he had made, but she meant to try. For her sake, as well as that of her sisters, she would try with all her might to find a way to break through her husband's intractable will.

A half hour later dinner was served, and without guests in attendance, the whole of the meal conducted by Sir Perran. He directed the food, seeing that it was offered when and to whom he wished; he broached the subjects he preferred at the time he wanted them discussed; he criticized each of the young ladies in turn—Caroline for not speaking enough, Elizabeth for speaking too much, and Julia for glancing at the clock on the mantel too frequently.

Julia didn't care. Her mind wandered aimlessly, waiting, waiting. Sir Perran rattled on about some occurrence or other at the Congress of Vienna. She had so little interest in political matters these days. What did politics have to do with love, with family, with learning to reside with an overbearing, dictatorial, yet cunningly elusive man? Nothing.

At last dinner was concluded and Sir Perran excused the ladies. Julia led her sisters to the Green Salon to await the arrival of the first carriage. When she attempted to apologize to both Elizabeth and Caroline for having brought Sir Perran's wrath falling down upon their heads, Elizabeth scoffed at her and Caroline stated flatly, "Don't be a goosecap! Your husband is an irritable old man, and though I dislike mentioning it, I have begun to wonder for some time if he might be bilious."

Elizabeth burst out laughing and Julia withheld her amusement with only the strongest effort. "He may very well be so," she returned, a chuckle escaping her throat. "But pray don't suggest the idea to him, at least not tonight. Somehow I am persuaded he would not take kindly to hearing you diagnose the cause of his ill-temper as an acute case of biliousness."

Caroline nodded gravely, ignoring Elizabeth's mirth. After a moment, she raised her finger aloft, the glow on her face indicating that a brilliant thought had just occurred to her. "But I do think a cleansing purge might be just the thing," she said, her blue eyes wide with hope. "What do you think?"

This was too much for even Julia, who let out a trill of laughter that overshadowed Elizabeth's whoops. Sir Perran and a cleansing purge. She laughed until she cried.

Julia wiped her eyes and smiled fondly on Caroline, who apparently still did not understand what she had said to cause her sisters so much amusement. "He is not bilious," she explained. "He is mean, and the cause of his meanness lies somewhere within his character, perhaps even in some injustice he suffered in the past, but not in his constitution."

Caroline accepted Julia's pronouncement with a resigned sigh and took a seat near the fireplace.

Elizabeth glanced toward the window and gave a sudden cry of delight. "It is snowing!" she cried. "How utterly perfect!"

"Indeed?" Caroline asked, rising from her chair instantly to join her sisters by the window. In the strong reflection of the candlelight from the windows shining on the shrubs, the scythed lawn, and the gravel drive below, snowflakes could be seen falling on the grounds.

"Annabelle will be utterly despondent when she sees that it is snowing," Caroline remarked wistfully. "She had so wished for it—and so near to Christmas. If only she had not challenged *the old man* tonight!"

Julia withheld another smile. Three months earlier, her sisters had all begun referring in private to Sir Perran as *the old man*. She would have rebuked them, but she knew they were as miserable as she with his conduct toward them, and it seemed to her that by referring to their brother-in-law in such a fashion they were better able to tolerate the oppressiveness of the situation. So, *the old man* he was.

"Annabelle knew better," Elizabeth stated, less sympathetically than her sister. "Who of us had not warned her a dozen times to keep her tongue in his presence? And tonight of all nights, she should have had more sense about her."

"It is my fault," Julia declared.

Both Caroline and Elizabeth groaned together. "Pray do not play the martyr this evening, Julia," Caroline said softly.

Julia glanced at her sisters and immediately apologized. Once each of them had come to understand both the enormity of the burden she had borne by herself since their mother's death, as well as the sacrifice she had made in wedding Sir Perran, they had been unrelenting in expressing a shared opinion that she should not have excluded them from her sufferings or her decision-making. Now, whenever she so much as hinted that the unhappiness of their circumstances was her fault, they set upon her with a vengeance.

"Oh, no, Caro," Lizzie responded facetiously. "Please don't stop Julia. I adore the aroma of burning martyr."

"You are wicked!" Caroline returned, shocked by Elizabeth's wretched choice of words. But her laughter spoiled her protest.

Julia looked through the falling snowflakes and down the drive. A wink of light could be seen in the distance. "I see a carriage!" she cried. Her sisters pressed from behind, anxious to see for themselves. Her heart rose quickly in her breast, like the sudden soaring of a flock of birds ever upward in the air.

He will be here soon, she thought.

She had never for a moment stopped loving Edward Blackthorn, and however much Julia had promised herself that once she was established in a daily routine as Sir Perran's wife she would forget all about Edward, each successive day seemed to give birth to an even greater longing for him than the day before.

Her sisters knew in part how horrendously she had erred in not waiting for Edward to return. But given that she had a more complete, more intimate knowledge of her husband's true char-

acter than her sisters would ever have—that had been revealed
to her the night of her wedding—no one could ever possibly
comprehend the depth of her regret for having trusted Sir Perran
instead of his nephew.

Before her wedding day, Julia had informed Sir Perran of her
unmaidenly state and he had responded to her revelation not
unkindly, saying he was not especially surprised since he knew
she had fancied herself violently in love with his nephew. He
had then adjured her not to give the matter a second thought.

On their wedding night, he had come to her in a fine burgundy
brocade dressing gown and had sat beside her on the bed. She
was glad he knew of her condition and was even more relieved
when he stated that until he could be certain she was not *increasing* with his nephew's child, he would refrain from coming
to her bed. The thought of permitting Sir Perran—even though
he was her husband—to touch her, to love her as Edward had
loved her, was an unsettling matter. Part of her had wanted to
get it over with, but another part of her was grateful that he had
decided not to consummate the marriage.

He had remained sitting on her bed, looking at her in what
she knew now to be his speculative, balancing expression. While
he weighed his thoughts, Julia had been tempted to tell him that
she already knew she was not with child, but somehow she could
not bring herself to explain to him just how she knew. The flow
of monthly blood that was part of every woman's life was never
an easy subject, even between women, let alone between husband and wife. She had chosen, therefore, to remain silent and
to let time be her interpreter.

What followed, however, had been the beginning of her unhappiness, when at last he spoke. "I trust you mean to be chaste,"
he had said, staring down at her, his gray eyes strangely hard.

She had been stunned, at first unable to credit he had said
such a thing to her. "Yes, yes, of course," she responded earnestly. "Sir Perran, I promise you that the only reason I succumbed to . . . to *him* was because I believed we would be
married soon afterward."

He had lifted a brow. "Well, we shall see, shan't we?"

Julia had watched him leave and had the strangest sensation she had stepped from a dream into a nightmare. Since the exchange had been short, she had initially dismissed the misgivings that had risen sharply to mind and had convinced herself that surely she had not understood him properly. After all, Sir Perran had known her for years. Surely he would not believe her capable of such wretched conduct.

Six months later, when he had still not made her his wife in the truest sense, when she had been the brunt of his many criticisms and manipulations, when she had begun to feel like a prisoner within the very house in that she had grown up, even her dreams had become filled with the very thing she had promised her husband she would never do. She was a woman of normal appetites. She needed to love and to be loved. Edward had soon become the object of every waking and sleeping thought.

So it was, two hours after a long stream of carriages had begun arriving, that Julia stood submissively beside her husband in the large rose receiving room on the ground floor of Hatherleigh, her heart longing for Edward to arrive. He was late, it would seem. Perhaps he had decided not to come after all.

Sir Perran was talking in serious tones with his good friend and companion Lord Yarnacott. The earl was a tall, thin man, some ten years Sir Perran's junior. His hair was an elegant silvered blond and his light blue eyes were the color of thin ice over a pool of clear, blue water. He carried himself in a slow, noble manner but shared with her husband a similar calculatedness of eye. Julia was never fully at ease with Lord Yarnacott, but fortunately rarely found herself in a situation where she was called upon to entertain him. The men were discussing Bonaparte's exile on Elba, each predicting that Napoleon would return to France before mid-summer.

Much Julia cared. All she wanted for the present was to see Edward cross the portals of the rose drawing room.

In the meantime, she remained at Sir Perran's elbow, a silent, obedient wife, as she surveyed the crowded chamber, her gaze never far from the entrance.

As though ushered into her home by her will alone, Edward suddenly appeared in the doorway, dressed in a black coat, white neckcloth, white starched shirt points of a medium height, a white waistcoat, black pantaloons, and black slippers. Julia nearly fainted at the sight of him. Her cheeks grew warm with pleasure of the sweetest kind, her heart quickening in her breast, her eyes smarting with sudden, unexpected tears.

She was dizzy with dread that she might betray to her husband, or anyone else present, the depth of her love for Major Blackthorn, yet for the first time in months, she felt truly alive. How dear he was to her. Julia suppressed a strong urge to run to him, to throw her arms about his neck, to hold him fast forever. Instead, she dug her nails into the palm of her hand and strove to compose her sensibilities. She took a deep breath, forcing herself to scan the assembled guests, and only when she was calmer did she permit her gaze to return to Edward.

How handsome he was, still dark from the Spanish sun. How odd that she did not remember he was so tall. Julia noted that even though he had been in England now for six months, he had still not clipped his hair short, which was the fashion. But this thought was unfortunate, for with it she remembered having untied the riband and released his long black hair. She had slipped her fingers into his hair, holding him close to her as they made love.

Desire, made more intense because of her disastrous marriage, flowed through her. She held her apricot lace fan up to her face, watching him over the spindles. He turned back to greet an older gentleman directly behind him, smiling at something the man said in return.

She loved watching him smile; she wanted to be with him, to touch his lips with her fingers, to make him smile, to kiss him, to make him smile a little more.

Julia's gaze was averted to a handsome woman, gowned in amethyst silk adorned with Brussels lace, who took the arm of

the gentleman next to Edward. She observed the attractive couple for several minutes and was struck by how familiar they both
seemed, in particular the tall, distinguished man who clapped
Edward affectionately on the shoulder and shook his hand. Who
was this man? she wondered. She could not remember having
met him before. He had a warm smile, a strong, though not
displeasing, aquiline nose, and his silvered temples against black
hair was most striking. He turned and whispered something into
the ear of the lady affectionately holding his arm. She opened
her eyes wide, rapped him with her fan, and Julia could read the
word *behave* on her lips. He again whispered in her ear. This
time, however, she did not admonish him, but gazed lovingly
into his eyes for a long moment, then turned her attention fully
and properly to Edward.

Julia was so filled with envy suddenly that a sense of raw
disappointment flooded her. Here was love, she thought despon-
dently. Even from across the room, the genuine affection flowing
between the man and the woman, undoubtedly husband and
wife, was evident. She wanted to turn away, to leave the rose
drawing room, to seek shelter in a dark corner until the surging
disappointment she felt should pass. Surely anyone observing
her would know the truth about her recent marriage—that her
disillusionment was vast, her unhappiness even more profound.

She took a deep breath and again strove to restore her spirits.
When she was less distressed, she returned her gaze to Edward.
Here she suffered a shock, for she found that he was watching
her, his gray eyes concerned, a frown troubling his brow. Had
he seen her unhappiness? He looked away from her almost at
once, and Julia sensed his disappointment in her all over again.
She felt small and ashamed. She turned her eyes from him, settling her vision instead upon the fine stitching on Lord Yarnacott's black coat. The lapel, in a careful *W* shape, was rather
exquisite. His waistcoat was fashioned of a pale beige and white
striped silk. His silk breeches, stockings, and slippers were all
black. Most of the men in the room were dressed in a similar

manner, with only fluctuating colors in their waistcoats setting them apart. Beau Brummell's influence had indeed triumphed.

How absurd to be thinking of Beau Brummell, Julia thought with a faint smile, yet how much safer than to be thinking of Edward. She wanted to continue dwelling on the prevailing fashions of the day, but her mind swooped inward. She recalled the expression on Edward's face the last time she had seen him, after he had been informed of her marriage to his uncle. He had blamed her for not having had faith in him.

How stupid she had been to think he would forgive her so easily, so readily. She had sacrificed Annabelle's evening for an absurdly hopeless hope. Why had she thought he could still love her after she had married his uncle?

If only she had received his letters when he left for Cornwall so many months ago. How many times had this thought risen from the depths of her mind to torture her? A dozen, a hundred, a thousand, ten thousand?

The day following Edward's return to Bath, Sir Perran had called upon the postmaster, but he had found no trace of any of Edward's letters. Their disappearance was a great mystery.

Tears of bitterness welled up in her eyes, tears she could not stop. Julia knew Sir Perran would be displeased with her, but she strongly suspected that if she did not instantly quit his side, she would fall into a fit of the hysterics.

With a murmured apology, her eyes downcast, she slipped away from him. She heard him call her name firmly, as though attempting to bring a dog to heel, but she wended her way quickly through the many guests in the drawing room, advancing in the opposite direction of Edward and his acquaintances.

Blinking away her tears, she passed through an antechamber in which four instrumentalists were busily playing a Haydn sonata, then entered the long blue drawing room, its dark blue ceiling adorned with cherubs descending from the heavens through drifts of pink and white clouds. Iced cups of champagne were being served steadily to a heated group of dancers who had just emerged from the ballroom beyond.

Julia slowed her pace a trifle, nodding to her acquaintances and to those whom she had met for the first time that evening. She moved into the long gallery laden with dozens of portraits of Delabole ancestors, pretending pleasure and enjoyment as she was complimented over and over on the grandeur and elegance of her Christmas ball. She saw Elizabeth standing beneath a sprig of mistletoe, which had mysteriously been hung over a doorjamb leading to the morning room, and watched as a young man lifted her sister's hand to his lips and kissed her fingers fervently.

How Elizabeth giggled, the laughter of innocence and harmless flirtation. Julia's sense of loss and envy increased. She turned away from the door leading to the morning room, in which tables had been set up for whist and silver loo. She passed through a tall archway that led back toward the entrance hall. Laughter, merriment, the sound of carolers in an antechamber on the other side of the stairs, rolled over her. Julia heard masculine voices emanating from the study, the place where she had found her father so many months ago.

She passed by the study, mounting the stairs in quick, light steps. The Green Salon was full of ladies listening rapturously to a strange young man, dressed *à la Byron* with wild hair and a Belcher neckcloth tied loosely about his neck, who was reading dramatically from Childe Harold's *Pilgrimage*. The crimson and gold drawing room was full of gossiping women and two young ladies performing a duet upon the pianoforte.

The library. Surely in the library she could find solitude. For a little while. She needed only a few minutes to compose herself. Julia opened the door and discovered, to her immense relief, that the square, rather dark chamber was empty. She moved quickly inside, then closed the door behind her with a snap. Leaning against the door, she let a deep sob shake her chest. She hadn't even known so much pain existed inside of her until now.

The library of Hatherleigh Park was smaller than the long chamber at The Priory. The viscounts Delabole had not been of a particularly scholarly turn, and the dark mahogany shelves, which did not rise to the ceiling as did Sir Perran's, were only partially filled with books. The draperies hanging to each side of two windows were of a brown velvet, and the sofa and two winged chairs that flanked the fireplace adjacent to the windows were covered in a gold brocade, a fabric belonging to the prior century.

For several minutes, Julia wept silently, tears streaming down her cheeks until she heard footsteps in the hallway just beyond the door. She swallowed hard and moved quickly toward the windows, wiping at her eyes quite ineffectually with her bare hands and arms.

Behind her, she heard the door open and a woman's voice call across the chamber to her. "I do beg your pardon, but are you Lady Blackthorn?"

Seventeen

Julia again wiped her face and cheeks with her hands, attempting once more to compose herself, but the effort was proving quite hopeless. She hadn't recognized the woman's voice but decided it hardly mattered. She had been caught in a dreadful indiscretion—tears at her first Christmas ball as Lady Blackthorn, wife of one of England's wealthiest men.

She turned around and sniffed. With some surprise, she found herself looking at the lady who had earlier been conversing with Edward. "Oh!" she cried, startled.

"My dear," the lady murmured, her warm brown eyes regarding her sympathetically. "It is not so easy being married to Sir Perran, is it?"

This unexpected observation, so full of quick understanding, brought a fresh bout of tears rushing to Julia's eyes.

When laughter was heard in the hallway, the woman quickly turned around and gave the key in the lock a hard twist. She then modestly lifted the skirts of her beautiful violet silk gown, found her pocket, which was sewn into the seam of her shift, and withdrew a very large embroidered kerchief. Dropping her skirts, she shook them out in a pretty, enthusiastic manner and crossed the room on a brisk, lively tread, pressing her kerchief into Julia's hand.

"Thank you," Julia murmured, the lady's kind attentions making it even harder than ever for her to compose herself. "I am become a watering pot," she complained as she dabbed at her eyes. "But I cannot blame my husband, ma'am. I . . . I suppose I am simply not in the habit of being anyone's wife."

"And especially not his, or do I much mistake the matter?"

"He . . . that is . . . oh, it doesn't signify. No fault can attach to him. I . . . I made a dreadful mistake, that's all." Julia then caught sight of the tearstains on her blue silk bodice and moaned.

The woman laughed at her and, in a kind, motherly manner, flipped open her painted fan and began vigorously wafting it over Julia's bosom. Julia began to laugh and the lady joined her.

What an odd beginning. Who was she, this lovely woman who was probably in her late forties? Julia wondered. She was not unlike her own mother—sympathetic, concerned, understanding, yet full of life.

"Who are you?" she asked boldly, watching the woman quizzically, the bizarre circumstance of their meeting causing her to forget her manners. The lady's brown eyes suddenly seemed familiar, as though Julia had looked into them before; yet she knew she had not. She had blond hair that was only faintly streaked with gray, hardly discernible in the candlelight. She was surrounded by an air of contentment, which immediately drew Julia to her.

"My husband calls me Margaret. But you may call me by my title, which is what our society deems appropriate. I am Lady Trevaunance."

Julia was dumbfounded, recalling instantly to mind her unfortunate experience with Lord Peter. She gasped and took a step backward, as though she had been touched by a hot coal.

"Now, why have I startled you, I wonder? Or do I know?" She smiled kindly, leveling her gaze squarely upon Julia as she stepped forward to again close the distance between them in order to continue fanning away the tearstains on her gown. "You see, once I received your husband's invitation, I felt I had to come. I am none too pleased with my son's conduct toward you. The very day he arrived in Brighton last summer—and quite unexpectedly, I might add—I received a letter in his hand, sent to me from Bath, though written a full sennight prior. He stated in his letter that he loved you, that he had offered for you in spite of his father's promptings against the match, and that regardless of anything we might say he meant to have you. Showing him his own letter and questioning him about what had happened to disrupt his plans—he never could tell a whisker properly!—I learned the truth. Your father's unfortunate demise deprived him completely of his courage. In my opinion, he behaved like a scoundrel and I have not let him forget it. Had he fulfilled his gentlemanly duty toward you, you would have at least been spared a . . . a difficult marriage and he would have gained a good wife." She paused for a moment, sighing faintly before continuing. "Though I suppose in one way I am glad you did not marry him, for I am persuaded then you would have been bound for a lifetime to a man you did not love. After all, my son is young and Sir Perran is not, if you get my meaning. Am I speaking too plainly? Do I offend your sensibilities?"

Julia shook her head and blew her nose. "No, not at all. I have not had much opportunity in recent years to permit my sensibilities full rein. I have had to be of a practical turn and for that, I suppose, I owe you an apology. But there was a time, early in your son's courtship, when I fancied myself in love with him. You must believe as much. And later, I promised myself I would make him the best wife possible . . ."

"And you would have, my dear. I am certain of it."

"How kind you are," Julia responded, frowning slightly. "I am very grateful for your confidence in me. I believe, in time, I would have grown to love Lord Peter . . . I promise you . . ."

Lady Trevaunance paused in her fanning efforts and took gentle hold of Julia's arm. "Do not look so fearful or guilt-ridden. Were I, or a dozen other ladies of quality, forced to endure all that you have endured, none of us would have acted any differently. You were doing what you believed best, especially for your sisters. Though a man might not so readily forgive such a motivation, with five sisters of my own and I the eldest, I have a thousand times blessed myself for having married well, if for no other reason than for their sakes. When you come to London—as I trust you will this spring—you will find a great deal of support you probably do not now believe exists."

"But the whole of it . . . my father's death—"

"—will in time be forgotten. But your mother's memory must and will be remembered and honored. I knew of her. Her reputation was impeccable. She was a lady of strength and dignity, just as you one day will be."

"You are terribly kind," Julia gushed. "I cannot thank you enough. You don't know the courage you are giving me."

"Yes I do. I once had a woman—some twenty-five years ago, now that I think on it—take me aside and impress the very same words upon me. One day you will return this favor, and in the meantime, will you write to me and tell me how you prosper?" Julia nodded. "Good. When you come to London, I expect you to pay a proper morning visit at the earliest opportunity."

"I will, I will," Julia assured her, determined now more than ever that she would somehow find a way to bring her sisters to London for the Season.

Lady Trevaunance looked down at the bodice of Julia's gown. "I can see that my task is complete." She lifted merry brown eyes to regard Julia.

Julia giggled.

"Much better. Now, come and speak to Major Blackthorn. The reason I pursued you in the first place was that I am in desperate need of your assistance. The silly fellow has been blue-deviled since we left Hertfordshire together, and to own the truth, I am sick to death of his megrims." She took Julia by the arm and guided her toward the library door. "I am persuaded that until you cheer him out of the sullens, he will forever look like a hound who has been deserted by his master."

Julia smiled. How much better to be laughing and smiling than to be wallowing in the wretchedness of her circumstances. She decided she would attempt to emulate Lady Trevaunance. She strongly suspected that that good lady did not waste many of her hours in self-pity or in wishings and longings that would never be fulfilled.

When they reached the door, Julia unlocked it, threw it wide, and straightened her shoulders. Before crossing the threshold and at the same time ascertaining that the hallway was empty, she confided in her new friend. "I am in love with him," she announced quietly.

Lady Trevaunance pinched her cheek. "I noted as much when we first entered your pretty drawing room. You were staring at him as though the gods had just delivered one of their number into your home. And he is not a god, I assure you, though at times even I can see a little of Mars in him." She smiled in her sweet manner and sighed. "He is quite handsome, isn't he?"

"You have such a manner of speaking!" Julia cried, feeling a blush creep up her cheeks.

Lady Trevaunance unfurled her fan and guided Julia into the hall. She nodded at an acquaintance who emerged from the crimson and gold drawing room. As they began their progress toward the stairs, she lifted her fan to hide her lips and whispered, "Have you kissed Major Blackthorn?" she asked.

Julia quickly flipped open her own fan of apricot-colored lace and covered her face past her nose. Whatever would Lady Trevaunance say if she knew the truth? She nodded in response to her question.

"Is there anything quite as wondrous as a kiss?" she queried softly, again nodding to another acquaintance.

"It is very pleasant," Julia responded, feeling both exhilarated and embarrassed by the conversation.

"When I first kissed Trevaunance—" the marchioness began wistfully.

Julia finished the thought for her, "—you felt as though you had just tumbled off a cliff."

The marchioness turned surprised eyes toward her young friend. "You are badly smitten, aren't you?"

"We knew one another when we were young. I always loved him. He used to take me up on his back when I was seven and he twelve. He went away to school the following year, and though I only saw him once after that, I had such dreams of him, of one day becoming his wife."

Lady Trevaunance nodded in response as they began their descent down the stairs, but addressed another subject entirely. "Now, tell me, what do you mean to do about this husband of yours?"

Julia turned her fan over in a helpless manner. "I don't know . . . he is an enigma to me. Before our marriage, he was all that was kind, but now . . ." She broke off, unwilling to reveal the particulars of her marriage.

"I see. Does he ever speak about what is in his heart?"

"No, never," Julia responded, turning to regard Lady Trevaunance's amiable countenance.

The marchioness turned to look at her, her eyes narrowed slightly. "Were I you, I would do everything I could to encourage his heart toward you. Kindness, dignity . . . these qualities will win the day if you are very clever, and I think you are."

Julia frowned slightly. "But does he even have a heart? After his conduct toward me these past six months, I have begun to wonder."

"Every man has a heart, even your husband. But I suspect that having given it once and having been quite brutally rejected, Sir Perran has since had difficulty both loving and being loved. Did you know that he was betrothed to Major Blackthorn's mother at one time?"

"No," Julia replied, "though I was aware she had had to choose between Lieutenant Colonel Blackthorn and Sir Perran."

Nearing the bottom of the stairs, where a number of guests were gathered, Lady Trevaunance lowered her voice. "He was deeply in love with her and then she eloped with his brother."

"How dreadful," Julia whispered as they reached the bottom of the stairs. "Yet how very much this would explain."

"Indeed," Lady Trevaunance returned with a nod. "I believe you are right. I never quite understood why Sophia spurned Sir Perran's love, but having known her as I did—she was an excellent friend of mine—I'm sure she must have had a sensible reason, though she never confided in me. But there is something more . . ." She paused, appearing uncertain whether she should continue.

"Yes? Please tell me whatever it is you are thinking."

"Well, I don't know. There was a time when Sophia suspected . . . that is . . ." But she got no further, for at that moment Edward and the Marquis of Trevaunance approached them.

Julia's attention was immediately diverted from the subject at hand. Edward had offered her his hand and a moment later he was placing a gentle kiss on her fingers. She looked up at him, her heart in her throat, scarcely able to breathe. "Edward," she murmured, unaware that she had addressed him by his Christian name.

His gray eyes grew soft and tender. "Hallo . . . Lady Blackthorn. May I introduce to you a most excellent friend, the Marquis of Trevaunance. You have, of course, already become acquainted with his wife."

Julia took a deep breath and turned her attention to His Lordship.

"Well met, Lady Blackthorn," the marquis said politely, the expression on his face as warm and as friendly as his wife's. "I was told you were a woman of exceptional beauty, but even such a description does not adequately convey the perfection of your face and figure."

"Why, thank you," Julia breathed, feeling her cheeks grow warm beneath his praise. She recalled his son to mind, realizing why when she had first observed the marquis at the entrance to the rose drawing room, she had felt as though she already knew him. Lord Peter, though he resembled his mother in the features of his face, carried himself with the courtly bearing of his father.

"Are you blushing?" the marquis queried on a half-smile. "Margaret, she is just like you!"

Lady Trevaunance quickly took her husband in tow, bidding him not to embarrass every young lady he met by offering fulsome compliments, then ordered him to lead her to the ballroom. "I wish to waltz with you, my darling," she declared. She then whisked him away, after he offered Julia a practiced bow and a teasing wink of his eye.

"What a delightful pair," she said, watching them wend their way through the crowds in the rose drawing room. The marquis leaned down and whispered something in his wife's ear, just as he had when Julia had first seen them. And again, Lady Trevaunance rapped his arm with her fan.

"They are marvelous," Edward agreed quietly. When Julia returned her attention to him, he regarded her from concerned eyes. "How are you, Julia? Has my uncle treated you kindly?"

Julia looked at him steadily, knowing that whatever she said to him would be a whisker. *I am miserable beyond speaking,* her heart cried. But she couldn't say as much to him. There would be no useful purpose in doing so. "Sir Perran tends to our every need," she replied at last. "In that, he has been all that is kind."

Edward's brow drew together in a faint frown. "I see," he said quietly. He held her gaze, the expression in his eyes scrutinizing, as though he was attempting to understand precisely what she meant.

Julia took a small step toward him. She wanted so very much to lay her hand on his arm, to touch him, but she knew she could not. She also did not want him to question her too closely about his uncle, so she changed the subject. "I was afraid you would not attend our Christmas ball," she began. "But Edward, I am so glad you've come. You've no idea."

An intense, almost hungry look entered his eye. "At first I rejected the notion of returning to Hatherleigh. But later I knew nothing could keep me away from you." When the crush near the stairs grew too great, he took her arm and guided her into the hallway leading back to the gallery. He leaned close to her as they walked, his breath warm on her ear as he whispered, "I will always love you, Julia. Always. You must remember that. And should you need me, you have but to send for me. I promise you, I will move heaven and earth if necessary to come to you."

Her whole being glowed with his words. Hope and happiness,

in the face of her current difficult marriage, were reborn within her heart. "You have forgiven me, then," she stated, looking up at him and searching his eyes carefully.

"Yes," he responded simply.

Julia's heart was now full to overflowing. Above all she had wanted his forgiveness, and he had given it to her. "I can be content now," she said, breathing a sigh of relief. A tension, which had fixed itself in her shoulders, began to dwindle away. She could feel her entire body relax as a measure of joy and serenity entered her heart.

With a smile, she asked, "Have you seen the ballroom? Annabelle and Elizabeth worked very hard, lacing together garlands of yew and holly. It is quite pretty."

When he confessed he had not yet made his way to the ballroom, she suggested he accompany her. Still holding her arm wrapped tightly about his, he declared, "Only if you will dance the waltz with me, which is the only proper and acceptable excuse I can have now for taking you in my arms. Please don't refuse, else I fear I shall fall into a decline!"

She laughed. Nothing could be more absurd than the picture of Edward Blackthorn, with his military bearing and sun-hardened face, succumbing to his sensibilities and languishing day after day upon a chaise longue. "Then I most certainly must oblige you," she returned, smiling up at him.

The moment was tender, convivial, flirtatious—all that Julia had wanted her reconciliation with Edward to be. But as they passed into the gallery and she gave his arm a friendly squeeze, Sir Perran chanced upon them.

Julia felt frightened and overset all at once. She tried to draw her arm from Edward's, but he wouldn't permit her to do so. Her anxiety increased.

"There you are, nephew," Sir Perran stated blandly. "What do you think of our home all dressed up in Christmas greens? Lovely, isn't it? And what of Julia? Doesn't royal-blue suit her complexion to perfection?"

"Yes, indeed," he responded, glancing sharply at Julia, the expression in his eyes a question.

Sir Perran glanced at the tangle of their arms, a faint lifting of his brow indicating his disapproval. He drifted his gaze over Julia's face. She found it difficult to look at him, but she forced herself. Guilt and fear rippled over her. She could not have felt worse if he had found them locked in an embrace.

"I won't keep you," he said, averting his gaze back to Edward. "I've a number of guests I wish to speak to at length. Do I trespass by asking you to see to my wife's amusements this evening?"

"Not in the least," Edward responded.

"Excellent. Well, then, I shall leave you to it."

Julia's heart was racing. As Sir Perran moved to pass by her, he whispered sarcastically in her ear, "Do not look so downcast . . . I trust you." He limped away before she could say anything in response, plying his cane with great care.

"You are trembling," Edward whispered as Sir Perran disappeared into the hallway and they began a slow progress down the long gallery toward the blue drawing room.

"It is nothing."

"Humbug. You are frightened nearly out of your wits. Has my uncle hurt you?" he asked, stroking her arm gently.

Julia looked up at him and saw the concern and sympathy in his eyes. She felt such a sudden yearning to be held by him, to be comforted by him, that for a long moment all she could do was look at him in painful despair. An answering gleam appeared in his eye, as though he understood her thoughts. She sensed that she had but to say the word and he would take her in his arms.

Feeling that she was in danger of succumbing to her love for him, Julia looked away from Edward and answered his question. "No, your uncle has not hurt me. He has merely proven to be a somewhat dictatorial spouse, and though I am endeavoring with all my heart to be a good wife to him, I am finding the task far more trying than I would ever have believed possible."

He drew her to the side of the long gallery, toward the windows overlooking the back terrace. Candlelight from the mansion's many windows spilled through the glass, causing the snowflakes to sparkle as they fell. A smooth blanket of snow now covered the grounds.

In a low voice, Edward said, "Elizabeth told me of your refusal to wear the gown of my uncle's choosing and of . . . of Annabelle's unfortunate speech afterward. You are unhappy here, aren't you?"

Julia wanted to tell him everything, to confide in him. What would he say, for instance, if he knew that his uncle had not yet touched her? She suspected, however, that she would be inviting disaster were she to reveal to Edward the deepest truth of her marriage. But precisely what was that truth? Why had he not yet come to her bed? Was he incapable of loving her in a physical way, as she had heard sometimes happened to men as they grew older?

With these thoughts, Julia decided it would be best to end the discussion of her marriage. "Whether or not I am happy is of little consequence of the moment. I want only to enjoy your company, for I strongly suspect that after tonight I will not be seeing you for some time."

Edward accepted her rebuff and guided her toward the blue drawing room. Beneath the dazzling light of the chamber's well-lit chandelier, Julia's spirits began to improve. On every table, on the mantel above the fireplace, at the base of the wall sconces, garlands and bows of sheer gossamer tulle, draped with row upon row of blue glass beads, lent a cool, wintry sparkle to the festivities.

When the carolers—a group of four full-voiced singers, two men and two women—moved into the chamber and began singing "Deck the Halls With Boughs of Holly," Christmas overtook the cares of the moment, affecting Julia as completely as an ocean wave breaking in the surf, then sliding over the sand in a gentle, final sweep. For the present, she was able to forget about her husband and give herself over to the enjoyment of the ball.

She danced with Edward, two sets only, for anything more would have set tongues a-wagging. Later, he led her in to supper, where all the guests dined on an array of food that would have pleased even the Prince Regent himself—Christmas goose, Yorkshire ham, roast beef, several fish, eel, lobster, turtle, quail, and partridges. Carrots, cabbages, turnips, peas, broccoli, and onions were served in a variety of sauces, from oyster to lemon. Several Christmas puddings, jellies, creams, sweetmeats, pies, tarts, cakes, and every fruit imaginable, including pineapple, weighed down the tables. Madeiras, ports, brandies, and champagne flowed around and around the gathered assemblage. Christmas cheer and well-wishing resounded from drawing room to antechamber, from ballroom to salon.

Lady Blackthorn's first Christmas ball was accounted a considerable success.

At length, as the early morning hours arrived, the guests began to leave. The gentle snow had stopped falling, and the coach lamps from dozens of carriages trailing toward Bath lit up the moonstruck, snow-laden countryside, like torches in a parade. The effect was magical, and Julia hurried up the stairs to the Green Salon to watch what soon became a bouncing and weaving of lights. She opened the window to better hear the jingle of the bells attached to the horses' harnesses. Her heart was full suddenly, of every Christmas she had ever experienced with her family.

Her mother, who made Christmas a particular time of reaching out to the many poor in and around Bath, had kept the singularly perfect meaning of the season alive for days and days. Her heart had been an endless flow of giving. Julia again recalled her parting words.

Make something beautiful for me.

What? What beauty could she create from the life she had both been given and had chosen to live? What beauty was here for her to bring to life? Was there a beauty she could coax out of her relationship with her husband? Julia didn't know.

She looked up at the stars above, then again at the dance of the coach lamps on the snow. The cold air struck her cheeks.

Make something beautiful.

Her throat constricted as a thought rent her heart in two. A child was beautiful. She could make a child, but not alone. Julia knew a conflict of sentiments. Would Sir Perran be willing to give her children? He had said he wanted children. Should she ask him? Could she bring herself to ask him? What would he say to her?

As the trail of coaches began to thin, she closed the window with a snap. The noise belowstairs had quieted. Most of the guests must have departed.

"There you are!" a familiar and beloved voice called to her from across the room.

Julia turned and was happy to see Edward, his greatcoat over his shoulders, standing in the doorway. "I couldn't resist watching the departure of the carriages," she said. "I know I should have been below to bid goodbye to the last few guests, but Elizabeth and Caroline were performing the task so sweetly. Are you leaving, then?"

The only sentiment that seemed to swell in her heart at the moment was one of pure affection. Somehow, during the course of the evening, she had been able to set aside the stronger, deeper feelings she had for Edward. Before her, instead of a lover, instead of the husband he could never be to her, was her playmate from childhood, almost a brother like the two she had lost, a concerned friend. He would always be these to her.

Julia crossed the chamber and when she reached his side, he teasingly looked up. She followed the line of his gaze and saw that another sprig of mistletoe had been mysteriously hung over yet another doorjamb. "Dare I?" he queried mischievously but harmlessly.

"Yes," she responded, knowing herself safe.

He placed a hand on each of her arms, leaned toward her, and kissed her on the cheek. "Good night, Julia, and goodbye. I hope to see you in London in the spring."

"Goodbye." Julia smiled softly as he released her arms.

"So this is how you repay my kindnesses!" Sir Perran's voice snapped from across the hall. "Taking advantage of my wife the moment my back is turned. I call that a despicable act!"

Before Julia could prevent him, Sir Perran had thrust himself between her and Edward, catching his nephew by the front capes of his thick black woolen coat and throwing him bodily against the door. The crashing sound was thunderous. "How dare you sport with my wife?" he cried, accusing Edward of something more than the innocent kiss he had given her.

Julia was horrified and her thoughts grew disjointed. How was it possible a man who limped and relied on a cane could move with such speed? How could he lift so strong a man as Edward almost off his feet? Why would he purposely provoke his own nephew, when anyone who had observed Edward's kiss would have known it was a gesture innocently meant? How ironic that all evening, with even the smallest encouragement, she could have persuaded Edward to kiss her passionately if she had so much as hinted at it. Why had a harmless kiss brought Sir Perran's accusations raining down upon his head?

"Release me, uncle!" Edward cried. "What manner of absurdity is this?" He grasped Sir Perran's wrists tightly. "Let me go, or I'll be forced to hurt you."

Julia could see by the redness in each man's face that they were caught in the heat of battle. Given their temperaments, as she understood them, she knew neither would relinquish the fight.

"Let Edward go!" she cried firmly. Julia moved to stand beside her husband, thrusting her hand under his arm and pushing hard against his chest. "Perran, he did nothing more than place a friendly salute on my cheek. A sisterly kiss, that is all! You said you trusted me! So pray, end this foolishness and release him!"

Sir Perran turned to look at her, surprised. He was breathing hard. She smelled brandy on his breath. His eyes had a wild appearance and it occurred to her that he wanted to do battle with his nephew.

"Let him go," she commanded. "Nothing unseemly happened. I would not use you so ill."

His breathing slowed as he continued to look at her. "I suppose I must take your word for it," he said at last.

"Indeed, you must," she responded, her gaze unflinching.

He blinked and slowly began to release his nephew, taking several steps backward. Edward's expression was grim, his gray eyes dark and fiery as he, too, stepped away from the door. He slipped his greatcoat apart at the front opening, tugging at his coat and waistcoat beneath. He never once took his gaze from his uncle. Julia looked from uncle to nephew, sensing that some greater conflict was present than her husband's fear that Edward had been flirting with her. She remembered what Lady Trevaunance had told her about Edward's mother and a broken betrothal. She felt uneasy, as though she was seeing a truth she had much rather not.

"But you wanted more from Julia than a mere kiss, didn't you, little Edward?" he asked, clearly taunting his nephew.

"I won't dignify that remark," Edward returned flatly, glaring at his uncle, his breath still coming hard through his nostrils. After a moment, he turned briefly toward Julia, bid her another farewell, then quickly left the room.

Julia's attention became fixed on her husband. He was standing very erect, and there was something in his bearing that put her so forcibly in mind of Edward that she suffered a mild shock. Physically, they were nearly identical—the same height, the same broad shoulders, narrow waist, firm thighs. Sir Perran had been looking down the hall, as though half expecting his nephew to return, when he shifted his gaze abruptly to her. He regarded her for a long moment, seeing her but not seeing her.

Julia was startled and confused. Where was the bent body she had grown accustomed to for so many years? What of his limp? How little she understood him.

His gaze slipped away from her, his expression changed, disintegrating. His shoulders seemed to collapse. He pressed his hand against his left hip and bent his knee. Without a word, he limped from the room, appearing to be in terrible pain.

Julia blinked. One moment he was limping, the next attacking his nephew with legs straight and strong, the next moment limping again.

If only she could come to understand her husband's mind.

Eighteen

A month later, as Julia watched her husband limp slowly into the morning room, she realized her attitude toward him had changed dramatically since Christmas.

She was seated on one side of the fireplace in a blue silk damask winged chair. He took up a chair opposite her, his lap desk under one arm as he sat down. Settling the small, angular cherrywood box on his lap, he bid her a good evening. She returned the same greeting, in the same cool manner, then lowered her gaze to the embroidery work resting on a pillow in front of her, pleased with her progress on the colorful, elegant peacock.

One of the things she had discovered about Sir Perran was his acute perception, probably the singular quality he possessed that was most nearly responsible for his success in restoring his family's fortunes. Julia had grown to admire that part of him, how he could look at anyone and seemingly determine what they were thinking and what sentiments were holding them captive.

With purposeful effort, she had begun to see the world through his eyes. It was a very different sort of world, a very different society in which he lived, breathed, and moved, as though if she were to say the tree was green, he would counter by saying the tree was a deep green with flecks of gold at the tips of the leaves, the undersides a lighter frosted green, the new growth pale and translucent.

Julia tried to think as he thought, to view everyone as he viewed them, and she was just now beginning to succeed in her efforts. Surprisingly, she had lost something in the process, something she had needed to lose, at least to a degree: her hitherto unrecognized belief that life could always be parceled into neat little boxes. Perhaps studying music could be relegated thusly, as might arranging a room of furniture to better suit longer summer days or colder winter evenings. But people were not disposed of so easily. Sir Perran, least of all.

She realized that since her marriage to the baronet, she had begun discarding her boxes one after the other. Her husband fit so few of the molds she believed constituted life and marriage. He had never made love to her, for one thing. She had always supposed, given the general manner in which men were always ogling the female body, that Sir Perran's first interest in her would have been physical. But not so. He had never even kissed her on the lips.

This had been the first object of her newfound interest in becoming an observer. She wanted to determine for herself precisely what Sir Perran thought on this subject. So she had watched him, noting that he never looked at any women, not even the buxom upstairs maid who had all the footmen stumbling over their feet whenever she was near.

But that was not exactly true. Julia had seen him look at her own bosom once. She had been intrigued by his apparent interest and watched him closely—no flushing of his complexion, not his cheeks, ears, or neck, as she had observed in other men; no shifting in his seat, as though a responsiveness within his body might betray his interest. When he scratched his cheek, then returned to the book he was reading and turned the page, she glanced down at her chest and saw that an errant string of deep red silk floss was looped on the bodice of her white gown.

Julia was faintly amused.

She wondered if he preferred men. So she had observed him a little more. After a week, when he elicited no telltale interest that she could detect, she decided her first observation about him early on in their marriage had been accurate: his pleasure was wholly in saying yes and no, in commanding his world.

Finally, she had tested him herself. She had had Gabrielle lower scandalously the décolleté of several of her gowns. He had noticed the change immediately and at first had been amused, yet still he had shown no particular interest. In the end, he admonished Julia for conducting herself immodestly, indicating that even old Grigson could scarcely keep his eyes from her bosom throughout dinner. If she did not at once repair the deficiency in her gowns, Sir Perran told her, he would confine her to her chambers.

Julia knew him well enough to believe he would carry out his threat if she did not comply. Gabrielle was exceedingly disappointed—by now she was fully conversant with the lack of amorous adventures in the master's bedchamber—and set to adding pretty lace ruffles and fichus to the improper bodices with a disapproving sniff.

So all men weren't the lascivious creatures she had believed them to be.

And what of marriage? Her girlhood daydreams would have seen her settled into a loving, affectionate relationship, yet here she was being told when to rise and when to retire, how to dress, how to speak, what pieces to play on the pianoforte. Nine days out of ten, Julia felt more like a naughty child than like a wife. Sir Perran had even taken away her housekeeping responsibilities. He had hired a housekeeper of his choosing, who was required to answer not to the mistress of the house but to him.

As Julia continued to ply her needle, and for the present let her husband believe she had no thoughts but for her embroidery work, she considered how changed she was, in such short a time, since Christmas—and how much better she was for it. In November, she had been so distressed by her unhappy marriage that she had lost her appetite and had found herself starting at every loud noise.

Now she no longer let her sensibilities rule her. Now she observed and waited. Somehow she would find a way of coming to terms with her husband, of coming to understand him, of gaining his trust.

"How is your embroidery progressing?" Sir Perran queried.

"I am convinced it more nearly resembles a pigeon than a peacock," Julia responded, lying, wondering if she could prevent him from discerning her whisker. She schooled her features and lifted her gaze to meet his.

Sir Perran never paid attention to fulsome gestures—throwing back the head to laugh, fanning oneself quickly, smiling, crying, arguing. He was an observer of the minute, of the smallest detail.

Julia lifted the piece for him to see, but she knew he wouldn't care about the embroidery. He didn't even shift his eyes away from hers while she held it up for his inspection. She met his gaze squarely and steadily, neither flinching nor smiling nor in any other manner betraying her thoughts or feelings to him.

Finally, he grunted, returning his attention to his lap box, in which he kept an ongoing pile of documents relating to his business affairs.

Julia made no quick movement, but resettled the embroidery slowly on her lap. She was immensely pleased. A few weeks ago, he would have caught her in the lie. But not tonight. After a moment, she stopped stitching and stared purposely at the carpet in front of her. She parted her lips infinitesimally, noting from her peripheral vision that when she did so he turned to look at her.

She settled back in her chair and again resumed her needlework. Yes, she was beginning to comprehend him.

Her thoughts spun sideways. How had he gained control over her? She had never really considered the whole of it before. What had he done? How had he uncovered her weaknesses?

Knowing him as she now did, Julia realized she must have been like an open book to him—and therefore easily manipulated. All he had to do was speak kindly to her, and she would reveal every tender spot where he could thrust a sword and bring her more closely into his web of control. But how could she have known he was this way, when his gaze was always tender, his words kind, his actions slow, steady, and fatherly—the very things she needed? Only Caroline had had a suspicion of the truth—an instinct, she had said. But her words of warning had come far too late, and with too little practical evidence to have even caught her attention at the time.

So instead of marrying the kind, thoughtful man she had believed him to be, she had married a man whose every objective seemed contrary to her happiness.

Her thoughts sped backward and an intriguing notion occurred to her, an instinctual thought, something that related to what Lady Trevaunance had told her at Christmastime about Sir Perran's past—about Blackthorn's mother—and about every man possessing a heart.

"Perran," she began, following her instincts and letting her hands settle on her embroidery. Julia grew very quiet as she looked at him, observing him, making use of her newfound powers. "What is it you want from me?"

He blinked swiftly, the only facial response she could detect that indicated she had surprised him. Julia set aside her embroidery.

She let a long moment pass, and after seeing that he was not inclined to answer her, she continued. "I know what it is I want from you—your kindness, your steadiness—those attributes you so benevolently gave to me after all the pain I had endured while watching my father disintegrate before my eyes. Edward insisted I should have waited forever for him, and for a long time I thought perhaps I had lacked courage in not waiting. But I believe I understand myself better now. I married you because I needed your steadiness more than anything else."

Julia rose from her chair and crossed the small distance between them. She sank to her knees in front of him, and after removing the small cherrywood desk and setting it on the floor beside his chair, she laid her head upon his lap. The warmth from the crackling wood fire was a pleasing sensation along her side. She heard him gasp faintly and she pressed her thoughts home. "I wanted your kindness, your consideration, your concern for my sisters' welfare. Why will you not give me these things? Have I so deeply offended you somehow that you have now found me unworthy of your tenderness?" Julia looked up at him and was pleased by the stunned expression he bore. "I have only one desire, Perran," she added. "To be an excellent wife to you. I could love you if you would permit me to. Only tell me what I have done, or if not I, tell me who then has so injured your heart that love has become your enemy?"

She could see that he was struggling, and that following her impulse to speak plainly and boldly from her heart had been the right course to take. For in his eyes, she saw great pain and longing. Was it of Sophia Kettering he was thinking? Julia then queried, "Will you not at least try, for your sake and for mine? I entered this marriage willing to please, wanting to be the best of wives. But if you keep your heart closed to me, I will never be your true wife. Never, no matter how firmly you bring me under your command, I will never truly belong to you. I will only be a signature on our marriage documents."

He shifted his gaze away from her. She knew he was seeing beyond her, beyond himself, perhaps deeply into the past.

Sir Perran was remembering himself as a young man, a passionate young buck not so very different from his nephew, full of ideals and of courageous schemes.

Once the quarry had been stripped from his family, he had bricked up his heart as firmly as if he had overlaid it with stone, until Sophia had entered his life. She was a vision, much of Blackthorn's fine looks reflective of her beauty. She wore her black hair powdered and smelling of roses. Her eyes were the keenest blue, full of sharp intelligence. He had met her at a Vauxhall masquerade. He had quickly stripped her of her mask; she had done the same of him. He had been in his late thirties when he met her. She had been so young, scarcely eighteen. The sensation of being with her was like watching the fireworks at the Gardens. She was all brilliant flashes, dazzling smiles, mischievous eyes. She made him pretend they were lost in the maze of paths that ran about the gardens. Secreted in the shadows, he had kissed her until he ached into his joints. The passionate love that rose up between them was sudden and powerful.

But he had not been alone in his pursuit of her. His younger brother, by nearly twenty years, had been smitten with her as well. He was a handsome captain with a brilliant future ahead of him.

When Sir Perran became betrothed to Sophia, he could want for nothing more. One night, a month before the wedding, he seduced her, purposefully, leading her with gentle caresses, sweet words of love and wickedness, his tongue everywhere that pleased her. The feel of her in his arms had been magical, his hearing dimmed by the excitement of taking her. He could not remember her protests or the feel of her biting into his hand when he covered her mouth. He did not remember covering her mouth.

When he realized he had hurt her, that she was weeping, he could not seem to console her. He had thought, he had believed she had wanted him. Surely, she had wanted him. Hadn't she enjoyed his kisses and caresses?

He still didn't know what he had done. He didn't want to know. He had tried to call on her, to speak to her. He confronted her angrily in public several times because it was obvious she was rejecting him. When she begged him to end the betrothal, he refused. How could he let her go when he loved her as he did—to the point of madness?

Three weeks later, she eloped with his brother. Three months later, when he found himself alone with her, he had begged her to tell him what had happened . . . why she had rejected him.

"My only desire was for your loving kindness and you withheld it from me," she said, tears pouring down her cheeks. "You put your hand over my mouth and kept it there until you were finished with my body, even though I bit you fiercely. I didn't know you until that moment—then I knew you too well."

"You are mistaken!" he had cried, trying to take her in his arms, but she pushed him away.

"Take care," she had warned him. "I am with child."

Sir Perran could listen no more to the memories that were shouting at him from across the years, accusing him. He could only look at the now-faded scars on the inside of his fingers. He didn't remember putting his hand over her mouth. He didn't remember the pain or the blood, only that he kept his fingers wrapped for three weeks in linen bandages. He told everyone that one of his hunting dogs had bitten him.

He looked down at Julia, who was still watching him with hopeful eyes. What was he supposed to tell her? That he was a kind man when he knew he wasn't?

He bid her leave him and was a little surprised that she did not protest, or beg, or in any other way try to force him into permitting her to stay. When she had closed the door, he leaned his head back and squeezed his eyes shut. He tried to envision a life with Julia other than the one he had planned for her for so long. His only present desire was to command her. Physically, it was as though he were dead, something he knew no woman could possibly comprehend.

Yet this marriage, which had brought under his domain all that he had schemed for—Julia, Hatherleigh Park, and the quarry—had not given him the satisfaction he had believed it would.

Initially, he had experienced a euphoria unequaled. The marriage settlements gave him the quarry and Hatherleigh in exchange for the settling of all of Delabole's debts. God knows there were twoscore of them. He smiled, for even then Delabole's debts had scarcely touched his fortune. That was perhaps the greatest irony of them all—that Delabole had perished for a sum that was insignificant to him.

But for some reason, as he brought Julia and her sisters firmly beneath his command, his euphoria dimmed in unhappy stages, to pleasure, pleasure giving way to warmth, which in turn lost its heat and left him daily with a sense of unrest and discontent he did not understand. He should have been the happiest man on earth knowing that he had vindicated his father and his father before him, that he had closed the circle that had robbed him of his inheritance early in his life.

But he was not. He was, in fact, very much alone.

And Julia had offered herself to him. He believed her to be sincere. He tried to imagine what it was she would then expect of him.

Kindness, she had said. He could be kind.

Consideration. He could be considerate.

Concern for her sisters. He could show concern.

But was that all she would want of him?

He sat alone by the fire for several hours, thinking, pondering. He would be taking a risk in acquiescing to her requests.

Could he love her? Could he be her husband truly? Would she indeed return his love? Thoughts of Sophia and the love he had lost became mixed in his mind with thoughts of Julia.

When the ormolu clock on the mantel struck the midnight hour, he came to a decision. He would try. For the present, he would try.

The next few weeks for Julia were immensely gratifying. Though Sir Perran did not broach the subject with her, she knew by his shift in demeanor that he wished to begin again. She saw no reason to provoke him into saying that which quite obviously he did not wish to say. She knew she had pushed him hard, in mid-January, speaking her heart to him, begging him to open his heart to her.

From that time, he had indeed been kinder to her, treating her less like a chess piece to be moved about at his whim and more like a woman with a good mind and a warm heart. She spoke of her love of Hatherleigh and the way it had been when her mother was alive—full of guests from Bath and the surrounding countryside, every chamber the family used day to day alive with fresh flowers and greenery. She told him how much she valued the immaculate attention to every housekeeping detail that his eye coveted. He actually smiled beneath her praise. He spoke of desiring to see the stables reestablished, receiving with another smile her enthusiastic exclamation that such a scheme would send Caroline *aux anges*.

He warmed toward her younger sisters, who in turn gentled their hearts toward him. As the snow began to melt in late February, the atmosphere at Hatherleigh began to relax. More young gentlemen were permitted to call upon the beautiful Verdell sisters, music from Julia's fingertips upon the pianoforte and Caroline's exquisite voice rising to the rafters.

Still, he had not kissed her or touched her. Julia wondered how to discuss such a delicate matter with him, especially when the mere thought of doing so brought a warm tingling to her cheeks. Yet she had always wanted children; a dozen of them would suit her to perfection. She could not imagine a more complete life—except for one in which a passionate love was possible. But even without such a love, Julia now believed she could be very happy, provided Sir Perran continued in his tenderness toward her and her sisters.

If he occasionally seemed elusive and dictatorial, she forgave him, especially when he came to her and apologized. She wondered if she ought to ask him about a London Season, but she was afraid to. Julia did not want him to think that her purpose in addressing him in January had been to coax him into reconsidering his refusal to take them to the Metropolis. At the same time, the subject was never far from her sisters, each one hoping that the baronet might somehow find it in his heart to relent.

While residing at Hatherleigh Park, Sir Perran maintained The Priory in full housekeeping staff. Once a week, on Saturday nights, he hosted his card soirées—just as he had prior to wedding Julia—an event that she knew to be of immense importance to him.

Saturday evenings had therefore, from the first, been the happiest for the sisters, especially in the difficult times before Christmas. On these evenings, they could rest assured they would not be criticized or directed to activities they disliked or in any other manner be required to please *him*.

In early March, on such a Saturday, the sisters were gathered in the Green Salon. Outside, a heavy rain pounded upon the windows, and the damp chill air had prompted Julia to see that a fire blazed in the hearth.

The sisters had rearranged the furniture so that a round table could be placed in front of the forest-green silk damask sofa. Presently, they were grouped around the table, over which a score of pages from *La Belle Assemblée* had been scattered. Each sister had with her several bandboxes full of fabrics of every sort, in her favorite colors. The discussion was lively, spirits were high, and the main topic—a London Season—was the object of the younger sisters' hopes and aspirations, especially Annabelle's.

"But I don't see why you have not asked him," Annabelle said, overlaying a bit of lavender sprigged muslin on a sketch of a delectable morning gown. She wrinkled her nose in dislike of the combination, then lifted her gaze to meet Julia's.

Julia had her elbow on the table and her chin propped in her hand. She sighed at the sight of a ravishing ball gown of burgundy silk, quite décolléte, the lady's hair adorned with a rosette of tulle. "I have not asked, because we have been getting along so famously I feared disturbing all by bringing forth a subject that would only remind him of . . . well, of my defiance at Christmastide."

Annabelle huffed a sigh of exasperation. "I detest it when you speak of him more as your father than as your husband."

"I don't want to brangle, Annabelle. I will ask him, but you must be patient, and if he refuses, you must be understanding."

"All this time we have been planning for a Season which I doubt will even come to pass," she returned petulantly.

Elizabeth pulled one of her long black curls and held it between her lips. She released it suddenly and it sprang back into a bouncing coil. "I should think it would be dreadful for you to have been so nice to him these many weeks and more, only to have your request refused. All your efforts would be to no avail whatsoever."

Julia thought she caught a fleeting movement near the door. Had the door closed, or was it her imagination? The light from the blazing fire certainly threw up oversized and constantly moving shadows. Deciding she had been mistaken, she turned back toward the window nearest her and watched a distant flash of lightning briefly illuminate the hills beyond. A terrible storm had overtaken the countryside. She hoped her husband had made it safely to The Priory.

Returning her attention to her sisters, she felt it necessary to rebuke Elizabeth's attitude. "You shouldn't say such things, Lizzie. I am not *being nice* to my husband so that he will give you a Season, and if you have failed to notice a complete alteration in his manner toward you and toward me, then you are more dim-witted than I had supposed."

Elizabeth sighed. "You are right, I know you are. And he has changed. I was being unkind and I do apologize."

"Thank you for saying so. Now, what do you think of this color against my hair?" She held up a swatch of bright pink silk, and much to her great satisfaction a groan went up about the table.

Sir Perran stood in the hallway outside the Green Salon, his cane in hand. He felt very foolish suddenly, as though he had been led merrily down the garden path like a silly halfling. The bridge that crossed the creek some two miles from Hatherleigh had been flooded and was impassable. He had returned, almost with a light heart, thinking how pleasant it would be to sit with Julia and her sisters through the evening. Perhaps they would sing duets for him. Caroline in particular had a voice to melt even the dullest pair of ears.

But when he had slowly opened the door, intending to give them all a fright, he had heard Annabelle complaining about the Season. He saw the bandboxes and was familiar with their contents—fabric pieces. He saw a sketch Elizabeth was holding up—Ackermann's, perhaps, or *La Belle Assemblée.* Well, women would always be more interested in fashion than would be men. But then he had heard Annabelle again, prompting Julia to ask him for a Season in London.

He thought Annabelle petulant and childish. But it was Elizabeth's remark that stilled his heart. *All your efforts would be to no avail.*

He walked down the hall and headed toward his bedchamber. *All your efforts would be to no avail.*

When he reached his finely carved oak door, Sir Perran gave it a strong kick with his hard Wellington boots, satisfied with the dent he had made in an acanthus leaf.

He turned the handle, gave the door a shove, and strode in. So Julia had played him like the fool he apparently was. He recalled to mind her pleading green eyes, the story she had told him of how glad she was she had chosen him, instead of his nephew, because of his steadiness.

And he had believed her! What a nodcock he was!

So, the ladies wished for a Season. Well, then, he would give them a season they would never forget.

Nineteen

London, England
20 March 1815

Julia watched Caroline and Annabelle laughing almost hysterically, but could join them by contributing only a faint smile. She should have been delighted that they were in London at last. Seeing her sisters' dreams of a season finally fulfilled should have pleased her enormously.

But from the time Sir Perran had graciously agreed to permit the sisters several weeks in the Metropolis during the spring, Julia knew something had gone awry. But what? She had searched her mind a dozen times, trying to determine what she might have done to have caused her husband's former distance to return, but so it had. But why?

"You are like a kitten that has fallen into a stream, only to spring out with its fur matted in clumps!" Annabelle cried, laughing at Caroline. Her sister's sable-trimmed bonnet and matching muff had gotten soaked in the process of running from Sir Perran's coach to the front door of their townhouse in Grosvenor Square. The rain was coming down so hard that none of them had been spared.

"And what of you?" Caroline responded, blinking up at Annabelle's wilting ostrich feather. "Rather like the pot calling the kettle black."

Annabelle peered up at the brim of her bonnet and started to laugh all over again as water dripped from the soggy feathers onto her nose. The sisters laughed together.

When Elizabeth, her bonnet tipped forward awkwardly and obscuring her vision, stumbled into the entrance hall exclaiming that she had been left outside to drown, Caroline and Annabelle fell into whoops. Even Julia could not keep from laughing, her present troubles dimming as Elizabeth took one step, slipped on the black-and-white tile floor that had become a lake of rain, and landed squarely on her backside.

Grigson, who had traveled to London with the family, came rushing from the nether regions full of apologies, and at least three footmen in tow to assist Elizabeth to her feet and to tend to the wet floor.

"We thought we could manage by ourselves so that the groom could get his poor horses into the stables," Julia explained, still laughing. "We were never so wrong. Would you please see that several hot baths and warming pans are brought upstairs immediately. We are laughing now, but if even one among us contracts a putrid sore throat—after so much effort in just getting to Mayfair—there will be no amusement for some time to come."

Grigson smiled, a rarity for him, and quickly issued orders to his footmen. The ladies went immediately upstairs and were helped out of their wet clothes and into hot baths in quick order.

As Julia sank into a porcelain tub of steaming rose water, she breathed in the lovely fragrance and sighed. They were in London at last—in this she would be content, for now she could truly begin to see her sisters well settled.

She leaned her head back and looked out the window of her bedchamber, which overlooked the square. The rain still pelted the Metropolis mercilessly and probably would do so for the remainder of the evening.

Julia had never been to London before and should have known an intense excitement, but instead, she admitted to herself at last, she was full of dread.

The stormy night that Sir Perran had returned unexpectedly early from his card soirée, Julia had joined him in the library and had asked him to relent in his decision not to permit a Season for her sisters. She had sat at his knees, as she frequently did, and had laid her head on his lap. He stroked her hair but remained quiet.

"I will understand, Perran, if you do not wish for it. After all, this was a decision you made in December because I did not obey your wishes regarding my gown of mourning."

"I paid a hundred guineas for that black gown," he stated, almost absently.

Julia frowned. His voice sounded strange to her ears. She lifted her head and looked up at him. "What is it?" she queried. "Have I offended you somehow?"

He shook his head but did not smile. She tilted her head slightly, still searching his face. He did not look at her, but rather over her shoulder, at seemingly nothing in particular.

"I should not have asked," she said. "You are displeased. I can see that you are."

"I am not displeased," he returned without emotion.

Julia sat back on her heels. "I know what it is. You are blue-deviled because you did not get to play at cards tonight. If you like, I shall play you as many hands of piquet as you wish."

He looked at her then. "You do not have to be so *nice* to me, Julia. I am not a child who needs to be coddled or entertained when I am, as you say, blue-deviled. The truth is, I have a slight headache, and if you wouldn't mind, I would rather retire for the evening." Only then did he smile, but even in his smile, he did not seem the same. "Please tell your sisters that I will give them, and you, a trip to London for the Season. Be prepared to leave in, let us say, a fortnight."

He had kissed her on the cheek and had then quit the library, leaning heavily on his cane. Julia watched him go, feeling vaguely ill at ease instead of overjoyed at his decision.

So, here she was, lying in a bath, trying to determine what was amiss. She had asked him several times if something was distressing him, but his answer was always the same. He would pose the question, "Am I not treating you with sufficient kindness?"

And she would respond, "Of course you are."

"Then you have nothing to worry about."

But she was worried, even though by all appearances his conduct toward her and her sisters had remained amiable. He was kind and attentive, agreeable in his choice of words. Yet it seemed to her that he had closed his heart to her. But why?

Julia sighed. All she could do at this juncture, since Sir Perran would not reveal to her what was troubling him, was to hope that somehow the future would solve itself.

Her thoughts were turned away from her husband when Gabrielle entered the bedchamber with fresh linens over her arm, her complexion pale, her expression stricken.

"What is it?" Julia asked, alarmed.

Tears welled up in Gabrielle's dark eyes. "I have just learned from Grigson that Bonaparte . . . he is in Paris. *C'est impossible!* The royal armies, they could not stop him."

"Oh, no," Julia breathed, her heart seeming to stop in her chest. She understood precisely what his presence in the French capital meant: War would resume. And war meant that Edward would yet again face an army across a battlefield. Tears of her own bit her eyes. She shivered, despite the heat of the steaming water.

She had, of course, known that in late February Napoleon had escaped from Elba, but it was hoped by all of England and by the allies that the French army would unite against their former emperor, would take him prisoner, and would banish him again from Europe—this time to a more distant place of exile than an island so near the coast of France. But it would seem the army could not forget the man who had given them the glories of so many victories. Now Bonaparte was in Paris, undoubtedly again preparing for war.

With thoughts of Edward, Julia found herself once more in a state of longing. She let the rose water seep through her fingers and tried not to think of him, but somehow he appeared in her mind, tall and handsome. She could hear his voice recalling his many professions of love. She could feel his lips on hers, as though he had kissed her yesterday instead of eight months ago. With her husband's increasing distance, Edward had begun to steal into her thoughts and dreams all over again. She knew from Sir Perran that his nephew was still in London and that she would probably see him when she arrived in the Metropolis. Julia closed her eyes, trying to push away thoughts of him, but they persisted. She wanted to see him so very much, but of what use would seeing him be except to torture her?

On the following afternoon, Julia ventured forth alone to pay a morning call upon Lady Trevaunance. She found the elegant marchioness seated on a gold and white striped silk sofa. Her Ladyship's drawing room was a reflection of ancient Greece and Rome. Egyptian caryatids were mounted on either side of the fireplace; the colors of the chamber were royal-blue, gold, and white; and several Empire chairs had been scattered about the long, rectangular room. The effect was almost military in color, form, and simplicity of decor. Draperies of royal-blue velvet, fringed with gold, hung on either side of the six long windows at the front and side of the chamber. The same fabric had been draped gracefully over valances adorned with bronze kestrels. The carpet on the floor was a blue, patterned with gold.

Lady Trevaunance was dressed in a light blue silk morning gown, frilled at the neck and at the wrists. Her blond hair, glowing delicately with silver, was caught atop her head and arranged in a flow of curls down her neck. She wore a paisley silk shawl in browns and blues, elegantly looped across her forearms. Pearl drops on her ears, a large sapphire ring, and white silk slippers completed a toilette that was utterly charming. She was in every respect a lady of fashion, enhanced even further by a young black page who stood over her shoulder, wafting a fan over her face, prepared to run errands for her on the instant. After greeting Julia, she whispered something into her page's ear, which sent the boy flying from the chamber.

Julia wore a white muslin morning gown trimmed with pale

green ribbons. Lady Trevaunance scrutinized her carefully. *"La Belle Assemblée,* only how clever to have added the point lace about the hem. Do turn for me," she directed Julia, "but quite slowly." Lady Trevaunance released a breath of appreciation. "The point lace ruff at the back of the neck and your auburn curls . . . very nice. The back of the gown gathered, and flowing and giving the appearance of a demi-train. Quite impeccable. Was this gown Sir Perran's choice?"

Julia shook her head. "My sisters and I have for many years created our own designs."

"How unfortunate that you are not a modiste. My dear, your costume alone will guarantee you the *entrée.*" She then smiled suddenly and brightly, and gestured for Julia to take up a black lacquered Empire chair opposite her. "Of course, my *sponsoring* you will not be a hindrance, either."

"My lady," Julia whispered, her heart beating quickly. "I had hoped you would, but I would not have presumed to ask!"

"Then I am glad I addressed the matter. But you must promise me never to be afraid to ask anything of me. It is my pleasure to be of assistance to you and your sisters. Now, tell me how you go on."

Julia arranged her skirts and told her everything—all the improvements at Hatherleigh, the increase in a social life for her sisters, her determination to comprehend her husband, her efforts to win him over, his initial change of heart, and his recent withdrawal from her.

Lady Trevaunance listened carefully and closely to all she said. "Then you have made excellent progress. Do not be dismayed if you suffer reverses now and again. Remember, Sir Perran is not a man used to the company of a woman." She smiled and then stated, in a firm, businesslike manner, "Are you ready to listen now to all that you must do this first sennight in order to bring your sisters into fashion?"

"Oh, yes," Julia sighed, greatly content. Here was the moment for which she had been working and sacrificing for nearly three years. Her sisters were in London, and with the marchioness's support, they would be well on their way to becoming firmly established in society.

Lady Trevaunance began. "First, you must always remember that you are at a disadvantage for two reasons: your father's unfortunate death and your decision to marry before you were out of black gloves."

"I understand," she responded with a nod.

"Good. Then you must be prepared to be shunned, though I trust you will never be given the cut direct. Believe me that if any use you so ill and it comes to my notice, heads will roll—dreadful expression, isn't it? At any rate, make it known to your sisters that regardless of the cold stares and the turned shoulders, they must always behave as though nothing untoward has happened. This is of the utmost importance. Having survived so many Seasons myself, I can assure you the worst scrapes and scandals can be overcome by simply smiling when you do not feel like smiling.

"Next. You must let me review every invitation you receive. There are many living on the fringes of society with whom neither you nor your sisters should become involved. This also is of the utmost importance. Though there are some soirées, fetes, and balls you must avoid, for the most part, if you wish to succeed, you must be seen at several every night. To fly from one to the other—especially *ensemble* with your siblings—will insure that the Verdell sisters are invited everywhere and therefore *must* be invited everywhere. Be seen at the opera frequently, and at Vauxhall gardens but not at the masquerades. Never go down St. James Street in the morning—the dandies wait in the bow windows of their clubs and pounce upon hapless young ladies who are ill informed of their intentions—but do shop to your heart's content in New Bond Street. Visit the museum, the Royal Academy, Hookham's Library. If you can possibly charm the eye of the Prince Regent, you will be made."

Julia noted that Lady Trevaunance's list was quite thorough except for one critical event. Had she forgotten it to a purpose? Undoubtedly, but Julia wished to know the marchioness's opinion anyway. Taking a deep breath, she posed the difficult question. "And what of the Almack Assembly Rooms?"

The marchioness sighed. "I am a lady with a great deal of influence. Unfortunately, Almack's is governed by a body of patronesses, most of whom are high-sticklers and must approve of everyone to whom they grant vouchers. I was unable to persuade even one of them—including Lady Cowper—to permit you to attend. I'm sorry."

Almack's was known as the Marriage Mart and was the surest way to a successful London season. Anything less, and Julia knew that the more eligible young gentlemen would be kept well away from the Verdell sisters. "Yet you still believe we will achieve success in spite of our exclusion from the assemblies?"

At that, Lady Trevaunance smiled. "Once Elizabeth and Caroline and Annabelle have been seen by one or two young men of birth and breeding, trust me when I say that Sir Perran will be besieged with callers."

Julia was not convinced, but since she could see by the clock that she had remained far beyond the requisite quarter hour, she rose to take her leave. Lady Trevaunance, however, was apparently not inclined to let her go just yet. She bid Julia retake her seat and seemed particularly animated when her page reappeared and took up his place over her shoulder, behind the sofa. She exchanged whispers with him, and again the lad whisked away at a run and disappeared from the chamber. He returned just as quickly, a beatific smile on his dark brown face. Again, he whispered to Lady Trevaunance.

She smiled at the child, pinching his cheek. To Julia, she said, "Forgive us our secrets, but we have a surprise for you."

A moment later, Edward stepped into the chamber.

Julia felt as though she had just crossed from reality into a dream.

Edward. Had she spoken his name aloud? She didn't know.

She could hardly breathe as she watched him advance into the chamber. His black hair was tied in a neat black riband. His shirt points just touched his cheeks and his white neckcloth was tied to perfection. He wore a dark blue coat, which set off his broad shoulders to advantage; his buff silk waistcoat showed in a thin line below the cutaway tails of his coat and black pantaloons; Hessian boots revealed the lean, muscled line of his legs. He was as handsome as ever, and as always, the sight of him brought her pulse racing wildly at her wrist and her throat. She could not take her gaze from him.

He approached her, smiling. He took her hand in his, speaking her name in his deep voice. "Lady Blackthorn," he said, kissing her fingers lightly and giving her hand an affectionate squeeze before releasing it.

Lady Trevaunance called to him. "Such wretched manners, Major! Who taught you to ignore your hostess?"

"I was doomed," he responded, turning to her and placing a mock hand against his heart, before crossing to her and also taking her hand lightly in his clasp. "For I knew that if I greeted you first, you would have rebuked me for having overlooked your special guest."

"You are right. But it is such fun to tease you."

"And thank you, my lady, for sending for me."

She smiled fondly upon Edward, then touched her hand to her cheek, her expression now one of pretended bemusement. "How very odd," she said in a theatrical manner. "For I have just remembered something I must attend to this very moment. Major Blackthorn, I know I impose on you sorely, but would you be so kind as to entertain Lady Blackthorn for me? I know it will be a severe trial for you, since she is quite dull-witted and ugly, but do be a dear and oblige me in this one thing."

Julia was a little shocked, both by how lightly and facetiously the marchioness spoke, and also by the fact that she meant to leave her alone with Edward. She wanted to protest, but when Edward turned back to her and looked at her in just that way, as though he were parched with thirst and she were holding in her hand a full glass of water, she resigned herself to the pleasure of his company.

Lady Trevaunance rose from the gold and white sofa and teasingly pulled her page's ear to lead him out of the room. Julia rose as well, bidding *adieu* to the marchioness who, before she passed into the hall, told Julia that she expected her to call upon her at least every other day to keep her informed of her progress and to review her invitations with her. She then threw Edward an object, which he caught and which turned out to be a key. She merely winked as she closed the door upon them.

Julia felt a warm blush creeping up her cheeks. "She cannot possibly mean—" She could say no more.

Edward smiled and moved to stand near her. "She is very wicked," he said, "but quite harmless. She knows very well I mean to behave myself, and I'm sure she knows that you will do the same." He looked deeply into her eyes, his expression warm and loving. "Though I must confess that for just a moment, when I first walked into the room, I felt as I did last July, when I had but to look at you and I would be overtaken by a longing to embrace you, to kiss you, to touch you. Julia, I will always love you."

Julia felt her heart warmed by his words. She laid her hand upon his cheek as she looked into clear gray eyes, wanting to fall into the deepness, the steadiness of his gaze and never return. "And for just a moment," she responded softly, "when you stepped into the room, I couldn't breathe, I couldn't think. I never expected to see you today. I was stunned. Thank heaven there were not other people present, else I would have betrayed to them all the true state of my heart where you are concerned." She felt she was speaking in great innocence to him, confessing harmlessly that even though she was married and was devoted to her husband, she would not deny, in a brief private moment, her love for him.

But before she knew what was happening, he had taken her into his arms and was kissing her, very lightly, very tenderly, her hand still resting upon his cheek. She stroked his sun-darkened skin, then slipped her hand to the back of his neck, the silk of the black riband that held his hair in place sliding along her fingers. The next moment he was searching her mouth ever so gently as he drew her tightly against him. Julia knew, from the sweet waves of desire that swelled and rippled over her, that she ought to push him away, that she ought to forbid him to kiss her in this manner, but she couldn't. For the moment, all she could think of was how much she wanted to feel his hands caressing her, touching her, his skin against her skin, his lips covering her in places she had dreamt about over and over since July.

Blackthorn did not understand why her closeness overset his every principle. He had not meant to kiss her or to take her in his arms so completely, and heaven help him he would do a great deal more before long given the least encouragement.

"Julia," he whispered softly in her ear. He heard his name returned to him and again he kissed her, deeply, passionately. He was quickly reaching a despairing, painful point of need. She must have felt the same or perhaps sensed his desperation, for she suddenly withdrew from him and moved to stand by the fireplace.

For a moment he stood still, letting the heat of his passion subside. But the sight of Julia as he turned to look at her—her downcast eyes, the slight slump of her shoulders—tore at his heart and he drew near her again, this time placing his hands on her arms.

"Oh, Edward," she whispered. "What a fool I was to have believed my own lies. All these months I have been telling myself that I could be content apart from you, but now, having you touch me and kiss me, I can scarcely bear the idea of walking from this room. Yet I must."

He kissed her hair and slipped his arms about her, holding her fast. She leaned her head back into his shoulder. "I love you," he breathed into her ear. "Julia, whatever are we going to do?"

She felt her throat grow painfully tight as he held her. Julia wanted to turn within his arms and permit him to kiss her again, but she feared what might ensue. She did not trust herself. "I am your uncle's wife," she responded. "I am determined to love him and to encourage his heart toward me. As much as I wish I could give myself to you, I can't. I have promised to be faithful to my husband and what I ask of you is that you help me to keep my promise."

He did not respond for a long time but held her close, continuing to place soft kisses in her hair. Finally, he said, "I will do whatever you want me to."

"Go now," she whispered, slowly disengaging his arms from about her. "Please. That is what I want."

"I will, but first there is something I must say to you. Please look at me." When Julia turned to face him, she lifted her gaze to his and felt tears start to her eyes. He touched her face with his hand and said, "I wanted you to live with me the rest of my life so that I might take you to bed every night if it so pleased you. I wanted you to bear my children; I wanted you to be their mother, to raise them, to care for them, to sew strong characters in their souls. When I leave you now, I need you to understand how hard this is for me . . . that I do not turn away from you easily. I am giving up the desires of my heart all over again, as I gave them up last summer. My heart is breaking. Do you understand?"

Julia felt her tears trickle down her cheeks, but she did nothing to stop them. She nodded in response to his question.

"With that said," he continued, "I honor you for wanting to remain chaste and to fulfill your vows to your husband. For that reason, whatever you want me to do I will do—you have but to instruct me."

"You must not approach me again," she told him. "When I meet you in public, I would be most grateful if you would treat me with polite distance. Anything more, and I fear—"

"I know," he whispered, leaning forward to touch his forehead against hers. "Very well. Polite distance it shall be." He then gently brushed his lips against hers and strode quickly from the chamber.

Soon afterward, Julia was safely ensconced in her husband's immaculate and comfortable town coach, bowling along Berkeley Square and heading back to Grosvenor Square. The sky was attempting to clear and in scattered places blue could be seen showing through a stubborn layer of gray clouds. The air smelled clean and fresh after such a hard rain of the night before. The smell of horses, however, had already begun to fill the city. Carts were everywhere, designed for the sole purpose of removing the collected offal and guided about the streets by strong-shouldered handlers. Another sight was rising into the air, a dark, cloudy smoke from the multitudinous coal-burning fireplaces. The buildings were dark gray and in places black, an indication of the constantly settling debris from the coal.

But Julia ignored what would likely be part of the Metropolis for centuries to come—horses and coal smoke—and enjoyed instead the sight and bustle of one of Europe's leading capitals. Carriages of every description passed by: Stanhope gigs, glossy curricles, phaetons en route to Hyde Park, town chariots, old-fashioned barouches, landaus. The pace of the city was fully alive and spoke to Julia of movement, of progress, of growth. In spite of Edward's disturbing presence, she was very glad to be in London after all.

The next week introduced a whirlwind of activities, beginning with the ball Lady Trevaunance gave as sponsor of the Verdell sisters. If Julia had had any doubts about her sisters' likely success in London, she was quickly reassured on that score. From the first, when the four ladies descended the stairs of the marchioness's home and made a dramatic presentation as contrasting auburn and raven-haired beauties, the younger sisters were positively besieged.

Julia might have collected a court about her, as well, but she chose to remain close to her husband, attendant upon him in every respect. He still seemed withdrawn much of the time, and occasionally she would catch him looking at her with a strange sadness in his eye. But yet he remained stoic and unmoved by her persistent and gentle queries. Whatever was troubling him he kept close to his heart.

Despite Sir Perran's unwillingness to impart his thoughts to

her, Julia was pleased with their London beginning. The first
two weeks progressed just as Lady Trevaunance had said they
would, Julia immediately finding herself shepherding her sisters
to no fewer than four engagements each evening. The front
knocker was rarely quiet and the townhouse soon resembled a
flower stall in the marketplace. The effects of the lack of vouchers to Almack's was not yet felt, since the Wednesday assemblies
had not yet begun. But until then, Julia hoped that all three of
her sisters would have sufficient time to let their characters,
dispositions, and the fine effects of their mother's teachings be
their *entrée*.

As for Edward, ever since her initial *tête-à-tête* with him, Julia
found she was able more and more to greet him in public without
experiencing a profound and nearly overwhelming impulse to
fall into his arms. Whenever she saw him, she reminded herself
of her duty to her husband and of her desire to win his heart if
she could. There could be no place for Edward in her life and
well she knew it. Besides, by June she would be returning to
Bath, and it was very likely she would not see Edward for
months, possibly years after that, particularly with the affairs in
Europe having taken a downward turn.

Keeping his word, Edward followed her lead. He rarely called
at Grosvenor Square, and when he asked her to dance for the
first time and she gently refused, he accepted her rebuff and did
not ask again. Though she chanced to meet him frequently during the round of events that characterized each day and evening,
Julia was never alone with him, even in conversation. Only occasionally would she permit herself the luxury of looking at him,
for there seemed to be some mystery at work within her, the
mere sight of him plucking at her heartstrings and causing her
to long for what could not be. She no longer tried to deny that
her heart was bound to him forever. Julia knew she would always
love him, but she hoped by being sensible, she could keep that
love from destroying her future happiness within her marriage
to Sir Perran.

Twenty

Early April found Julia sitting with her sisters in the large front receiving room of Sir Perran's townhouse in Grosvenor Square. The chamber was a brilliant scarlet study, accented in black lacquer and gold. Crimson velvet draperies, drawn back with gold tasseled braid, flanked each of four windows. Scarlet silk damask covered the walls, sofa, and several of the black lacquer chairs. A harp and pianoforte awaited skilled fingers in the corner of the chamber opposite the windows.

Julia listened to Caroline and Annabelle arguing over the design for a new bonnet, which involved a poke covered in artificial red cherries and white rhododendron flowers. The size of the poke was under serious scrutiny, Annabelle insisting it should be larger than usual, and Caroline, whose tastes were considerably more subdued, championing a smaller, less curved brim. Auburn and black curls tangled together, they examined a sketch Annabelle had made.

Julia was about to inquire what color ribbons the ladies intended to use and precisely what Gabrielle's opinion was of the sketch, when Grigson appeared in the doorway and announced Ladies Trevaunance and Cowper, and Lord Peter.

Julia's gaze flew swiftly to Lord Peter's face, her heart sinking in her breast. She had not seen him since last June in Bath. When she had first arrived in London, she had learned he was visiting friends in Lincolnshire and had been exceedingly relieved not to have had to meet with him in *tonish* society. If only someone had warned her he had returned from the north.

Lady Trevaunance, in her habitually enthusiastic manner, swept into the room. Julia greeted her patroness and Lady Cowper. As her sisters came forward to also welcome their visitors and afterwards to direct them to comfortable seats near the fireplace, she turned to extend her hand to Lord Peter.

She noted, with faint amusement, that his ears were pink with embarrassment against his blond hair and his brown eyes were riddled with guilt. "Well met, Lady Blackthorn," he murmured, quite chastened.

As he bent over her proffered hand, she couldn't help but smile, in spite of having been startled by his sudden arrival, for he was as sheepish as a dog who had chewed up his master's favorite Moroccan slippers. Giving his hand an encouraging squeeze before she released it, she asked politely, "How do you go on? I am so glad you have come to call. I recently received a letter from Mary Brown, who was asking after you. You must tell me what you've been doing to occupy your time since we last met, so that I might have something with which to fill my next lines to her."

At this friendly speech, she could see that she had succeeded in putting him at ease. Surely he had been dreading an encounter with her as much as she had been.

"You must tell Miss Brown," he responded politely and amiably, "that I had come to London specifically to help Mama bring you and your sisters into fashion, only to find, to my utter delight, that the deed had already been done. The Misses Verdell and Lady Blackthorn can have no use for me after all." They had remained standing near the doorway, and as he shot a quick glance toward his mother and found that she and Lady Cowper were busily critiquing Annabelle's drawing, he lowered his voice. "You must also tell Miss Brown that I should never have left Bath as I did and that I have regretted having done so ever since. It was very wrong of me."

The expression in his eyes was pleading. Julia understood his cloaked request for forgiveness and she forgave him. But really there was nothing to forgive. Lady Trevaunance had been right:

Lord Peter would have found himself wed to a woman who did not love him. How much better that he had had the courage to play the coward after all.

"You will think me quite addled, I am sure, for saying so, My Lord, but I can't imagine to what you are referring. Again, let me say that I am glad you have come to call and that I trust I will always be able to count you among my friends."

He seemed so relieved, as he let out a great sigh, that she could have laughed. Instead, she smiled up at him and for his sake drew him to the lively feminine group clustered about his mother. Her sisters greeted him in a warm, friendly manner, each in turn, much to her approbation, and the conversation continued along the lines of fashion.

When presented with Annabelle's sketch, Lord Peter refused to give an opinion. "For I know what will follow!" he cried. "Either Miss Annabelle will refuse to dance with me at the next ball, or Miss Caroline will. And since I would be utterly cast down were either circumstance to occur, I shall refrain from remarking on the sketch. You will have to make up your minds without benefit of my hints, suggestions, approval, or criticisms."

Annabelle protested, saying that he was fainthearted, but Caroline expressed her belief that Lord Peter had spoken in a completely sensible manner. Julia thought it possible that each of her sisters was right.

When the sketch of the bonnet had been thoroughly examined, Lady Cowper, a beautiful young woman and a favorite among the *beau monde,* withdrew a missive from her reticule and handed it to Julia. Julia was surprised and looked at the sealed letter with sharply rising excitement. It could only mean one thing. She felt her cheeks grow quite warm. A silence fell over the drawing room as she broke the seal with trembling fingers. Within the folded sheet of paper were vouchers to Almack's.

"Oh, my lady," she breathed, tears starting to her eyes. She lifted her gaze to Lady Cowper. "Thank you ever so much. Thank you."

"Vouchers?" Elizabeth cried, glancing from Lady Cowper to Lady Trevaunance, then back to Julia.

Julia nodded and her sisters all spoke at once, an excited chattering reminiscent of a flock of happily clucking hens, as they clustered about Lady Cowper and showered her with their heartfelt thanks. Julia looked at the marchioness and shook her head in wonder, her heart full to overflowing. She expressed her thanks to her sponsor and felt she could now want for nothing more.

Her mind shot back to the past summer. She remembered the painful agitation she had endured for so many weeks, before her father's death, of waiting and wondering what would become of her and of her sisters.

Now she was in London and had even quite miraculously been granted vouchers to an assembly that would ensure her sisters' futures. In this moment, all that she had sacrificed had proven completely worthwhile. She could not remember feeling happier in ages.

A quarter of an hour later, the ladies and Lord Peter rose to take their leave. Julia followed her guests onto the landing at the top of the stairs, again expressing the depth of her appreciation for the vouchers. To her surprise, Lady Cowper begged the marchioness and Lord Peter to excuse her for just a moment, as she wished a private word with Lady Blackthorn before she departed. Lady Trevaunance did not seem in the least surprised and, taking her son's arm, said they would await her in the carriage.

Lady Cowper watched them descend the stairs, and when they had accomplished half the flight, she turned to smile sweetly upon Julia. "You have quite a champion in Major Blackthorn," she said quietly. "Will it surprise you to learn that he hounded me until I agreed to push for your acceptance? I can refuse that man nothing, if the truth be known. He is quite a favorite of mine."

"Major Blackthorn persuaded you?"

"Yes, he did," she responded. "Though I suspect he had his

own reasons for conducting his campaign on your behalf. I . . . I know it is impertinent of me to say so, but I sympathize very much with your particular situation. Permit me to advise you as my mother has advised me: you must always support the man you love, even if he is not your husband."

Julia had heard rumors of a certain association between Lady Cowper and another gentleman, who was not her husband. Her words, therefore, struck her heart deeply. She wanted to say something to Lady Cowper, but words seemed to fail her. "Thank you" was the most she could achieve, and even then she spoke in a whisper.

"You are most welcome on every score, Lady Blackthorn. I trust you will enjoy the assemblies. I bid you good day and good luck." With that, she began a slow, graceful descent down the stairs.

Julia watched her go, her thoughts a mixture of marvel at her good fortune and a wish that she could indeed support Edward as she wanted to, but she was unable, for the life of her, to see how she could.

Later that evening, when she met Edward by chance at a soirée in Park Lane, Julia broke her former rule of never permitting herself to be alone in conversation with him. She drew him aside and thanked him for his efforts on her behalf. "For you must know that above all things, I had wanted vouchers for my sisters."

He stood beside a palm tree, the fronds almost touching his cheek as he looked down at her. "I know," he responded. "And your appreciation is all that I have sought. I can do so little for you at present; I can't even express my love for you in silly presents or bits of trumpery. But I knew the assemblies would give you what you have strived for these many months and more."

He took her hand in his and placed a fervent kiss on her fingers. Julia had not been this close to him in three weeks and she found the sensation heady. A warmth curled within her and she sighed deeply as he released her hand at last.

He met her gaze and she found herself leaning toward him, her lips parted. "Edward," she whispered, taking a step toward him and placing a hand on the sleeve of his black coat.

Misery entered his gray eyes as he looked down at her. "You mustn't," he whispered. "Remember?"

Julia devoured him with her eyes, setting each precious feature to memory. "I know. It is just that I miss you dreadfully. A dozen times a day my thoughts turn toward you. I sometimes wonder if you can feel my thoughts, my longing to be with you."

They were standing in a dimly lit antechamber, between two formal receiving rooms. A steady flow of people moved from one room to the next, oblivious to all but their own concerns.

Edward held her gaze steadily. "I will be leaving for the Continent before the month's end," he said earnestly. "Would to God you could come with me. In Europe, we could—"

Julia placed her fingers on his lips for a brief second, then let her hand fall away. "Do not torture me, Edward, for I promise you I could never conduct my life in such a wicked fashion, even if my heart begs to do so. I could not."

"I should not have said such a thing." He took a deep breath, and after letting his hand slide the length of her arm, a gesture hidden from the crowds flowing past them, he continued. "Perhaps . . . perhaps it would be best if you left me now, Julia. I fear if you stay much longer, I shall likely take you in my arms and then we would be in the basket, indeed."

Edward smiled down at her and she forced herself to look away. "Goodbye," Julia whispered. Like a leaf caught up in a swiftly moving current, she stepped into a crowd of several noisy young ladies, moving from the antechamber into a beautiful rose and green drawing room beyond.

On the following evening, Sir Perran watched his wife carefully, his eyes cloaked, his fingers gripped about the edges of his newspaper. Julia's head was bent over a sheet of writing paper, the delicate scratching of her quill the only sound in the

small yellow salon at the back of the townhouse. He was reading
The Times, or pretending to.

The chamber was decorated *en suite* in yellow silk damask,
contrasted with molding, tables, and chairs in a gleaming cherrywood. A warm, glowing fire, at odds with the coldness in his
heart, kept a chill from the room. Julia sat at a writing desk near
the doorway, the letter she was composing illuminated by a
branch of candles. Outside, the black night was made blacker
still with fine sheets of a steady rain.

It was Sunday evening and guests were forbidden in his house.
From the large crimson receiving room at the front of the house,
he could hear Elizabeth, Caroline, and Annabelle practicing duets. He should have been exceedingly content. Instead, his
thoughts had become singular and fixed: precisely how he was
to bring the Season to a swift end.

So he was watching Julia and pondering how the deed might
be done, instead of reading his paper. The day before she had
been *aux anges* with her news of having received vouchers for
Almack's from Lady Cowper. As he considered what he might
be able to contrive, somehow the vouchers kept coming to mind.
A scandalous confrontation at Almack's, perhaps. He withheld
a smile of amusement. Yes, that would do to a nicety.

At his elbow was a cup of tea, half full. "Will you pour me
a little more tea?" Sir Perran asked. He was perfectly capable
of performing the task himself, but he wanted to observe her.

"After I . . . finish . . . this thought," Julia replied, her attention fixed on the letter she was writing to her friend, Mary
Brown, in Bath. A few seconds passed, she returned her quill to
the silver tray in front of her, and rose to her feet.

She was so pretty in pale blue muslin. Her smile was warm
as she moved to the round table near the window on which sat
a silver pot of tea, silver bowls for cream and sugar, and a large
arrangement of pink roses. She moved to the table beside him,
carrying the silver pot, and poured the fragrant eastern brew.
She did not remark on his half-empty cup. An air of contentment
seemed to emanate from her.

He watched her return the teapot to the table, then cross the room in her elegant stride. How much he despised her. Hatred had replaced what for a time had been a strong blossoming of love for her. She had used him ill by pretending her kindnesses over the past three months, when in truth her only objective had been to manipulate him into taking her sisters to London. Yet somehow he knew that his hatred for her had its roots in some-thing else—or perhaps *someone* else.

Last night, he had seen Julia with his nephew. He had watched the sway of her silk skirts of a lovely golden-brown—an exqui-site color against her apricots and cream complexion and auburn hair—as she moved into the drawing room beyond. He had been standing in the shadows of the doorway of the opposite room, his view of Julia and his nephew unobstructed. Even then, hatred had begun to swim in him—through his brain, into his throat, his chest. He hated Julia and he despised Edward Blackthorn, as he always had. Seeing him make pretty love to Julia last night, bowing over her hand, kissing her fingers, staring down at her like the lovesick moonling he was, brought every ill feeling ris-ing up within him all over again, as though if he but turned around, Sophia would be there mocking him with her worthless apologies.

As he watched Julia now, again bent over her letter, Sir Perran came to realize that he despised her because she would never truly love him. He thought it ironic that he had never considered love part and parcel of his marriage to her. He had wanted only to be in possession of Hatherleigh, of the quarry and of the last Delabole descendant. He had wanted to rule her, and therefore her sisters, as if to say to his peers he had at last vanquished those who had stripped him of his rightful inheritance so many years ago. But now that he was wed to her, how much he had come to crave her utter devotion, her affection, her love.

But perhaps from the time he had observed his nephew taking what should have been his own prize—Julia's innocence—a kind of mad, jealous rage had slowly begun to take hold of him. He had never quite comprehended why, once having defeated Delabole and married Julia, a sense of fulfillment had not sustained him over the ensuing months. After all, what was Julia to him but only a symbol? Why now did he want from her something she could not give him, either physically or from her heart?

She had hinted to him that she would welcome him in her bed, but he had firmly turned aside her hints. She had spoken of children, of wanting to fill Hatherleigh with as many as she could bear. Something deep inside him had twisted and burned when she had said as much. Children. His children. Her brief encounter with Blackthorn had not resulted in a child. So now she wanted him to provide her with children.

His heart grew fiery with feelings he couldn't understand, especially since Julia was in the room with him. He couldn't stay in the room much longer. His heart was aching. He slowly began folding up the paper on his lap, then rose to his feet. He limped, plied his cane, and refused to answer her when her voice reached him from across the room. "Perran, are you all right?"

He hated the compassion in her voice. He hated her.

Once on the landing, he tucked his cane beneath his arm and descended the stairs quickly and easily, since no one was about to witness the truth of his lameness. He went directly to the small chamber at the back of the house, which he had converted into a private study. The small chamber consisted of two winged chairs covered in burgundy silk, draperies to match, and a desk and chair of fine mahogany. He began to pace the room. His hands were trembling. Rage roared in his chest, but he could give no expression to it. He did not even understand from where so much anger had come.

What was the matter with him? What had happened to his stoic sense of mastery of his world?

She had happened. She had knelt before him in January and he had opened up his heart to her, fool that he was. For a time he had allowed himself to believe that he could love and be loved, but then he had learned of the purpose behind her sweetness to him: a London Season.

Now Blackthorn was again attempting to seduce her. He hated

them both. Well, there was only one thing to be done: ruin the pair of them.

As his thoughts took this new and decidedly more pleasurable turn, a calm gradually came over him. After a few minutes, he was at peace with himself once again.

He crossed the chamber to his polished mahogany desk, and after withdrawing a small key from the pocket of his waistcoat, he unlocked the bottom right-hand drawer. From the drawer he withdrew a packet of letters tied up with a black silk ribbon.

He flipped his thumb along the edges of the letters, feeling an exhilaration not unlike lovemaking steal over him. He had read each of the letters more than once, especially whenever he felt happiness eluding him as it was this evening. At random, from the center of the packet, he withdrew one of them. He unfolded it on the desk and began to read.

My darling Julia . . .

"Am I disturbing you?" his wife called to him from the doorway. Why hadn't he heard the door open? Good God, he had forgotten to lock the door!

A flush of fear swept over him. He felt his face grow hot and suspected that his complexion was by now a lovely shade of pink. He quickly refolded the letter and, with a single swipe of his hand and arm, swept the packet onto his lap. "Indeed you are!" he cried angrily. He could see by the sudden shock in her eyes that his manner and his words had stunned and overset her. He was not surprised that with a murmured apology, she closed the door. He could hear her steps echo down the hallway.

Sir Perran sat in stunned silence for a moment. Had she seen enough to identify the writer of the letters? How much would she be able to surmise from his uncharacteristic conduct? With palms apart, he pressed his long fingers together in the shape of a steeple and stared at a globe of the world from the tips of his manicured nails. She would be able to surmise nothing. It was not in Julia's nature to believe him, or anyone, capable of such terrible deceit—even though he had already proven to her that for years he had been deceiving her. Julia would probably always believe the best of him, just as she believed the best of everyone around her.

With a smile, he slowly replaced the letter among the others, then returned the packet to the bottom drawer, once again locking away the evidence of his crime.

Well, well! Life could certainly be intriguing at times. Now, how ought he bring about the social demise of his wife and of the lover she wished was hers?

Twenty-one

The evening before the first ball at the Almack Assembly Rooms, Julia sat in the yellow salon, reviewing the past week. She sighed deeply, well aware that a darkness had fallen over the townhouse, even though a succession of sunny spring days had arrived to delight the Metropolis.

Sounds originating from the crimson drawing room informed her that her sisters were practicing the pianoforte and harp, and were occasionally reviewing the more difficult portions of their favorite ballads with a singing instructor. With her feet situated comfortably on a footstool and warmed by a glowing fire in the hearth, she threaded her needle carefully with a vivid blue silk floss. Setting her first stitch into the eye of a peacock feather, she cast her mind backward.

The night she had followed her husband down to his study on the ground floor and had interrupted his reading of an unfamiliar packet of letters, Julia had finally begun to face the truth regarding her relationship with him. For several weeks she had permitted herself to believe that with a little more time and effort, his former warmth toward her could be renewed. But that night, when she had posed the question *Am I disturbing you* and had seen the responding enraged expression on his face, Julia knew a sense of despair that had begun to alter her perception of him yet again.

Had Sir Perran come to her following the incident and apologized for his display of temper, she would have been more hopeful. Instead, she had seen a full return of the man whose cloistering commands had afflicted her, as well as her sisters, last summer. Sir Perran barked his commands, refused to permit her sisters to attend half the balls and soiréss Lady Trevaunance had pronounced requisite for success in Mayfair, and ordered the Verdell sisters about with his former high-handedness.

Julia's sense of distress had mounted, made worse by Edward's uncanny ability to discern that something had gone awry. At a soirée in Upper Brook Street only two night's past, he had begged her to confess her unhappiness and to tell him all. Grateful that he wished her to unburden her heart, she revealed a little of her concerns, mentioning as well the incident of having followed his uncle into his study. When she told him of the letters, Julia added, "I am beginning to suspect that he is keeping a mistress. I believe I have been very naive, but tell me, do you think it possible?"

Edward had merely looked at her with a quizzical expression in his gray eyes. "A packet of letters?" he asked. "Are you sure?"

Julia nodded. "Yes, quite sure. And for just a moment, before I made my presence known to him, there was such a look in his eye that I could not help but think, *He is in love*. Edward, I had never before considered the possibility that your uncle might be in love with another woman—perhaps a lesser-born female to whom he could not offer his name. Only pray, tell me, what do you think?"

Edward shook his head. "I don't know. The truth is, I was never well acquainted with my uncle. He always treated me with a measure of disdain, which I believe was connected to my mother's elopement with my father."

Julia nodded, and after becoming aware that her husband was watching her from the shadows of the doorway, she quickly ended the conversation and moved on.

When a scratching on the door of the salon brought her brief reveries to an end, the muscles along her shoulders constricted painfully. If that was her husband, what order did he mean to impart to her this time? What gentle instruction would he lay at her feet? What blatant criticism would he make of her hair, of her gown, of the shade of her slippers?

Fortunately, it was only Grigson who entered. To her surprise, however, he brought forward one of Lady Trevaunance's footmen, who stammered out a verbal message, his complexion pale. "My Lady Trevaunance requests that you come to Berkeley Square," he stated. "She wishes me to inform you that it is most urgent."

Julia stared at the footman, who did not look her directly in the eye. A sheen of sweat glistened on his forehead and his powdered wig was slightly askew. "She did not, perchance, give you a letter for me?"

"Nay, m'lady, she did not. She awaits a reply and has asked that you attend her at eight of the clock."

"Th . . . thank you. Pray tell Her Ladyship—no, never mind. I shall pen her a quick missive." She began to set aside her embroidery when the servant took a step forward.

"Nay, m'lady," he interjected quickly. He seemed oddly nervous to Julia as he finally met her gaze, his blue eyes frowning and worried. "She doesn't want a letter. She made that quite clear to me. So, if you please, what shall I tell her?"

"Tell her that of course I shall come to her," she returned. "At eight o'clock."

He bowed to her. "Very good, m'lady."

For a few minutes after the footman left, Julia remained plying her needle. A certain thought struck her—that the marchioness might be acting on Edward's behalf. Of course, such a conjecture was probably the wishes of her heart making themselves known to her yet again, and she smiled at how silly she could be.

Yet, why the urgency, and worse, how was she to leave Grosvenor Square without being observed? Her husband had been in the habit of taking supper at White's whenever he forbid the ladies to leave the house, and Julia knew he intended to do so this evening. But she also knew that he had spies watching her. If she had had any doubt on that account, Gabrielle had informed her some time past of the tittle-tattle among the servants—it would seem Lady Blackthorn was to be followed everywhere.

For a moment, as she steadily worked the blue silk floss into the fine mesh of her embroidery cloth, Julia considered not going to Berkeley Square, since she would probably be followed. However, some devilment was at work within her, causing her to delight in the notion of disobeying her overbearing husband. All she had to do now was to wait for him to leave and afterward—tomorrow, undoubtedly—to suffer the consequences of her recalcitrant conduct.

When a half hour had passed, Julia was grateful for the abilities she had acquired from living with her husband. She was able to stitch her peacock, without the smallest trembling of hand, while she bid him to enjoy his supper at White's. He had eyed her curiously for a moment, and she would perhaps have felt a great deal more distress than she did had he been in the habit of treating her with even a semblance of kindness over the past several weeks. She was able therefore to ignore his penetrating gaze as she steadily threaded three more strands of floss through her needle.

At last, when he quit the yellow salon and a moment later the wheels off his carriage could be heard on the cobbles, Julia retired swiftly to her bedchamber, full of both dread and excitement. She considered explaining her intent to her sisters, but on second thought decided not to involve them in a situation that was likely to infuriate Sir Perran. Far better to leave them out of it entirely. Her sisters, having been instructed to again practice their musical instruments as well as their ballads, could still be heard singing and playing in the scarlet drawing room. She knew they would have known of Sir Perran's departure, but because they were held captive by a well-paid and quite loyal vocal master, they remained at their task.

At half past seven, with a black silk hooded cape covering her forest-green velvet gown and the hood of her cape disguising her brilliant auburn hair, Julia found herself in a hackney coach

bowling along the dark, misty streets of London, heading toward
Berkeley Square.

From the confines of his traveling coach, hidden in the shadows of several coaches waiting in front of a nearby townhouse,
Sir Perran watched his wife's hackney sway as it turned the corner of the square. He smiled with pure satisfaction and ordered
his postilion to follow the coach. He had been informed by one
of his spies—a footman in his household—that Lady Trevaunance's servant had come to deliver a message to Lady Blackthorn. The same spy would have listened at the door, but for
some reason Grigson had remained outside the yellow salon
while the footman spoke with Julia. He could only guess at the
nature of the message, but had every reason to assume that the
marchioness was scheming to bring Edward and Julia together.

Sir Perran had never counted Lady Trevaunance among his
friends. She was scornful of him—in a polite way, of course.
He had never known precisely what he had done to offend her,
but so it would seem he had. He therefore believed she would
not hesitate to champion Cupid's cause and arrange for Julia to
meet Edward in a clandestine setting.

If such was the case tonight, he would have precisely the
ammunition he needed with which to destroy Julia's *tonish* career. It was one thing for a married woman to take a lover, but
quite another for her to be caught by her husband in the act of
infidelity. He could only trust that tonight was to be one such
arrangement.

With the carriage traveling at a brisk pace toward Berkeley
Square, Sir Perran leaned back against the squabs, his cane in
hand, and sighed with great contentment. Very soon, tomorrow
perhaps, he would be taking his wife back to Bath.

Julia stood on the threshold of Lady Trevaunance's drawing
room of military hues and stared at Edward, disbelieving her

gaze. The marchioness's butler had already informed her that
Lady Trevaunance was not at home, but that Major Blackthorn—
with Her Ladyship's knowledge—awaited her in the blue drawing room. A quick glance about the chamber assured her that
the draperies had been drawn. Edward stood by the fireplace, a
booted foot on the hearth, his gaze fixed on the glow of coals
before him. The butler had not announced her, and it would seem
he was so deep in thought that he was still unaware of her presence. To her surprise, Julia saw that he was not wearing evening
dress, but rather sported a blue coat, buff breeches, and gleaming
Hessians, as though he was ready to travel.

A sudden dread filled her as she watched the tightness about
his eyes and the workings of his jaw. He was clearly upset.

"What is it, Edward?" she queried as she quickly crossed the
chamber to greet him.

He turned toward her, sliding his foot from the brick hearth
as she walked into his arms. "Thank God you've come," he
whispered into her ear, holding her fast.

"I didn't know you would be here—the message came to me
from Lady Trevaunance."

"For your protection," he replied. He looked down at her hungrily, stroking her cheek with his thumb. Without so much as a
word, he leaned toward her and kissed her hard on the mouth.

Julia had lost her will to refuse him. She felt as she always
did when he assaulted her, as though she were falling from a
cliff when she was in his arms. She returned his embrace and
parted her lips, permitting him to possess her mouth. All was
forgotten in this moment—her husband, her sisters, the proprieties. She loved Edward Blackthorn so much. Would that she had
waited for him in July. Would that she had not succumbed to
Sir Perran's persuasions of comfort and peace. Would that she
was Edward's wife even now.

After a long moment, he drew back and took her shoulders
in his hands, holding her firmly and forcing her to look at him.
"I am leaving for Brussels shortly, in the early hours of the
morning, in fact. Julia, I want you to come with me. I need you

with me. I don't know what is going to happen in France, or when or if I shall ever return. But now that Napoleon has regained the throne and the allies have declared war upon him, a battle must follow. Wellington speaks of June, which is two months away. Only come with me to Brussels. I shall find a place for us to be together."

Julia squeezed her eyes shut. She wanted to go with him more than life itself, yet she knew she could not. "What you are asking of me is impossible. Utterly impossible. Beyond the fact that I cannot conceive of how we would live once we arrived in the Netherlands, what would become of my sisters? Do you suppose that your uncle would magnanimously continue to care for them once it was learned I had run away with his nephew?"

He looked down at her, his gray eyes troubled. "I have refused to think beyond my love for you, Julia," he whispered. "I want only to be with you . . . to know that whatever happens when I return to my rooms, you will be waiting for me."

"Edward, would to God I could oblige you. I want nothing more than to live as your wife."

He kissed her again and her every thought became fixed on him—on the softness of his lips, on the strength of his soldier's arms as he embraced her, on the feel of his thighs pressed hard against hers. She was saying goodbye to him, perhaps for the last time, which served to make every touch of his hands, every kiss that cascaded like ripples in a stream over her face, her neck, her lips, every search of his tongue, bittersweet and painful.

Was she breathing? She didn't know. Were her feet touching the carpet? She couldn't tell. Was it night or day, spring or fall, April or September? She wasn't sure. Time stopped, yet seemed to move at a startling speed. Her life did not exist, except that which was returned to her in his whispers of love. For the moment, only Edward was real as she clung to him, stroking the skin of his face, feeling the muscled strength of his arms through his coat. With his hands, he caressed her in places he shouldn't have and she let him, all the while wondering if she would ever see him again. A powerful longing came over her.

Through a fog of desire, Julia heard faint sounds of movement belowstairs. Something nagged at her, yet she didn't want to stop tasting of Edward's love as he kissed her over and over.

Louder movements, voices this time, intruded. She promised herself this kiss would be the last, but her hearing dimmed and she let him kiss her again, the warmth of his lips becoming a trail of fire on her lips, her cheek, her ear, and down her neck.

Finally, just as she was pushing him away, intending to tell him she must leave now, the door burst open. Julia stood next to him, her body tense with passion, her legs pressed against his, one of his hands holding her arm and preventing her from drawing away from him, his other hand caressing her cheek.

The sight of both her husband and Lady Trevaunance's now-red-faced butler caused the former richness of her blood to run thin and cold.

"How utterly charming," Sir Perran drawled, leaning forward on his cane as he looked from one to the other. Holding Julia's gaze, he queried, "And is this how you keep your promise to me? I was on my way to White's when I suddenly remembered that I had forgotten my snuffbox. Of course I had to return to Grosvenor Square, but think how astonished I was to see my wife entering a hackney. *Where is she going?* I asked myself. My curiosity forced me to follow you, my dear, and do but look to what it has led me. Do you think me a fool? Well, well, we shall soon see who is the fool, for I don't hesitate to tell you that the patronesses of Almack's will not tolerate your conduct, so unbecoming in a young bride, and I shall see that Princess Esterhazy is duly informed of what has transpired here tonight. I have little doubt that the vouchers you have so cherished will be rescinded without hesitation." He clucked his tongue and shifted his gaze to his nephew.

Julia had been horrified by his arrival, but the look of pure hatred in his eye, as he met Edward's gaze, caused her to feel dizzy with fear. She tried to intervene. "I . . . I was saying goodbye to your nephew," she stammered. "He is leaving for Brussels on the morrow. I won't be seeing him again."

Sir Perran lifted a brow and turned back to her, as he waved the butler away and moved into the lofty chamber. "Perhaps you won't at that," he said. "Perhaps he will be killed in battle."

Summoning every ounce of courage, she spoke firmly. "Take me home, Perran. Nothing good can come of further conversation."

As she started to pull away from Edward, he held her back with a firm grasp on her arm. "Don't go," he told her.

"Don't go," Sir Perran cried mockingly, moving to stand but a few feet in front of Edward. "Don't go. And where, then, is my wife to go? With you, when you haven't two tuppence to rub together? A pretty picture indeed. Or do you mean to keep her in a little cottage somewhere in Brussels, a little rat-infested love nest—what could be more romantic, eh? And what of her sisters? After tonight, do you think for a moment they will not suffer from my wife's scandalous indiscretion? Do you think, then, that you shall be able to provide husbands for them all?"

"You dare to provoke me," Edward cried, "when you stole Julia from me! Don't deny that you did. I've come to understand you better in these past several months, ever since the last card game with Delabole. You baited him, over and over, and kept his glass filled while you watched him lose the remainder of his fortune without even the vestige of a conscience. And what of my letters to Julia, for I have now come to believe that you somehow managed to intercept them? How did you do it, Sir Perran? How much did you pay the postmaster in Bath to see that my letters never reached her?"

Julia's mind reeled backward. She could see every vivid detail: her husband's study; Sir Perran sitting at his mahogany desk; a branch of candles illuminating a packet of letters, one of the letters open before him. Julia felt her stomach turn over once, then twice. She felt extremely ill and pressed her fingers to her lips.

Edward's letters. Of course.

She swallowed hard and forced her stomach to obey her, to grow calm. She ordered her mind to a familiar stillness.

As Edward stared angrily at Sir Perran, she felt his grip on her arm slacken. She pulled away from him, and in his anger, he did not protest. Stepping away from both men, Julia let her gaze settle upon her husband.

She waited, she observed.

Edward's letters.

She noted a slight flush on Sir Perran's cheeks, a flinching of a nerve beside his eye, the erratic rising and falling of his chest. Julia saw not the righteous anger of one offended unjustly, but the ire of one who hates, of one who is caught in his lies and deceits.

"You have no proof!" he returned scornfully.

"What of the letters Julia saw you reading the other night?" Edward asked, taking a step toward his uncle.

"Well, it hardly matters at this eleventh hour, now, does it?" Sir Perran retorted, his features twisted. "Whether I prevented them from reaching Julia or not, she is still my wife. She will do as I bid her. She shall return to Bath, along with her sisters. As for you, Major Blackthorn—"

Julia stopped listening. She had heard enough. She believed Edward's accusation was true, that her husband had somehow intercepted Edward's letters. She felt numb, stunned beyond feeling at how badly he had betrayed her. Turning away from both men, who were now arguing hotly, Julia let their voices flow over her as she left the chamber, her departure apparently unnoticed. She floated down the stairs as if in a dream. Her thoughts were disjointed: Edward's letters were in her husband's study; Sir Perran had all but handed her father the pistol that killed him; how would she now go about securing her sisters' futures?

Dazed, she quit the townhouse, securing a hackney to return to her husband's house. Her mind was so liquid, her thoughts unceasing and unrelenting, that before she knew it, Julia was walking through the front door, bidding Grigson to settle the fare. She ran to the study, rounded the beautiful desk, and pulled open each of four unlocked drawers. The letters were not there, which meant they had to be in the locked bottom right-hand drawer. She picked up a heavy bronze figurine, which sat on the desk, and with careful aim, Julia swung hard into the lock, smashing at the wood over and over until the drawer pulled free.

She removed the letters and found what she already knew to be true. Edward had been right: the letters were addressed to her; they were his letters, the very same ones missing from last summer. Everything now made sense to her, as though the letters had themselves been the final piece of a puzzle that had been troubling her for the past nine months. Her marriage was over.

When she lifted her gaze, she saw that Sir Perran was standing in the doorway, a look of astonishment on his face.

"You had no right—" he began coldly.

Julia laughed scornfully. "I had no right? Don't be absurd, Perran. I had every right, as you very well know. And now I will say to you what you said to Edward last summer: *I do hope you mean to be a gentleman about this.*"

He started forward, his gray eyes filling again with rage. "How dare you!"

"I dare because I have no reason now to oblige you in anything. I shall be leaving you, Perran, my sisters with me. We shall be gone by morning."

Clenching and unclenching his fists, each breath he took a harsh rasp through his nose, Sir Perran struggled to compose himself. He did not meet her gaze, but stared at the letters she held in her hand. After a moment, when he was obviously calmer, he spoke. "I am going to my club and I expect you to be here when I return. Lest you have forgotten, you are quite penniless and couldn't support a mouse, let alone your sisters. Tomorrow, we shall return to Bath as planned."

Julia did not try to argue with him. Instead, she gave voice to the most prominent thought in her heart. "You are a fool," she said. "You could have had everything from me—my love, my body, my devotion, my children. Instead, you forfeited all, for what? Why have you punished me? What have you achieved? Do you sleep at night, I wonder? How curious that I thought your character above reproach in every respect before I married you, and now I realize the only character you have is that which suits your intentions of the moment. I was willing to do anything for you, but now, you get nothing from me."

His jaw worked strongly as he again strove to compose himself. He was clearly biting back words he did not wish to speak. "Again, I expect you to be in your bed when I return home. That is all I will say. Good night."

With that, he turned on his heel and strode, quite limpless, down the hall.

Twenty-two

Julia took the parcel of letters to her bedchamber. Sitting in a chair near her carved oak wardrobe, she began to read, light from a single candle at her elbow illuminating the thin sheets of paper. She was transported by Edward's professions of love. No longer was it spring in London but summer in Bath, and she was sitting on the terrace outside the long gallery of Hatherleigh, sipping a glass of lemonade while she read and reread his letters.

She recalled the feeling of desolation that had characterized the previous summer and transposed over this remembered sentiment how she would have felt instead had she been reading of Edward's love, of his attempts and successes at acquiring contracts for Delabole stone, of his hopes that one day she would be able to accompany him to his next posting. She read in his letters of his wish to one day serve in India, the country where Wellington had gained his first military experience.

How strange now to think not only of her marriage to Sir Perran, but also of war returning to Europe once again. How differently the future had played out for both Edward and herself.

There were fifteen letters in all, each full of adoration, the later ones showing an increasing concern that she had not written to him. When she had read most of them, Julia heard a scratching on the door, followed by Grigson's quiet voice as he begged admittance.

"Come," she called out to her family's most faithful retainer. When he entered her bedchamber with a worried light in his eye, she queried, "What is it?"

"My lady," he began slowly and carefully. "I beg you will not take it amiss if I say that I could not help but overhear your recent conversation with Sir Perran."

"Ah," Julia remarked with an amused sigh.

"Yes," the butler stated, bowing slightly. "Pray forgive my impertinence, but I was wondering if your ladyship had a particular destination in mind?"

"I rather thought Grillon's hotel would suffice for the present. After that, I intend to hire a townhouse for the remainder of the season."

He lifted his brows in some surprise. Julia knew it was believed by the staff that she hadn't a feather to fly with. "But how?" he queried. "That is, I don't mean to bring forward so delicate a matter, madame, but . . . how shall you discharge the, er . . . debts incurred at such an establishment?" His face was pinched with fatherly concern.

Julia smiled. "My mother shall pay for them all . . . for everything, in fact."

Grigson eyed her as though she had just gone mad. "Your mother, madame?" he asked.

Julia laughed outright. "I mean to sell her ring."

"Ah, I see," he responded, his face relaxing into a smile. He was silent for a time, shifting his feet slightly before continuing. "There is one more thing, however. Is . . . is it possible you might have need of me, Lady Blackthorn, in any particular capacity over the next few weeks or so?" He eyed her hopefully.

Julia held his gaze for a long moment, then nodded, her heart full of gratitude. "Oh, yes, Grigson, very much so."

"Then I shall happily see that your trunks and portmanteaus are quickly packed. I shall also arrange all the details for the hotel, if it should please you."

"It pleases me very much. You are a good friend." When he opened the door to leave, she added, "Will you send my sisters to me?"

"Of course, madame."

Julia watched the door snap shut, and as she pressed one of

Edward's letters to her lips, a thought struck her. She might not be able to go with him to Brussels, since her duty to her sisters must keep her in London, but she could at least say goodbye to him. Her heart began racing at the thought of seeing him one last time before he left. She would let him kiss her, and tonight she would refuse him nothing.

A moment later, her sisters entered her bedchamber. Elizabeth appeared first, her black hair swept up into a pretty chignon and dressed with a single white ostrich feather. Caroline followed her, her similar raven's hair flowing in a cascade of curls down the back of her head and threaded with ribbons and seed pearls. Annabelle entered last, her long, curly auburn hair braided and tucked into a coil atop her head. A jaunty fringe of curls across her forehead gave her a playful look so very much in keeping with her wild temperament.

Julia beamed at them. "I have some news of no small import to relate to you. This evening, I was caught kissing Major Blackthorn and have fallen into disgrace with my husband. Unfortunately, he intends to remove us to Bath, ostensibly because of my indiscretion, but I say we ought to take a holiday and stay at Grillon's instead. But do tell me what you think. Do you wish to return to Bath?"

Elizabeth's blue eyes were wide with astonishment. "I never thought you had the courage to kiss Blackthorn! Julia, how . . . how wicked. How utterly marvelous for you!"

"I am in love with him," Julia returned simply. "I believe I always shall be. Only tell me, Lizzie, do you wish to return to Hatherleigh?"

"No, of course not, at least not yet. But what else can we do?"

Julia ignored her last question and addressed Caroline. "And what of you, Caro? Do you wish to return to Bath?"

Caroline shook her head. "No, I don't," she responded with a worried frown. "The truth is, I never thought I would enjoy the Season as much as I have. But Sir Perran must have been very angry. Are you not afraid he will be even more so when you tell him you do not intend to obey his wishes?"

Julia shook her head. "No," she answered firmly. "I don't know how it has come about, but I don't fear him anymore. In fact, I have no feeling for him at all. I have only an intention of living my life separate from him."

She then looked at Annabelle and smiled. "Well?" she queried.

Annabelle stamped her foot. "I shall never return to Bath! Not when I have just discovered London! But how can we afford to reside at a hotel . . . and Grillon's is so very dear?"

"The truth is, my darlings, we are in the devil of a fix. I have not quite sorted out all that we will need to do in order to maintain our place among the *haut ton,* but first I intend to sell Mama's emerald ring. No, no, don't repine. I believe she would have wanted me—us—to do so. You must understand, however, that Sir Perran will not take kindly to our leaving the . . . er . . . *protection* of his home, but I shall seek out Lady Trevaunance's advice as soon as possible and see what might be contrived. For now, however, there is something I wish you to know about Sir Perran." She looked down at the letters on her lap and explained all that had happened since last summer.

When she was finished, her sisters gathered about her and consoled her. "He was not worthy of you," Caroline stated at last. "For I know your heart was well disposed toward him. That he could not respond lovingly to the proper advances of your heart . . . well, I am sorry for him, but he must now live with the results of the complete and utter hardness of his heart."

Julia was grateful for her sister's kind words. Taking a deep breath, she again addressed the difficulties before them. "I believe we shall be able to live for several months on the proceeds of the sale of mother's ring, but beyond that . . ." She frowned deeply and shook her head, not knowing what else to add.

"Beyond that," Elizabeth cried quite emphatically as she placed her hand on Julia's shoulder, "we shall manage something. We are not Mama's daughters for nothing, after all. Surely there is enough intelligence among us to see to our futures without your husband's manipulations, connivings, or his wealth."

Julia smiled up at her. "I am grateful for your strength, Lizzie, and I do believe you have the right of it. But for now, we must leave as quickly as possible. The longer we remain, the longer Sir Perran will have to work his wiles against us. Once we are gone, however, I believe he will have a very difficult time putting any scheme into effect—certainly not without creating a horrific scandal, which would harm him as much as us."

Since Grigson returned at that moment with a host of footmen and all the ladies' personal maids, conversation about the future was brought to a close and the entire house was soon aflutter with the activity of packing.

An hour later, just before eleven o'clock, Julia and her sisters left Grosvenor Square.

When Sir Perran returned to his townhouse, his mind dimmed from the effects of two bottles of claret, he found his home peacefully and wonderfully quiet. He was a little surprised, too, when a footman opened the door instead of Grigson, but he didn't care. He'd been able to fleece a stupid young man from the north of five hundred pounds, and nothing pleased him more than taking money from a fool.

He retired to his bedchamber and fell asleep instantly, enjoying the sleep of a contented child who has been given everything his heart desires.

Once Julia saw her sisters settled in the hotel, she immediately hired a hackney to take her to Edward's rooms on Half Moon Street. As the small carriage bowled along the dark streets, she watched light fall from the gas lamps, gathering in faint yellow circles on the stone flagways. The ever-present fog—a clammy mixture of coal-smoke and mist from the Thames and from the persistent layer of clouds overhead—clung to the alleyways and obscured the horizon of rooftops in a dense curtain of gray gauze. In its way, the mist was beautiful, the edges of buildings softened, shadows becoming an intriguing flow of moving shapes, the lamplight seeming to hang in the air, suspended momentarily until a coach would pass by and send the light into a dancing, swirling plume of mist.

Julia felt curiously at peace as she listened to the steady clip-clop of the horses. Midnight was upon Mayfair, laughter echoing at every corner where gentlemen gathered or raced by in open gigs and curricles—so absurd at night in the mist. She felt as if she were returning home after a long, long journey at sea.

When the hackney drew up before Edward's rooms, he was on the sidewalk, a many-caped greatcoat snug upon his shoulders, his hat low on his head. Her heart became flooded with affection as the carriage drew to a stop some ten feet from him. He was directing his batman in the arrangement of his portmanteaus, his head downcast. He did not seem to notice that another carriage was present. But then, at all hours of the day and night, carriages flew about Mayfair, releasing passengers, taking them up. Of course he wouldn't notice.

Even when she stepped down from the hackney and paid the driver, he was still engrossed in his task. "Better to put it at my feet, then," she heard him say.

Was she in a dream? She heard her footsteps echo on the flags; she could feel the cold, damp mist on her cheeks; she knew that her heart was hammering in her chest. But was any of it real?

Julia remained a few feet away, standing, staring, wondering. He was so tall. His black hair was tied neatly with a riband, his hat pressed firmly on his head. His voice in the dark and the mist was the rich, mellow sound of a violoncello. She closed her eyes and listened.

"The devil take it!" he cried, much to her amusement. "We'll be crammed together tighter than a flea's arse! I knew I should've hired a second chaise, just for the luggage."

Julia bit her lip. *A flea's arse.* She wanted to laugh and then was too embarrassed to do so. She had never heard him speak so basely and was reminded suddenly that he was a soldier. What would he do when he discovered she had heard him?

"Edward," she said softly, deciding it was quite time she made her presence known.

He turned around abruptly, his mouth dropping open. "Julia!" he cried. "Good God—whatever are you doing? I was just about to depart—how long have you been standing—? Oh, dear, you will have to forgive me, I never would have said—"

"I don't give a fig for any of it. Only that I arrived in time to say goodbye."

He drew her away from his man and toward the door of his townhouse. He spoke to her in a whisper. "Why did you come? How pretty you are in the streetlight." He ran a thumb across her cheek. "Are you all right? My uncle was very angry when I left him."

Julia ignored the fact that another coach was coming down the street and that Edward's servant was eyeing her curiously. With no thought for her reputation or the proprieties, she took one of his gloved hands and brought it up to her cheek. She then kissed him lightly on the lips. "I had to see you," she said.

She found herself afraid suddenly. Her own troubles had kept her so forcefully removed from Edward's concerns that only now, with his baggage being arranged in the boot of a traveling coach, did she truly comprehend that he was leaving for Brussels to rejoin his regiment.

"Julia, what is it?" he pressed her. "What has happened? Oh, I knew I should've followed him . . . you! Did he . . . did he hurt you?"

"No," Julia replied, shaking her head and looking deeply into loving, concerned eyes. "I was only thinking just now of your leaving for the Continent and what that means: war."

"I will be all right," he announced firmly, taking both her hands in his and holding them close to his chest. "You must believe me. I never take unnecessary risks." He paused and smiled crookedly before adding, "Well, at least not too many."

Julia sighed. "I know this will sound absurd, but I am just now realizing you are a soldier." For a brief moment, she felt her heart grow quite cold and still. Was this how most officer's wives felt when they kissed their husbands goodbye? She shook her head slowly. "How is it possible I never understood as much before?"

He did not try to give her an answer, but instead placed a warm, soft kiss on her lips. She was comforted by the gesture, and given how little time she had left with him, Julia set her fears aside and gave herself up to the pleasure of being so close to him. For a long time, he kissed her while the mist swirled about them. She would have let the moment continue forever, but she wanted to tell him what had happened after she left Lady Trevaunance's house.

Drawing back from him slightly, she said, "Edward, I found them—the letters, your letters. I had had only one objective upon returning to Grosvenor Square: to search your uncle's desk. I found the packet of letters he had been reading the other night and they were all yours, dating from last summer, the very letters you wrote to me from Plymouth and elsewhere. He has had them all this time. I still find it so hard to believe."

"I knew it," Edward responded. "The moment you told me you had seen him with a packet of letters, I knew they were mine."

"But it was so wicked of him. How can he be so very bad, so unconscionable? There is something more. I . . . I left him, Edward. We all did. We are at Grillon's for the present. I find I can be his wife no longer."

"Julia!" he cried, releasing her hands and catching her up tightly about the waist. "Do you know what you are saying? Dare I hope?"

"Yes," she breathed, smiling up at him.

A look of joyous expectation rushed over his face. "My darling," he said, sweeping her fully into his arms. She gave a faint cry and his mouth was hard upon hers. He kissed her fiercely as she slipped her arms around him. Again and again he pressed his lips to hers, professing his love for her, his belief that they would be together always, from this day forward.

For the first time in many months, Julia permitted herself to give her heart completely to him. "I love you," she returned ardently as he kissed her eyes, her cheeks, her lips.

"You are coming with me," he whispered in return. "You must come with me. Julia, tonight our life begins."

Tears trembled on her lashes, then slid down her cheeks. For the present, she did not have the heart to disillusion him. "Take me inside," she whispered as he kissed her tears away. "Please."

Edward seemed confused, as though for a moment he did not know where he was or what he ought to do. He turned to his man. "How much time do we have before we need to depart?"

"An hour, perhaps two," the servant replied. "The packet sails with the tide, and the tide won't wait."

Edward looked down at Julia, his gray eyes intense, considering. "Come," he said, drawing her arm about his and guiding her up the steps.

Once inside his rooms, the door closed and locked, he jerked his hat from his head and tossed it on a nearby chair. After lighting a branch of five candles, the room now awash with a soft, yellow light, he unbuttoned his greatcoat, threw it off his shoulders, and let it land in a heap behind him. He then accosted her forest-green velvet pelisse.

Julia let him struggle with each small button for a few minutes, laughing at his hurried, clumsy efforts, finally suggesting he remove his gloves of York tan. He laughed, kissed her once quite fiercely, then ripped off each glove in turn. While he deftly gained command of the buttons, she touched his face, kissing his brow, his cheeks, his lips.

He hurried her out of the pelisse and kissed the swell of her breasts just above the décolletage of her velvet gown. She pulled on the riband restraining his hair, letting it free. She tugged on the knot of his neckcloth, then began unwinding the creation until it fell in a wrinkled, starched heap beside him.

He slipped his arm about her waist and, picking up the branch of candles in one hand, drew her into the bedchamber. After setting the candelabra on a small writing desk across from the bed, he closed the door and again attacked her clothing, this time wreaking vengeance on the buttons of her gown. Again he mastered them, and her dark green gown fell into a circle about her feet. Her thin muslin shift, her garters, her stockings, and her velvet slippers remained. He bade her sit on the bed and, slipping his hands beneath her shift, pushed it up to her knees, then began to untie each garter.

Julia looked down at him, at the candlelight glistening on his raven-black hair, her heart overcome with pleasure at being touched by him, at the feel of his hands on her thighs, then on her knees, as he began rolling the silk down to her slippers. These he slid off her feet, then the stockings. All that remained was her shift.

He did not immediately rise from his knees, but buried his face in her lap and hugged her close about her waist. He kissed her and bit at her, his hands beginning to rove, his lips a search on every curve of her body, rising until, through the muslin, he began kissing her breasts.

Pleasure spiked within her, at being touched and kissed, at having him close to her, possessing her.

Edward rose from Julia and began to undress, removing his coat and waistcoat. He then sat next to her and, with no small degree of effort, removed his snug top boots. She touched his back through his white linen shirt, both of her hands running from his neck to his waist, then gliding around to the front. Leaning against him, she hugged him.

Julia felt his hands on hers as he responded to her embrace. He turned his head back toward her. "Julia," he whispered, the sound of her name on his lips like a fresh breeze on a hot summer's day.

She moved lithely around his shoulder and met his lips in a quick, fiery kiss. He shifted swiftly, turned into her, and, a moment later, was lying on top of her, kissing her passionately, his tongue possessing her. Her arms became tangled in his as she sought his hands. Finding them, she gripped them tightly. He drew back slightly from her, his gray eyes intense and demanding.

"I love you," he whispered, his breathing ragged.

"Edward," she breathed in his hair, into his ear, along his cheek as he rolled her over onto him. She looked down into his face, still holding his hands. She kissed him, her body moving over him restlessly.

Loving him was like being turned and tossed in a small boat on a wind-drifted lake. She felt dizzy and strange, exhilarated.

"When we are in Brussels, I will make love to you a score of times," he murmured.

She kissed him hard, unwilling to tell him that she would not be going with him. For the present, she wanted only to love him, to make love with him, to take him inside her, so that no matter what happened in the ensuing months, she would have no regrets.

Julia slipped her hands beneath his shirt and touched the coarse masculine hairs of his chest. He was hard beneath her. She wanted him so much. She wanted to be part of him, now and forever. He moaned at the feel of her fingertips, at her nails on the skin of his chest. Rolling her over onto her side, he removed his shirt. She touched him over and over, letting her lips drift across his cheek, his jaw, his neck, and down the length of his chest.

Her hands were everywhere. His hands responded, touching, fondling, exploring. Julia could hardly breathe. How many times had she dreamt of being with him again? How many times had she awakened full of an aching that remained with her the entire day? Too many times.

He slid her shift up to her waist, over her breasts and arms, and finally slipped it over her head. He tossed it onto the floor. He lay on top of her, stroking her thighs. Julia thought nothing could be as pleasant as the feel of his warm body against hers, soothing, satisfying, endearing.

Edward slid off her and removed his pantaloons and stockings. He lifted her from the bed and pulled her into a tight embrace, kissing her fully, completely.

Pulling back the bedcovers, he laid her down, then joined her, easing into her, kissing her, touching her.

Julia's mind became loose. Her heart rose to a place of sweetness and bliss she had never known. How smooth the rhythm was as he moved, pulsing to the beat of life in an endless song of desire, of wonder, of pleasure. She shed tears, her heart wondrously full. Again he kissed away her tears and asked if he was hurting her. She held him close, explaining she was crying because she was so deeply satisfied. He kissed her harder still, moving into her with wildness and strength. She loved him so much, beyond words, beyond expression. Julia raked his back with her nails, her blood racing in her head, sending pulses of pleasure deep within her.

She gasped as he moved more quickly. Pleasure began pouring through her, over her. She cried out. He grasped her tightly about the waist and brought her pleasure soaring higher and higher, until she cascaded along the winds and circled the heavens. Her mind was a great white expanse that turned a brilliant crimson, then violet, then blue, and finally settled into a deep green, an emerald-green, a place of exotic peace and contentment. She was back in Eden, pure, whole, unashamed.

All her troubles were worth this one moment, she thought. All of them. To be so greatly and richly loved by a man was worth every consequence she could conceive.

She lay beneath him, feeling the quick rise and fall of his chest, knowing he was satisfied, and let her contentment dwell richly in her blood. More tears streamed from her eyes. He was her lover. He would always be the man she loved. In her heart, in her mind, Edward Blackthorn was her husband and would always be her husband, no matter how hard life strove to keep him from her.

When his breathing had settled into a gentle rhythm, she heard him say, "We should be going. Immediately. Wellington is expecting me in Brussels tomorrow. I cannot disappoint him. We will stop by Grillon's and tell your sisters, then—"

She placed her hand on his mouth. "Edward, I love you so very much, but—" she paused for a moment to gather her courage, "but I cannot go to Brussels with you. Not now."

She felt his body grow very still. "What do you mean?"

"I can't go. I have to care for my sisters."

He gently withdrew from her and eased himself up beside her, so that he could look into her eyes. Julia touched his cheek with her hand. "I am not going to Brussels. I cannot go with you, not this time. Perhaps later. But you have to understand. I must make provisions for all of them immediately."

He sat up, his face ashen. He appeared as though she had thrust a sword in his side. "You are not coming with me," he announced. "I see. I comprehend fully. Your loyalty will never be with me, will it? I begin to understand." For a long moment he sat there, breathing heavily. Finally, he got up from the bed and began to care for himself, then to dress.

Julia watched him in silence. She knew there was nothing she could say to ease his anger or his pain. With his coat flung over his shoulder, he went into the other room. She could hear him cursing his neckcloth. She knew what a sore trial the long length of linen could be for a man. In his temper, she supposed it would be nearly impossible to get the cravat into a happy state.

She almost smiled at the thought, as she remained in the bed. But she couldn't. Her heart was too heavy with missing him already, with wondering if he would ever forgive her for choosing duty over love.

Edward returned to the bedroom, to the side of the bed. She rolled on her back and looked at him. He was fully dressed, just as he had been when she arrived on Half Moon Street, his great-coat fitting to perfection his broad shoulders. He was so strong, a soldier, everything she loved and admired.

"I am going now," he stated coldly.

She looked at him steadily and posed a question she was certain would set him off balance. "Why are you leaving me?" Julia asked.

He seemed taken aback. "I am going to Brussels, of course. I am needed there."

"I need you here," she returned without expression.

Edward narrowed his eyes slightly. "You know I can't stay."

"You could if you loved me," she retorted, holding his gaze, forcing him to think through his arguments against her decision to remain behind in London.

"What are you saying?" he snapped.

"I think you know. I have not asked you to stay before because I understand why you are going. So why won't you understand why I am staying?"

"It is not the same thing."

Julia looked away from him. "Then we have nothing further to discuss, do we?"

He stood by the bed for what seemed like an eternity. She did not look at him, but she knew he was still bitterly angry. When he spoke, his voice was cold. "I shall fetch you a hackney. Please get dressed. I can't leave until I see you safely away." Then he wheeled from the room and left.

A few minutes later, Julia joined him on the flags below. He did not kiss her or in any way show her compassion or affection as he handed her up into the hackney coach. Julia leaned her head against the squabs. She dismissed his anger, refusing to remember him that way. Instead, she closed her eyes and let her mind drift to that place of emerald brilliance and peace that had consumed her when she had been locked within his arms, when pleasure and love had been her companions.

What would the future hold? she wondered.

Would she ever see him again?

Sir Perran did not awaken until the sun was on his face. As he lay in bed, recalling the night's many successes, he felt utterly gratified, a sensation he had not experienced in many weeks.

He smiled, tendrils of pleasure curling into every joint of his body. Revenge could be sweet. Indeed, it could.

Julia's insistence that she would leave his house he disregarded as an idle threat. She had nowhere to go, her dignity would be her first objective in order to preserve her place in society, and she had no money.

He sighed contentedly. Yes, revenge could be very sweet. He would begin today by calling upon Princess Esterhazy and relating last night's events to her. No doubt the princess would see to it that his wife's vouchers were rescinded immediately, and given the social disgrace that would follow, Sir Perran would be obliged to take Julia and her sisters back to Bath.

Of course, the real pleasure would come when he would see the sour look upon Annabelle's face, hear Caroline's long-suffering sigh, and receive Elizabeth's fearless, haughty stare as he stuffed them all into a coach and four, along with Julia, and asked them sarcastically if they had enjoyed their London Season.

As he lay in bed, however, something nagged at him, but for a long moment he didn't know what was amiss. He heard the traffic outside, for even in the morning the square bustled with the comings and goings of the gentry and the aristocracy at play. All seemed as it should.

He listened to his house. He heard a few rumblings. Not many. Not nearly as many as there usually were. His shoulders grew tense. Why? Why was it so quiet? Perhaps Julia had told her sisters of the incident. Perhaps all the sisters feared facing his wrath this morning, as well they should.

Whatever the case, he now felt ill at ease. Yet, he shouldn't. Yet, he did.

When his valet entered the chamber with a footman in tow, his qualms grew. For one thing, where was Grigson, and for another, why was the footman bearing a silver salver upon which rested a suspicious missive?

Sir Perran blinked at the tray, then looked at the footman. "Where is Grigson? Is he ill?"

The footman swallowed hard. "No, Sir Perran. The last I saw of him, he was in excellent health."

Sir Perran looked back at the letter. Somehow he knew it was from Julia. As he lifted it from the tray, he recognized her handwriting and knew she was gone. How odd he felt, as though he had just been dealt a hard blow across his face. He permitted his valet to settle several pillows behind him before dismissing both servants.

How could she have gone? She hadn't the funds with which to support herself—he had seen to that.

He took a deep breath and turned the missive over in his hands once, twice, a third time. His fingers were actually trembling as he broke the red wax seal.

My dearest Sir Perran,
  You will not credit what has happened! Last night, after you had left for White's, I was just preparing for bed when the whole house was suddenly overrun with rats. There were at least seven upstairs and five more downstairs, not to mention a dozen in the servants's garrets. We—my sisters, Grigson, our personal maids, and myself—have removed to Grillon's until we have found another residence. You may call upon us if you wish, but trust me when I say that I shall never return to your townhouse in Grosvenor Square.
                                    Your wife, Lady Blackthorn.

Sir Perran read the letter three times. He found the notion of using an infestation of rodents as her reason for having left the protection of his roof an incredibly brilliant maneuver. Rats would provide her with everything—an acceptable reason for leaving her husband and for engaging a separate domicile. The notion was so cleverly lighthearted that even those who did not approve of Julia's conduct would find themselves tittering in spite of themselves. Should he so much as attempt to smudge her impeccable reputation with a recounting of having found her in his nephew's arms—coupled with the story of the rats—he

would find himself the laughingstock of all Mayfair before the
day was out.

Brilliant.

Utterly brilliant.

He leaned his head against the pillows and closed his eyes.
Where the devil had Julia learned such cleverness? Rats.
Damme, if he wasn't so nearly affected by the situation, he would
find nothing but admiration for her. Instead, his mind became a
swirl of rage, at being cuckolded, duped, and now outwitted. For
several minutes, he permitted his anger to rule his mind and his
heart. He breathed deeply, letting the fury first bed within him,
then leave him through each exhale. After an hour had passed,
he had settled his anger into a pocket of his heart, where he
could nourish it at will. His mind was again clear. Now it was
time to think, to observe, to wait, and to plan.

Having had his valet confirm that the Verdell sisters—all of
them—were indeed gone, he sipped a cup of hot coffee and
opened his copy of *The Morning Post*. He let his mind roam
about freely as he read the paper. He did not pursue ideas, he
let them come to him. After a time, he knew what to do. He
would begin his counterattack by hiring someone to spend every
day for weeks scouring his house for rats. He would purchase
rattraps and discuss with anyone willing to listen the horrible
plague that had torn his family from his bosom.

If he was to be laughed at, he intended to disconcert anyone
who dared so much as snigger in his presence. He might even
give hints that he had heard the black plague was again sweeping
Europe. Was it possible?

He knew people.

A sennight later, the plague was on everyone's lips, and those
of a more gullible turn had their homes searched for rats as well.

Twenty-three

"This will do to a nicety!" Julia exclaimed, twirling about in a circle, her heart at ease for the first time in ages. She felt alive and strong. If only she had conceived such a notion before ever having accepted Sir Perran's hand in marriage.

Julia stood, along with her sisters and Gabrielle, in the middle of an empty shop on New Bond Street. It was seven o' clock in the morning, early enough for her to be certain of not being observed by the *haut ton*. In a few hours, New Bond Street would be inundated with genteel shoppers, and if she and her sisters were seen engaging in trade, their combined hopes for the continuation of their Season would end abruptly.

The whole scheme was a gamble. But Julia was learning that sometimes gambling was a far sight better than trying to do the orderly and safe thing.

She had sold her emerald ring, with only a pang of regret, to Lady Trevaunance for the handsome sum of three thousand pounds. The marchioness had listened sympathetically to Julia's tale, of having been caught in a scandalous *tête-à-tête* with Major Blackthorn, of having found Edward's letters in her husband's possession, and of having subsequently removed to Grillon's. Upon learning the extent of Sir Perran's terrible scheme of last summer, Lady Trevaunance approved of Julia's departure from Grosvenor Square and of her intention to set up her own establishment. She offered to help in any way she could, and when asked to recommend a jeweler who might be interested in purchasing the emerald, she had insisted on buying it from Julia herself.

Julia had used a portion of the money to hire a house on Upper Brook Street, along with the servants, furniture, linens, and dishware needed to properly sustain a household. She had for so long managed Hatherleigh Park—except for the time Sir Perran had hired his own housekeeper—that within a few days, with Grigson's help, all the arrangements had been made to everyone's satisfaction.

She also had not seen her sisters so happy in ages. The death of her father and subsequent disastrous marriage had taken a toll on all their spirits. But the happy outcome of the *rat missive,* as Julia called it, along with the sale of her emerald to Lady Trevaunance, had so encouraged the Verdell sisters that singing and laughter could be heard through the halls at all hours of the day and night.

In addition, Julia made certain that from the first, she and her sisters continued meeting their social obligations among the *ton*—the opera, Drury Lane, morning calls, their own "at homes," balls, fetes, soirées, even Almack's. Julia did not know why her husband had not carried out his largest threat—of seeing their vouchers rescinded—but she rather thought he had come to the conclusion that to do so would have placed him in an awkward position.

The night following her removal to Grillon's was the evening of the first Almack's assembly. Having garnered Lady Trevaunance's support, Julia and her sisters attended the ball, though not without trepidation. She soon found, however, that the marchioness's powers were significant, and before long, as she watched Annabelle perform a waltz approved by Lady Jersey, Julia knew that this final path of social success had been opened to her. She could want for nothing now.

Even her husband had attended the assembly, but to his whispered threats, delivered while leaning upon a cane that she knew he didn't need and pronounced behind a smile that he offered for all the world to see, she responded, "How kind of you to have attended our first assembly, Perran. We are now made. But as for returning to Grosvenor Square and your intention of exposing my love for your nephew if I refuse, I can only demur. For I have an impossible fear of rats, which I cannot seem to overcome, and since I know that one very large rodent still resides most contentedly beneath your roof, I simply won't subject myself to the spasms and palpitations that I have little doubt would ensue were I again to take up residence with you. Ah, I see Lady Cowper beckoning me. She has been most kind. Pray, excuse me." She had left her husband's side then, ignoring his cold glances, which he did not hesitate to direct toward her the remainder of the evening.

During the next few days, Julia had set her mind to solving her most pressing difficulty: how she was to support herself and her sisters once she had completely used up the three thousand pounds. Remembering a suggestion Elizabeth had made last summer about opening a millinery shop, she began evaluating the idea, even consulting Lady Trevaunance.

A fortnight later, Julia was prepared to present her idea to her sisters and found the proper moment when they were gathered on a quiet Sunday evening, in their neatly appointed light blue and gold drawing room.

Annabelle had introduced the subject by posing a question. "What are we to do once our funds are gone?" she asked. "I would seek out a wealthy husband, but what if he turned out to be as . . . well, as big a rat as Sir Perran!"

Julia at first stared at her in surprise, then burst out laughing. "Oh, Annabelle! You always could make me laugh so! I wish I were of a literary turn. I should write a novel about *Sir Perran, the Rat*. Perhaps a charming children's tale of a rodent who posed as a nanny and chewed off the children's fingers, one at a time, when they were very bad."

Elizabeth laughed until her sides ached. Annabelle fell into stitches. Even Caroline, who had opened her eyes wide at the truly horrid thought of a huge rat posing as a Nanny, set aside her disapproval and giggled.

When Julia's laughter had subsided, she rang for Gabrielle. After returning to her pale blue silk damask winged chair, which was settled comfortably by the fireplace, she addressed her sisters. "You are very right, Annabelle," she said, setting feathered stitches along the edges of her peacock's exquisite tail. "Even with the greatest care applied to our resources, I believe we should not have funds to last a year."

The younger sisters groaned together. What were they going to do?

"We had all best get husbands, then," Caroline suggested softly, glancing from Elizabeth to Annabelle. They were grouped around the fireplace, each sister enjoying the warm glow of coals as they engaged in a variety of pleasures: Julia worked on her peacock, Annabelle and Elizabeth played at piquet, and Caroline read from a book of sermons.

Julia set a stitch in royal-blue floss and smiled. "Annabelle was also right about fearing that her husband—or yours, Caroline, or yours, Elizabeth—might be as bad as Sir Perran, then we would be in the basket yet again. No, I think I have had enough of attempting to make use of a man in order to protect our futures, to quite last me a lifetime. So, I have been considering another scheme entirely, one over which only this morning Lady Trevaunance was kind enough to exclaim when I laid the whole of my plans before her."

"Indeed," Elizabeth remarked, turning her eyes upon Julia.

"Yes," Julia said with a teasing smile. "But I shan't say another word until Gabrielle arrives."

Fortunately for the suspense of the ladies, the French maid arrived in quick order, all eyes becoming fixed upon her, then shifting in quick darts from Julia and back again to Gabrielle.

"Bon soir, madame," she said in her pretty French accent. "What is it you wish of me?"

"Gabrielle," Julia began, letting her hands rest on her lap, "how would you like to become the proprietress of a quite fashionable shop on New Bond Street and engage in the creation of charming millinery for ladies of fashion?"

The younger sisters gasped as one. Gabrielle placed a hand upon her cheek. "What a wonderful idea!" she cried. *"C'est merveilleux!* But how? When?"

Julia smiled. "I found the shop only yesterday morning. I have hired it until the end of the summer. I had meant to wait until I had more of the details settled before presenting the notion to you or my sisters, but somehow it seemed appropriate to discuss the idea tonight. So tell me, do you think you could take charge of such a shop? Could you hire ladies to work for you? Of course, I intend to secure a man of business to attend to the management of the accounts, but the bonnets would be your domain exclusively."

"Oui . . . yes! . . . it could most certainly be done. I have three friends in London . . . all refugees of the Revolution. And Laure is particularly clever with artificial flowers and feathers. Oh, *mon coeur,* he is pounding fiercely. Tell me this is not a dream. I have wished for something like this for so long."

Now, as Julia stood with her sisters in the empty shop on New Bond Street and watched Gabrielle pass through the doorway leading to the back rooms, she turned to her sisters. "What do you think? The location seems quite excellent, since there is a modiste but a few doors away and that truly wretched millinery across the street. I have heard everyone complain of their failing workmanship and lack of design. I am convinced we shall succeed."

"It is perfect!" Elizabeth cried.

"What shall you call the establishment?" Caroline queried, turning about in stages and carefully examining each aspect of the shop.

"I know precisely what it should be called!" Annabelle offered.

"What?" Julia asked, not having given the smallest consideration to a name for their millinery.

Annabelle beamed. "Olivia's, of course," she breathed.

Julia heard her mother's name and tears immediately started to her eyes. Elizabeth and Caroline exclaimed over the perfection of Annabelle's choice, and the decision was made as easily as if the name had been dropped from the heavens.

"I am recalling to mind what Mama told me just before she died," Julia said. "Do you remember, Annabelle? *Make something beautiful for me.* I cannot imagine anything prettier than all the ladies of Mayfair walking about the streets or traveling in open landaus in Hyde Park wearing Gabrielle's bonnets."

Caroline's eyes filled with tears as well. "She would be so pleased."

The sisters agreed. And so the shop was called Olivia's.

By the end of April, Olivia's enjoyed a fine patronage, in part because the beautiful Verdell sisters wore only bonnets created at Olivia's, and in part because Gabrielle was a genius with flowers, feathers, ribbons, silks, felt, and straw. If the tittle-tattle, whispered behind lace fans, was that Lady Blackthorn was in actuality the proprietress, anyone daring to suggest aloud such a notion was soon pushed to the fringes of *tonish* society. If it seemed strange for a young lady to have hired a male secretary who was seen frequently at Olivia's as well, it was no one's concern after all.

Lady Trevaunance was proving to be a masterful sponsor among the *haut ton*. In spite of the fact that once it was known for certain that rodents no longer resided in Grosvenor Square and Lady Blackthorn still did not return to her husband, the *beau monde* was quite willing to accept the arrangement. Her independence was tolerated, in part because both Ladies Trevaunance and Cowper stood firmly behind Lady Blackthorn, and in part because there was not a hostess in Mayfair who did not fear that were the beautiful Verdell sisters absent from one of their fetes, social disaster might quickly follow.

The weeks began piling up, one atop the other, and the London season drove steadily through the month of May. If Sir Perran treated her respectfully and with a sort of courtly dignity when they would meet in public, Julia was not fooled for a moment. When he hinted he would mend his ways if she would only return to his home, she had but to look into his cold gray eyes to know he was attempting to deceive her yet again. She therefore kept her discourse with him lighthearted and distant, and always disengaged herself from his presence as soon as possible whenever they met. Once, when he had pressed her most forcefully to come home, saying that as always he found London intolerable but even more so because she was not with him to warm his hearth in Grosvenor Square, Julia had suggested flatly that if he was so blue-deviled, he ought to return to Hatherleigh. He responded immediately that he would only return to the Park when she and her sisters were ready to leave London.

Julia had looked at him strangely. "I shall never return to Hatherleigh," she announced. "So long as we are married."

He had seemed stunned for a brief moment, then bowed to her and walked away. After that, he had been less eager to speak with her, though frequently she found him watching her closely at the opera or the theater or at any number of shared social events. What was he thinking? she wondered. Or worse, planning?

As June drew steadily closer, Julia found, much to her pleasure, that between Olivia's, her sisters, and their many social engagements, she had little time to bother her head about her husband. Her life was very full, and her only pain and disappointment resided in the fact that never did an hour pass that she did not think of Edward and wish he had been able to forgive her. Since she had written to him time and again yet had not once received an answer, she could only assume that he was still angry and his heart remained closed to her.

Calling upon Lady Trevaunance on the first of June, Julia again expressed her gratitude for the marchioness's help.

"Yes, yes, that is all very well and good," Lady Trevaunance responded impatiently, at the same time waving a letter before Julia. "But not once in the past two months—though I have nearly expired time and again with curiosity—have you told me of Major Blackthorn. I find I can no longer keep silent, especially when after having received a letter from him, I find it carries not a single word of you. So tell me, have you heard from him these many weeks and more? Goodness, it has been two months since he left London!"

Julia was so taken aback by the introduction of a subject so near to her heart that for a moment she merely stared at Lady Trevaunance, her lips parted. "Not a word," she said at last, her voice barely above a whisper. Her throat was painfully constricted as she continued. "I have written to him a score of times, but he was very angry when he left. I fear . . ." Julia could not complete her thought. She did not want to let her darkest concerns float in the air. She was certain that if she gave voice to her anxieties, they would take physical shape and strike at her.

"I see," Lady Trevaunance replied with a frown.

"He doesn't understand the duty I have toward my sisters."

"His concerns for the present involve matters of enormous consequence—for England and for Europe. It would be foolish to suppose he could comprehend what must seem to him your less important affairs. You must somehow help him see that you had to stay, that you could no more turn your back on your sisters than he could dismiss Bonaparte's presence in France."

Julia shook her head. "I tried to the last night I saw him. But sometimes I wonder, was he right? Should I have left London and joined him in Brussels when he wanted me to?"

Lady Trevaunance shook her head vigorously. "I believe you had to stay, at least for these several weeks, perhaps a little longer yet. Had you left with him, Sir Perran would probably have seen that your scandalous conduct with his nephew became known to the world and your sisters would have been sunk in disgrace. What then would they have done had you left them kicking their heels at Grillon's with nowhere to go, their London careers ruined? No, you had to stay. But perhaps you ought to consider going sometime soon. Olivia's is prospering, your sisters are welcomed everywhere, and were you to hire a suitable companion in order to enjoy the gaieties of Brussels while all of Europe is again preparing for war, your conduct would not be regarded as improper. Rumors will always persist, but as long as you are discreet, none of it matters."

"I don't think I could," Julia declared, trying to imagine her sisters going about London without her guidance.

"Trevaunance and I are going, I think in a week or so. Why don't you consider accompanying us? I know you believe Elizabeth, Caroline, and Annabelle still have great need of you, but I also think you underestimate their resilience and resourcefulness."

"You are very kind," Julia responded immediately, her heart quickening. She wanted nothing more at that moment than to accompany Lady Trevaunance to Brussels. "I will consider your invitation. Believe me, I want nothing more than to go."

"Just think about it," she said, taking Julia's hand and patting it kindly.

Twenty-four

Sir Perran stood on the threshold of Julia's drawing room, a bandbox tucked beneath his arm. Much to his surprise, he found that his heart was beating rapidly. He was anxious to see her again, more than he ought to be for his purposes. He took a slow, measured breath and brought his pulse under control. Grigson had shown him to the drawing room, though obviously under strong protest. He moved into the elegant chamber and noted that the butler would still not meet his gaze. When the aging retainer quit the chamber and the door was closed behind him, Sir Perran surveyed his wife's drawing room with great interest.

He had never before been inside Julia's home on Upper Brook Street. What he saw pleased him. She was a woman of excellent taste and obviously possessed keen management abilities. As a lady's receiving room, the furnishings were simple, pleasing, and completely lacking in the ostentatious use of gilt that ladies of little discernment frequently employed.

The walls were decorated in a light blue silk damask. The windows, overlooking the busy Mayfair street, were hung with gauzy muslin underneath and gold silk damask in two pieces, which overall consisted of a single drape pulled diagonally across the window and tied back with a gold tasseled cord, topped by a valance. With the draperies tied back, a lovely but unusual May sunshine streamed into the chamber and lit up a patterned Aubusson carpet in varying shades of blue and gold.

The fireplace sat opposite the door. A large embroidered screen was set to the right of the hearth and a warm glow of coals kept the perpetual spring chill from the chamber. Deep in the corner to the left of the fireplace sat a rosewood pianoforte. Four of Annabelle's quite masterful watercolors portraying landscapes of the countryside around Bath were mounted on the wall beside the pianoforte.

Opposite the pianoforte, on the wall to the left of the door, a sideboard of mahogany gleamed in the morning light. A vase of white roses flanked by jaunty pansies adorned the sideboard, along with a large silver candelabra. To his right was a writing table upon which sat a silver filigreed inkwell, a pen tray, and another large candelabra. Grouped in front of the fireplace were two sofas in the same blue silk damask as the fabric on the walls, a matching winged chair, and two black lacquer Empire chairs in gold and white striped silk.

Occasional tables of a fine mahogany had been placed for convenience throughout. He noted several volumes of poetry scattered among the tables. Caroline's book of piano music was open on the pianoforte, and Julia's embroidery hoop, peacock scissors, and several lengths of floss rested on a table next to the winged chair. The flowery embroidered pillows scattered about turned the sofas into summery gardens. Not even the most exacting eye could find fault with this chamber.

With the bandbox still under his arm, Sir Perran limped forward, cane in hand, and seated himself in the Empire chair closest to the fire. He held the bandbox on his lap while he waited for his wife. He felt strange, as though he had stepped into a world he was only now beginning to comprehend—the world of females. Let him be with men, especially men of large affairs and concerns, and he was greatly at ease. He knew the rules well and played them to perfection. But this Season in London, because of Julia's tremendous support from Ladies Trevaunance and Cowper, had seen him the recipient of a dozen haughty stares and cold greetings from more than one influential hostess. A fortnight after his wife had left Grosvenor Square, he realized she was being protected by a muslin and silk brigade as powerful as any of Wellington's forces. He could no more touch her socially than he could enter a Mayfair drawing room in a state of undress.

But here, in her drawing room, she would not have the marchioness to defend her. He knew himself to be more than Julia's equal and believed that with a little careful persuasion, he could bring her home. Sir Perran was confident of his abilities.

Then why the devil did he feel like bolting?

The door opened. Julia stood in the doorway, her head high and proud, her auburn hair dressed in a tight chignon, pearl ear-bobs dangling from her ears. She wore a high-necked morning dress of apricot silk, trimmed with a fine cream-colored lace. She appeared in every respect a Lady of Quality, and it seemed to him she had matured a dozen years since he had led her to the altar last summer.

"Sir Perran," Julia said by way of acknowledgment.

He rose unsteadily, clutching the bandbox in his hand. Her gaze drifted to his legs. He watched her expression grow speculative and disapproving, then fade to disinterest as she advanced into the chamber. She seated herself in the pale blue winged chair opposite him. Clever. She didn't settle into a sofa, but rather met him squarely on her terms.

"What may I do for you?" she queried formally.

"I have brought you a gift." He offered her the bandbox.

Julia did not take it, but instead folded her hands on her lap. When he withdrew his present and set it on the floor beside her chair, she spoke. "Why are you here, Perran?"

"I wanted to see my wife," he returned, watching her closely. He noted that a faint color dappled her cheeks. Perhaps she was more distressed by his visit than she appeared.

"I am not your wife any longer," she said.

He drew in a sharp breath. "Whatever do you mean?" he asked, frowning. "What nonsense is this? You are my wife. You will always be Lady Blackthorn so long as I am alive." Already his temper was besting him. Sir Perran took a deep breath, trying to calm himself. Why the deuce was he so angry?

She eyed him coolly. "You know precisely what I mean. You manipulated me into wedding you—"

"There I must beg to differ. You were anxious for my fortune. After all, you had your sisters to care for."

"You manipulated me into marrying you by withholding Edward's letters. For that—and for the coldness of your heart toward me—I shall never forgive you."

"My heart was not always cold," he retorted, again to his surprise. A strange sensation came over him. His heart began beating rapidly and his words came out in a rush, so unlike him. "I can love . . . I can love you. In my way I always have." What was he saying? Why was he speaking these words to her? He rose to his feet and watched his cane slide off his knee and fall to the floor. He did not limp as he crossed the small distance between them and fell to his knees before her.

Another being inside him took over as he grasped her hands and began weeping, kissing her palms, her wrists. He begged her to return to Grosvenor Square. "You are my life. How can I live without you?" He looked up and saw Julia's auburn hair turn an exquisite raven's black, her emerald eyes becoming as blue and as clear as a West Indies island sea. "You shouldn't have left me for him, my darling. What can he give you? Nothing. I can give you everything, the world, every desire of your heart. We can have children together, a dozen if you wish for it."

She was so beautiful, so desirous.

Sophia, his heart cried out.

He rose from his knees and bent to kiss her. She turned her face away, so different from the last time. He forced his kiss upon her, then he began touching her breasts, stroking them, kneading them. Slipping his arm about her waist, Sir Perran lifted Julia easily to her feet. He felt her striking at him but he embraced her roughly, kissing her brutally hard. He moved his hand from her waist to her buttocks and pressed himself against her.

Suddenly, he felt a sharp pain in his arm. He released her

abruptly. She fell back, onto the floor at the foot of the chair. In her hand was an absurdly small pair of peacock scissors with a telltale smear of blood on the blades.

He gripped his arm where she had stabbed him, pain slicing through him in sickening waves. The blade had sunk deeply into his muscle. "What have you done?" he cried, his vision clearing, Sophia's black hair returning to a gleaming auburn. He blinked as panic seized him. What was happening to him? "I was only kissing you!" he cried. "You are my wife! I am allowed such a liberty."

"You are allowed nothing," she returned hoarsely, rising to her feet and still holding the scissors, as though she would attack him again if need be. "Now get out and don't ever come to my house again. There was a time when I had hoped that you could love me, but I have come to understand that you are incapable of even the smallest of honorable sentiments. Now get out!" Tears rolled down her cheeks. He picked up his cane and moved to stand over her.

He felt violently ill. He looked down at her and was consumed with rage. He saw her, he saw Sophia, both of whom had betrayed him. He wanted to hurt her as deeply as she had hurt him. He could take her life. He could strike her with his cane until she breathed no more.

But his thoughts began to form a clear and straight line, until he saw a more perfect means of destroying her. He smiled faintly. "Enjoy your bonnet," he said, gesturing toward the unopened bandbox. "I purchased it from Olivia's, if you must know."

With that, he quit the townhouse.

Julia sank down into the chair behind her, remaining there for a long time as she stared into the fire. She still gripped the scissors tightly in her hand. His anger had reddened his eyes and for a moment he had appeared as though he meant to kill her.

More than anything, Julia wished Lady Trevaunance had not left for Brussels. She needed to speak with her, she needed her advice. It seemed that the depth of Sir Perran's hatred was only now just surfacing. She wanted to seek a divorce from him. But divorces weren't granted except by an act of Parliament. As she collected her thoughts, Julia concluded she would begin pressing her husband for a divorce regardless of the consequences. She needed to separate herself from a man whose conduct toward her was a straightforward promise that he meant to continue to harass her until she bowed to his will.

She considered going to his house, but given his recent assault while under her roof, Julia knew she would not be safe with him. She decided, then, to seek him out in a public setting, perhaps meeting him at a soirée or at a ball, by chance, and to let the safety of the surroundings protect her while she asked him for a divorce.

Her mind made up, Julia sought him everywhere, day after day, but he was never present at the events she attended. She wondered if the wound she had inflicted on him had perhaps become infected, and her heart seemed to fail her. How had things come to such a pass? She had never intended to hurt Sir Perran, but then never would she have believed he could have used her so ill.

A week, then ten days passed, and June was well upon London. Julia continued to look for him, laughing whenever anyone asked her slyly whether the rats had all left Grosvenor Square.

Even Lady Cowper teased her one night at Almack's. "So now that the largest rat has left Grosvenor Square, do you intend to give up your home on Upper Brook Street?"

Julia laughed, pretending an amusement she did not feel. She then thought over what Lady Cowper had said. "I am wondering if I heard you properly. Did you say, *the largest rat* had gone?" Had Sir Perran left London after all?

"Well, yes. I suppose you are teased to death about Sir Perran and the rats, but now that he is gone, I could not help but wonder what you meant to do. Or do you enjoy having your own establishment?"

Julia stared at her blankly. For a long moment she could not put two thoughts together. She was stunned by the news Lady Cowper was, in fact, conveying to her.

She fanned herself and drew near to her. "I didn't know he had left the Metropolis," she whispered, her heart beginning to thrum in her ears. "Only tell me, do you know where he has gone?"

"Why, to Brussels—or at least that is the latest *on-dits*— with Lord Yarnacott and Mr. Loxhore."

Julia felt queasy and dizzy all at once. "I fear I am going to faint," she murmured, dread seizing her. "There can be only one reason—"

Lady Cowper led her to a chair near the doorway and bid her sit down. "For you do appear as though you are like to swoon." The assembled guests moved past them, a perpetual flow of chatter and laughter obscuring her words so that only Julia could hear. "What is it I have said?" she asked, seating herself next to Julia and speaking in a low voice. "Or did you not know Sir Perran has gone to Brussels? Certainly, under the circumstances, you can't be unhappy that he is no longer here."

She looked at Lady Cowper and responded, "Anywhere but Brussels, yes. But you see, his . . . his nephew is there. When last they met . . ."

Lady Cowper's eyes opened wide. "Oh, I see your concern now. Good heavens! What do you mean to do?"

"I don't know. It is so difficult for me to leave London at the present."

Lady Cowper placed her hand on Julia's arm. "If I were you, I would move heaven and earth to get there, do you hear me? For one thing, private duels are not frowned upon so severely in Europe as they are here, even between father and . . . er . . . that is, even between uncle and nephew."

"You are right, I must go," she declared. "You are so kind."

Lady Cowper regarded her sympathetically. "Did you ever suspect your life would be so complicated when you were a schoolgirl learning your letters?"

Julia shook her head. "No, never."

"Just take my advice—go to Brussels, the sooner the better!"

The next morning, Julia went to Elizabeth's bedchamber with the intent of asking her sister to take over the management of the house. When she found Lizzie in tears, her eyes puffy and red from crying, her resolve began to slip. She knew her sister had been distressed for some time over the horrifying circumstances of a childhood friend of hers who had been captured some months ago by Algerian corsairs. Julia's opinion, which she kept to herself, was that Lizzie's friend had long since been sold into slavery and had undoubtedly disappeared into the darkness of the vast Turkish Empire. Seeing her thus dispirited, she found she could not prevail on Elizabeth to help her after all.

Wondering what next she ought to do, Julia moved into the hallway, only to find her youngest sister waiting for her, a frightened light in her eye.

Drawing Julia away from Elizabeth's door, Annabelle said, "I wasn't certain if I ought to mention it to you, but Lizzie has been speaking wildly of late. Only last night she spoke of cutting off her hair and signing aboard a sailing vessel with the intent of somehow getting to Algiers. I don't usually listen to Elizabeth when she rails against injustice in this or that quarter, but there is just such a light in her eye, of holy purpose, that when she spoke of going to sea, I began to think it possible she might just do it. What do you make of it? Is there cause for worry?"

Julia pressed her hand to her head and squeezed her eyes shut. It seemed impossible to concentrate on Annabelle's concern for her sister when her heart was besieged with fear for Edward's life. "I don't know what to think," she responded. Opening her eyes, she regarded Annabelle and, with a sigh, spoke. "Pray, don't distress yourself. I promise you I shall speak with her later, when she is feeling more the thing. I'm sure she would never do anything as absurd as cutting off her hair and joining the navy."

At that, Annabelle seemed relieved and shortly afterward parted from Julia, explaining she meant to go to Hookham's

Library. "I knew I could rely on you, Julia," she called over her shoulder as she headed for the stairs.

Julia remained standing in the hallway, not knowing what to do next. She had meant to entrust Elizabeth with the management of the household, but it was quite obvious that her sister was not capable of it at the moment.

"Julia?" she heard a whisper from down the hall.

Turning, she saw Caroline, still dressed in a white muslin morning gown, beckoning to her from her bedchamber door.

"Do come and talk with me for a moment," she said, smiling in soft encouragement.

Julia went to her sister somewhat reluctantly, wondering what difficulty Caroline was experiencing that now required her attention. She began to feel that Brussels might as well have been on the other side of the world, instead of across the English Channel.

"Sit down, Julia, won't you?" Caroline queried in her soft manner as Julia entered the amber and green bedchamber. "I can see that you are greatly distressed. You have been ill at ease since we left Almack's last night. Only tell me what is wrong? Perhaps I can be of some help to you."

Julia looked at her in surprise. "Oh . . . that is, I thought . . . that is, you are not perchance suffering from some indisposition and require my advice?"

"No," Caroline responded with a smile. "Poor, responsible Julia. How is it in the course of the past year you have failed to notice we are all of us grown up now? The truth is, I knew you were unhappy, and what I wish to know is how I can be of use to you? You have been shouldering our troubles far too long and I thought perhaps there might be something I could do to help. Will you let me?"

Julia was so surprised that she did not immediately answer, but instead permitted her sister to lead her to an amber velvet chaise longue by the window. They sat down together and Julia looked at her sister almost as if for the first time, and began to see that what Caroline had said was true: Her sisters were indeed grown up.

When Caroline took her hand and begged her to unburden herself, Julia took a deep breath and proceeded to relate everything to her, including Sir Perran's attack on her in the drawing room the previous week, as well as the fact that she had protected herself from his advances by stabbing him.

Caroline, of a sensitive nature, had shed tears at the horror of the situation. After that, however, her thoughts and insights took a decidedly practical turn. "So now that you have learned your husband has gone to Brussels, you are convinced that he means to harm Major Blackthorn. Do I have the right of it?"

Julia nodded. "Precisely so. If you could have seen the look in his eye, so full of hatred . . ."

"Isn't it strange? Caroline mused, her eyes taking on a faraway expression. "I mean it is almost a story out of mythology, don't you think?"

"Whatever do you mean?" Julia asked.

"Well, it seems that frequently the Greek and Roman myths involve family members who do not know they are so closely related. I can only suppose then that if Sir Perran is intent on harming Major Blackthorn, he cannot possibly be aware of their closer connection."

Julia shook her head in confusion. "He is Blackthorn's uncle," she stated, wondering what Caroline could possibly mean by a *closer connection.*

"You don't know, do you?" Caroline breathed, her complexion paling.

"Whatever are you talking about?" Julia queried, her heart beginning to pound in her breast.

"I thought you knew . . . I never meant . . . oh, dear." She laid a hand on Julia's arm. "I don't know how to say this except straight out. You see, I learned some time past that Major Blackthorn is not Sir Perran's nephew. He is, in fact, his son."

Julia stared at her sister blankly for a long moment, a dizziness assailing her. At the same time, her vision became blurred, as though she were seeing Caroline through a heavy fog. "His son?" she questioned.

"Julia, don't look at me like that. Oh, dear . . . I wish I hadn't told you."

Julia ignored her sister's agitation. "You mean Sophia Kettering and Sir Perran . . . ?"

Caroline nodded.

Julia shook her head again, unable to credit what she was hearing. "But where . . . I mean, how did you learn of this? Oh, Caroline, I am now filled with the worst sort of dread. Are you absolutely certain?"

"Yes," Caroline breathed, her blue eyes full of anguish. "I can see I have given you a terrible shock. I am so sorry, so terribly sorry." She placed a hand on Julia's arm. "When we first came to London, I happened to be standing behind Lady Trevaunance—she couldn't have known I was there, else she would not have begun speaking of it. She was talking in a low voice to Lady Jersey. I didn't mean to eavesdrop, but I was in the middle of it before I could leave without making matters worse. At any rate, she told Lady jersey that Sophia had once told her the whole history: that she had loved Sir Perran quite violently but he had frightened her by . . . that is, by taking her innocence when perhaps he should not have, even though they were betrothed; and that she had married Harry Blackthorn, only later to discover she was carrying Sir Perran's child—his son—Edward, in fact."

Still feeling dizzy, Julia rose to her feet and moved to the empty fireplace across from her sister's bed. Taking a deep breath, she let her hand rest on the rounded edge of the mantel. Tears of fright burned her eyes. Why did this knowledge change everything in her mind? She felt as though she were caught in a whirlpool, spun around and around, pulled deeper and deeper into some fathomless, endless circle. Her fears mounted.

Edward was Sir Perran's son.

The man she loved was her husband's son.

How sordid it seemed, how bizarre. Then, Sir Perran had violated Edward's mother. Had he vindictively assaulted her or lost himself in his passion?

Julia had looked into Sir Perran's heart more than once. She had seen how twisted and cold were his sentiments. Yet there had been a time in late February when she knew his heart was softening toward her. Was it possible that beneath the hardness of his heart was a man not wholly beyond redemption?

"I must go to Brussels," she stated, turning back to hold Caroline's gaze steadily.

Her sister had remained sitting on the chaise longue but now rose to her feet. She regarded her anxiously but nodded. "Yes, you must go. You must. I believe I know what you are thinking—and I believe you are right. He means to harm his son. Given everything you've said to me, I am convinced he intends to exact some sort of revenge."

"Caroline, I am persuaded he doesn't know that Blackthorn is his son. If he did, if he had known all along . . . well, I wonder if any of this would have happened. Perhaps he would never have prevented his letters from reaching me."

"I am not certain it would have made one whit of difference," Caroline pressed. "Something has gone awry in Sir Perran's heart, something very old and painful has kept him imprisoned. Don't suppose that at this eleventh hour he will suddenly become forgiving of either you or Blackthorn."

"Hope dies hard with me, Caro," she said. "He can't be all bad—no one is."

"Perhaps not, but he may be beyond salvation. Please be careful. If he could have used you so badly in your own drawing room, he is capable of anything. But now, go to Brussels. I will manage everything here. You may trust me to follow to the letter whatever instructions you give me." When Julia hesitated, Caroline slipped her arm about her waist and added, "I won't let you down, I promise you. Please let me help."

"If you truly wish for it," Julia declared.

"Indeed, I do," Caroline assured her. "But tell me what you mean to do once you are in Brussels?"

Julia smiled. "Lady Trevaunance extended me an invitation to join her in Brussels no fewer than a dozen times before she left. I hope once I arrive, she doesn't suddenly regret her kind offer."

Her decision made, Julia took Caroline to her office and began going over in detail all the matters relating to the household and to Olivia's. In the morning, when her secretary arrived, she reviewed everything again in his presence. Afterward, Julia informed her new abigail, Hetty, of her journey, and the maid who would accompany her set to the task of packing the best of Lady Blackthorn's wardrobe into several portmanteaus and trunks.

For the sake of propriety, a distant and impoverished cousin of Lady Cowper's was hired to serve as a companion to Elizabeth, Caroline, and Annabelle in Julia's absence.

Only one task remained to be done before Julia felt she could leave with even a semblance of peace and that was to address Elizabeth's distress over the kidnapping of her friend. But when she posed her concerns to Lizzie, she was informed by Elizabeth not to be a goose, that though she might speak of cutting off her hair or of signing aboard a sailing vessel, she was not so henwitted as to actually do anything as foolish. Julia regarded her sister closely and saw that there was a calmness in Lizzie's demeanor that indicated she had come to accept her inability to help her friend in his dire predicament. She knew now she could leave London without fearing her sister would act upon any of her outrageous schemes.

The parting was a tearful one, because Caroline stated the heretofore unrecognized truth: Since their mother's death, the sisters had never once been separated. Not once.

"It is an ending," Annabelle said in a whisper, giving voice to the sentiment that seemed to rest heavily in the air. "I know it is. We shall never be together again like this. Somehow I feel it to be true."

Julia felt a spattering of gooseflesh creep down her neck. They were all in tears now, and Julia held each one in turn in a long embrace. She sensed the future as well, perhaps because of her own pressing need to be with Edward, or perhaps because Elizabeth was solemn and mournful over her friend, or perhaps because Caroline seemed to have grown two inches taller since having taken over the management of the household. Whatever the case, when she climbed aboard the carriage and looked back at her sisters one last time, Julia knew that when she saw them again, all would be changed forever.

Life was such a mystery, she thought, as the wheels began to turn and the figures of her beloved sisters grew smaller with each onward press of the horses. The whole business of living was a flow of strange parts, of comings and goings, of givings and takings, of bad and good, of wildness and dullness. Now she was separated from her siblings and leaving the orderliness of her country, and Brussels awaited her. What would she find once she arrived there?

Twenty-five

Sir Perran pushed back a sheer muslin underdrape and looked out the window of his bedchamber, letting his gaze drift over the city of Brussels. The sun was setting upon the bustling, cobbled streets and baroque buildings of the ancient, busy Metropolis situated in the heart of the Low Countries. The Upper and Lower Town areas of the city, in the center of Brussels, had for centuries been kept apart by ramparts built around a five-mile perimeter and housing seven gates. A few years ago, however, Bonaparte had ordered the ramparts destroyed, and the edges of this internal island were becoming increasingly blurred as wide avenues replaced the ramparts.

Ordinarily, Sir Perran chose to lease a townhouse in Upper Town, which housed European aristocracy. But for his purposes, he elected to take rooms near the extraordinary Grand Place in Lower Town, where he could easily escape notice. In the more privileged Upper Town, where every manner of social fete had been enlivening the city since Europe first began mobilizing against Bonaparte, in no manner could he have avoided the natural social intercourse that would have ensued given his wealth and rank.

Besides, he did not want his nephew to know he was in Brussels. Not yet, at any rate.

As he watched the sun dip slowly in the west, he let his senses reach out to the city and to the countryside beyond. The window of his chambers faced south and west. Several miles beyond Brussels was a forest of beech trees planted by the Austrian Hapsburgs, known as the *forêt de Soignes,* and beyond that was an extensive corn plain upon which, it was predicted, the battle against the French would take place. Like everyone else in Brussels, Sir Perran had for days since his arrival been trying to ascertain from which direction Napoleon would attempt to reconquer the City and vanquish his opponents. The Prussian and combined Dutch and British forces were stretched in a line across all the major roads leading into the capital city from every southerly direction.

Daily, British forces arrived from England, joined by veteran regiments from the Peninsular campaigns, which were just now returning from America. Blucher's Prussian forces numbered nearly one hundred thirteen thousand, a figure matching France's army. The forces under Wellington's command were estimated at eighty thousand. The French Emperor seemed to be outnumbered and most certainly would be if the estimated half million additional men arrived—contributions from the remaining sovereigns of Europe—who were reputedly marching toward Brussels even as Sir Perran surveyed the city.

Brussels and the Low Countries were safe, or so the rumors abounded. But Sir Perran knew better, if not from the information he had received from his spies then from his intuition. Bonaparte would certainly have a reasonable knowledge of the whereabouts of the armies not yet arrived in Brussels, and common sense dictated he attack the capital before they had a chance to join the Prussian or British combined forces. Sir Perran was convinced only a day or two would see a major assault by the old master of war and the battle would be inflicted on an enemy perhaps a little too confident in its numbers.

He drew in a breath, letting the warm, humid air flow into his nostrils. There seemed to be a certain electricity all about him as he inhaled deeply. He had felt this way once before, aboard one of his merchant ships in the Orient. An hour later the edge of a typhoon had caught his ship, tossing the vessel and his crew about like a helpless leaf for hours on end. Powerful waves had swept a number of his crew overboard as all strived to keep the vessel from foundering. Once the storm had passed, he had fallen in intense fatigue, in the very spot where he had labored, and had slept the sleep of the dead. The next day he had awakened on deck in calm waters, a hot sun on his neck and back.

The air felt the same way to him now, as though a typhoon were about to descend on the reveling soldiers scattered about the Netherlands. War rested just beyond the horizon. He could feel it as surely as if it were a tangible thing. If only he were a younger man, how much he would have enjoyed going into battle, not unlike his nephew.

Edward Blackthorn. God curse him.

Well, soon enough to settle that score, unless God did it for him.

How strange, though, yet not inappropriate, that Julia had arrived only that afternoon. His spies had witnessed her pass through the Grand Place, her reported awe of the exotic baroque fronts of the guild houses a reminder of what he had lost to his nephew when she had quit Grosvenor Square. For weeks he had missed her, deeply and intensely, as though in her departure from his home she had taken part of his soul with her. One way or the other, he would make her suffer for deserting him.

For the present, he knew her to be residing in Upper Town in the Marquis of Trevaunance's townhouse. His spies would follow her every movement, and once she betrayed him with his nephew—as he was certain she would—he would take his revenge.

Later that evening, Julia entered a fashionable townhouse in Upper Town alongside Lord and Lady Trevaunance. Her heart was in her throat, her knees were weak with excitement. It would seem that in a scant few minutes, the fondest desire of her heart would be realized: She would be with Edward Blackthorn again.

According to the marquis, Edward would be in attendance, along with the Duke of Wellington and many of his officers.

Upon entering the townhouse, Julia was struck first with the presence of so many languages—Dutch, French, German, Italian, and of course English. The core of European *haut* society was present, along with a brilliant display of a score of contrasting military uniforms. The initial impression was dazzling and not less so for Julia, since the object of her heart would be wearing one of those uniforms.

The ladies responded to the presence of the officers by wearing their finest gowns, many adorned with the intricately crafted Brussels lace. Jewels of every hue glittered beneath the glowing candle-lit chandeliers. Smiles were excited and flirtatious; the air was filled with a camaraderie and goodwill Julia found exhilarating. It would seem all of Europe had come to Brussels to support her armies.

For herself, Julia wore a dark green silk gown with puffed sleeves and an underdress of white silk. Pearls adorned her earlobes and her neck. In addition, she had entwined a rope of matched pearls about her wrist. She fanned herself as she moved beside Lord and Lady Trevaunance and greeted all those to whom she was introduced. If she heard a few whispers and titters about a certain *tonish* rat, she could not help but smile behind her gently wafting fan.

The truth was, she had little interest in anyone present. Her gaze drifted purposely about each chamber and antechamber through which she passed, always seeking the one face that would warm her heart. Each step brought her pulse quickening. Surely around the next corner she would find him.

At last the sight she had so long awaited was before her. Edward's fine soldierly bearing greeted her eyes, and it was as though a window had just been opened and a breeze suddenly rushed over her and enveloped her. How she loved him! But would he forgive her?

He appeared to distinct advantage in a dark blue military coat trimmed with red facings and silver braid, his broad shoulders tapering to a narrow waist, his strong, athletic legs encased in white silk breeches and stockings. Several young ladies nearby ogled him with good reason. He was clearly the handsomest man in the chamber.

"He is here," she whispered to Lady Trevaunance, leaning toward the marchioness.

Lady Trevaunance followed the line of her gaze. "And he is with Wellington. Goodness! Two such fine men! Even my own heart is palpitating. Come. You ought to meet the man who holds Blackthorn's career in the palm of his hand."

Julia moved toward Edward, who stood to the side of a fireplace in one of the chambers at the back of the narrow house. An orchestra in an adjoining chamber could be heard playing a bright waltz, the sounds of which were muffled by the chatter of all the personages around her. Edward was laughing at something Wellington was saying to him. He was so deucedly handsome, she thought. Would she ever tire of looking at him? Never.

She smiled. He still hadn't seen her, and to her knowledge he did not know she had arrived in Brussels. Though she had continued writing to him, Julia had not told him she intended to join Lady Trevaunance. How would he respond? Would he be angry or grateful she had come?

She glanced at the Duke of Wellington and noticed with some pleasure that he was watching her with a distinctly admiring expression in his blue eyes. *What an attractive man,* she thought. Though he had a rather large nose, he was still in her opinion a very handsome, appealing man. He was tall, his hair was brown, and his complexion well bronzed like Edward's. Having caught her eye, he smiled at her and inclined his head to her. She watched him lean toward Edward and whisper something to him.

Edward in turn glanced in her direction, started slightly, then spoke her name. A moment later, his complexion pale, he was introducing Julia to His Grace, the Duke of Wellington.

She curtsied to the famous general and felt peculiar suddenly. Here was the man who, as field marshal in command of the allied armies, would very soon be meeting in battle the one man who had succeeded during his career to conquer most of Europe. How at ease Wellington seemed, so self-assured, confident, good-humored. Julia had the oddest sense that she was staring her future in the face. A prickling went up along her back. What was it he was saying? . . . "From all reports you are a woman of uncommonly good sense and strong mettle. You would have made an excellent officer's wife." He smiled faintly, the lines at his eyes crinkling. "How stupid of Major Blackthorn to have let you get away when he did." He then directed a rather penetrating glance at Edward, returned his gaze for a fraction of a second to Julia, then begged Lady Trevaunance to dance with him.

Julia watched him go, feeling unabashedly awestruck. "It is no wonder you are willing to do whatever he says," she whispered to Edward. "I vow I have never met such a man before."

"There is no one like him," she heard Edward say.

Shifting her gaze back to him and meeting his gray eyes squarely, she saw at once that he was angry. His next words altered the subject entirely. "I can't imagine why you've come," he began curtly, his nostrils flaring slightly. "Although I suppose like many others you've arrived in Brussels for the sheer amusement of watching our armies prepare for war."

Julia's mind began to move very quickly. Her first thought was that she needed to tell him that his uncle—his father—had come to Brussels and that she believed his intent was evil. But because Sir Perran, though seen by many, had not chosen to partake of the pleasures of Brussels society, she set aside her initial impulse. Whatever Sir Perran's intentions, they were not imminent. She then picked up and discarded any number of possible responses to his decidedly caustic remark, but found she had no answer that she believed would either appease him or allay his temper.

In the end, she chose to offer a facetious retort. "How well you know me after all," Julia said, dipping her lashes and fluttering her fan. "Of course I have come for my own amusement. What other purpose could I have had?" She then dropped him a quick curtsy, turned on her heel, and strolled away.

Julia knew he would not follow her. To some degree, she believed he was in shock at her sudden appearance. So she began to flirt, quite outrageously, with every gentleman who showed her the least amount of interest. She danced until her feet ached; she engaged in absurd banter until her brain was fatigued from being clever; she made use of the languages she had studied for years—French, Italian, and German.

But the whole time she appeared to be amusing herself, Julia knew precisely where Edward was, when he would leave the ballroom after watching her go down a country dance, when he would return, how frequently he himself danced, which was at least every third set, and how often, through her lashes, she caught him watching her, staring at her. Yet he did not approach her the rest of the night.

The later the hour became, the more careful Julia was to keep her sights fixed on him. She wanted to leave when he left. She knew he was not indifferent to her, and all she wanted was to be alone with him for a few minutes to see if she might break through the fortress about his heart.

At two o'clock in the morning, she watched him speak briefly with Wellington. A farewell, surely. She instantly exclaimed to her waltzing partner that her head had begun to ache and that she must seek out Lady Trevaunance at once.

When the gentleman left her with the marchioness, Julia whispered to her hostess that she meant to follow after Edward, that she believed he was leaving. Lady Trevaunance smiled faintly in response and, rather than rebuking her conduct, merely wished her well.

Julia had no need to explain her intent to the worldly-wise marchioness.

Leaving Lady Trevaunance, she found Edward in the entrance hall just as the butler was opening the door for him. When he passed through, she followed immediately after him.

He climbed lightly aboard a hackney and, with the door open, was leaning out and giving the driver, who rode postilion, his direction. In a pointed manner he completely ignored Julia, but just as he was about to sit down, she rushed toward him, gave him a push backward onto the squabs, and leaped within the hackney as the horses moved forward.

"Julia!" he cried as she closed the door behind her. "What the devil—?"

He was half off the seat, half on, when she threw herself upon him and began kissing him. She smelled his skin and caught the fragrance of his soap. Rubbing her cheek against his, she cooed. Julia felt his hand take strong hold of her arm and force her backward as he tried to right himself, but the coach took a turn and he again lost his balance.

Her legs were tangled with his and she giggled, slipping her hand under his coat and feeling the heat of his skin through his linen shirt. She kissed his neck, catching the soft lobe of his ear between her teeth. Pleasure at being so close to him rolled over her in delicious waves, even if he was resistant to her advances.

"No, you mustn't," he whispered angrily, sliding himself more fully onto the seat. "This is absurd. You know nothing can come of our being together. Where are you staying? What hotel? I'll see that you get home."

She was kissing his ear softly, letting her tongue rim the edges. His breathing grew ragged and he no longer struggled to push her off him. "Be sensible," he said weakly.

"I am being sensible," she returned gently. "Given the circumstances, the most sensible thing I could do was to come to Brussels to be with you."

"But only for a time," he stated, taking hold of her chin and forcing her to look at him. His eyes were a question in the dark shadows of the hackney.

Julia shook her head. "I don't know. I can't make any promise but this one." She then placed her lips hard upon his and kissed him again.

She tasted of his lips and thought that for this brief moment, she could be completely happy. The touch of his skin against her lips, the feel of his lips upon hers, the warmth of his body through the thin fabric of her gown, all gave her a sense of completeness she could not explain. She was simply at home in his arms.

He embraced her fully, surrendering to her assault at last, and for the present accepted what she could give him.

"I have missed you so much, Julia, you've no idea," he whispered into her hair as he slipped the puffed sleeves of her gown off her shoulders. "I wanted to answer your letters a dozen times, but I thought it best I try to forget you."

His strong hands were on her neck and the exposed skin of her back, traveling in a possessive line to the swell of her breasts. With each dizzying touch of his hands, she began to feel as though she were disappearing into him. Julia embraced Edward as best she could in the awkward confines of the coach. She stroked the length of his arms and twice the rope of pearls entwined about her wrist became caught in the fabric of his military dress coat. A third catch, as she reached up to touch his face, broke the strand. The pearls popped over his face and chin, falling over the edge of the seat and dancing on the floor of the hackney. The deep, melodious timbre of his laughter echoed through Julia's heart.

"The best music I've heard all evening," she said, as she kissed him again. "You were so somber every time I stole a glance in your direction. You are very angry with me still."

"I wish you hadn't come," he declared, touching her face lightly with the tips of his fingers. He raised himself slightly to kiss her lips, her neck, her breasts, which were still held captive by the gown and the shift underneath.

There was precious little room within the small hackney. He tried to undo the buttons of her gown, but the fabric was stretched taut across her back because the sleeves were pulled off her shoulders. If he tugged any harder, he would begin ripping her gown to pieces.

"I want you," he whispered, holding her fast and again kissing her hard. "God help me, I want you."

When the carriage began to slow and the horses drew to a

stop, he asked, "Will you come to my rooms? Will you be with me tonight?"

Julia nodded in the dim light. She lifted herself off him and rose to a sitting position.

Edward gathered up as many of the pearls as he could find and stuffed them into his pocket. Assisting Julia from the carriage, he led her up the stairs to his rooms, which consisted of a spare sitting room and a bedchamber. The sitting room contained a small sofa, a fireplace with an empty grate, and a scarred writing table upon which sat a candelabra, an inkwell, and a bent silver pen.

Julia glanced at the adjoining bedchamber. "Will your batman attend to you?" she queried, frightened by the idea of having anyone else present while she was with him.

"No," he answered, stepping past her to light the branch of candles. "He has strict instructions to go to bed when I am gone so late. I am perfectly capable of removing my dancing slippers at night."

Edward turned to look at her and smiled, his gaze taking in her hair, her face, her dark green ballgown, her white slippers. "I can't believe you're here," he murmured. When she closed the small distance between them, he slipped an arm about her waist and pulled her to him. With his hand he felt the shape of her features, her brow, her cheekline, her chin. He kissed her. "I adore you. Dear Julia, don't leave me."

"I won't leave you tonight," she said.

He picked up the branch of candles and guided her into his bedchamber. Once inside, he kicked the door closed with his foot and the wall rattled.

Julia noted that the bedchamber was as sparsely furnished as the sitting room. A four-poster bed hung with ancient red brocade draperies, a tall screen behind which Julia presumed the chamber pot was placed, a small wood chair, a chest of drawers, a narrow wardrobe, and a table bearing a washbasin were the sole and quite uninteresting inhabitants of the room. His shaving gear was spread out neatly and precisely on the table beside the basin.

The orderliness of his shaving gear struck Julia.

Spartan furnishings. An officer's bedchamber.

An officer. Julia felt a nerve of anxiety contort within her breast. What was it she feared? She turned to watch Edward and the sight of him soothed away her fears.

He set the candelabra on the chest of drawers. Shadows jumped about the walls with each movement of his hands. He looked at her and again smiled. The world, Brussels, even Edward's bedchamber, began to disappear. Moving to stand behind her, he began unfastening the numerous silk-covered buttons that ran down to the waist of her pretty gown. She had only a thin muslin shift underneath.

Julia felt his hands slip inside the back opening and slide around to touch her breasts. She leaned into him and let her head rest into his shoulder and against his neck as he touched her through the thin muslin. His hands moved lower, onto her stomach, descending over her curves, which caused her to moan with pleasure. She turned her face into his neck and kissed him. He withdrew his hands and began to peel off her gown, until it became a pool of green silk about her feet, kissing her all the while.

After a moment, Edward released her in order to pick up the gown from the floor and drape it over the chair. Even in his lovemaking, he was orderly. When he returned to her, he began pulling at the pins in her hair, settling each one on the dresser in a tidy row beside the candelabra, along with her pearl necklace and earrings. He tugged at her curls until her hair was flowing around her shoulders and down her back. When he took her in his arms and kissed her fully, his tongue rippling over hers, the sensation caused her to feel as though she were disappearing and becoming part of him.

"I love you, Julia," he whispered hoarsely. "To the point of madness. Is this a dream? Are you truly here with me?"

"I feel as though I am dreaming, too," she responded in a faint whisper.

Julia closed her eyes as he dropped to his knees and slid his hands beneath her shift, stroking her legs in a long, slow rhythm. He then untied her garters, sliding her silk stockings down her legs and off her feet, her slippers along with them. She watched with a smile as he set the slippers just under the chest of drawers, covering them with the stockings and the garters.

A soldier's precision. As before, fear worked within her, a fear that she might lose him again.

She felt tears prickle her eyes as she reached down and began lightly stroking his long black hair. He was still on his knees as he embraced her, his arms about her legs. She felt him shudder as he kissed her thighs through the muslin.

She thought of the armies gathering and converging to the south of Brussels, beyond the *forêt de Soignes*. She thought of the long war in which Edward had engaged campaign after campaign. Her heart began to ache with a dread her own difficulties in London had for so long diverted. Julia could no longer avoid a truth she now realized she had refused to face.

Edward Blackthorn was a soldier by profession and by temperament.

He could die in the ensuing conflict.

She didn't want to think about it. Julia blinked back her tears and concentrated instead on the feel of his hands as he slid them up beneath the shift, bunching up the thin fabric and exposing her legs. His lips were upon her skin, her thighs. Desire began moving over her as his hands moved over her, exploring every curve slowly, erotically, until she thought she would faint from the pleasure he aroused within her. Julia could hardly breathe as he tasted of her. She pulled at the locks of his hair and untied the black ribbon that held it back. Sliding her fingers deeply into his hair, she echoed his movements in splayed strokes.

She barely noticed the coldness of the chamber until she shivered. He rose from his kneeling position. "I'm sorry," he said, taking her by the hand and kissing her fingers. "You're cold."

"I suppose I am a little, but to own the truth, I barely noticed." She quickly caught his face in her hand and kissed him thoroughly, deeply. He embraced her, throwing his arms about her and catching her off the floor.

"Thank God you've come," he breathed, then kissed her again. His hands supported her buttocks and he pressed himself against her until she moaned. Again he pressed into her. She held him tightly, everything disappearing except Edward, the smell of his skin, the feel of his body against hers, the rhythmic movements that sent wave after wave of desire pouring over her.

After a moment, he released her and pulled back the red brocade covers. He bid her climb between the sheets before she contracted an inflammation of the lungs. With a laugh, Julia gratefully obliged him. He then quickly divested himself of his uniform and joined her.

His body was warm on hers, the hair of his chest, arms, and legs a comforting sensation as he kissed her and touched her. Julia stroked his arms and his back, then began to place whispery kisses on his lips. He parted his lips and she gently took his upper lip between her teeth. His breath—or was it hers?—rolled over her cheek. She teased him until he couldn't bear it. He drove his tongue into her mouth and possessed her. She clung to him. Edward parted her legs, completing his vanquishing of her body, of her soul, of her heart.

Her mind slipped away as she became one with him. Julia moved with him in an ancient rhythm, her breathing becoming his, his becoming hers. She held him locked in an embrace that forced the air from her lungs. His mouth was hard on hers as he moved quickly, strongly, into her. Pleasure began rising, dipping, rising again. She heard a voice moaning. Was it his or hers? Time ceased. All sensations—the dull sounds of traffic outside, the candlelight, the feel of the sheet beneath her—disappeared. There was only movement and pleasure, his body joined to hers, the knowledge that she had taken this man to be her husband in the truest sense.

Pleasure exploded through her body and into her mind. She

shed tears, she groaned, her thoughts a prayer that he would never be taken from her again. Julia belonged to him. She had given herself to him, she had received him into her. She belonged to him, now and forever.

Several hours later, Julia awoke, feeling satiated. A bright morning light shone through a thin break in the worn crimson curtains over the window. She felt Edward beside her, naked and warm. Holding the sheet to her neck, she recalled the night and the early morning hours.

He had loved her more than once. The second time had been wild and rough. Julia had felt part of some great primal world in which all proprieties had been stripped away, and there was only her body and his. She had become fascinated by every sensation, by the pounding of his hips against hers and the wealth of pleasure each rhythmic movement created. Wrapping her legs wantonly about his hips, she felt like a wild beast rutting with complete abandon. His teeth had raked her neck, shoulders, and breasts. The bed shook, shuddered, and struck the wall. He had driven her to the edge of a cliff and pushed her off. Julia had fallen into a place of pleasure so great, she wanted never to return.

But the third time was what had left her this morning feeling fearful of the future. He had kissed her softly, then whispered in her ear: *The battle will begin soon, very soon. I didn't want you to come. But words can't express how grateful I am that you are here with me now.*

He had looked at her then and she knew he was saying good-bye. Julia remembered having thought of every officer's wife, every foot soldier's bride who had ever bid her husband farewell on the doorstep of war. For so long she had been consumed with her own concerns, with Elizabeth, Caroline, and Annabelle, that she had never considered what being Edward's wife would mean.

Now she could no longer ignore the bare truth.

Edward was a soldier.

Julia permitted the thought full rein in her heart. A blinding fear shook her to the roots of her comfort, disturbing the visions of what she believed her life with Edward would be.

When he awoke and kissed her cheek, she pretended to be asleep. He slipped quietly from bed. He had told her he would be joining his regiment to the south of Brussels that morning, so she was not surprised that he began to prepare to depart. She could hear him in the sitting room speaking with his batman. A few minutes later, he moved his personal articles from the bed-chamber to afford her a degree of privacy, for which she was grateful. Clearly, his thoughts were all for her comfort and for what little dignity a woman could possess who was found in a bed not her husband's.

After an hour of lying on her side and fearfully pondering the future, Julia wondered how she could be so fainthearted that the thought of Edward going to war could undermine all the tendernesses he had whispered in her ear the night before. She wished she were anywhere but here in his rooms. She wished she couldn't hear his voice as he spoke in hushed tones to his valet. She wished she were back in England. A terrible dread had seized her, which she could not shake off, of death hovering over the four-poster bed, of Edward being torn from her.

She had known death before. That was the rub. Julia was too well conversed with how completely death could overturn one's life. She thought of her mother and the carriage accident at the mouth of the quarry, of her brothers never returning from the sea. She squeezed her eyes shut. Burning tears forced their way through her closed lids. She rolled on her back and flung her arms across her face. A sob escaped her. She didn't want Edward to die; she couldn't bear it if he did.

Julia heard the door open, then close. She heard his footsteps, and all she could do was hold her arms more tightly over her face. She felt his hands on her arms. "What is it, Julia?"

She hated the sound of his voice. She hated his compassion. She couldn't speak, even though she wanted to shout at him to go away, to leave her, to never return. She rolled on her side away from him, her throat choked with tears.

"My darling, you are crying," he said. She felt his weight on the side of the bed.

"Go away," she finally uttered on a sob.

But he didn't leave. Instead, he slipped his arm underneath her shoulders, and before she could protest, he had gathered her to his chest. It was not his uniform beneath her face that she felt, but rather the cool, thin cambric of his shirt. Julia slipped her arms about his waist, and though her neck was caught at an awkward angle, she held him fast. "Don't go," she pleaded.

She heard him chuckle softly as he stroked her hair and her bare shoulders. "Vandeleur will have my head. As it is, I am already two hours late. I must go. I've only come in to say good-bye and to tell you that I have sent word to Lady Trevaunance asking her to send you your abigail, your hairbrush, and a morning gown."

Julia looked up at him, scarcely able to make out his features through the veil of her tears. "No, I mean don't go to war, Edward. Stay with me. We can go somewhere else. To . . . to America, perhaps. Only please don't go. I . . . I don't want you to die."

He stroked her face with his hand and leaned down to place a kiss on her lips. He tasted of coffee and smelled of shaving soap. "I have sworn to die for England if I must, in order to rid Europe of Bonaparte forever. Would you have me recant my vow?"

"If you don't like America," she said irrationally, "what of the West Indies? We could purchase a plantation; we could raise our children there, hire tutors and governesses for them . . . oh, Edward!"

He placed his fingers on her lips and again pressed her close to his heart. "I will do everything in my power to come back to you, Julia. But right now I need you to be strong. Just as you have been valiant in protecting your sisters from disaster, now I need you to be strong for me. Do you think I do not fear the army approaching us from the south? Do you think there is one among us who is not riddled with panic? Knowing my duty is all that keeps me from bolting when I am astride my horse and facing the enemy. But you've a duty as well right now, to dry your tears and to kiss me goodbye. I need you to do as much, Julia. Now."

Julia heard the firmness and command in his voice. She hated him for demanding what was so hard for her to give. Somehow she reached deep within herself and ordered her body to grow calm. The pain in her throat subsided, her breathing grew even, her tears waned. She sat back and looked at him.

He smiled, half in amusement, half in such adoration that her fears melted away. How could anything so perfect as the love between them be touched by earthly concerns? He touched her breasts, leaned over, and kissed her cheeks. She caught him about the neck and kissed him passionately in return.

"When your duty is completed, I will be waiting for you at Lady Trevaunance's townhouse," announced Julia.

"I shall come to you there," he said. Edward looked at her one last time, his eyes full of love. Then he released her, slipped from the bed, and was gone.

Julia stared at the door for a long time, the lower half of her body tangled in the sheets, the upper half bare to the cold air of the chamber. What an ugly door, she thought with a laugh. It had been painted a dark blue at one time and was now chipped, scratched, and appeared as though someone had kicked at it in a fit of rage.

The tears began to fall at the sight of the door and would not stop. She cried until the sheet on her lap was soaked through and through.

An hour later, Hetty arrived and tended to her. Once bathed and dressed in a cream-colored silk morning gown, she glanced about the empty chamber, which Hetty had tidied. Julia looked at the threadbare red brocade bedcover and felt a chill go through her.

Would she ever see Edward again?

She couldn't bear the sight of the bed any longer and quickly left Edward's rooms. A few moments later she was crossing the threshold of the front door, where a hackney was waiting. Only as she settled herself on the seat did Julia realize she had completely forgotten to tell Edward of Sir Perran's presence in Brussels and of her belief that he meant to harm him. But in the face of the forthcoming battle, somehow the threat Sir Perran represented did not signify.

Sir Perran watched his wife descend the narrow steps of the boardinghouse and enter a hackney. He had only one prayer: that the war would not strip him of his right to take his nephew's life.

Twenty-six

Julia bid farewell to Lord and Lady Trevaunance as they left their townhouse to attend the Duke of Richmond's ball. She had no heart for gaieties, not when Edward was already returned to his regiment. Many of the British and allied officers were in attendance at the ball, but an equal number were not. Edward was among the latter.

She spent the evening in the doldrums, her spirits caught between a terrible anxiety that Edward would soon see battle and all the attending sublime sentiments that attached to her frequent recollections of being loved by him. Every once in awhile, she caught the scent of him from a wisp of her hair or on her wrist—shaving soap, mostly. She missed him already, and he had been gone less than ten hours.

She entertained herself with a book of Wordsworth's poetry. But the letters formed long chains that made no sense to her, try as she might to concentrate on the words in front of her. If the lines spoke of the magnificence of trees, she would immediately think of the *forêt de Soignes* to the south, a fine, thick beechwood, which separated her from the man she loved. A mention of corn kept her mind fixed on the cornfields north of the River Sambre, and an instant vision of soldiers fighting among young stalks would sweep through her brain. An allusion to any four-legged beast in nature brought forward line upon line of cavalry, mounted officers, and soldiers, blades glinting in the sunlight. She finally set the volume aside. Never would she have believed Wordsworth could have teased her of war.

Julia tugged on the bellpull and when the butler arrived, she requested a glass of port. With the wine in hand, she let the rich flavor dwell in her mouth, and very soon her nerves did not jangle as loudly. When the glass was empty, she closed her eyes. Later, she awoke, startled, unaware she had fallen asleep in her chair.

What had awakened her? she wondered. She heard noises outside in the street below. Checking the clock on the mantel, Julia saw that it was three o'clock in the morning. How strange to have slept so long and so soundly, though she admitted to herself she was worn out from worrying.

The noises in the street grew louder. Something was amiss. Julia blinked back the sleep that still clogged her mind and listened intently. She thought she could hear shouting from outside. Certainly, she heard the rumble of carts and the sounds of horses dashing by. Voices belowstairs rose to the drawing room on the first floor. She recognized Lady Trevaunance's voice and a moment later she heard steps on the stairs.

Julia rose to her feet. She clutched the carved arm of the chair and waited, listening to the approach of her host and hostess along the hallway outside the door. She watched the doorknob turn, the door open, and the marchioness, splendid in a gown of the deepest sapphire, walk into the room, her complexion ashen.

"It has all happened so quickly," she said, disoriented and breathless. "Wellington is gone. Trevaunance spoke with him briefly before he quit the ball. We followed suit shortly after. Julia, the French have crossed the Sambre!"

Julia wavered on her feet. "Whatever do you mean? How is it possible they could be so near to Brussels? Did anyone know they had advanced this far north?"

Trevaunance entered the chamber at that moment and closed the door behind him. "No. Bonaparte is up to his tricks again. Very clever, if you ask me, not permitting the armies to assemble. Mark my word, he means to see the Prussians crushed before they can join up with Wellington. God curse Napoleon. Our forces are spread so thin—there will be the devil to pay."

Julia felt violently ill and sank back down into her chair. No one had expected this to happen. The allies had planned upon enacting a grand invasion of France around the first of July, once the combined European forces had all been assembled. At the same time, there had been a general hope that the French people would rise up and cast Bonaparte out before war truly became necessary. Now the French army had crossed the Sambre and war had become inevitable.

Julia clasped her hands tightly on her lap and stared down at the smooth apricot silk of her gown. Watching dispassionately as her knuckles grew white, she tried to unclench her hands but they wouldn't obey her. She heard the marquis speaking but his words made no sense to her ears; she tried to keep from staring but her eyes refused to blink. Julia forced herself to breathe. War. Why couldn't she think clearly? Why did she feel as though her whole body had just been bound by a dozen strong ropes? Her shoulders ached with fear.

Would Edward come home?

Lady Trevaunance crossed the chamber to kneel beside Julia, her long fingers covering the younger woman's whitened hands as she stared up at her. "Julia?" the marchioness said.

Julia heard Lady Trevaunance as though separated from her by a thick wall. She shifted her gaze to look into the marchioness's warm brown eyes. How much she looked like her son, Lord Peter. How long ago her brief betrothal to him now seemed, as though it had occurred centuries in the past instead of just last year. If only she had married Lord Peter, she would not now be filled with a panic so great her thoughts refused to be ordered.

But she hadn't loved Lord Peter.

She loved Edward. Slowly, she blinked and read the compassion in the marchioness's eyes. "He might be killed," she murmured.

"Yes," Lady Trevaunance responded quietly. "Or he might return to you. The future is in God's hands."

"God's hands aren't big enough," Julia responded absently.

"I won't argue the point, except to say that he's given us to each other to show the breadth of his care. Courage, my dear. The man you love is an excellent soldier."

"I know."

Lord Trevaunance called from the window. "The armies are assembling. I can see some of the Brunswickers in their black uniforms from here. Good God, I never expected—"

Julia turned to look at him, having heard the catch in his throat. He appeared to be completely overcome as he shaded his eyes with his hand.

The reality of the forthcoming battle was beginning to settle in with a vengeance.

The sixteenth of June was hot and airless, but Julia moved through the townhouse with hands and feet that remained painfully cold the whole day. Fear had wrestled with her and won. Muffled cannonading could be heard in the distance coming from the direction of Quatre Bras some twenty miles to the south of Brussels down the Charleroi road. What was happening? No one knew for certain.

On the seventeenth of June, torrential rains replaced the heat of the day before. The Marquis of Trevaunance danced a jig, saying, "See if Boney can move his cannon now!"

Julia cried all night. The wounded from the battles of Quatre Bras and Ligny had begun arriving in Brussels. She had only heard of the suffering following an assault by the enemy. For the first time, she was seeing what she had only read about in *The Times* or heard about from those who had themselves been in battle. Considering how much had not been revealed to her, she could only conclude that Edward had failed completely in translating the true horror of war to her—the smell of gunpowder, the sight of missing limbs, the moans of those in excruciating pain.

In addition, rumors abounded that Napoleon had guaranteed

his soldiers the sack of the city, which meant only one thing for any woman. Currents of fear drove through Brussels. Many tried to escape north by road and waterway to Antwerp. But every vehicle had been requisitioned, and by the following day, Sunday, June 18, Julia knew her fate was sealed in Brussels. In the early afternoon, cannonading to the south could be heard from the vicinity of the villages of Waterloo and Mont St. Jean, a mere twelve miles from Brussels. By three o'clock, soldiers began galloping into the city proclaiming that all was lost, that the French would soon be in the city. Over and over they arrived with news that Bonaparte had defeated Wellington's forces.

Julia sat with Lady Trevaunance, huddled together on a settee while the marquis guarded the door with a primed pistol in hand. Waiting became unbearable. Julia wanted to scream, but was afraid if she dared open her mouth and emit even the smallest sound, she would never stop screaming. So she held her kerchief to her lips and rocked silently beside the somber-faced marchioness.

At dusk, the cannonading simply stopped.

By nine o'clock, contrary to all previous reports, word came flooding into Brussels that the Prussians had arrived just before dusk, and combined with the failure of the Imperial Guard to break through the British and allied line, Napoleon had been vanquished.

The ladies wept together. Lord Trevaunance sank into a chair near the settee and buried his face in his hands.

On the following day, Julia was seated in the drawing room with both Lord and Lady Trevaunance, attempting to occupy herself with her embroidery but failing to achieve one proper stitch in two. She had just rethreaded her needle when the butler opened the door and somberly announced "Major Edward Blackthorn." Julia gasped, as did Lady Trevaunance, then set aside her peacock. She rose from the settee of rose and white striped silk and watched Edward enter the room on his firm tread, as though he had never been away.

He had obviously gone first to his rooms to bathe and to shave. She had seen many returning soldiers, but their faces had been blackened from gunpowder, their clothing muddy and stained with blood. Edward was clean and fresh in appearance, though his eyes clearly betrayed his true state. They were slightly sunken from fatigue and were a brilliant red from the battle of the day before.

"Edward," she whispered, wondering if she were dreaming or seeing some sort of ghostly apparition.

"Julia, my darling," he returned, smiling faintly as he moved toward her.

"Where did you come from?" she queried. "How—? Are you really here?" She could not credit that here he was, alive, in the marchioness's drawing room.

As he approached her and she could see that he was neither a dream nor a ghost, Julia fell into his arms, holding him tightly for a long, long moment. When he deemed it necessary to release her, he turned and embraced Lady Trevaunance, who did not attempt to hide her tears as she fell on his neck. Afterward, he received a fatherly embrace from Lord Trevaunance.

The marchioness expressed her impatience to hear about the battle, which was being generally referred to as Waterloo since Wellington's headquarters had been in the village of the same name. She hurried him to sit in a black lacquer and gilt Empire chair, which she drew forward quite close to the settee. Once he sat down, at her insistence, she seated herself opposite him and bid Lord Trevaunance to join her, which he readily did. She begged Julia to take up a chair next to Edward, but the younger woman declined her kind offer and instead moved to stand by the window, from which vantage point she was able to observe Edward's profile.

If he seemed a little surprised by her conduct, he was quickly diverted by Lady Trevaunance's request to pray tell her all.

Julia wasn't certain why she chose to stand apart from them

all. She had been waiting for hours to hear word of him, and when she had learned that his regiment had been ordered immediately to Paris following the battle, she had not expected either to hear from him or to learn of his actual fate for days. For all she knew, he could easily have been one of the incredible number of casualties streaming into Brussels.

Now he was here, having arrived so unexpectedly that Julia didn't know what to think or to feel. She was overwhelmed with a variety of emotions.

The greatest, however, began to surface: that she was overjoyed he had survived the battle, having not perished as so many had, especially since the initial reports indicated the British had suffered losses nearing ten, possibly fifteen, thousand. But here he was, unharmed save a bump on his head, or so he was telling the marquis.

"I don't remember a thing after charging the French once the Imperial Guard had broken and the army began to scatter. A musket ball caught the side of my head and knocked me from my horse. Though the wound wasn't serious by half, in falling, my head struck something hard, a rock perhaps, I don't really know. I was carried from the field eventually and here I am."

"You were very fortunate," Lady Trevaunance breathed, a hand to her chest.

"And well I know it," Edward responded seriously.

"We wish to know everything, m'boy," the marquis declared, his expression grave. He sat forward on the settee, a forearm draped across his knee, the other hand placed on his upper thigh.

Edward shifted his gaze away from the marquis, staring at nothing in particular as his attention turning inward. When he spoke, his voice was solemn and deliberate. "We were only twice engaged in a major assault—once in support of Ponsonby's heavy cavalry brigade, which had overrun its mark in shattering the initial French infantry charge. The brigade—the Royals, Greys, and Inniskillings—had actually reached the French line in the heat of their pursuit, which proved to be a dreadful mistake, for they were quite understandably pursued immediately by enemy Lancers. They were all but cut to pieces. We were ordered to support the brigade, which we were anxious to do. You can't imagine the confusion. But being a light cavalry regiment, we were able to move swiftly and we soon drove the French back, along with the 12th, to their line of infantry, and saw as many of Ponsonby's men returned to safety as possible." He paused and sighed deeply. Julia could see tears brimming in his blood-red eyes. For the next few minutes, he explained the position of his regiment on the battlefield, serving in support of Picton's infantry division.

He then spoke of the second assault, in which the 16th Light Dragoons had taken part. "Later, it was dusk. The Imperial Guard had made its final assault and was simply overpowered. Wellington lifted his hat in the air and galloped past one worn, tattered regiment after the next, encouraging his army to pursue the enemy. The French cannons ceased soon afterward, as enemy post after post was deserted.

"As the smoke drifted away from the ridge, we saw what Wellington had seen through his telescope: the whole French army in utter chaos and disappearing into the cornfields beyond, leaving behind piles of arms. You see, the Prussians had finally arrived and were flooding onto the corn plain. We had been expecting them all day, but their march from Wavre had been hindered miserably by the mud from the rains of the day before. The heavy guns were nearly impossible to move through the muddy lanes as the army worked its way toward Mont St. Jean. At any rate, we charged the remaining French cavalry, as well as those of the Imperial Guard who had quite loyally remained behind to continue fighting in order that Bonaparte might effect his escape. We charged and countercharged, until finally even the Old Guard gave way before us.

"You cannot imagine the exhilaration of chasing the French from the field." He shook his head, almost in disbelief. Julia saw the tears begin to course down his cheeks. "It's over at last. Napoleon Bonaparte cannot rise again, not after this defeat."

By now, tears were rolling down the marquis's cheeks as well, and he brushed them away as he clapped Blackthorn's shoulder with a firm hand. "Well done, my lad," he said hoarsely. Lady Trevaunance leaned forward, her tears considerably more bountiful as she embraced Edward again, her unrestrained sobs causing Julia's own chest to constrict painfully. But for some reason she could not give way to her tears. It all seemed so unreal.

After a time, when Lady Trevaunance had released Edward and was blowing her nose quite thoroughly, begging pardon and laughing, the marquis gave the subject a lighter turn. "You must forgive my curiosity, Blackthorn, but tell me, where was Wellington positioned? Did you ever see him during the course of the conflict, for you were on the far left of the line behind Picton's infantry? Do I have the right of it?"

"Yes, next to Vivien's brigade. As for Wellington, he was everywhere at once, or so it seemed. The line was fully two miles long, but every officer with whom I have spoken says the same thing: When the fighting was hardest, Wellington was there, encouraging the men to stand fast."

The marquis nodded and smiled, his eyes gleaming with pride. "I hear he refuses to wear a uniform coat, and instead has adopted a gray single-caped greatcoat and a rather obscure low cocked hat for battle dress, as it were. Quite odd, don't you think?"

"I suppose," Edward responded, smiling. "But given the propensity to military fineness among the officers, it is fairly impossible to mistake Wellington for anyone else. There's not a bit of pretension in him. Even his words are plain. When Boney's cannons were at their worst, I heard him say: *Hard pounding this, gentlemen, but we will see who can pound the longest.*"

Lord Trevaunance gave a crack of laughter. "Plain indeed, and such a great man! Really, it is quite amazing. Though I admit he is precisely the same in a ballroom, a man of few words, when he speaks, he says what needs to be said and little more." He sighed and regarded Edward with an expression of profound relief. "So what do you do next? I understand your regiment is in pursuit of the French to Paris."

"Yes, and I should have been with them," Blackthorn said, touching his head gingerly. "But Vandeleur wouldn't have it. Told me to return to Brussels, that whether I wished for it or not, his brigade could manage to get to Paris without me. In a few days, I shall join them, of course."

Precisely when Julia stopped listening to Edward she didn't know, nor even that she had turned away from Lord and Lady Trevaunance and the man she loved. Her thoughts were filled with death, especially the deaths she had known so recently in her life—her mother's, father's, brothers'. How absurd! Why had she not realized before how frightened she was of death and of loss? All this time, she had been so certain that her only possible reason for not immediately agreeing with and holding fast to Edward's desires for their joint future was her responsibility toward her sisters. But now Julia saw a side of herself she had never before acknowledged.

Edward Blackthorn was a soldier and would be one the remainder of his life. He had said as much to her, but somewhere in her thoughts had been the belief that he would sell out and retire to Bath to be with her. But already he was speaking of his need to join his regiment in Paris.

"Julia?"

She heard Edward whisper her name very near her ear. She didn't even know she was staring out the window and down into the busy street below, until she felt a hand on her arm. Julia blinked several times, clearing her vision and her mind. Celebrations of the momentous victory had already drawn throngs of people into the streets.

She turned to look at Edward and saw that his gaze was direct and concerned.

"Are you all right?" he asked, still whispering.

She looked behind her and saw that they were now alone in the drawing room. "I don't know," she responded. "I just never thought . . . never realized until the past several days, that you were truly a soldier, prepared to give your life for your country. I suppose I understood a little of it when you left me before the battle had begun, but for some reason only now am I beginning to comprehend the whole of it."

"I have come home to you, Julia," he said, searching her eyes. "Right now, that is all that matters."

Julia needed him to understand what she was feeling, but she didn't know how to continue.

He lifted her hand to his lips and kissed her fingers fervently. "My darling, return to my rooms with me."

She lowered her gaze, feeling strange and queasy. He kissed her fingers again, then the palm of her hand. His touch worked against her fears, but still she felt ill. Though he had bathed, he still smelled of gunpowder and horses. She couldn't breathe. She felt his lips on her cheek. She let him kiss her, but she couldn't feel anything except the turning of her stomach. Julia began to tremble.

"What is it?" he asked, his voice sounding terribly distressed.

"I . . . I am not feeling well," she answered. "I suppose it was the suspense of waiting. Now that you're here, I can't believe it's real, not when so many were lost." She looked up at him, her eyes blinded by tears. "You're alive. I can't believe you are alive."

He released her hand, slipped his arms about her waist, and drew her close to him in a tight embrace. She didn't want to tremble, but she couldn't seem to stop. Tears now rolled down her cheeks. "I was so frightened," she murmured into his coat.

He began kissing her hair, her ear, her forehead. His lips were gentle and soothing. She clung to him as her fears poured through her in strong, pulsing waves. His lips were upon hers, warm and gentle, until the trembling began to subside. Her fears metamorphosed into a sudden and profound gratitude that he had been returned to her when so many had been lost.

Relief spread through her veins, warming her, drawing her thoughts away from death, placing her mind upon the feel of his lips. She began kissing him in return, deeply, roughly. He pressed his legs against hers, his arms holding her closer still, his tongue possessing her mouth. For the present, she saw only him, felt only his arms and his lips, heard nothing but his professions of love as they drifted through her hair, into her ear, and across her cheek.

"Julia, my love," he breathed again and again.

Julia lost herself in his affection, slipping an arm about his neck, stroking his hair, giving him kiss for kiss.

"Come with me," he whispered.

She wanted to desperately. She wanted nothing more than to oblige him. "I can't," she whispered. "I am promised to Lady Trevaunance . . . several engagements . . ." He kissed her, silencing her.

"She will release you. I know she will."

Julia laughed and kissed his cheek. "Of course she will. Besides, the whole of Brussels is in chaos. I don't know what I was thinking."

A few moments later, her cheeks pink with embarrassment as she explained her intention to Lady Trevaunance, Julia was in a hackney alongside Edward.

The streets were crowded, and the sight of any uniform brought a round of huzzas pouring through the masses. Carriages were decorated with bay and laurel. From the windows, flags of the combined forces were displayed everywhere. Going was slow, but since Edward held her tightly against him with an arm slipped about her waist, she felt secure and comforted and didn't mind the frequent interruptions to the progress of the carriage.

When at last they arrived at his rooms, Julia found some of her courage restored and nothing of her love for him lost. Once inside the sitting room, the key turned protectively in the lock, Edward caught her by the hand, swept her into a warm embrace, and again set to kissing her passionately. He paused only to remove her bonnet trimmed in dark blue silk, tossing it with great disinterest on the floor.

All the hours and days spent waiting, either without news or with the erroneous news that Wellington and Blucher had been defeated and the French would soon be swelling the streets of

Brussels, overtook Julia again. Perhaps because he still smelled so nearly of war, her mind began to turn over and over as he kissed her. Her eyes burned with the gunpowder smoke that descended over soldiers locked in battle. The sound of the guns roared in her ears. She could hear the officers shouting orders, the moans of the wounded, the screams of the horses as they were shot, the thud of the earth being pummeled by two enormous armies.

She didn't know precisely where she was. Perhaps on the sofa in the front room. All she knew was that he was on her, in her, his hands moving roughly over her as she wrapped her arms and legs about him and clung to him with her gloved fingers. Again the cannons roared, the cavalry thundered through her head. She held him tightly, the rapid, fitful rise and fall of his body over hers echoing the strange visions in her mind.

The images began to shift, to slide away, to disappear, as pleasure rose within her. She touched his arms, still sheathed within his coat. He was real. He was alive. A sudden and overwhelming spike of pleasure forced her mouth open and she let out a great cry. She could hardly breathe, the pleasure was so sharp, the relief so great. Again, as before, tears poured from her eyes, unbidden. His groans drifted into her ear as his movements became less forceful and intense. Still, she clung to him.

Again, as before, he asked if he had hurt her. Julia laughed, though she didn't feel like laughing. "No, of course you didn't," she replied, her eyes closed as he nuzzled her neck and kissed her below the ear.

Only after a long moment, when her breathing became even and regular, did she realize they were tangled up on the sofa. Julia began to feel a pinch here and another there. "Where are your legs?" she asked, since the sofa was rather short and his legs were long.

He chuckled into her neck. "My left knee is bent and my ankle is resting on the armrest of the sofa. My other foot is on the floor."

Julia craned her head to see. How strange that now he felt

heavy on her and she was beginning to feel pinched and uncomfortable, when only a few minutes ago, she didn't even know
where she was.

She looked about the dark little room. The momentary relief
she had felt in his arms began to dissipate quickly as her gaze
shifted from the cold grate, the writing desk—if the rectangular,
straight-legged, scarred collection of wood could be termed
such—the pewter candelabra. Light shone from the window in
a patch on the floor. A length of red brocade only a few inches
wide lived in pretense as a drapery and hung to the side of the
window.

Julia sighed, her arms wrapped tightly about Edward's shoulders. Her heart became a stone in her chest. She seemed devoid
of sentiment as she began to wonder if she truly loved him after
all. "I must leave," she whispered.

"No, you must stay," he responded, again nuzzling her neck.
"I'm certain Lady Trevaunance will understand if you do not
return tonight."

He lifted off her slightly and looked into her eyes. Julia was
surprised at the change her heart underwent the moment he but
looked at her. Butterflies suddenly raced about in her stomach.
He kissed her, and she returned his kiss.

Of course she loved him. She would always love him.

Then what was wrong?

After a moment, he rose from her and went into the bedchamber. Julia remained on the sofa, turning on her side and slipping
a hand beneath her cheek. She felt tears welling up into her
throat and climbing to her eyes. She couldn't keep them from
slipping across the bridge of her nose and down the side of her
face, to slide into her hair.

She couldn't stay. She couldn't, and she knew Edward would
never understand. When he returned a few minutes later, Julia
went into the bedchamber to tend to herself. When she was done
and her hair was restored to a reasonably tidy state, she remained
standing in the middle of the floor facing the bed, looking at the
threadbare red brocade bedcover. Her heart felt threadbare.

Could she purchase new threads and repair her heart? Why was she so sad?

She turned to walk back into the other room and saw that Edward was standing by the window holding his saber dangling from his hand. He was looking down into the street.

Julia glanced at the sword and for the barest second, as though a nightmare had just crept into her thoughts, she saw it sliding into the flesh of the enemy, blood pouring from the wound.

She took a step backward and swallowed a silent gasp.

I must go, she thought. Panic overtook her body. She couldn't breathe. She quickly circled the sofa and passed in front of the fireplace, her thoughts jumbled about.

"I'm leaving now," she announced, her voice a pitch higher than normal.

He turned to look at her, his brows lifted in surprise. "You can't go," he stated, taking a step toward her. She picked up her bonnet from the floor and dusted it with her gloved fingers.

"I told you I had to. I have numerous obligations. I must go."

He took another step toward her, a frown now creasing his brow. "Julia," he pleaded, laying his saber on the scarred wooden writing desk. "I don't understand. What the devil is the matter with you?"

"You needn't curse at me," she said, her gaze fixed to the saber as she slipped the blue bonnet over her auburn curls. "I will always have obligations to others, Edward, no matter . . . well, that is, I must go. I can't stay."

She wheeled around and began twisting the key in the lock, but no matter which way she turned it or how many times it flipped over in her hand, Julia couldn't unlock the door. She heard him cross the room behind her; she felt his hands on her arms. She stiffened, released the key, and pressed a hand to her face. She bit back the tears.

"Julia, my darling, whatever is the matter? . . . I know what it is! You've never been so close to the war before, have you? It is a terrible business, but I am here. . . . I am uninjured, God be praised."

Julia knew she couldn't make him understand. "It . . . it isn't the war," she replied, knowing this was partially true but not entirely. "It is just that I believe I have discovered I am not fit to be a soldier's wife. I used to think only my duty to my sisters prevented me from coming to you sooner in Brussels, but I now realize I was wrong. I . . . I cannot follow the drum."

She again tried to turn the key in the lock, but it kept spinning around and around without once fitting into its proper place. She felt his hand on her hand, staying her fitful movements. Julia withdrew her hand and he gently slid the key farther in, turned it once, and opened the door.

She was surprised that he did not stop her or try to argue with her. She ran from his rooms, to the landing and down the stairs, tying the ribbons of her bonnet at the same time. When she was outside, she breathed in deeply and strongly of the damp, humid air. The streets were as crowded as ever. Julia knew she couldn't get a hackney but didn't care. She turned to the right and began making her way on foot back to Lady Trevaunance's home. In the midst of the jubilation, she knew she would pass unnoticed.

Sir Perran, Lord Yarnacott, and Mr. Loxhore watched silently as Julia, having turned the corner, disappeared from sight. "Well, gentlemen," Sir Perran said quietly, his eyes heavy-lidded. "Will you accompany me to my nephew's chambers?"

"Yes," Lord Yarnacott answered firmly.

"You have settled my doubts," Mr. Loxhore stated. "Despicable conduct for an officer and a gentleman. Your own nephew! By God, it's the outside of enough. I will happily serve as your second."

Blackthorn sat down on the sofa where he had so recently made love to Julia. He could still feel her warm, yielding body beneath his, the touch of her gloved fingers roughly on his coat, his face, his neck, his back. He had let her go because there was no point in forcing her to stay. He had seen the look in her eyes upon his return, a deadness caused by severe strain. But he had hoped that the sensations would pass, particularly if they were together for a time before he had to leave again. Apparently, he had been wrong.

He let his head drop in his hands. Edward felt as though these thoughts were ripping his heart, his life, his mind apart. He wanted to tear about his rooms, to stomp, to dash every loose article from its wood surface onto the floor. Instead, he remained where he was, breathing hard, trying to work out of his blood the agony that was clawing at him.

But how could he let her go? How could he forget her? When he had been joined to her, somehow his life made sense to him. His purpose for rising in the morning, for dropping to sleep at night, and for all the absurd or critical activities that filled his day thrummed in strong rhythm to his life when Julia was its main thread. He could not explain it, any more than he could explain why so many poems, plays, and common ballads had only one theme: man's love and need for woman.

Entering her, taking her, possessing her, was like bringing her into himself. He was alive and whole when he was with her. Apart from her he performed his functions, his duties, though with precision and meticulous care, also without joy, without the wonder of life flowing through him.

That was what Julia was to him, the wonder of life. Having known her, having experienced such sublimity, such joy, how could he then live without her?

He had been with other women before. But the cold act of love was about as wondrous as the writing desk opposite the sofa. Utilitarian, yes, but hardly a joy. These were mysteries his soldier's existence hadn't before permitted him to grasp. He didn't know what to do. Should he go after her now? Should he browbeat her into staying with him, into being an officer's wife, into setting aside her fears so that he could be joyful?

Edward leaned back into the sofa. Riding back to Brussels

after the battle, he had had only one thought: to nestle himself safely into her arms. This was the worst action he had seen. He had refused to think of it while astride his horse. He had only wanted to take Julia in his arms. He still couldn't believe he was alive after so many officers and soldiers had perished.

He had found the refuge he had sought in her arms, but now she was gone.

Just as he closed his eyes, trying to press all the memories away, a sharp rapping sounded on the door.

It so startled him, sounding like the crack of rifle fire, that Edward was immediately on his feet and crouched over before he realized someone had simply knocked rather briskly on his door.

He gave himself a shake, then strode quickly to the door and opened it. He was stunned to see his uncle regarding him coldly. When had Sir Perran arrived in Brussels? Edward stepped back, holding the door wide, a gesture of politeness bred into him by his society.

The two men who accompanied his uncle he knew well from Bath. Their expressions were grim as they strode in. Edward realized they had witnessed, probably to a purpose, Julia's departure from his rooms, and comprehension of the unexpected visit flooded him. How strange to have just come from the worst battle of his career, only to face another with his uncle.

He closed the door and straightened his shoulders. Sir Perran, his back to the window, his features cast in shadow, glared at his nephew from half-closed lids. "I see the battle left you unscathed," he declared, his tone imperious and cold.

Blackthorn watched him guardedly. From across the room, he felt his uncle's enmity. His own suppressed hatred for the man who had stolen Julia from him prickled over his flesh. He touched the absent sword at his side. "You have not come here to congratulate me on my survival. I would suppose, then, that you had some other business of significance to conduct." He paused for a moment and smiled sardonically. "Let me guess.

You wish to make me, as your closest relative, heir to your fortune."

Sir Perran started, his cane thumping once. "You dare!" he snorted. "You will never see a tuppence of my lands or my wealth."

Blackthorn despised him. "I never wanted a farthing of your acquisitions. You know that."

"You were always so proud," he remarked. "Stephen and George were wont to ask for the moon when I took them to Bath, but you . . . you folded your arms over your chest and stared out the window when I would beg you to tell me what would please you."

"You were cruel to my mother. I have never forgiven you for that. Stephen and George were too young to know of your unkindnesses toward her, but I saw you strike her once, and from that moment on, you were nothing to me except a man she bade me promise to do my duty by. I never understood her attachment to you, but even after you hit her, she was insistent that I not hold a grudge. She used to tell me that you had given her something very precious and that for that reason alone, I was supposed to hold you in respect and devotion. Her heart was far more forgiving than mine, for I don't hesitate to say now that I have always despised you. Your money was everything to you and her honor nothing, but until you prevented my letters from reaching Julia, I kept my promise to my mother. But no more. Since London, no more. You may go to the devil, and be quick about it, for all I care."

Sir Perran, leaning on his cane, began stripping one of his hands of its glove. He then slowly crossed the room and stood before his nephew.

Blackthorn held his gaze, staring into gray eyes. He knew his uncle's abilities with dueling pistols. In his lameness, he could scarcely lift a sword, but even a man with a bad leg could wield a pistol with great accuracy. He felt his heart begin to beat strongly. He was staring at death as surely as he had been a day ago. Blood rushed to his head, pounding in his temples.

Sir Perran simply dropped the glove at his feet. "You have but to name your seconds. I shall meet you at dawn in three days' time, in the *forêt de Soignes.*"

"It will have to be at dawn tomorrow morning," Blackthorn returned. "I am expected to join my regiment in Paris as soon as possible. Our business with Bonaparte is not yet finished, not until he has left the Continent."

Sir Perran's gaze never wavered. He nodded faintly. "So be it," he said calmly. "Tomorrow morning, at dawn, then."

Blackthorn understood in that moment, by his uncle's bearing, by his calmness, by the unwavering coldness of his eye, that he meant to kill him. He bent to retrieve the glove, tossed it to Mr. Loxhore, then turned and opened the door.

Sir Perran passed through without another word.

Twenty-seven

Near midnight, Julia was awakened by emphatic voices coming from the study, which was directly below her bedchamber. Sleep curled about her brain, she covered her head with her pillow, hoping to recapture her dreams, but still the argument reached her. Gradually, sleep drifted away from her completely and she uncurled herself, lying on her back and staring up at a large blue silk rosette, which formed the center of the canopy over her bed. Her mobcap covered her auburn curls and the long skirts of her fine cambric nightgown were twisted awkwardly about her knees.

The voices grew louder. She could hear Lord Trevaunance nearly shouting at another man. But who? Both his sons were in England. The other man spoke fiercely, the line of his speech direct and intense. If only she could hear the words.

Suddenly, she sat bolt upright as recognition dawned on her. *Edward.* Before she had mentally decided to leave her bedchamber, her bare feet were already running across the planked wood floor. She jerked the door open and listened. All was quiet.

Then the front door slammed and she quickly closed her door as though she might be seen, which was quite impossible, since she was on the first floor of the townhouse in the farthest chamber from the stairs. She heard footsteps and knew that Lady Trevaunance was running down the hall. Whatever was the matter?

She had no window overlooking the street. Julia had to know

what was happening, but her window wouldn't permit her to see more of what was happening.

She went to her wardrobe and withdrew a shawl from its depths. Slipping it about her shoulders, she left her room and ran in Lady Trevaunance's wake, whose footsteps she now heard on the stairs. Instead of descending the stairs, however, Julia went into the rose drawing room, which overlooked the street, hurried to one of the two windows, and looked up and down.

Edward was gone.

She felt panicky. Why had he come? Why was he arguing with the marquis?

She turned slowly around, trying to arrange her thoughts. Had he come to beg to speak with her? Had Trevaunance refused? But why?

Julia walked to the doorway and heard the marquis and his wife whispering in the entrance hall at the base of the stairs. Moving into the hallway, she leaned over the railing and, seeing the marchioness, queried softly, "Why was he here?"

The marquis moved into view, after which both Lord and Lady Trevaunance looked quickly up at her. Distress was written in their eyes and on their faces. Lady Trevaunance pressed her husband's hand and began walking quickly back up the stairs. When she reached the landing, she said, "Come back to bed, Julia. It is nothing. I promise you."

"I know Edward was here. Did he wish to speak with me?"

"Yes, but Trevaunance wouldn't have it. He . . . he told him to return in the morning and . . . and speak to you before he left for . . . for Paris."

The marchioness gently took Julia's arm and led her back down the hallway. Behind her, Julia heard Trevaunance curse loudly, a circumstance unusual for him. She glanced at the marchioness and frowned. "Something is wrong," she stated. "Please tell me what is happening."

Lady Trevaunance pressed her lips together. She seemed angry. "Men and their honor!" she snorted. "But there isn't anything you can do about it. They will behave like simpletons! I, for one, mean to sleep well tonight, and you shall do the same. Pay no heed to this . . . this ridiculous business!"

"I don't understand," Julia responded.

But Lady Trevaunance refused to be pressed further. Instead, she patted Julia's hand and ushered her to her bedchamber. She then tucked her between the sheets as though she were a little girl. She blew out the candle, refusing steadfastly to answer a single question, crossed the room, and closed the door firmly behind her.

Julia was left in the dark to surmise and to wonder. Had Edward come to take her away and had Trevaunance refused? Of course, she had told both the marquis and his wife of her intention of breaking forever with Edward and of returning to England on the morrow. Perhaps they were merely honoring her wishes in this instance.

Still, she wondered. Why had Edward come? As her thoughts turned toward him, her heart was suddenly filled with dread. Perhaps it was the night hours, or the creeping damp that seemed to slink beneath her window at night, or the strange shadows that the light from the city played through her bedchamber, but all her thoughts became dark, tangled, and fearful. Had she made the right decision to return to England? What if the allies fought another battle with the French? What if Edward were killed?

If he were killed, then so be it, but she would not be here to receive the news and to cry over his body. No, she was going back to London tomorrow.

Julia fell into a fitful sleep that was disturbed time and again, until she was fully awakened just before dawn by a loud clattering that resounded in the hallway, followed by Lord Trevaunance's curses. She threw back the bedcovers and leapt from her bed, just as she had done earlier in the night.

Men and their honor. What had Lady Trevaunance meant by that?

Terror suddenly seized her. More was going forward than just Trevaunance's refusal to permit Edward to speak with her—if indeed, he had done any such thing.

She again raced across the wood floor, drew the door open, and, at the end of the hallway, saw Lord Trevaunance, carrying a candle in one hand and a square wood case in the other, reach the landing and descend the stairs. His shadow moved in a wild, monstrous form on the ceiling and on the wall long after he had disappeared from Julia's sight.

She listened and heard him issue an order to his butler.

Julia closed the door and leaned her forehead against the cold panels, her palms pressed against the door. Her heart was hammering in her chest.

The case.

Men and their honor.

A duel! Undoubtedly between Edward and Sir Perran!

Julia felt her heart nearly burst in her chest as she crossed the bedchamber on a run and pulled a dark green woolen morning gown from her wardrobe. She tore at the ribbons of her night-dress, ripping the mobcap from her head as she scrambled out of her sleeping garb.

She could hardly breathe. She knew precisely what was happening. A duel. Then Sir Perran was in Brussels after all, and he had found Edward and had called him out. She dressed herself rapidly, stuffing her auburn curls beneath a straw bonnet tied hastily below her ear.

Julia stepped into leather slippers, but did not bother putting on stockings and garters. Withdrawing an inappropriate but serviceable apricot silk cape from her wardrobe, she left the room on a dead run.

She hurried to the rose drawing room again and peered out the window. She watched Lord Trevaunance climb aboard his coach and give the postilion the orders to start. Whirling around as the faint clatter of the coach's wheels echoed up to the drawing room windows, she again ran, her heart racing in her chest, through the chamber and down the hall to Lady Trevaunance's bedchamber. She did not scratch on the door, but pushed it open.

Julia heard a gentle snoring and crossed the darkened chamber to the marchioness's bed. She had to shake the woman to awaken her and then had to calm her after Lady Trevaunance began screaming that she was being attacked. Five minutes later, with a sketchy direction of the location of the duel, Julia left the townhouse in a hackney the butler had procured for her.

Blackthorn sat on the edge of the floor of Lord Trevaunance's traveling chariot, his legs hanging over the side, his booted feet planted awkwardly on the bottom step. He held the marquis's dueling pistol in his hand. The firearm was a finely balanced weapon and would undoubtedly serve its purpose to a nicety. The long barrel was still hot from having been fired once by the marquis, who had insisted upon testing it for him.

They had not spoken to one another the entire journey southeast from Brussels to the *forêt de Soignes*. A morning mist crept through the tree trunks; dead leaves from last winter carpeted the ground; a musty smell of fungus and pungent ferns rose from the earth. How strange to have returned so soon to the beechwood forest. Was it only two days ago that he had passed through the forest at night, following the Battle of Waterloo? So much had happened in so few days that Blackthorn could scarcely make any sense of it all. All he knew was that he missed Julia dreadfully.

One of the horses snorted, another stamped its foot. Sir Perran had not yet arrived.

Blackthorn stared down at the pistol, his thoughts suddenly growing strangely full of his mother. He didn't know why he was thinking of her just now. After all, though it was possible his life would soon be at an end, this would not be the first time he had confronted death, and he could recall no previous occasion before a battle when his thoughts had turned toward his beloved parent.

But for some reason, she was in possession of his mind as he held the pistol in his hand. Perhaps it was because he was finally confronting Sir Perran in battle. In a way, he was glad this day had come. From the first, when his mother had brought him to

Sir Perran's home, he had been at odds with his uncle. He could remember a time when he had hoped one day they would come to fisticuffs. He could think of no greater joy than to plant his despised uncle a facer. But that day had passed with Sir Perran's growing lameness and his advancing age.

Now they would do battle with pistols—a battle to death. And he would be breaking his vow to his mother to always love and honor Sir Perran Blackthorn.

Why had she insisted he show a respect and devotion he did not feel? Edward had never understood this part of her, especially when Sir Perran had used her so ill.

His throat grew tight with thoughts of his mother. He had loved her so much, but he confessed he had never really understood her or her complicated relationship with his uncle. Whenever Sir Perran was mentioned, her initial reaction was always the same: She would jump or flinch as though she had been startled by a loud noise. Then her eyes would grow distant and strange. Sometimes she would smile when she thought no one was looking, sometimes she would leave the room. Once he had followed her, curious what her thoughts might be, and, to his dismay, had found her dropped to her knees beside her bed, sobbing. Only then had he come to suspect that she had truly been in love with Sir Perran at one time. He had always known she had made a choice between the brothers, but it seemed to him—and this was so dishonorable to his father—that she had regretted her choice.

There was a missing page in his life called Sir Perran Blackthorn, and Edward did not understand what was on that page.

Perhaps his uncle would die today, or perhaps he would face his own death. One thing he knew for certain: Today he would break his vow to his mother. If he could, he meant to kill Sir Perran, to avenge his father, perhaps, or to punish him for having robbed him of Julia's hand in marriage, which had ultimately cast the woman he loved into the role of his mistress rather than his honored wife. Yes, he wanted Sir Perran dead just as surely as his uncle wanted him dead.

He felt irritable. He ran his fingers the length of the pistol. The barrel was cool now and he handed the pistol to the marquis, who began priming the pan.

Blackthorn's gaze became fixed on the dead leaves at his feet. Something nagged at him. His mother, Sir Perran, his father. The veriest conception of a thought began rising up through the layers of his mind. His mother, Sir Perran, his father.

He frowned, blinked, feeling more agitated.

He heard the jingling traces of an approaching carriage, along with the measured gallops of the horses' hooves. A few moments later, a handsome coach appeared, in gleaming burgundy and black, with Sir Perran's coat of arms emblazoned on the side. The coach lamps were still lit and the carriage possessed an air of magic as Sir Perran descended slowly from the steps. He was dressed all in black, from head to toe, his black cape swirling to the ground about his ankles.

Blackthorn leaped lightly to the ground and turned to face his uncle. How calm he appeared in the gray early morning light. Calm and at ease, as though he felt assured of success. Blackthorn searched his every feature for a telltale sign of anxiety—a twitch of his eye or cheek or lip, a constriction of the muscles in his face, a rapid blinking of the eye. But he saw nothing that might indicate Sir Perran was anything less than confident.

His boldness irritated Blackthorn and he flipped back his cape, over his shoulder, to reveal a target he had prepared for his uncle. His black cape was lined with red silk, and the brilliant scarlet swathe would guide Sir Perran's malevolent eye to his heart. Fury seized Blackthorn suddenly as he reviewed again all his uncle's past insults toward his mother and toward himself. He had used his mother ill and he had stolen Julia from him. Sir Perran had no heart and he had no honor. He wished him dead. He willed him dead.

The proper offices were quickly performed. The seconds attempted to reconcile the principals. The pistols were primed and approved by both duelists. They stood back to back, and with pistols held pointing upward, Edward began marching away

from Sir Perran. The count began—ten paces. Death was sure
to follow. One. Two. Three.

The sound of another carriage approaching caused Blackthorn to look to his left as the counting continued.

Eight. Nine. Through the mist, horses appeared down the lane,
then the black outline of a hackney. What the devil!

Ten. He turned. He saw Sir Perran turn. He lowered his pistol,
but the carriage bowled into the clearing and placed itself between the duelists.

Julia scrambled down from the hackney, falling to her knees
when her apricot silk cape got caught in the door.

"Julia!" Blackthorn cried, averting his pistol and immediately
walking toward her. "What the deuce are you doing here?"

"You can't fight Sir Perran."

"I can and I will."

"No, you can't," she cried. "He . . . he is not who you think
he is."

"Julia!" Sir Perran snapped, also approaching her. "Climb
back aboard the hackney and return to Lady Trevaunance's
home, at once. You are not wanted here. This is our business,
not yours."

Lord Trevaunance approached her and took her by the arm.
"Come with me, Julia. I'll see you home. You can have no effect
here, as you should very well know by now."

"I can," she responded, jerking her arm out of his grasp. "And
I will." Turning to address Edward, she said, "Whatever the
provocation, you cannot fire upon Sir Perran. You cannot."

Edward frowned at her. "Why do you try to protect him?
Because he is your husband? Go away. You already made your
decision, now let me conduct my life as I deem best."

He turned away from her and she followed, catching him by
the arm, circling him to look him full in the eye. "You don't
know the truth, do you?" she queried. "I couldn't be sure, but
now I am. Sir Perran isn't your uncle at all."

He narrowed his eyes. She saw coldness there, even anger. "What do you mean? Of course he is."

"I learned recently from my sister, who overheard a conversation between Lady Trevaunance and Lady Cowper, that Sir Perran is your father. Not your uncle, but your father. Do you understand? Your father."

Blackthorn stared at her blankly for a long moment. He felt as though his thoughts had become like leaves that had been tossed in the air and were now floating slowly to earth. And until his thoughts made their way to the ground, he would be unable to move or to speak. He waited for one to land, and then another and another. He thought of his mother and her odd conduct where Sir Perran was concerned. Glancing over at the man who had dogged his heels ever since he could remember, he saw a face white with shock. He scrutinized Sir Perran from head to foot and saw himself reflected in his uncle—his father.

"You are mistaken," Edward said flatly. "You must be. Lady Trevaunance and Lady Cowper were merely gossiping. Your sister misunderstood what she heard." It couldn't be true.

"You have his bearing, his will, his temper," Julia responded. "You are his son."

"A nephew could have as much likeness," he returned. "I won't place any stock in such tittle-tattle." He walked away from her. Most of the leaves had not yet fallen to lay on the ground of his mind. He could hardly breathe. Anger swelled over him. He remembered his mother's tears. Good God, it was true!

Suddenly, his feet shifted, his body moved swiftly, and he was running before he realized what he was doing. When he reached Sir Perran, he dropped the pistol and swung at nearly the same time. His fist caught Sir Perran at the jawline, sending the older man flying backward into the chest of Mr. Loxhore.

Sir Perran staggered, half falling to his knees, then caught himself. He held his jaw and glared at Blackthorn. Mr. Loxhore lifted Sir Perran to his feet and Blackthorn felt Lord Yarnacott quickly take hold of his arms, trying to keep him from assaulting his uncle—his father—again. Blackthorn broke free and took

another swing at him, but Mr. Loxhore had perceived his intent
and managed to swiftly move Sir Perran out of his range.

"You've gone mad!" Sir Perran cried.

Blackthorn tried to control his rage, but it seemed to surround
him in a maddening whirlwind. "Only tell me this, *uncle,* can
there be even the smallest chance that you are my father? Tell
me! I want to hear you say it!" He heard his voice return to him
from the beech trees and the mist. Blackthorn struggled against
the arms that had again pinioned him, his boots clawing through
the leaves and mulch beneath his feet. He wanted Sir Perran
dead. "Did she choose your brother, or was it simply that you
wouldn't marry her? What did you do to her?"

"What rubbish are you speaking now?" Sir Perran asked, rubbing his jaw.

"Think back!" he shouted. "You can recall twenty-eight years
ago, can't you? What did you do to my mother?"

"I won't listen to this." Sir Perran shifted his gaze away from
Blackthorn. His mind rolled back into the past. He pushed Mr.
Loxhore away and stumbled to his coach. He felt ill, desperately
ill, as though he had eaten rotten meat and was just now experiencing the effects of it. He moved to his horses and leaned his
head against the warm flank of the one nearest him. The horse's
muscles rippled in an uncertain spasm beneath his hands and
head. He didn't want to remember, but the images came never-
theless—of Sophia, of speaking words of love to her, of touching
her, of becoming overwhelmed with passion, of ignoring her
protests. *Oh, God, it was true. All of it.*

And Edward was the result of that union.

He had had a son by Sophia Kettering and he never knew it.

A shaft of wonder appeared for the barest moment within his
heart, like a ray of unexpected hope and life. Of course Edward
was his son. Sophia must have hinted as much to him a dozen
times, but he had failed to see it. He hadn't wanted to know the
truth.

But what was the truth, really?

Hope dimmed.

The truth was, he had been robbed again. He saw it as clearly as he felt the coarse chestnut horsehairs prickling the skin of his forehead as he leaned against the horse. He had given his seed to Sophia, she had conceived a son, and then she had taken that son from him.

The truth was, Edward Blackthorn was no more his son than either Stephen or George had been.

A flatness drove through him, ending the sickness in his stomach, depriving him of emotion.

Whatever the truth, he had no son. He had no son.

He leaned away from the horse and straightened his shoulders. When he turned around, everyone was watching him—the surgeon sitting in readiness within Trevaunance's coach; the marquis, who had taken Julia aside and now held her tightly about her shoulders; his friends; and Edward Blackthorn, who had again taken up his appointed place in the duel. He could see that Blackthorn was calmer now. He smiled faintly, wondering what Julia had hoped to achieve by revealing the irrelevant truth to either of them at this eleventh hour.

Sir Perran walked slowly back to his friends. "Where is my pistol?" he queried. "I seem to have lost it."

"I have both pistols here. They should be checked and reloaded," Lord Yarnacott said slowly, a pinched frown between his brows. "But if I may say so, Sir Perran, you don't mean to continue, do you? After all, if—"

"I think you will agree that whether he is my nephew or my son, he has betrayed me. And unless Major Blackthorn objects, I intend to continue."

Blackthorn bowed to him, moving to wait by the surgeon until the pistols had been primed again and reloaded.

Sir Perran watched him indifferently. He ignored his wife's protests and tears. How much better this is, he thought. So much more perfect, really. He would be able to settle all his scores in one accurate placement of a very small pistol ball. He thought of the fourth viscount Delabole, who had seen the quarry stripped from his family. He thought of Sophia, who had so badly betrayed him. Her seed and his brother's would disappear from the face of the earth forever after this morning's work.

He felt a peace envelop him. Mr. Loxhore presented him with the restored pistol. He held it aloft and moved to stand again back-to-back with Blackthorn. He walked slowly, still feigning his limp, as the paces were counted. Eight, nine, ten. He turned and waited.

Blackthorn leveled his pistol at him. They were scarcely twenty feet apart. Such a small, insignificant space of distance and time. He held Blackthorn's heated, angry gaze.

He watched his nephew—his son—blink once, then twice. He watched in some surprise as the anger in his gaze began to dissipate. Blackthorn slowly lifted his arm high in the air and fired. Sir Perran smiled with immense satisfaction. Blackthorn had chosen, quite stupidly, to delope. The pistol ball whirred through the mist and was gone. He lowered his arm and stood waiting steadfastly.

"Thank God," Julia cried.

"Yes, yes!" Lord Trevaunance exclaimed. "That's the way of it. Good lad. Good lad!"

But Sir Perran was as unmoved by their remarks as by his son's display of chivalry. He aimed his pistol at Edward. His heartbeat picked up its cadence. He knew this was the moment, the real moment, he had been waiting for his entire life. He had always hated Edward Blackthorn. Now he understood why.

He squeezed the trigger.

His son.

No, he couldn't do it!

He lifted his arm quickly in the air, but the priming pan had fired a split second earlier. The ball whirled from the barrel, and a moment later he watched his son spin around and drop to the ground on his face, remaining motionless. Through the sudden tears that burned his eyes, he heard Julia scream and run to him. The surgeon brought his bag to Edward's body; the marquis began preparing his coach to take Sir Perran's son back to Brussels.

Mr. Loxhore took Sir Perran by the arm and led him away to his coach. He stumbled blindly beside him.

"We must get back to England," Lord Yarnacott said as he, too, assisted Sir Perran into his coach.

"Yes," Sir Perran said. "Yes, I wish to return to England at once." He felt very old, suddenly, and very tired.

Twenty-eight

"Do you understand, Sir Perran?" Julia asked. She was standing in front of her husband, and when he would not respond, she lifted his face with her hands to look into his eyes. He was seated slumped over in the same black lacquer and gilt Empire chair that Edward had occupied but a few days earlier, and Julia was having no small degree of difficulty speaking with her husband. Looking into tortured gray eyes, she continued. "The surgeon does not know whether he will live or not. It has only been three days and the fever has not yet broken."

He blinked and a tear trickled down his cheek. Searching her eyes, he queried, "Have you been sitting with him every night? You look very tired."

"Of course I have," Julia responded, a tear of her own matching the one on his cheek.

Sir Perran had not left Brussels after all. He had called every day since the duel. He had secured the best surgeons in the city, even one serving on the staff of the Prince of Orange, and had sent them to Lord Trevaunance's townhouse one after the other. He had begged to speak with Julia a score of times, but she had refused. Finally, Lady Trevaunance had convinced her that the only way the household would have the least bit of peace was if Sir Perran was granted his interview with her.

Julia had been cold at the outset, staring at him woodenly, her fingers balling into claws at the sight of him. But little by little she began to realize that the duel, and Sir Perran's awareness that Edward was his son, had finally broken him. He seemed to have aged a dozen years. His white hair was streaked with yellow, his eyes red-rimmed from weeping, his cheeks sunken. His tears were for himself, for his son, and as he had said over and over, for all the lost years.

He looked at her now and, shifting his cane from one hand to the other, took her hand in his. "You must forgive me, Julia. You must."

Julia did not know what to say to him. She wanted to say, of course, that it was her duty as a Christian to forgive. But her mind kept reviewing his schemes: her father's death, the stealing of Edward's letters, her unhappy marriage to him, his overbearing treatment of her sisters. And now he had perhaps cost her what she valued most: his son's life.

She did not try to disengage his hand from hers. His grasp was hard and desperate. Instead, she seated herself next to him on the rose and white silk settee. "I had meant to make you the best of wives, Sir Perran," she began. "You had always seemed so kind and understanding. I would have given you sons and daughters if you had but shown me the smallest measure of love."

"I know. I know," he murmured, tears now streaming down his face. He withdrew a cambric kerchief from the pocket of his coat and wiped his eyes. "I can't seem to stop this curst weeping. I've become an old woman." He took a deep breath. His shoulders sagged. He leaned his head on the back of his hand, which covered his cane. Shaking his head back and forth, he kept on crying. "I've been so foolish. So stubborn, so irascible. I was bent on vengeance, but look what I have: nothing. I have gained nothing. I didn't mean to kill him. That is, I had intended to, even after I learned he was my son. But at the very moment I leveled my pistol at him, I promise you I had not meant to fire. It was an accident, I tell you, an accident! A curst accident!" At that he sobbed uncontrollably, until his face grew slippery against the back of his hand.

Julia looked down at his white head. A dram of compassion entered her heart, which she didn't completely understand. She placed her hand on his shoulder. "Blow your nose, Sir Perran," she directed with a sigh. "You look awfully silly right now."

He obeyed her.

As she watched him, again wiping his eyes, his nose, his face, Julia understood something she had not comprehended before. All these years Sir Perran had been trapped within himself, within his own hatreds. All these years he could have known and loved his son had he not been filled with rage that the woman he loved had married another man. Instead, he had so permitted his anger to rule him that he had nearly killed the child of his body. With her, as well, he could have known love; instead, he had been bent on mischief of the worst kind from the very beginning.

"I am sorry for you, Sir Perran," she said at last.

"I have made my own bed," he responded. "I don't deserve your forgiveness or anyone else's. I have been a fool."

"Yes, a very great one, it would seem."

He glanced at her, then looked away. "Is there nothing I can say to redeem myself, nothing I can do?"

Julia shook her head. "I will forgive you, but you must realize that the pain you have caused me will not permit me to readily accept your friendship. I would, however, ask that you grant me a divorce."

"Of course," he responded quietly. "I will return to England and begin proceedings at once. You have my word on that."

Julia finally disengaged her hand from his. "I must return to Edward," she told him. "It would seem that my presence, even in his feverish state, is beneficial."

She rose from the settee, and as he gained his feet, he asked, "May I . . . may I see my son?"

Julia's throat grew clogged with tears. "Yes, but just for a moment, and perhaps it would be best if you did not speak to him."

She would have immediately led him to Edward's bedchamber, but first he held her back and pressed a small package into her hand. "I wanted you to have this, Julia, as a token of my sincere regret for all the pain I have caused you. It is your mother's ring."

"The emerald?" she queried, stunned. "But it belongs to Lady Trevaunance."

"I had always suspected you had been able to create Olivia's by the selling of your mother's ring. When I approached Lady Trevaunance about it yesterday in order to discover its where-abouts, much to my relief I found that it was in her possession. She did not hesitate to come to terms with me once she knew of my intentions. Please take it, won't you?"

Julia unwrapped the package and when she saw the sparkle of the green emerald, she felt her throat tighten. Her mother's ring had come home to her. "Thank you," she whispered. "You've no idea how much this means to me."

"I'm glad, Julia," he answered softly.

She lifted her gaze to look into his red-rimmed gray eyes and again saw a man who had been deeply humbled by life. "Come," she said. "You will want to see Edward now."

Julia led the way to the bedchamber across the hall from hers. She opened the door and saw that Lord Trevaunance and the surgeon were bending over the bed. The chamber was lit dimly with a branch of three candles. "Oh, no," Julia murmured. She forgot about Sir Perran as she walked quietly into the room.

The smell of sickness was heavy in the air.

Lord Trevaunance turned and looked at her, his expression grim. "We found him like this not a moment ago. I'm sorry, my dear."

Julia covered her mouth with her hand, restraining the cry that wrestled in her throat. She moved beyond the screen that blocked the doorway from the bed. She saw the pallor of Ed-ward's face and emitted a faint cry. He was deathly pale, his body still. The surgeon's head was against his chest. After a moment, the surgeon stood upright. "No, my lord, he is not dead," he stated, addressing the marquis. "In fact, I believe I may safely say the worst is behind us. The fever is broken."

"God be praised," Lord Trevaunance murmured.

Julia circled behind the doctor and stared down at Edward's face. Dark circles lay beneath his eyes. His complexion was bluish gray. He hardly appeared to be breathing. It was no wonder the marquis had thought him dead.

She knelt beside the bed and drank in the vision of life as it now lay on Edward's brow. How ironic that what Waterloo had not touched a duel with his father had nearly stormed.

Remembering that Sir Perran wished to see his son, she turned to beckon him forward, but he was already gone. She glanced at Lord Trevaunance. "Does he know Edward is alive?"

The marquis nodded. "He was simply overcome."

Later, in the dark hours before dawn, Julia awoke to the gentle sounds of her name. She had been sitting in a chair placed by the bed, slumped forward next to Edward's arm, when the sound awakened her.

"Julia."

She lifted her head and wondered what the doctor wanted, but found she was alone in the chamber. She glanced at Edward and saw that he was watching her. Julia smiled and reached her hand out to touch his cheek.

"I am supposed to be with the army," he said, struggling to speak. "Wellington will not like one of his officers—"

"Hush. You've been four days now with fever. Lord Trevaunance dispatched a letter to Vandeleur informing him of your *illness* some time ago."

"Excellent." He smiled faintly. "Four days. I suppose that means I will live."

"Yes, you will live."

"I'm so thirsty."

Julia poured him a glass of water, then turned to find he was wincing in pain as he tried to sit up. "No, no, you mustn't. You were shot deep in your shoulder. You'll be bleeding again if you try to move. Let me fetch a footman to help you."

"I'm as weak as a kitten," he returned, settling back into the pillows.

Julia's voice grew suspended with tears. "You've been very

ill." She then turned away from him and bid the footman, who was asleep in a chair in the hall, to assist her.

Several days later, with the fever gone and his wound healing according to his doctor's wishes, Edward was sitting up in bed eating a thin gruel. Julia watched him now and again as she attempted to finish the last few stitches on her peacock. His hand no longer trembled as it had initially when he tried to do anything. Every hour, it seemed, he grew stronger, and she judged it time to discuss Sir Perran's visit.

As she began, she could see that anger cloaked his eyes as he continued to dip his spoon into the steaming bowl and lift the gruel to his lips. Julia omitted nothing, however, finally ending with, "And he has granted me a divorce and has given his word as a gentleman that he will see it through."

Edward grunted with scorn. "He is no gentleman. There is no honor in him."

"You may be right," she responded.

At that moment, a servant entered bearing a letter for Edward on a shiny silver salver. Julia took it and dismissed the servant. She recognized the handwriting at once. "It is from . . ." she hesitated, ". . . your father."

"Burn it," Edward stated. "He may be my father, but I will have nothing to do with him, not now, not ever."

Julia turned the letter over in her hands. The grate was behind her and she could feel the warmth of a coal fire on the back of her legs. She turned and was preparing to toss it in the fire, when he called out, "Wait. Let me have it. I confess I am curious to see what the old man would say to me."

She flipped the missive to him, a silly, childlike act that made him smile. "Are you too fatigued from your embroidery to rise from your chair?"

She lifted a brow and continued to ply her needle with an unconcerned air. "You have become sullen and peevish. I no longer mean to offer all my tender ministrations. I command you to regain your strength because I've done with you."

He chuckled, then broke the seal of the letter and began to read. When he was finished, Julia lifted her gaze from the last stitch of her peacock and watched him carefully. A deep frown had creased his brow. He spoke, but did not look at her. "It would seem he was her lover, at least once. He confesses he believes he hurt her, frightened her. He was too hasty." Julia watched his jaw move strongly. "He raped her."

Julia took the letter and read it through carefully, then folded it up and set it aside. "Edward," she began slowly, "I have heard that for some women the first time is so painful that they wish never to repeat it. I know it was not that way for me—in truth, I didn't know any pain at all. You cannot be sure he took her entirely against her will. How did your mother seem to feel about him in later years?"

At that, he lifted the linen from his chest and wiped his chin. "That's the rub, I suppose. He was very mean to her. He struck her once; I saw it. But she never spoke a harsh word against him."

"For your sake?" she asked.

He shook his head. "I don't know. I believe she loved him. I believe she blamed herself."

"Could his unkindnesses to her, then, have been the result of his bitterness in her choice and not an evil in his character?"

"I don't know. It was her wish, however, that I honor him. When I pressed her as to why I should give a groat of respect or tolerance to a man who had slapped her, she had responded that he had once given her a most precious gift and that he would always hold a special place in her heart because of it. I suppose she was referring to me. But that was the first I suspected she had once been in love with him, but I never dreamed she had been with him."

"It is still so strange to think of him as your father."

"Yes, indeed it is."

* * *

Three weeks passed, and every day saw Edward's health changing and improving in great strides. One afternoon, in mid-July, Julia sat with him on the rose and white striped silk settee, the warm summer light streaming into the rose drawing room through thin muslin drapes, which cast the elegant, tall-ceilinged chamber in a bright glow. The day was warm, the windows were open, and the fragile muslin billowed gently as a cool breeze swept over the city of Brussels.

Julia watched Edward now, as he quickly read a brief letter from Wellington, which had only just arrived. A smile was already on his lips and she sensed that something momentous had occurred.

"My God," he whispered. "I've been given command of a regiment. I suppose I knew the day would come, but now that it has, I find I am stunned."

"You've worked very hard for this," Julia said. "Only tell me, what will your rank be?"

"Lieutenant colonel." He lifted his gaze from the letter and regarded her steadily.

"Oh, Edward," she breathed, responding to his promotion as the good friend she hoped she was to him. "I'm so happy for you, my darling." Julia quickly leaned over and embraced him gently, sliding an arm about his waist and taking great care to avoid hurting his tender shoulder.

He slipped his arm about her and returned her embrace. He then kissed her hair and her forehead, and when she lifted her face to his, he kissed her lips. She found herself as always responding fully to the touch of his lips upon hers. Desire rose within her and she felt his embrace grow tighter.

"Julia," he murmured into her ear. "My love. There is only one thing lacking."

She drew back from him and knew what it was he meant. His words sobered her and she felt her former fears surface. "I don't know what to say."

"Will you not at least consider the possibility?" he queried.

"You are better suited to this task than you know. I wish I could help you to see that."

"I have the courage of a black beetle," she stated, tears brimming in her eyes.

He chuckled but at the same time withdrew his arm from about her. Julia saw resignation in his face. Impulsively, she reached over and touched his cheek. "Thank you for not pressing me, Edward. Now tell me, where is your new regiment? In Paris, awaiting you? One of Vandeleur's, perhaps? I am so happy for you."

He frowned slightly. "I didn't say before?" he asked, not looking at her.

"No, you did not." Her heart seemed to stop beating. She knew the answer already by the expression on his face.

He drew in a deep breath. "The post I've always wanted—India."

"No," she murmured, tears flooding her eyes. He would be so far away. Were he to serve in Europe, she could see him whenever she wished for it. But India! India was on the other side of the world.

"You must listen to me," he said. "Hear me out just this once and I promise you I will say no more. I know you, Julia. I've known you since you were a child. You are as ripe for adventure as any officer I've known. India is the very place for you. You've proven yourself—your courage, your inventiveness in the face of quite difficult circumstances—over and over again. You weren't born to remain an idle observer of life, but to partake of its fullest, richest portion. I tell you, you have sufficient courage to come with me, to share in my life in an exotic land. Will you at least try to believe that what I say is true?"

Julia regarded passionate gray eyes and wanted to believe him, but how could she when all she had to do was think back to June 18 to know that she could never endure such a day again, of waiting, of wondering, of such terrible fears and dreads? She was about to reiterate her opinions, when the door suddenly burst open and a sight greeted Julia's eyes that rendered her speechless.

"Hallo, Julia!" two feminine voices called to her in unison.

"Annabelle!" she cried, recovering her senses. Rising from her seat, she quickly crossed the room to greet her sisters. "Caroline! Oh, my dears! How wonderful it is to see you, you've no idea! But how . . . when did you get here? Where is Elizabeth? Oh, let me look at you!" She embraced them both and found that tears were coursing down her cheeks.

Only when she began wiping them away with a kerchief Caroline had retrieved from her reticule and handed to her did she notice that Sir Perran was with them, though he had remained standing in the doorway. She saw that he was waiting to be invited in.

"Sir Perran," she said, nodding to him by way of acknowledgment. She didn't know what to say to him and felt that his presence cast a dark shadow over their sweet reunion. Sir Perran glanced at Edward, who had risen to his feet but remained silent, watching him from a cool, unwelcoming gaze. She wondered if he was angry that Sir Perran had come.

It was Annabelle who broke the tension by pulling away from her and moving to stand beside Sir Perran. Slipping her arm through his, she then drew him forward and began to speak. "Sir Perran was kind enough to come to London and bring us to you, Julia. He knew you would want us to be with you, and so here we are. He . . . he has been all that is kind, generous, and quite, quite humble. So I hope that you do not mind overly much that we have brought him along with us."

Julia was dumbfounded by the alteration in her sister's attitude toward Sir Perran. Annabelle, above all, had held the greatest animosity toward the baronet. Somehow it would seem that in the course of the past three weeks, he had been able to completely restore her good graces toward him.

"And look," Caroline added, as she, too, crossed to the baronet and took up his other arm. "He has given up that silly cane of his." Caroline then looked very hard at Julia.

Whatever ambivalence Julia had felt toward Sir Perran seemed to dissipate in the absence of his cane. She understood that in giving up his cane, he had relinquished his former self. How her heart changed toward him as she observed the pleading expression in his eyes. Though she would never have thought it possible, she forgave him—for everything.

"You are most welcome to join us," she declared, addressing the baronet. "And thank you for bringing my sisters to me." She then approached him and kissed him on the cheek.

"Thank you, my dear," he whispered as he disengaged his arm from Annabelle's and embraced Julia. "You are very kind to a foolish old man."

He then released her and cleared his throat. Moving forward away from the sisters, he approached a position by the windows on the wall juxtaposed to the settee, and with a glance that shifted uneasily to his son and back to Julia, he said, "Pray be seated, won't you, all of you? I have a few matters of business to discuss that won't take long, I promise you, but which must be addressed. Then, if you wish for it, I shall leave and will never bother you again."

Julia regarded Sir Perran for a moment, wondering what sort of business he was referring to. She then directed her sisters to greet Edward carefully, since he was still in some pain from his wound. Afterward, when Julia took up a seat in the Empire chair, she directed her sisters to each take a place on either side of Edward, which they were glad to do, since from the beginning of their acquaintance with him the past summer, he had been a favorite with them.

When everyone was comfortable, Sir Perran quickly explained his intentions, which left both Julia and Edward in a state of wonder and disbelief. He was restoring Hatherleigh Park to Julia and the quarry to the sisters jointly. He had dowered each of the sisters, including Julia, quite handsomely, then divulged his finest achievement: He had succeeded in procuring an annulment—his marriage to Julia Verdell was as if it had never been.

"I would also confess my numerous faults to you, but the list is so long I daresay I wouldn't be able to finish it in the course of a lifetime, and then where would we be? I ask only for your forgiveness." These words he directed first to Edward, then to Julia.

"I do forgive you, Sir Perran," Julia said quietly.

"Even—" the baronet began unsteadily, his voice breaking. "Even my hand in your father's demise?" His tone was harsh and self-recriminating.

Julia looked away from him, allowing her gaze to rest on the embroidered white muslin of her gown. Prettily stitched blue-bells were scattered over the thin, summery fabric. She was remembering her father and her heart was suddenly full of sadness. "He was a gamester," she said at last. "You must live with your conscience in regard to how much you took advantage of his greatest vice, but I cannot pretend that his life would have ended differently. Mama kept him anchored. When she was taken from us, it seemed nothing could console him or again provide the strong moorings that he needed." She shifted her gaze back to Sir Perran and smiled faintly. "You must make your own peace with God on this score, I'm afraid."

"Yes," he murmured, his entire demeanor laden with a weight Julia thought it likely would never quite disappear from his countenance again. Giving himself a mental shake, he then straightened his shoulders and addressed his son. "As for you, Edward, I have taken steps to do what I should have done many years ago. I have legally made you and your progeny heirs to my lands and fortunes, without restriction. All attending legal papers shall be delivered to you by Mr. Ladock within the next two days for your signature. Edward, I don't expect you to forgive me for all that I've done, for I know I've hurt you deeply"— his voice broke and his eyes again filled with tears as he continued—"so I will merely say goodbye and may God be with you."

He then turned on his heel, obviously overcome, and began walking toward the door, upright, limpless, caneless.

Annabelle and Caroline looked at Julia hopefully. She knew they wanted her to stop him, to invite him back. But Julia was looking at Edward, who still appeared to be in a state of shock. When he finally met her gaze, she felt she could read his thoughts and was not surprised when at last he rose to his feet and, just as Sir Perran reached the door, called out, "Father, won't you stay for a glass of sherry."

"Oh," Caroline murmured, pressing a hand to her mouth. Annabelle sniffled. Julia again held Caroline's kerchief to her eyes as she rose to observe Edward move to greet his father. Caroline and Annabelle also left their seats, rising to join Julia, slipping their arms about her waist. Annabelle whispered, "Sir Perran is so changed. We did not know him when he came to Upper Brook Street."

Julia spoke quietly. "I believe he is the man he always was, in truth, in the depths of his heart. He had only been playacting all these years. It seems to me he has come home."

Edward, for his part, felt that each step he took was as though he were marking off five years of his life. He was no longer a man but a boy, as he met his father for the first time. Over the past few weeks, he had given great consideration to all that had happened and he had been convinced that he would never truly be able to forgive Sir Perran for his many hurtful acts. But when Sir Perran had arrived and Edward had looked into his broken gray eyes, his heart had begun to undergo an unexpected transformation. Somehow in his father's contrition, the past began to make sense. He could forgive him now. For that reason, he embraced Sir Perran Blackthorn and held him close for a long, long time.

"Good lad," Sir Perran murmured.

Sometime later, while everyone was enjoying a platter of rich summer fruits and sipping sherry and lemonade, Julia was in the midst of answering Annabelle's question about what it had been like to be in Brussels on the day of the Battle of Waterloo, when she was suddenly struck by the absence of her next eldest sister. Interrupting her own cataloging of that fateful day, she blurted out, "Where is Elizabeth? It has just now occurred to me that you have said nothing of her. Why was she unable to come? She is not ill, is she?" Julia found herself suddenly concerned, and not less so than when Annabelle, Caroline, and Sir Perran all suddenly appeared quite conscious.

"Oh, dear," she murmured. "What is it this time?"

Annabelle bit her lip. "She is gone to Italy, Julia. We didn't want to say anything right away because we didn't wish to distress you. She means to help her friend who was captured by Algerian corsairs."

Julia stared at Annabelle, disbelieving what she was hearing. "She intends to go to North Africa, to the Barbary Coast, doesn't she?" Both Caroline and Annabelle nodded.

Turning to Sir Perran, she queried, "Did you know of this?"

Sir Perran shook his head. "She had been gone over a sennight when I arrived in London. There isn't much we can do at this point, I'm afraid."

Julia felt strange suddenly, almost dizzy. Her initial inclination was to set in motion a whole army of efforts designed to retrieve and protect her sister. But now, after she let the impulse pass through her, she realized Lizzie was all grown up and had made a decision that no one had the right to overturn, no matter how well intentioned. So instead of issuing a mountain of orders, she excused herself and went to her bedchamber, where she retrieved her mother's emerald ring. Julia smiled as she looked at it and knew precisely what she wanted to do.

When she returned to the drawing room, she gave it to Sir Perran and asked him to see that it was delivered to Elizabeth *posthaste*. He looked up at her quizzically. She seated herself and said, with a smile, "I think Elizabeth will understand my intention."

Annabelle cried, "You don't mean to rescue her?"

"Not by half," Julia responded. She turned to look at Caroline and continued. "For I was informed a few weeks past that all my sisters were grown up now. Elizabeth has always been a pillar of sheer strength of will, and I had much rather her will be extended toward North Africa than against me in my attempts to bring her home."

Both Annabelle and Caroline laughed, and Sir Perran promised to see that the ring was delivered safely to her.

Julia then let her gaze settle on Edward. He met her eyes with a smile, and an understanding passed between them. Julia thought to herself, *Where in all of this, in the past hours since the time of my sisters' and Sir Perran's arrival, had the decision been made?* Aloud, she announced, "But I refuse to be outdone by Elizabeth. I wish to inform you that in a month's time, I will be sailing, hopefully with Edward as my husband, to India. He has just been given a regiment. You are now looking at Lieutenant Colonel Edward Blackthorn."

Annabelle shrieked, leaped from her seat on the settee, and hugged both Edward and Julia in quick succession. Caroline again dissolved into tears. Sir Perran rose to his feet and lifted his glass of sherry by way of a toast.

Julia sipped her sherry and let her gaze rest on Edward's face. She was at peace finally. Love for him flowed through her, in much the same way the sherry did, warming her veins, softening her heart, and undoubtedly bringing a glow to her complexion.

That night, after a cherished evening of celebration with Lord and Lady Trevaunance, Edward and his father, and her sisters, Julia finally found herself alone with Edward and in his arms. He kissed her deeply, and she received his kisses with a profound sense that she had been given a second chance to know love well and to experience life to its fullest.

After a time, Edward released her slightly. "You won't regret your decision, Julia, I promise you," he said earnestly.

Julia could not keep from laughing. "Don't be silly," she told him. "I have little doubt I shall regret it every day of my life, for I am the most hen-hearted creature ever born."

He seemed taken aback. "But, Julia—"

She silenced him with a quick kiss. "I suppose what I am

trying to say to you is that I don't expect to go to India, and to be an officer's wife, without experiencing a great deal of regret, fear, and a whole host of spasms and palpitations, so it is you who must now prepare yourself! But don't think you have the power to relieve me of my worries and fears, for you don't."

"Oh, my darling, if this is how you truly feel, then I will take great pains to ensure your happiness."

"Edward, there's not a thing you can do for me, so don't even try. But if you will promise to love me a little, now and again, then I will promise that you shall never hear me once complain about being your wife."

He kissed her again, and this time Julia let her mind drift to a place of wondrous peace that soon became filled with visions of elephants and tigers, of a dark-skinned, sloe-eyed people in exotic costumes, speaking a rhythm of language as unfamiliar to her as the skill of navigating a ship by the stars.

To her surprise, now that the decision had been made, Julia found she could hardly wait for the adventure to begin.

About the Author

Valerie King is the author of twelve Regency romances. *Vanquished* is her first historical Regency romance. Valerie lives with her family in Glendale, Arizona, and is currently working on her next Zebra Regency romance, *Bewitching Hearts,* which will be published in October 1995. Valerie loves hearing from her readers and you may write to her c/o Zebra Books. Please include a self-addressed stamped envelope if you wish a response.